FLIGHT PATTERNS

FLIGHT PATTERNS

A CENTURY OF

STORIES

ABOUT FLYING

EDITED BY

DOROTHY SPEARS

 OPEN CITY BOOKS

New York

Introduction and Afterword copyright © 2009 by Dorothy
Spears. Additional copyright information on page 545.

Printed in the United States of America

FIRST EDITION

Design: Nick Stone
Cover: Gretchen Hupfel, *Horizontal Stabilizer*, 2001.
Inside cover: Chris Jordan, *Jet Trails, 2007.*

Library of Congress Control Number: 2009925055
ISBN-10: 1-890447-51-X
ISBN-13: 978-1890447-51-9

OPEN CITY BOOKS
270 Lafayette Street
New York, NY 10012
www.opencity.org

09 10 11 12 13 14 15   10 9 8 7 6 5 4 3 2 1

CONTENTS

INTRODUCTION

DOROTHY SPEARS

On a cold, wind-swept morning in December 1903, Wilbur and Orville Wright introduced the world's first human flying machine to a small group of onlookers near the ocean in Kitty Hawk, North Carolina. With Orville riding solo in its open-air helm, the Wrights clocked an official hang-time of twelve seconds. It hovered at an altitude of around ten feet, for a distance of 120 feet, before plummeting to the ground. Orville escaped injury, and although the plane suffered some minor damages under its rudder, it was quickly repaired. By the end of the day, the Wright brothers had extended their flight time to fifty-nine seconds, traveling a record distance of 852 feet along the sandy dunes.

The Wright brothers' early experiments in sustained human flight, which offered physical evidence of abstract relationships between weight, power, and speed, ushered in such rapid developments in aviation that only thirty years later, Wiley Post, in a feat of extraordinary endurance, flew solo around the world, covering 15,596 miles in a mere seven days in his single engine Lockheed Vega. Eleven years after that, in 1944, an atomic bomb was unleashed from the belly of the B-29 Superfortress over Hiroshima. And by 1969, the astronauts Neil Armstrong and Buzz Aldrin had displayed enough of the so-called right stuff to withstand 195 hours, eighteen minutes and thirty-five seconds of total travel time, on the first manned round-trip flight to the moon.

Still, while reports of the triumphant—and tragic— escapades of pilots, flight crews, and airplane passengers have proliferated on the shelves of libraries and bookstores over the course of aviation's relatively brief history, a selection of these stories has yet to be collected in a single volume. *Flight Patterns: A Century of Stories about Flying* attempts to remedy this. Indeed, in isolating air travel as a recurring motif among intrepid authors of the last century, this anthology shows that the spirit of experimentation, which first led humans to the skies, has been deftly matched by extraordinary feats of writing.

The fiction, nonfiction, poetry, and diaristic accounts collected in *Flight Patterns* fall into several distinct categories. Stories told from the cockpit are represented by a chapter from Amelia Earhart's haunting compilation of writings, *Last Flight*, published after her disappearance in the South Pacific in 1937. The final chapter of Beryl Markham's memoir *West with the Night* vividly articulates how "the earth hurries to meet me," at the end of her fateful transatlantic journey from, as she puts it, Abington, England, to "a nameless swamp" in Cape Breton—nonstop. An excerpt from Antoine de Saint-Exupéry's award-winning novel, *Night Flight*, describes the impact of a unexpected storm on a mail courier flying over the Andes. A story from Roald Dahl's darkly magical story collection *Over to You*, and a chapter from master stylist James Salter's memoir, *Burning the Days*, evoke an infinite array of emotions, aspirations, and absurdities endured by military combat pilots.

The ground crew assumes center stage in Mary Lee Settle's chilling account of a control tower mishap during World War II, excerpted from her 1966 memoir, *All the Brave Promises: Memories of Aircraft Woman Second Class 2146391*. James Dickey's 1981 poem "Falling" telegraphs the final thoughts of a flight attendant sucked out the door of a flying aircraft. Meghan Daum's "Inside the Tube" offers a dry send-up of the twenty-first century flight attendant as "somehow blonde even when she's not blonde, a girl even when she's a guy. Part bimbo and part Red Cross." And in Bill Broun's "Heart Machine Time" a baggage attendant seeks solace while walking on a conveyor belt.

Romantic notions about pilots—and flying—on the part of spouses, lovers, best friends, and starry-eyed children play out in surprisingly different ways in an excerpt from Tom Wolfe's seminal book of reportage, *The Right Stuff*, and in short stories such as Alice Munro's "How I Met My Husband," Barry Hannah's "Testimony of Pilot," and Tobias Wolff's "Flyboys."

Parsing personal-boundary violations, rote intimacies, and, yes, also, sexual opportunities that arise when passengers find themselves in close proximity to total strangers are Jerry Stahl's "The Age of Love," recounting a fourteen-year-old's in-flight romp with a widow older than his mother; Mary Gaitskill's seething "The Girl on the Plane"; the opening chapter of Walter Kirn's frequent flier parody, *Up in the Air*; and David Sedaris's hilariously awkward "Cry Baby."

While presenting the unfolding of the flight motif over time, *Flight Patterns*, which is organized chronologically, according to the era depicted in each story, also reveals parallel developments—in world history, gender politics, popular culture, and even design and fashion.

In the opening chapter of his memoir, *The Spirit of Saint Louis*, for example, Charles A. Lindbergh reports on the early days of U.S. airmail, describing an incident in 1926 when, after ejecting from a mail carrier over a field in Illinois, he follows a rutted road to the home of a farmer. Finding the farmer's party telephone line "jammed" with locals gossiping about a nearby plane crash, Lindbergh breaks into the twittering phone line with a gruff announcement: "I was the pilot." The incident not only spurs Lindbergh to dream up plans for his legendary nonstop solo flight from New York to Paris, it conjures a Normal Rockwell–like moment in latter day telecommunications.

Decades later, in 1961, Joseph Heller's groundbreaking novel *Catch-22* connects the confused mental states of combat pilots to war's inherent absurdities. *Flight Patterns* includes the chapter of Heller's novel that invokes the term "catch-22" for the first time. The phrase has since earned the status of noun in English dictionaries, permeating all walks of life in the English-speaking world. Also of historical note: the first chapter of Erica Jong's 1973 novel *Fear of Flying* finds its protagonist Isadora Wing fantasizing about fellow passengers en route to a psychiatrist's convention in Hamburg. The result: Jong defines the term "zipless fuck," and establishes *Fear of Flying* as a feminist classic.

In her 1977 piece "On the Road," from *The White Album*, Joan Didion reports that during her first book tour, accompanied by her eleven-year-old daughter, "We spoke not of cities, but of airports. If rain fell at Logan, we could find sun at Dulles. Bags lost at O'Hare could be found at Dallas/Fort Worth." In airports, as in television interviews, the specifics of Didion's surroundings are regularly submerged into a catch-all generality: "*where are we heading?*" The question applies as much to her whirlwind travels as it does to the underlying sense of purposelessness besetting America in the late 1970s. By the end of her tour, Didion writes, "I began to see the country itself as a projection on air, a kind of hologram, an invisible grid of image and opinion and electronic impulse."

An excerpt from Linda Yablonsky's novel *The Story of Junk* captures the barbarity of smuggling heroin from Thailand, while evoking the zeitgiest of New York's East Village subculture of the 1980s. Sheila M. Schwartz's award-winning "Afterbirth" reveals the 1990s phenomenon of the Supermom, and the opening chapter of Brad Kessler's 2006 novel *Birds in Fall* portrays an aircraft cabin as a microcosm of more recently emerging globalism.

Flight Patterns also includes previously unpublished stories and personal essays. In "Dark Man at the Airport," Saïd Sayrafiezadeh offers a wry twist on racial profiling post–9/11. John Bowe laments a missed opportunity for a chat with a fellow passenger in "My Friends: There Is No Orchestra So Old It Cannot Be Enlivened by the Addition of a New and Heartfelt Player." Thomas Beller's short story "The Baggage Carousel" examine a teenager's bittersweet induction into the Mile High Club. In "Jack, the Road, and Me," Gary Horn conjures Jack Kerouac's adventurous spirit, even after a diving accident has confined him to life in a wheelchair. Aviation history meets a Hollywood happy ending in "The Adventures of *Hazy Lily*," Bernard Chabbert's poignant account of his sixty-eight-year-old Electra's escapades en route to the filming of *Amelia*, a 2009 movie starring Hilary Swank as Amelia Earhart.

Lastly, in "Pilot, Co-Pilot, Writer," Manuel Gonzales offers a horrifying—and often hilarious—portrayal of a hijacked plane condemned to circling an airport for twenty years.

Over the last century air travel has evolved from a high-risk experiment involving a few visionary pioneers to an efficient—and often irritating—means for distributing masses of people to the far reaches of the globe. Whether gridlock in the sky signals progress is debatable. But what becomes clear upon reading the letters, diaries, memoirs, poems, and fictional stories of pilots, flight attendants, crew members, and passengers included in *Flight Patterns* is that flight requires a state of suspension. This suspension is of real life as much as of disbelief, and during the hundred-year history of human air travel it has yielded writing that is, by turns, heroic, dreamy, subversive, and utterly dire.

This anthology promises an entertaining refuge for frequent fliers and a gateway to dreams for nighttime readers. *Flight Patterns* exudes the primal fear and cool perspective that can only come from seeing the world— and one's own life—from a great distance. Appealing to a wide swath of readers, these stories present an accumulation of voices and experiences. As Saïd Sayrafiezadeh remarked recently, "We are never more ourselves than when we're in an airplane." *Flight Patterns* renders airplane travel as a time capsule of modern life.

HOW I LEARNED TO FLY

ORVILLE WRIGHT

I suppose my brother and I always wanted to fly. Every youngster wants to, doesn't he? But it was not till we were out of school that the ambition took definite form.

We had read a good deal on the subject and we had studied Lilienthal's tables of figures with awe. Then one day, as it were, we said to each other: "Why not? Here are scientific calculations, based upon actual tests, to show us the sustaining powers of planes. We can spare a few weeks each year. Suppose, instead of going off somewhere to loaf, we put in our vacations building and flying gliders." I don't believe we dared think beyond gliders at that time—not aloud, at least.

That year—it was 1900—we went down to North Carolina, near Kitty Hawk. There were hills there in plenty, and not too many people about to scoff. Building that first glider was the best fun we'd ever had, too, despite the fact that we put it together as accurately as a watchmaker assembles and adjusts his finest timepiece. You see, we knew how to work because Lilienthal had made his tables years before, and men like Chanute, for example, had verified them.

To our great disappointment, however, the glider was not the success we had expected. It didn't behave as the figures on which it was constructed vouched that it should. Something was wrong. We looked at each other silently, and at the machine, and at the mass of figures compiled by Lilienthal. Then we proved up on them to see if we had slipped somewhere. If we had, we couldn't find the error; so we packed up and went home. We were agreed that we hadn't built our glider according to the scientific specifications. But there was another year coming and we weren't discouraged. We had just begun.

We wrote to Chanute, who was an engineer in Chicago at the time. We told him about our glider; we drew sketches of it for him; we set down long rows of figures.

And then we wound up our letter by begging him to explain why the tables of Lilienthal, which he had verified by experiments of his own, could not be proved by our machine.

Chanute didn't know. He wrote back it might be due to a different curve or pitch of surfaces on the planes, or something like that. But he was interested just the same, and when we went down to Kitty Hawk in 1901 we invited him to visit our camp.

Chanute came. Just before he left Chicago, I recall his telling us, he had read and OK'd the proofs of an article on aeronautics which he had prepared for the *Encyclopedia Britannica*, and in which he again told us of verifying Lilienthal's tables.

Well, he came to Kitty Hawk, and after he had looked our glider over carefully he said frankly that the trouble was not with any errors of construction in our machine. And right then all of us, I suspect, began to lose faith in Lilienthal and his gospel figures.

We had made a few flights the first year, and we made about 700 in 1901. Then we went back to Dayton to begin all over. It was like groping in the dark. Lilienthal's figures were not to be relied upon. Nobody else had done any scientific experimenting along these lines. Worst of all, we did not have money enough to build our glider with various types and sizes of planes or wings, simply to determine, in actual practice, which was the best. There was only the alternative of working out tables of our own. So we set to work along this line.

We took little bits of metal and we fashioned planes from them. I've still a deskful in my office in Dayton. There are flat ones, concave ones, convex ones, square ones, oblong ones, and scores and scores of other shapes and sizes. Each model contains six square inches. When we built our third glider the following year, ignoring Lilienthal altogether and constructing it from our own figures, we made the planes just 7,200 times the size of those little metal models back at Dayton.

It was hard work, of course, to get our figures right; to achieve the plane giving the greatest efficiency—and to know before we built that plane the exact proportion of efficiency we could expect. Of course, there were some books on the subject that were helpful. We went to the Dayton libraries and read what we could find there; afterward, when we had reached the same ends by months and months of study and experiment, we heard of other books that would have smoothed the way.

But those metal models told us how to build. By this time, too, Chanute was convinced that Lilienthal's tables were obsolete or inaccurate, and was wishing his utmost that he was not on record in an encyclopedia as verifying them.

During 1902 we made upward of 1,400 flights, sometimes going up a hundred times or more in a single day. Our runway was short, and it required a wind with velocity of at least twelve miles an hour to lift the machine. I recall sitting in it, ready to cast off one still day when the breeze seemed approaching. It came presently, rippling the daisies in the field, and just as it reached me I started the glider on the runway. But the innocent-appearing breeze was a whirlwind. It jerked the front of the machine sharply upward. I tilted my rudder to descend. Then the breeze spun downward, driving the glider to the ground with a tremendous shock and spinning me out headfirst. That's just a sample of what we had to learn about air currents; nobody had ever heard of "holes" in the air at that time. We had to go ahead and discover everything for ourselves.

But we glided successfully that summer, and we began to dream of greater things. Moreover, we aided Chanute to discover the errors in Lilienthal's tables, which were due to experimental flights down a hill with a descent so acute that the wind swept up its side and out from its surface with false buoying power. On the proper incline, which would be one parallel with the flight of the machine, the tables would not work out. Chanute wrote the article on aeronautics for the last edition of that encyclopedia again, but he corrected his figures this time.

The next step, of course, was the natural one of installing an engine. Others were experimenting, and it now became a question of which would be the first to fly with an engine. But we felt reasonably secure, because we had worked out all our own figures, and the others were still guessing or depending upon Lilienthal's or somebody's else that were inaccurate. Chanute knew we expected to try sustained flights later on, and while abroad that year mentioned the fact, so we had competition across the water, too.

We wrote to a number of automobile manufacturers about an engine. We demanded an eight-horse one of not over two hundred pounds in weight. This was allowing twenty-five pounds to each horsepower and did not seem to us prohibitive.

Several answers came. Some of the manufacturers politely declined to consider the building of such an engine; the gasoline motor was comparatively new then, and they were having trouble enough with standard sizes. Some said it couldn't be built according to our specifications, which was amusing, because lighter engines of greater power had already been used. Some seemed to think we were demented—"Building a flying machine, eh?" But one concern, of which we had never heard, said it could turn out a motor such as we wanted, and forwarded us figures. We were suspicious of figures by this time, and we doubted this concern's ability to get the horsepower claimed, considering the bore of the cylinders, etc. Later, I may add, we discovered that such an engine was capable of giving much greater horsepower. But we didn't know that at the time; we had to learn our A, B, C's as we went along.

Finally, though, we had a motor built. We had discovered that we could allow much more weight than we had planned at first, and in the end the getting of the engine became comparatively simple. The next step was to figure out what we wanted in the way of a screw propeller.

We turned to our books again. All the figures available dealt with the marine propeller—the thrust of the screw against the water. We had only turned from the solution of one problem to the intricacies of another. And the more we experimented with our models the more complicated it became.

There was the size to be considered. There was the material to be decided. There was the matter of the number of blades. There was the delicate question of the pitch of the blades. And then, after we had made headway with these problems, we began to scent new difficulties. One pitch and one force applied to the thrust against still air; what about the suction, and the air in motion, and the vacuum, and the thousand and one changing conditions? They were trying out the turbine engines on the big ocean liners at that time, with an idea of determining the efficiency of this type. The results were amazing in the exact percentage of efficiency developed by fuel and engine and propeller combined. A little above 40 percent, efficiency was considered wonderful. And the best we could do, after months of experimenting and studying, was to conceive and build a propeller that had to deliver 66 percent of efficiency, or fail us altogether. But we went down to Kitty Hawk pretty confident, just the same.

There were the usual vexatious delays. But finally, in December 1903, we were ready to make the first flight. My brother and I flipped a coin for the privilege of being the first to attempt a sustained flight in the air. Up to now, of course, we had merely taken turns. But this was a much bigger thing. He won.

The initial attempt was not a success. The machine fluttered for about a hundred feet down the side of the hill, pretty much as gliders had done. Then it settled with a thud, snapping off the propeller shaft, and thus effectually ending any further experiments for the time being.

It was getting late in the fall. Already the gales off Hatteras were beginning to howl. So I went back to Dayton personally to get a new shaft, and to hurry along the work as rapidly as I could.

It was finished at last. As I went to the train that morning, I heard for the first time of the machine constructed by Langley, which had dropped into a river the day before. You see, others were working just as desperately as we were to perfect a flying machine.

We adjusted the new shaft as soon as I reached Kitty Hawk. By the time we had finished it was late in the afternoon, with a stiff wind blowing. Our facilities for handling the machine were of the crudest. In the past, with our gliders, we had depended largely upon the help of some men from a life saving station, a mile or two away. As none of them happened to be at our camp that afternoon, we decided to postpone the next trial till morning.

It was cold that night. A man named Brinkley—W. C. Brinkley—dropped in to warm himself. He was buying salvage on one or more of the ships that had sunk during a recent storm that raged outside Kitty Hawk Point. I remember his looking curiously at the great framework, with its engine and canvas wings, and asking, "What's that?" We told him it was a flying machine, which we were going to try out the next morning, and asked him if he thought it would be a success. He looked out toward the ocean, which was getting rough and which was battering the sunken ships in which he was interested. Then he said, "Well you never can tell what will happen—if conditions are favorable." Nevertheless, he asked permission to stay overnight and watch the attempted flight.

Morning brought with it a twenty-seven mile gale. Our instruments, which were more delicate and more accurate than the Government's, made it a little over twenty-four; but the official reading by the United States was twenty-seven miles an hour. As soon as it was light we ran up our signal flag for help from the life-saving station. Three men were off duty that day, and came pounding over to camp. They were John T. Daniels, A. D. Etheridge and W. S. Dough. Before we were ready to make the flight a small boy of about thirteen or fourteen came walking past.

Daniels, who was a good deal of a joker, greeted him. The boy said his name was Johnny Moore, and was just strolling by. But he couldn't get his eyes off the machine that we had anchored in a sheltered place. He wanted to know what it was.

"Why, that's a duck-snarer," explained Daniels soberly. North Carolina, of course, is noted for its duck shooting. "You see, this man is going up in the air over a bay where there are hundreds of ducks on the water. When he is just over them, he will drop a big net and snare every last one. If you'll stick around a bit, Johnny, you can have a few ducks to take home."

So Johnny Moore was also a witness of our flights that day. I do not know whether the lack of any ducks to take away with him was a disappointment or not, but I suspect he did not feel compensated by what he saw.

The usual visitors did not come to watch us that day. Nobody imagined we would attempt a flight in such weather, for it was not only blowing hard, but it was also very cold. But just that fact, coupled with the knowledge that winter and its gales would be on top of us almost any time now, made us decide not to postpone the attempt any longer.

My brother climbed into the machine. The motor was started. With a short dash down the runway, the machine lifted into the air and was flying. It was only a flight of twelve seconds, and it was an uncertain, wavy, creeping sort of a flight at best; but it was a real flight at last and not a glide.

Then it was my turn. I had learned a little from watching my brother, but I found the machine pointing upward and downward in jerky undulations. This erratic course was due in part to my utter lack of experience in controlling a flying machine and in part to a new system of controls we had adopted, whereby a slight touch accomplished what a hard jerk or tug made necessary in the past. Naturally, I overdid everything. But I flew for about the same time my brother had.

He tried it again, the minute the men had carried it back to the runway, and added perhaps three or four seconds to the records we had just made. Then, after a few secondary adjustments, I took my seat for the second time. By now I had learned something about the controls, and about how a machine acted during a sustained flight, and I managed to keep in the air for fifty-seven seconds. I couldn't turn, of course—the hills wouldn't permit that— but I had no very great difficulty in handling it. When I came down I was eager to have another turn.

But it was getting late now, and we decided to postpone further trials until the next day. The wind had quieted, but it was very cold. In fact, it had been necessary for us to warm ourselves between each flight. Now we carried the machine back to a point near the camp, and stepped back to discuss what had happened.

My brother and I were not excited nor particularly exultant. We had been the first to fly successfully with a machine driven by an engine, but we had expected to be the first. We had known, down in our hearts, that the machine would fly just as it did. The proof was not astonishing to us. We were simply glad, that's all.

But the men from the life-saving station were very excited. Brinkley appeared dazed. Johnny Moore took our flights as a matter of course, and was presumably disappointed because we had snared no ducks.

And then, quite without warning, a puff of wind caught the forward part of the machine and began to tip it. We all rushed forward, but only Daniels was at the front. He caught the plane and clung desperately to it, as though thoroughly aware as were we of the danger of an upset of the frail thing of rods and wings. Upward and upward it lifted, with Daniels clinging to the plane to ballast it. Then, with a convulsive shudder, it tipped backward, dashing the man in against the engine, in a great tangle of cloth and wood and metal. As it turned over, I caught a last glimpse of his legs kicking frantically over the plane's edge. I'll confess I never expected to see him alive again.

But he did not even break a bone, although he was bruised from head to foot. When the machine had been pinned down at last, it was almost a complete wreck, necessitating many new parts and days and days of rebuilding. Winter was fairly on top of us, with Christmas only a few days off. We could do no more experimenting that year.

After all, though, it did not matter much. We could build better and stronger and more confidently another year. And we could go back home to Dayton and dream of time and distance and altitude records, and of machines for two or more passengers, and of the practical value of the heavier-than-air machine. For we had accomplished the ambition that stirred us as boys. We had learned to fly.

THE ST. LOUIS–CHICAGO MAIL

CHARLES A. LINDBERGH

Night already shadows the eastern sky. To my left, low on the horizon, a thin line of cloud is drawing on its evening sheath of black. A moment ago, it was burning red and gold. I look down over the side of my cockpit at the farm lands of central Illinois. Wheat shocks are gone from the fields. Close, parallel lines of the seeder, across a harrowed strip, show where winter planting has begun. A threshing crew on the farm below is quitting work for the day. Several men look up and wave as my mail plane roars overhead. Trees and buildings and stacks of grain stand shadowless in the diffused light of evening. In a few minutes it will be dark, and I'm still south of Peoria.

How quickly the long days of summer passed, when it was daylight all the way to Chicago. It seems only a few weeks ago, that momentous afternoon in April, when we inaugurated the airmail service. As chief pilot of the line, the honor of making the first flight had been mine. There were photographs, city officials, and handshaking all along the route that day. For was it not a milestone in a city's history, this carrying of the mail by air? We pilots, mechanics, postal clerks, and business executives, at St. Louis, Springfield, Peoria, Chicago, all felt that we were taking part in an event which pointed the way toward a new and marvelous era.

But after the first day's heavy load, swollen with letters of enthusiasts and collectors, interest declined. Men's minds turned back to routine business; the airmail saves a few hours at most; it's seldom really worth the extra cost per letter. Week after week, we've carried the limp and nearly empty sacks back and forth with a regularity in which we take great pride. Whether the mail compartment contains ten letters or ten thousand is beside the point. We have faith in the future. Some day we know the sacks will fill.

We pilots of the mail have a tradition to establish. The commerce of the air depends on it. Men have already died for that tradition. Every division of the mail routes has its hallowed points of crash where some pilot on a stormy night, or lost and blinded by fog, laid down his life on the altar of his occupation. Every man who flies the mail senses that altar and, consciously or unconsciously, in his way worships before it, knowing that his own next flight may end in the sacrifice demanded.

Our contract calls for five round trips each week. It's our mission to land the St. Louis mail in Chicago in time to connect with planes coming in from California, Minnesota, Michigan, and Texas—a time calculated to put letters in New York City for the opening of the eastern business day.

Three of us carry on this service: Philip Love, Thomas Nelson, and I. We've established the best record of all the routes converging at Chicago, with over ninety-nine percent of our scheduled flights completed. Ploughing through storms, wedging our way beneath low clouds, paying almost no attention to weather forecasts, we've more than once landed our rebuilt army warplanes on Chicago's Maywood field when other lines canceled out, when older and perhaps wiser pilots ordered their cargo put on a train. During the long days of summer we seldom missed a flight. But now winter is creeping up on us. Nights are lengthening; skies are thickening with haze and storm. We're already landing by floodlight at Chicago. In a few more weeks it will be dark when we glide down onto that narrow strip of cow pasture called the Peoria airmail field. Before the winter is past, even the meadow at Springfield will need lights. Today I'm over an hour late—engine trouble at St. Louis.

Lighting an airport is no great problem if you have money to pay for it. With revolving beacons, boundary markers, and floodlights, night flying isn't difficult. But our organization can't buy such luxuries. There's barely enough money to keep going from month to month.

The Robertson Aircraft Corporation is paid by the pounds of mail we carry, and often the sacks weigh more than the letters inside. Our operating expenses are incredibly low; but our revenue is lower still. The Corporation couldn't afford to buy new aircraft. All our planes and engines were purchased from Army salvage, and rebuilt in our shops at Lambert Field. We call them DHs, because the design originated with De Havilland, in England. They are biplanes, with a single, twelve-cylinder, four-hundred-horsepower Liberty engine in the nose. They were built during the war for bombing and observation purposes, and improved types were put in production in the United States. The military DH has two cockpits. In our planes the mail compartment is where the front cockpit used to be, and we mail pilots fly from the position where the wartime observer sat.

CHARLES A. LINDBERGH

We've been unable to buy full night-flying equipment for these planes, to say nothing of lights and beacons for the fields we land on. It was only last week that red and green navigation lights were installed on our DHs. Before that we carried nothing but one emergency flare and a pocket flashlight. When the dollars aren't there, you can't draw checks to pay for equipment. But it's bad economy, in the long run, to operate a mail route without proper lights. That has already cost us one plane. I lost a DH just over a week ago because I didn't have an extra flare, or wing lights, or a beacon to go back to.

I encountered fog, that night, on the northbound flight between Marseilles and Chicago. It was a solid bank, rolling in over the Illinois River valley. I turned back southwest, and tried to drop my single flare so I could land on one of the farm fields below; but when I pulled the release lever nothing happened. Since the top of the fog was less than a thousand feet high, I decided to climb over it and continue on my route in the hope of finding a clear spot around the airmail field. Then, if I could get under the clouds, I could pick up the Chicago beacon, which had been installed at government expense.

Glowing patches of mist showed me where cities lay on the earth's surface. With these patches as guides, I had little trouble locating the outskirts of Chicago and the general area of Maywood. But a blanket of fog, about eight hundred feet thick, covered the field. Mechanics told me afterward that they played a searchlight upward and burned two barrels of gasoline on the ground in an effort to attract my attention. I saw no sign of their activities.

After circling for a half hour I headed west, hoping to pick up one of the beacons on the transcontinental route. They were fogged in too. By then I had discovered that the

14

failure of my flare to drop was caused by slack in the release cable, and that the flare might still function if I pulled on the cable instead of on the release lever. I turned southwest, toward the edge of the fog, intending to follow my original plan of landing on some farmer's field by flarelight. At 8:20 my engine spit a few times and cut out almost completely. At first I thought the carburetor jets had clogged, because there should have been plenty of fuel in my main tank. But I followed the emergency procedure of turning on the reserve. Then, since I was only fifteen hundred feet high, I shoved the flashlight into my pocket and got ready to jump; but power surged into the engine again. Obviously nothing was wrong with the carburetor—the main tank had run dry. That left me with reserve fuel for only twenty minutes of flight—not enough time to reach the edge of the fog.

I decided to jump when the reserve tank ran dry, and I had started to climb for altitude when a light appeared on the ground—just a blink, but that meant a break in the fog. I circled down to twelve hundred feet and pulled out the flare-release cable. This time the flare functioned, but it showed only a solid layer of mist. I waited until the flare sank out of sight on its parachute, and began climbing again. Ahead, I saw the glow from a small city. I banked away, toward open country.

I was five thousand feet high when my engine cut the second time. I unbuckled my safety belt, dove over the right side of the fuselage, and after two or three seconds of fall pulled the rip cord. The parachute opened right away. I was playing my flashlight down toward the top of the fog bank when I was startled to hear the sound of an airplane in the distance. It was coming toward me. In a few seconds I saw my DH, dimly, less than a quarter mile away and about on a level with me. It was circling in my direction, left wing down. Since I thought it was completely out of gasoline, I had neglected to cut the switches before I jumped. When the nose dropped, due to the loss of the weight of my body in the tail, some additional fuel apparently drained forward into the carburetor, sending the plane off on a solo flight of its own.

My concern was out of proportion to the danger. In spite of the sky's tremendous space, it seemed crowded with traffic. I shoved my flashlight into my pocket and caught hold of the parachute risers so I could slip the canopy one way or the other in case the plane kept pointing toward me. But it was fully a hundred yards away when it passed, leaving me on the outside of its circle. The engine noise receded, and then increased until the DH appeared again, still at my elevation. The rate of descent of plane and parachute were approximately equal. I counted five spirals, each a little farther away than the last. Then I sank into the fog bank.

Knowing the ground to be less than a thousand feet below, I reached for the flashlight. It was gone. In my excitement when I saw the plane coming toward me, I hadn't pushed it far enough into my pocket. I held my feet together, guarded my face with my hands, and waited. I heard the DH pass once again. Then I saw the outline of the ground, braced myself for impact, and hit—in a cornfield. By the time I got back on my feet, the chute had collapsed and was lying on top of the corn tassels. I rolled it up, tucked it under my arm, and started walking between two rows of corn. The stalks were higher than my head. The leaves crinkled as I brushed past them. I climbed over a fence, into a stubble field. There I found wagon tracks and followed them. Ground visibility was about a hundred yards.

The wagon tracks took me to a farmyard. First, the big barn loomed up in haze. Then a lighted window beyond it showed that someone was still up. I was heading for the house when I saw an automobile move slowly along the road and stop, playing its spotlight from one side to the other. I walked over to the car. Several people were in it.

"Did you hear that airplane?" one of them called out as I approached.

"I'm the pilot," I said.

"An airplane just dove into the ground," the man went on, paying no attention to my answer. "Must be right near here. God, it made a racket!" He kept searching with his spotlight, but the beam didn't show much in the haze.

"I'm the pilot," I said again. "I was flying it." My words got through that time. The spotlight stopped moving.

"*You're the pilot?* Good God, how—"

"I jumped with a parachute," I said, showing him the white bundle.

"You aren't hurt?"

"Not a bit. But I've got to find the wreck and get the mail sacks."

"It must be right near by. Get in and we'll drive along the road a piece. Good God, what went wrong? You must have had *some* experience! You're sure you aren't hurt?"

We spent a quarter hour searching, unsuccessfully. Then I accompanied the farmer to his house. My plane, he said, had flown over his roof only a few seconds before it struck the ground. I asked to use his telephone. The party line was jammed with voices, all talking about the airplane that had crashed. I broke in with the statement that I was the pilot, and asked the telephone operator to put in emergency calls for St. Louis and Chicago. Then I asked her if anyone had reported the exact location of the wreck. A

17

number of people had heard the plane pass overhead just before it hit, she replied, but nothing more definite had come in.

I'd hardly hung up and turned away when the bell rang—three longs and a short.

"That's our signal," the farmer said.

My plane had been located, the operator told me, about two miles from the house I was in. We drove to the site of the crash. The DH was wound up in a ball-shaped mass. It had narrowly missed a farmhouse, hooked one wing on a grain shock a quarter mile beyond, skidded along the ground for eighty yards, ripped through a fence, and come to rest on the edge of a cornfield. Splinters of wood and bits of torn fabric were strewn all around. The mail compartment was broken open and one sack had been thrown out; but the mail was undamaged—I took it to the nearest post office to be entrained.

The Illinois River angles in from the west. Lights are blinking on in the city of Peoria—long lines of them for streets; single spots for house and office windows. I glance at the watch on my instrument board—6:35. Good! I've made up ten minutes since leaving St. Louis. I nose down toward the flying field, letting the air-speed needle climb to 120 miles an hour. The green mail truck is at its usual place in the fence corner. The driver, standing by its side, lifts his arm in greeting as my plane approaches. And for this admiring audience of one, I dive down below the treetops and chandelle up around the field, climbing steeply until trembling wings warn me to level off. Then, engine throttled, I sideslip down to a landing, almost brushing through high branches on the leeward border.

The pasture is none too large for a De Haviland, even in daytime. We'll have to be doubly careful at night. If a pilot glides down a little fast, he'll overshoot. To make matters worse, a small gully spoils the eastern portion of the field for landing, so we often have to come in with a cross wind.

I taxi up to the mail truck, blast the tail around with the engine, and pull back my throttle until the propeller is just ticking over. The driver, in brown whipcord uniform and visored cap, comes up smiling with the mail sack draped over one arm. It's a registered sack, fastened at the top with a big brass padlock. Good! The weight of that lock is worth nearly two dollars to us, and there was registered mail from Springfield and St. Louis too. Those locks add an appreciable sum to our monthly revenue.

I toss the sack down onto aluminum-faced floor boards and pass out two equally empty sacks from St. Louis and Springfield. A few dozen letters in, a few dozen letters out, that's the Peoria air mail.

"No fuel today?"

"No, plenty of fuel," I answer. "I've had a good tail wind."

It's a relief to both of us, for twenty minutes of hard labor are required to roll a barrel of gasoline over from our cache in the fence corner, pump thirty or forty gallons into the DH's tank, and start the engine again. That is, it takes twenty minutes if the engine starts easily; an indefinite time if it doesn't.

Leaving the engine idling, we walk over to inspect the field-lighting equipment which has been improvised for the night landings of winter. Since the Robertson Aircraft Corporation keeps no mechanics at intermediate stops between St. Louis and Chicago, all the assistance we have comes from the mail truck drivers. They help us with refueling and starting, keep the wind sock untangled, and hold on to a wing when taxiing is difficult. For whatever the pilot can't do alone, he has to call upon them. It's not part of their work; they get nothing for it, but they're always ready to give us a hand. Now we'll have to depend on them to arrange the lights for our night landings.

Electric floodlights cost too much, so our Corporation bought flares instead. The first shipment has just arrived. The driver unlocks a plank box near the gasoline barrels and takes out a long, cylindrical flare. On one end there's a spike that can be stuck into the ground to hold it upright, like a piece of Fourth of July fireworks. We selected a type that would burn for nearly two minutes—long enough if lighted at the right moment, and much less expensive than the larger ones.

I show the driver where it should be placed with different directions of wind—always on the leeward end of the landing strip, with a curved sheet of tin behind it for a reflector and to keep the intense light from blinding the pilot as he glides down. A flare is not to be set off, I tell him, unless he sees the plane's navigation lights blink several times. On moonlit nights we can economize by not using one at all.

I'm an hour and ten minutes behind schedule, taking off. The trees at the far end of the field have merged into a solid clump in thickening dusk, have lost their individual identity. The moon, just past full, is rising in the east. I didn't notice it before I landed, but now it seems to be competing with me for domination of the sky—just the two of us, climbing, and all the world beneath.

I welcome the approach of night as twilight fades into brilliant moonlight. The day has been crystal clear and almost cloudless; perfect for flying. It's been almost too perfect for flying the mail, for there's no ability required in holding your course over familiar country with a sharp horizon in every quarter. You simply sit, touching stick and rudder lightly, dreaming of the earth below, of experiences past, of adventures that may come. There's nothing else to do, nothing to match yourself against. There hasn't been even an occasional cloud near enough to burrow through. Skill is no asset. The spirit of conquest is gone from the air. On such an evening you might better be training students. It's an evening for beginners, not for pilots of the mail—no tricks of wind, no false horizons. Its hours were shaped for beauty, not for contest.

The last tint of pink disappears from the western sky, leaving to the moon complete mastery of night. Its light floods through woods and fields, reflects up from bends of rivers, shines on the silver wings of my biplane, turning them a greenish hue. It makes the earth seem more like a planet, and me a part of the heavens above it, as though I too had a right to an orbit in the sky. I look down toward the ground, at the faintly lighted farmhouse windows and the distant glow of cities, wondering what acts of life are covered by the weird semidarkness in which only outlines can be seen. Around those points of light are homes and men— family gatherings, parties, doctors at births and deathbeds, hope and despair, youth and age. That line of six glowing dots—is it a barroom, church, or dance hall? And all those myriad lights, all the turmoil and works of men, seem to hang so precariously on the great sphere hurtling through the heavens, a phosphorescent moss on its surface, vulnerable to the brush of a hand. I feel aloof and unattached, in the solitude of space. Why return to that moss; why submerge myself in brick-walled human problems when all the crystal universe is mine? Like the moon, I can fly on forever through space, past the mail field at Chicago, beyond the state of Illinois, over mountains, over oceans, independent of the world below.

Suppose I really could stay up here and keep on flying; suppose gasoline didn't weigh so much and I could put enough in the tanks to last for days. Suppose, like the man on the magic carpet, I could fly anywhere I wanted to— anywhere in the world—to the North Pole or to China or to some jungle island if I wished. How much fuel *could* a plane carry if its fuselage were filled with tanks? But Fonck tried that out in his big Sikorsky biplane, only a few days ago, and crashed—crashed into flames on a New York field, taking off for a nonstop flight to Paris. Why does fuel have to be so heavy? If gasoline weighed only a pound per gallon instead of six, there'd be no limit to the places one could fly—if the engine kept on running.

If the engine kept on running! The schooled habit of periodic instrument readings brings me back to the mechanics of human flight. One can't be following a satellite's orbit and watching these dials at the same time. I return abruptly to earthly problems of temperature, oil pressure, and rpm. I contended for a moment, but the moon has won. Independent of the world? Only as long as the engine runs smoothly and the fuel holds out. I have fuel enough for another two hours at most. But long before that I'll have to be down at Chicago; my DH safely in the hangar; the mail sorted, resacked, and most of it in the cockpit of an eastbound transcontinental plane, headed for the Alleghenies and New York City.

I'm annoyed at the thought of landing. It's a roundabout method anyway, this flying the mail to Chicago to get it east. Why shouldn't we carry it direct to New York from St. Louis? True, there aren't enough letters in that wilted sack to pay for a direct service, but the mail will grow in volume as aircraft improve and people learn to use them. The more time we save, the more letters we'll get. If we flew direct, we could wait until the business day closed before collecting St. Louis mail, and still land at New York City before offices opened the next morning. Such a service would really be worth the cost of extra postage. We might even be able to fly from St. Louis to New York nonstop, eventually. Not with these salvaged Army DHs—they can't reach Chicago against a headwind without refueling—but with new planes and new engines—

The lights of a small city emerge behind my right wing—Streator. Ottawa is ahead and a few miles to the left. I make a mental note of my position, glance at the instruments, and let the plane bore its way on toward Chicago.

Those new Lairds the Northwest pilots are flying, for instance—they have only half the power of our DHs, but they're faster and they carry a bigger load. And there's that Wright-Bellanca. It has taken off with an incredible weight on some of its test flights. With three planes like the Bellanca we could easily carry the mail nonstop between St. Louis and New York, and on clear nights possibly two or three passengers besides.

But the cost—it would take ten or fifteen thousand dollars to buy just one Wright-Bellanca. Who could afford to invest so much money in a single airplane, to say nothing of the three that would be needed for a mail route? Our Corporation has a hard enough time keeping going with the DHs, and they cost only a few hundred dollars apiece.

I grow conscious of the limits of my biplane, of the inefficiency of its wings, struts, and wires. They bind me to earth and to the field ahead at Chicago. A Bellanca would cruise at least fifteen miles an hour faster, burn only half the amount of gasoline, and carry double the pay load of a DH. What a future aviation has when such planes can be built; yet how few people realize it! Businessmen think of aviation in terms of barnstorming, flying circuses, crashes, and high costs per flying hour. Somehow they must be made to understand the possibilities of flight. If they could see the real picture, it wouldn't be difficult to finance an airline between St. Louis and New York, even at the price of three Bellancas. Then commercial pilots wouldn't have to fly old army warplanes or make night landings with flares instead of floodlights.

If only I had the Bellanca, I'd show St. Louis businessmen what modern aircraft could do; I'd take them to New York in eight or nine hours. They'd see how swiftly and safely passengers could fly. There are all kinds of records I could break for demonstration—distance, altitude with load, nonstop flights across the country. In a Bellanca filled with fuel tanks I could fly on all night, like the moon. How far could it go if it carried nothing but gasoline? With the engine throttled down it could stay aloft for days. It's fast, too. Judging from the accounts I've read, it's the most efficient plane ever built. It could break the world's endurance record, and the transcontinental, and set a dozen marks for range and speed and weight. Possibly—my mind is startled at its thought—I could fly nonstop between New York and Paris.

New York to Paris—it sounds like a dream. And yet— if one could carry fuel enough (and the Bellanca might)— if the engine didn't stop (and those new Wright Whirlwinds seldom do stop; they aren't like our old Liberties)—if one just held to the right course long enough, one should arrive in Europe. The flying couldn't be more dangerous or the weather worse than the night mail in winter. With fuel enough, a pilot would never have to land in fog; if he got caught, he could simply keep on going until he found clear weather. Navigation?—over the Atlantic and at night, boring through dark and unknown skies, toward a continent I've never seen? The very thought makes me rise to contend again with the moon—sweeping over oceans and continents, looking down on farms and cities, letting the planet turn below.

Why shouldn't I fly from New York to Paris? I'm almost twenty-five. I have more than four years of aviation behind me, and close to two thousand hours in the air. I've barnstormed over half of the forty-eight states. I've flown my mail through the worst of nights. I know the wind currents of the Rocky Mountains and the storms of the Mississippi Valley as few pilots know them. During my year at Brooks and Kelly as a flying cadet, I learned the basic elements of navigation. I'm a Captain in the 110th Observation Squadron of Missouri's National Guard. Why am I not qualified for such a flight?

Not so long ago, when I was a student in college, just flying an airplane seemed a dream. But that dream turned into reality. Then, as a two-hundred-hour pilot barnstorming through the country for a living, the wings of the Army Air Service seemed almost beyond reach. But I won them. Finally, to be a pilot of the night mail appeared the summit of ambition for a flyer; yet here I am, in the cockpit of a mail plane boring through the night. Why wouldn't a flight across the ocean prove as possible as all these things have been? As I attempted them, I can—I will attempt that too. I'll organize a flight to Paris!

I sit contemplating my decision. The magnitude of the undertaking overwhelms me for a time. This idea which has come upon me, this vision born of a night and altitude and moonlight, how am I to translate it into an actual airplane flying over the Atlantic Ocean to Europe and to France?

The important thing is to start; to lay a plan, and then follow it step by step no matter how small or large each one by itself may seem. I haven't enough money to buy a Wright-Bellanca. Could any other plane make the flight—the Fokker, or the new Travel Air? They might not cost as much. Maybe I could raise the money in St. Louis. I can put up some myself. Other people might be willing to take part when they realize all the things that could be done with a Bellanca. Then there's the Orteig prize of $25,000 for the first man to fly from New York to Paris nonstop—that's more than enough to pay for a plane and all the expenses of the flight. And the plane would still be almost as good as new after I landed in Europe. In fact, a successful trip to Paris wouldn't cost anything at all. It might even end up a profitable venture.

There must be men of means with enough vision to take the risk involved. The problem is to find them, and to get them to listen to my plan. Maybe the Wright Aeronautical Corporation itself would back the project. What could be a better advertisement for their plane and engine than a nonstop flight across the ocean? New York to Paris nonstop! If airplanes can do that, there's no limit to aviation's future.

The Chicago beacon flashes in the distance. In ten minutes I must land.

WEST WITH THE NIGHT

BERYL MARKHAM

I have seldom dreamed a dream worth dreaming again, or at least none worth recording. Mine are not enigmatic dreams; they are peopled with characters who are plausible and who do plausible things, and I am the most plausible amongst them. All the characters in my dreams have quiet voices like the voice of the man who telephoned me at Elstree one morning in September of 1936 and told me that there was rain and strong head winds over the west of England and over the Irish Sea, and that there were variable winds and clear skies in mid-Atlantic and fog off the coast of Newfoundland.

"If you are still determined to fly the Atlantic this late in the year," the voice said, "the Air Ministry suggests that the weather it is able to forecast for tonight, and for tomorrow morning, will be about the best you can expect."

The voice had a few other things to say, but not many, and then it was gone, and I lay in bed half-suspecting that the telephone call and the man who made it were only parts of the mediocre dream I had been dreaming. I felt that if I closed my eyes the unreal quality of the message would be re-established, and that, when I opened them again, this would be another ordinary day with its usual beginning and its usual routine.

But of course I could not close my eyes, nor my mind, nor my memory. I could lie there for a few moments—remembering how it had begun, and telling myself, with senseless repetition, that by tomorrow morning I should either have flown the Atlantic to America—or I should not have flown it. In either case this was the day I would try.

I could stare up at the ceiling of my bedroom in Aldenham House, which was a ceiling undistinguished as ceilings go, and feel less resolute than anxious, much less brave than foolhardy. I could say to myself, "You needn't do it, of course," knowing at the same time that nothing is so inexorable as a promise to your pride.

I could ask, "Why risk it?" as I have been asked since, and I could answer, "Each to his element." By his nature a sailor must sail, by his nature a flyer must fly. I could compute that I had flown a quarter of a million miles; and I could foresee that, so long as I had a plane and the sky was there, I should go on flying more miles.

There was nothing extraordinary in this. I had learned a craft and had worked hard learning it. My hands had been taught to seek the controls of a plane. Usage had taught them. They were at ease clinging to a stick, as a cobbler's fingers are in repose grasping an awl. No human pursuit achieves dignity until it can be called work, and when you can experience a physical loneliness for the tools of your trade, you see that the other things—the experiments, the irrelevant vocations, the vanities you used to hold—were false to you.

Record flights had actually never interested me very much for myself. There were people who thought that such flights were done for admiration and publicity, and worse.

But of all the records—from Louis Blériot's first crossing of the English Channel in 1909, through and beyond Kingsford Smith's flight from San Francisco to Sydney, Australia— none had been made by amateurs, nor by novices, nor by men or women less than hardened to failure, or less than masters of their trade. None of these was false. They were a company that simple respect and simple ambition made it worth more than an effort to follow.

The Carberrys (of Seramai) were in London and I could remember everything about their dinner party—even the menu. I could remember June Carberry and all her guests, and the man named McCarthy, who lived in Zanzibar, leaning across the table and saying, "J. C., why don't you finance Beryl for a record flight?"

I could lie there staring lazily at the ceiling and recall J. C.'s dry answer: "A number of pilots have flown the North Atlantic, west to east. Only Jim Mollison has done it alone the other way—from Ireland. Nobody has done it alone from England—man or woman. I'd be interested in that, but nothing else. If you want to try it, Burl, I'll back you. I think Edgar Percival could build a plane that would do it, provided you can fly it. Want to chance it?"

"Yes."

I could remember saying that better than I could remember anything—except J. C.'s almost ghoulish grin, and his remark that sealed the agreement: "It's a deal, Burl. I'll furnish the plane and you fly the Atlantic—but, gee, I wouldn't tackle it for a million. Think of all that black water! Think how cold it is!"

And I had thought of both.

I had thought of both for a while, and then there had been other things to think about. I had moved to Elstree, half an hour's flight from the Percival Aircraft Works at

Gravesend, and almost daily for three months now I had flown down to the factory in a hired plane and watched the Vega Gull they were making for me. I had watched her birth and watched her growth. I had watched her wings take shape, and seen wood and fabric moulded to her ribs to form her long, sleek belly, and I had seen her engine cradled into her frame, and made fast.

The Gull had a turquoise-blue body and silver wings. Edgar Percival had made her with care, with skill, and with worry—the care of a veteran flyer, the skill of a master designer, and the worry of a friend. Actually the plane was a standard sport model with a range of only six hundred and sixty miles. But she had a special undercarriage built to carry the weight of her extra oil and petrol tanks. The tanks were fixed into the wings, into the center section, and into the cabin itself. In the cabin they formed a wall around my seat, and each tank had a petcock of its own. The petcocks were important.

"If you open one," said Percival, "without shutting the other first, you may get an airlock. You know the tanks in the cabin have no gauges, so it may be best to let one run completely dry before opening the next. Your motor might go dead in the interval—but she'll start again. She's a De Havilland Gipsy—and Gipsys never stop."

I had talked to Tom. We had spent hours going over the Atlantic chart, and I had realized that the tinker of Molo, now one of England's great pilots, had traded his dreams and had got in return a better thing. Tom had grown older too; he had jettisoned a deadweight of irrelevant hopes and wonders, and had left himself a realistic code that had no room for temporizing or easy sentiment.

"I'm glad you're going to do it, Beryl. It won't be simple. If you can get off the ground in the first place, with such an immense load of fuel, you'll be alone in that plane about a night and a day—mostly night. Doing it east to west, the wind's against you. In September, so is the weather. You won't have a radio. If you misjudge your course only a few degrees, you'll end up in Labrador or in the sea—so don't misjudge anything."

Tom could still grin. He had grinned; he had said: "Anyway, it ought to amuse you to think that your financial backer lives on a farm called 'Place of Death' and your plane is being built at 'Gravesend.' If you were consistent, you'd christen the Gull 'The Flying Tombstone.'"

I hadn't been that consistent. I had watched the building of the plane and I had trained for the flight like an athlete. And now, as I lay in bed, fully awake, I could still hear the quiet voice of the man from the Air Ministry intoning, like the voice of a dispassionate court clerk: "The weather for tonight and tomorrow . . . will be about the best you can expect." I should have liked to discuss the flight once more with Tom before I took off, but he was on a special job up north. I got out of bed and bathed and put on my flying clothes and took some cold chicken packed in a cardboard box and flew over to the military field at Abingdon, where the Vega Gull waited for me under the care of the RAF. I remember that the weather was clear and still.

Jim Mollison lent me his watch. He said: "This is not a gift. I wouldn't part with it for anything. It got me across the North Atlantic and the South Atlantic too. Don't lose it—and, for God's sake, don't get it wet. Salt water would ruin the works."

Brian Lewis gave me a life-saving jacket. Brian owned the plane I had been using between Elstree and Gravesend, and he had thought a long time about a farewell gift. What could be more practical than a pneumatic jacket that could be inflated through a rubber tube?

"You could float around in it for days." said Brian. But I *had* to decide between the lifesaver and warm clothes. I couldn't have both, because of their bulk, and I hate the cold, so I left the jacket.

And Jock Cameron, Brian's mechanic, gave me a sprig of heather. If it had been a whole bush of heather, complete with roots growing in an earthen jar, I think I should have taken it, bulky or not. The blessing of Scotland, bestowed by a Scotsman, is not to be dismissed. Nor is the well-wishing of a ground mechanic to be taken lightly, for these men are the pilot's contact with reality.

It is too much that with all those pedestrian centuries behind us we should, in a few decades, have learned to fly; it is too heady a thought, too proud a boast. Only the dirt on a mechanic's hands, the straining vise, the splintered bolt of steel underfoot on the hangar floor—only these and such anxiety as the face of a Jock Cameron can hold for a pilot and his plane before a flight, serve to remind us that, not unlike the heather, we too are earthbound. We fly, but we have not "conquered" the air. Nature presides in all her dignity, permitting us the study and the use of such of her forces as we may understand. It is when we presume to intimacy, having been granted only tolerance, that the harsh stick falls across our impudent knuckles and we rub the pain, staring upward, startled by our ignorance.

"Here is a sprig of heather," said Jock, and I took it and pinned it into a pocket of my flying jacket.

There were press cars parked outside the field at Abingdon, and several press planes and photographers, but the RAF kept everyone away from the grounds except technicians and a few of my friends.

The Carberrys had sailed for New York a month ago to wait for me there. Tom was still out of reach with no knowledge of my decision to leave, but that didn't matter so much, I thought. It didn't matter because Tom was unchanging—neither a fairweather pilot nor a fairweather friend. If for a month, or a year, or two years we sometimes had not seen each other, it still hadn't mattered. Nor did this. Tom would never say, "You should have let me know." He assumed that I had learned all that he had tried to teach me, and for my part, I thought of him, even then, as the merest student must think of his mentor. I could sit in a cabin overcrowded with petrol tanks and set my course for North America, but the knowledge of my hands on the controls would be Tom's knowledge. His words of caution and words of guidance, spoken so long ago, so many times, on bright mornings over the veldt or over a forest, or with a far mountain visible at the tip of our wing, would be spoken again, if I asked.

So it didn't matter, I thought. It was silly to think about.

You can live a lifetime and, at the end of it, know more about other people than you know about yourself. You learn to watch other people, but you never watch yourself because you strive against loneliness. If you read a book, or shuffle a deck of cards, or care for a dog, you are avoiding yourself. The abhorrence of loneliness is as natural as wanting to live at all. If it were otherwise, men would never have bothered to make an alphabet, nor to have fashioned words out of what were only animal sounds, nor to have crossed continents—each man to see what the other looked like.

Being alone in an airplane for even so short a time as a night and a day, irrevocably alone, with nothing to observe but your instruments and your own hands in semi-darkness, nothing to contemplate but the size of your small courage, nothing to wonder about but the beliefs, the faces, and the hopes rooted in your mind—such an experience can be as startling as the first awareness of a stranger walking by your side at night. You are the stranger.

It is dark already and I am over the south of Ireland. There are the lights of Cork and the lights are wet; they are drenched in Irish rain, and I am above them and dry. I am above them and the plane roars in a sobbing world, but it imparts no sadness to me. I feel the security of solitude, the exhilaration of escape. So long as I can see the lights and imagine the people walking under them, I feel selfishly triumphant, as if I have eluded care and left even the small sorrow of rain in other hands.

It is a little over an hour now since I left Abingdon. England, Wales, and the Irish Sea are behind me like so much time used up. On a long flight distance and time are the same. But there had been a moment when Time stopped—and Distance too. It was the moment I lifted the blue-and-silver Gull from the aerodrome, the moment the photographers aimed their cameras, the moment I felt the craft refuse its burden and strain toward the earth in sullen rebellion, only to listen at last to the persuasion of stick and elevators, the dogmatic argument of blueprints that said she *had* to fly because the figures proved it.

So she had flown, and once airborne, once she had yielded to the sophistry of a draughtsman's board, she had said, "There: I have lifted the weight. Now, where are we bound?"—and the question had frightened me.

"We are bound for a place thirty-six hundred miles from here—two thousand miles of it unbroken ocean. Most of the way it will be night. We are flying west with the night."

So there behind me is Cork; and ahead of me is Bere-haven Lighthouse. It is the last light, standing on the last land. I watch it, counting the frequency of its flashes—so many to the minute. Then I pass it and fly out to sea.

The fear is gone now—not overcome nor reasoned away. It is gone because something else has taken its place; the confidence and the trust, the inherent belief in the security of land underfoot—now this faith is transferred to my plane, because the land has vanished and there is no other tangible thing to fix faith upon. Flight is but momentary escape from the eternal custody of earth.

Rain continues to fall, and outside the cabin it is totally dark. My altimeter says that the Atlantic is two thousand feet below me, my Sperry Artificial Horizon says that I am flying level. I judge my drift at three degrees more than my weather chart suggests, and fly accordingly. I am flying blind. A beam to follow would help. So would a radio—but then, so would clear weather. The voice of the man at the Air Ministry had not promised a storm.

I feel the wind rising and the rain falls hard. The smell of petrol in the cabin is so strong and the roar of the plane so loud that my senses are almost deadened. Gradually it becomes unthinkable that existence was ever otherwise.

At ten o'clock p.m. I am flying along the Great Circle Course for Harbour Grace, Newfoundland, into a forty-mile headwind at a speed of one hundred and thirty miles an hour. Because of the weather, I cannot be sure of how many more hours I have to fly, but I think it must be between sixteen and eighteen.

At ten-thirty I am still flying on the large cabin tank of petrol, hoping to use it up and put an end to the liquid swirl that has rocked the plane since my takeoff. The tank has no gauge, but written on its side is the assurance: "This tank is good for four hours."

There is nothing ambiguous about such a guaranty. I believe it, but at twenty-five minutes to eleven, my motor coughs and dies, and the Gull is powerless above the sea.

I realize that the heavy drone of the plane has been, until this moment, complete and comforting silence. It is the actual silence following the last splutter of the engine that stuns me.

I can't feel any fear; I can't feel anything. I can only observe with a kind of stupid disinterest that my hands are violently active and know that, while they move, I am being hypnotized by the needle of my altimeter.

I suppose that the denial of natural impulse is what is meant by "keeping calm," but impulse has reason in it. If it is night and you are sitting in an airplane with a stalled motor, and there are two thousand feet between you and the sea, nothing can be more reasonable than the impulse to pull back your stick in the hope of adding to that two thousand, if only by a little. The thought, the knowledge, the law that tells you that your hope lies not in this, but in a contrary act—the act of directing your impotent craft toward the water—seems a terrifying abandonment, not only of reason, but of sanity. Your mind and your heart reject it. It is your hands—your stranger's hands—that follow with unfeeling precision the letter of the law.

I sit there and watch my hands push forward on the stick and feel the Gull respond and begin its dive to the sea. Of course it is a simple thing; surely the cabin tank has run dry too soon. I need only to turn another petcock . . .

But it is dark in the cabin. It is easy to see the luminous dial of the altimeter and to note that my height is now eleven hundred feet, but it is not easy to see a petcock that is somewhere near the floor of the plane. A hand gropes and reappears with an electric torch, and fingers, moving with agonizing composure, find the petcock and turn it; and I wait.

At three hundred feet the motor is still dead, and I am conscious that the needle of my altimeter seems to whirl like the spoke of a spindle winding up the remaining distance between the plane and the water. There is some lightning, but the quick flash only serves to emphasize the darkness. How high can waves reach—twenty feet, perhaps? Thirty?

It is impossible to avoid the thought that this is the end of my flight, but my reactions are not orthodox; the various incidents of my entire life do not run through my mind like a motion-picture film gone mad. I only feel that all this has happened before—and it has. It has all happened a hundred times in my mind, in my sleep, so that now I am not really caught in terror; I recognize a familiar scene, a familiar story with its climax dulled by too much telling.

I do not know how close to the waves I am when the motor explodes to life again. But the sound is almost meaningless. I see my hand easing back on the stick, and I feel the Gull climb up into the storm, and I see the altimeter whirl like a spindle again, paying out the distance between myself and the sea.

The storm is strong. It is comforting. It is like a friend shaking me and saying, "Wake up! You were only dreaming."

But soon I am thinking. By simple calculation I find that my motor had been silent for perhaps an instant more than thirty seconds.

I ought to thank God—and I do, though indirectly. I thank Geoffrey De Havilland who designed the indomitable Gipsy, and who, after all, must have been designed by God in the first place.

A lighted ship—the daybreak—some steep cliffs standing in the sea. The meaning of these will never change for pilots. If one day an ocean can be flown within an hour, if men can build a plane that so masters time, the sight of land will be no less welcome to the steersman of that fantastic craft. He will have cheated laws that the cunning of science has taught him how to cheat, and he will feel his guilt and be eager for the sanctuary of the soil.

I saw the ship and the daybreak, and then I saw the cliffs of Newfoundland wound in ribbons of fog. I felt the elation I had so long imagined, and I felt the happy guilt of having circumvented the stern authority of the weather and the sea. But mine was a minor triumph; my swift Gull was not so swift as to have escaped unnoticed. The night and the storm had caught her and we had flown blind for nineteen hours.

I was tired now, and cold. Ice began to film the glass of the cabin windows and the fog played a magician's game with the land. But the land was there. I could not see it, but I had seen it. I could not afford to believe that it was any land but the land I wanted. I could not afford to believe that my navigation was at fault, because there was no time for doubt.

South to Cape Race, west to Sydney on Cape Breton Island. With my protractor, my map, and my compass, I set my new course, humming the ditty that Tom had taught me: "Variation West—magnetic best. Variation East—magnetic least." A silly rhyme, but it served to placate, for the moment, two warring poles—the magnetic and the true. I flew south and found the lighthouse of Cape Race protruding from the fog like a warning finger. I circled twice and went on over the Gulf of Saint Lawrence.

After a while there would be New Brunswick, and then Maine—and then New York. I could anticipate. I could almost say, "Well, if you stay awake, you'll find it's only a matter of time now"—but there was no question of staying awake. I was tired and I had not moved an inch since that uncertain moment at Abingdon when the Gull had elected to rise with her load and fly, but I could not have closed my eyes. I could sit there in the cabin, walled in glass and petrol tanks, and be grateful for the sun and the light, and the fact that I could see the water under me. They were almost the last waves I had to pass. Four hundred miles of water, but then the land again—Cape Breton. I would stop at Sydney to re-fuel and go on. It was easy now. It would be like stopping at Kisumu and going on.

Success breeds confidence. But who has a right to confidence except the Gods? I had a following wind, my last tank of petrol was more than three-quarters full, and the world was as bright to me as if it were a new world, never touched. If I had been wiser, I might have known that such moments are, like innocence, short-lived. My engine began to shudder before I saw the land. It died, it spluttered, it started again and limped along. It coughed and spat black exhaust toward the sea.

There are words for everything. There was a word for this—airlock, I thought. This had to be an airlock because there was petrol enough. I thought I might clear it by turning on and turning off all the empty tanks, and so I did that. The handles of the petcocks were sharp little pins of metal, and when I had opened and closed them a dozen times, I saw that my hands were bleeding and that the blood was dropping on my maps and on my clothes, but the effort wasn't any good. I coasted along on a sick and halting engine. The oil pressure and the oil temperature gauges were normal, the magnetos working, and yet I lost altitude slowly while the realization of failure seeped into my heart. If I made the land, I should have been the first to fly the North Atlantic from England, but from my point of view, from a pilot's point of view, a forced landing was failure because New York was my goal. If only I could land and then take off, I would make it still . . . if only, if only . . .

The engine cuts again, and then catches, and each time it spurts to life I climb as high as I can get, and then it splutters and stops and I glide once more toward the water, to rise again and descend again, like a hunting sea bird.

I find the land. Visibility is perfect now and I see land forty or fifty miles ahead. If I am on my course, that will be Cape Breton. Minute after minute goes by. The minutes almost materialize; they pass before my eyes like links in a long slow-moving chain, and each time the engine cuts, I see a broken link in the chain and catch my breath until it passes.

The land is under me. I snatch my map and stare at it to confirm my whereabouts. I am, even at my present crippled speed, only twelve minutes from Sydney Airport, where I can land for repairs and then go on.

The engine cuts once more and I begin to glide, but now I am not worried; she will start again, as she has done, and I will gain altitude and fly into Sydney.

But she doesn't start. This time she's dead as death; the Gull settles earthward and it isn't any earth I know. It is black earth stuck with boulders and I hang above it, on hope and on a motionless propeller. Only I cannot hang above it long. The earth hurries to meet me, I bank, turn, and sideslip to dodge the boulders, my wheels touch, and I feel them submerge. The nose of the plane is engulfed in mud, and I go forward striking my head on the glass of the cabin front, hearing it shatter, feeling blood pour over my face.

I stumble out of the plane and sink to my knees in muck and stand there foolishly staring, not at the lifeless land, but at my watch.

Twenty-one hours and twenty-five minutes. Atlantic flight. Abingdon, England, to a nameless swamp—nonstop.

A Cape Breton Islander found me—a fisherman trudging over the bog saw the Gull with her tail in the air and her nose buried, and then he saw me floundering in the embracing soil of his native land. I had been wandering for an hour and the black mud had got up to my waist and the blood from the cut in my head had met the mud halfway.

From a distance, the fisherman directed me with his arms and with shouts toward the firm places in the bog, and for another hour I walked on them and came toward him like a citizen of Hades blinded by the sun, but it wasn't the sun; I hadn't slept for forty hours.

He took me to his hut on the edge of the coast and I found that built upon the rocks there was a little cubicle that housed an ancient telephone—put there in case of shipwrecks.

I telephoned to Sydney Airport to say that I was safe and to prevent a needless search being made. On the following morning I did step out of a plane at Floyd Bennett Field and there was a crowd of people still waiting there to greet me, but the plane I stepped from was not the Gull, and for days while I was in New York I kept thinking about that and wishing over and over again that it had been the Gull, until the wish lost its significance, and time moved on, overcoming many things it met on the way.

41

A PILOT GROWS UP

AMELIA EARHART

Pilots are always dreaming dreams.

My dream, of owning a multi-motored plane, probably first took form in May 1935.

I was flying nonstop from Mexico City to New York. The straight-line course, from Tampico to New Orleans, took me over about seven hundred miles of the Gulf of Mexico. There weren't many clouds, so for once what lay below was quite visible. It did seem a good deal of water.

Previously I'd been by air twice across the North Atlantic, and once from Hawaii to California. All three voyages were flown chiefly at night, with heavy clouds during most of the daylight hours. So in the combined six thousand miles or more of previous over-ocean flying it happened I'd seen next to nothing of ocean.

Given daylight and good visibility, the Gulf of Mexico looked large. And wet. One's imagination toyed with the thought of what would happen if the single engine of the Lockheed Vega should conk. Not that my faithful Wasp ever had failed me, or indeed, even protested mildly. But, at that, the very finest machinery *could* develop indigestion.

So, on that sunny morning out of sight of land, I promised my lovely red Vega I'd fly her across no more water. And I promised myself that any further over-ocean flying would be attempted in a plane with more than one motor, capable of keeping aloft with a single engine. Just in case.

Which, in a way, was for me the beginning of the world flight project. Where to find the tree on which costly airplanes grow, I did not know. But I did know the kind I wanted—an Electra Lockheed, big brother of my Vegas, with, of course, Wasp engines.

Such is the trusting simplicity of a pilot's mind, it seemed ordained that somehow the dream would materialize. Once the prize was in hand, obviously there was one flight which I most wanted to attempt—a circumnavigation of the globe as near its waistline as could be.

Before writing about the preparation for that flight, and of the journey itself, it seems well to set down briefly the career, such as it is, of a girl who grew up to love flying—the who, when, and why of this particular pilot.

At the age of ten I saw my first airplane. It was sitting in a slightly enclosed area at the Iowa State Fair in Des Moines. It was a thing of rusty wire and wood and looked not at all interesting. One of the grown-ups who happened to be around pointed it out to me and said: "Look, dear, it flies." I looked as directed but confess I was much more interested in an absurd hat made of an inverted peach basket which I had just purchased for fifteen cents.

What psychoanalysts would make of this incident, in the light of subsequent behavior, I do not know. Today I loathe hats for more than a few minutes on the head and am sure I should pass by the niftiest creation if an airplane were anywhere around.

The next airplane which impinged upon my consciousness was about the time of the armistice. Again I found myself at a Fair, this time the great exposition held at Toronto in Canada. A young woman friend and I had gone to the Fair grounds to see an exhibition of stunt flying by one of the aces returned from the war. These men were the heroes of the hour. They were in demand at social teas and to entertain crowds by giving stunting exhibitions. The airplanes they rode so gallantly to fame were as singular as they. For aviation in those days was very limited. About all a pilot could do was to joy-hop. That is (1) taking a few hardy passengers for short rides; (2) teaching even hardier students to fly; and (3) giving exhibitions.

The idea that airplanes could be transportation as today entered nobody's noggin.

My friend and I, in order to see the show, planted ourselves in the middle of a clearing. We watched a small plane turn and twist in the air, black against the sky excepting when the afternoon sun caught the scarlet of its wings. After fifteen or twenty minutes of stunting, the pilot began to dive at the crowd. Looking back as a pilot I think I understand why. He was bored. He had looped and rolled and spun and finished his little bag of tricks, and there was nothing left to do but watch the people on the ground running as he swooped close to them.

Pilots, in 1918, to relieve the monotony of never going anywhere, rolled their wheels on the top of moving freight trains; flew so low over boats that the terrified occupants lay flat on the deck; or dived at crowds on the beach or at picnics. Today of course the Department of Commerce would ground a pilot for such antics.

I am sure the sight of two young women alone made a tempting target for the pilot. I am sure he said to himself, "Watch me make them scamper."

After a few attempts one did but the other stood her ground. I remember the mingled fear and pleasure which surged over me as I watched that small plane at the top of its earthward swoop. Common sense told me if something went wrong with the mechanism, or if the pilot lost control, he, the airplane, and I would be rolled up in a ball together. I did not understand it at the time but I believe that little red airplane said something to me as it swished by.

I worked in a hospital during the war. From that experience I decided that medicine interested me most. Whether or not medicine needed me I did not question. So I enrolled at Columbia University in New York and started in to do the peculiar things they do who would be physicians. I fed orange juice to mice and dissected cockroaches. I have never seen a cockroach since but I remember that the creature has an extraordinarily large brain.

However, I could not forget airplanes.

I went to California for a summer vacation and found air meets, as distinct from wartime exhibitions, just beginning. I went to every one and finally one day came a chance to ride. Frank Hawks took me on the first hop. He was then a barnstorming pilot on the west coast, unknown to the fame he later acquired. By the time I had got two or three hundred feet off the ground I knew I had to fly.

I think my mother realized before I did how much airplanes were beginning to mean to me, for she helped me buy the first one. It was secondhand, painted bright yellow, and one of the first light airplanes developed in this country. The motor was so rough that my feet went to sleep after more than a few minutes on the rudder bar. I had a system of lending the plane for demonstration so as not to be charged storage. Hangar rental would have annihilated my salary.

After a year my longest hop was from Long Beach to Pasadena, about forty miles. Still I all but set off to cross the continent by air. The fact that I couldn't buy gasoline myself forced me to compromise and drive a car with Mother along. I am sure I wouldn't be here to tell the tale if I had carried out the original plan.

I did what flying I could afford in the next few years and then the *Friendship* came along. I was working in Denison House in Boston, one of America's oldest social settlements.

"Phone for you, Miss Earhart."

"Tell 'em I'm busy." At the moment I was the center of an eager swarm of Chinese and Syrian neighborhood children, piling in for games and classes.

"Says it's important."

So I excused myself and went to listen to a man's voice asking me whether I was interested in doing something dangerous in the air. At first I thought the conversation was a joke and said so. Several times before I had been approached by bootleggers who promised rich reward and no danger—"Absolutely no danger to you, Leddy."

The frank admission of risk stirred my curiosity. References were demanded and supplied. Good references. An appointment was arranged for that evening.

"Would you like to fly the Atlantic?"

My reply was a prompt "Yes"—provided the equipment was all right and the crew capable. Nine years ago flying oceans was less commonplace than today, and my own experience as a pilot was limited to a few hundred hours in small planes which work and finances permitted.

So I went to New York and met the man entrusted with the quaint commission of finding a woman willing to fly the Atlantic. The candidate, I gathered, should be a flyer herself, with social graces, education, charm, and, perchance, pulchritude.

His appraisal left me discomforted. Somehow this seeker for feminine perfection seemed unimpressed. Anyway, I showed my pilot's license (it happened to be the first granted an American woman by the F.A.I.) and inwardly prepared to start back for Boston.

But he felt that, having come so far, I might as well meet the representatives of Mrs. Frederick Guest, whose generosity was making the flight possible, and at whose insistence a woman was to be taken along. Those representatives were David T. Layman, Jr., and John S. Phipps, before which masculine jury I made my next appearance. It should have been slightly embarrassing, for if I were found wanting in too many ways I would be counted out. On the other hand, if I were just too fascinating, the gallant gentlemen might be loath to risk drowning me. Anyone could see the meeting was a crisis.

A few days later the verdict came. The flight actually would be made and I could go if I wished. Naturally I couldn't say "No." Who would refuse an invitation to such a shining adventure?

Followed, in due course, after weeks of mechanical preparation, efforts to get the monoplane *Friendship* off from the gray waters of Boston Harbor. There were chill before-dawn gettings-up, with breakfasts snatched and thermos bottles filled at an all-night lunch counter. Brief voyages on the tugboat *Sadie Ross* to the anchored plane, followed by the sputter of the motors awakening to Mechanic Lou Gordon's coaxing and their later full-throated roar when Pilot "Bill" Stultz gave them the gun—and I crouched on the fuselage floor hoping we were really off.

Thrice we failed, dragging back to Boston for more long days of waiting. Waiting is apt to be so much harder than *going*, with the excitement of movement, of getting off, of adventure around the corner.

Finally one morning the *Friendship* took off successfully, and Stultz, Gordon, and I transferred ourselves to Newfoundland. After thirteen days of weary waiting at Trepassey (how well I remember the alternating diet of mutton and rabbits!) the Atlantic flight started. Twenty hours and forty minutes later we tied up to a buoy off Burryport, Wales. I recall desperately waving a towel; one friendly soul ashore pulled off his coat and waved back. But beyond that for an hour nothing happened. It took persistence to arouse interest in an itinerant trans-Atlantic plane.

I myself did no piloting on that trip. But I gained experience. In London I was introduced to Lady Mary Heath, the then very active Irish woman flyer. She had just made a record flight from London to Cape Town and I purchased the small plane she had used. It wore on its chest a number of medals given her at various stops she made on the long route.

After the pleasant accident of being the first woman to cross the Atlantic by air, I was launched into a life full of interest. Aviation offered such fun as crossing the continent in planes large and small, trying the whirling rotors of an autogiro, making record flights. With these activities came opportunity to know women everywhere who shared my conviction that there is so much women can do in the modern world and should be permitted to do irrespective of their sex. Probably my greatest satisfaction was to indicate by example now and then, that women can sometimes do things themselves if given the chance.

Here I should add that the *Friendship* flight brought me something even dearer than such opportunities. That Man-who-was-to-find-a-girl-to-fly-the-Atlantic, who found me and then managed the flight, was George Palmer Putnam. In 1931 we married. Mostly, my flying has been solo, but the preparation for it wasn't. Without my husband's help and encouragement I could not have attempted what I have. Ours has been a contented and reasonable partnership, he with his solo jobs and I with mine. But always with work and play together, conducted under a satisfactory system of dual control.

I was hardly home when I started off to fly the continent—my 1924 ambition four years late. Lady Heath's plane was very small. It had folding wings so that it actually could fit in a garage. I cranked the motor by standing behind the propeller and pulling it down with one hand. The plane was so light I could pick it up by the tail and drag it easily around the field.

At that time I was full of missionary zeal for the cause of aviation. I refused to wear the high-bred aviation togs of the moment. Instead I simply wore a dress or suit. I carried no chute and instead of a helmet used a close-fitting hat. I stepped into the airplane with as much nonchalance as I could muster, hoping that onlookers would be persuaded that flying was nothing more than an everyday occurrence. I refused even to wear goggles, obviously. However, I put them on as I taxied to the end of the field and wore them while flying, being sure to take them off shortly after I landed.

That was thoroughly informal flying. Pilots landed in pastures, race courses, even golf links where they were still enough of a novelty to be welcome.

In those days domestic animals scurried to the fancied protection of trees and barns when the flying monsters roared above them. Now along the airways there's not enough curiosity left for a self-respecting cow even to lift her head to see what goes on in the sky. She's just bored. Stories of that happy-go-lucky period should be put together in a saga to regale the scientific, precision flyers of tomorrow.

Nineteen-twenty-nine was the year of the women's derby from California to Cleveland, the first time a cross-country race had ever been sponsored for women alone. I felt I needed a new plane for this extraordinary sporting event. So I traded in the faithful little Avion for my first Lockheed Vega. It was a third-hand clunk but to me a heavenly chariot.

I crossed the continent again from New York to California to stop at the Lockheed factory. I thought possibly there might be a few adjustments necessary before I entered the race. There I met the great Wiley Post for the first time. Wiley Post had not then had his vision of stratosphere flying, and was simply a routine check pilot in the employ of the Lockheed company.

It fell to him to take my airplane up for test. Having circled the field once, he came down and proceeded to tell everyone within earshot that my lovely airplane was the foulest he had ever flown. Of course the worse he made the plane, the better pilot I became. The fact that I should have been able to herd such a hopeless piece of mechanism across the continent successfully was the one bright spot in the ensuing half hour.

Finally Lockheed officials were so impressed by my prowess (or so sorry for me) that they traded me a brand new plane. The clunk was never flown again.

The Derby produced one of the gems which belong in the folklore of aviation. Something went wrong with her motor and Ruth Elder made a forced landing in a field thickly inhabited by cattle. The bovine population crowded around her plane and proceeded to lick the paint off the wings—there seemed to be something in the "doped" finish that appealed to them. Meanwhile, Ruth snuggled down in the safety of the cockpit. "You see," she explained, "I didn't know much about such things and was uncertain as to the sex of the visitors. My plane was red—very red. And I'd always heard what bulls did to *that.*"... Apparently the cows were cows.

After the *Friendship* flight I did not immediately plan to fly the Atlantic alone. But later as I gained in experience and looked back over the years I decided that I had had enough to try to make it solo. Lockheed #2 was then about three years old. It had been completely reconditioned and a new and larger engine put in. By the spring of 1932 plane and pilot were ready.

Oddly, one of my clearest memories of the Atlantic solo concerns not the flight itself but my departure from home. On May 19th the weather outlook was so unpromising we had abandoned hope of getting off that day. So I had driven in to New York from our home in Westchester. Just before noon an urgent message caught up with me immediately to get in touch with Mr. Putnam at the Weather Bureau.

Our phone conversation was brief.

"It looks like the break we've waited for," he said. "Doc Kimball says this afternoon is fine to get to Newfoundland—St. John's anyway. And by tomorrow the Atlantic looks as good as you're likely to get it for some time."

I asked a few questions. A threatening "low" on the first leg of the route had dissipated to the southeast; a "high" seemed to be moving in promisingly beyond Newfoundland.

"Okay! We'll start," I said. Mr. Putnam agreed he would corral Bernt Balchen, my technical adviser who was to go with me to Newfoundland to be sure that everything was as right as could be before I hopped off. I explained I would have to rush back to Rye to get my flying clothes and maps. We arranged to meet at two o'clock at the city end of the George Washington Bridge, which leads across the Hudson toward Teterboro Airport in New Jersey, where my plane waited.

As fast as I dared—traffic cops being what they are— I drove the twenty-five miles to Rye. Five minutes was enough to pick up my things. Plus a lingering few more to drink in the beauty of a lovely treasured sight. Beside and below our bedroom windows were dogwood trees, their blossoms in luxuriant full flower, unbelievable bouquets of white and pink flecked with the sunshine of spring. Those sweet blooms smiled at me a radiant farewell . . . That is a memory I have never forgotten.

Looking back, there are less cheering recollections of that night over the Atlantic. Of seeing, for instance, the flames lick through the exhaust collector ring and wondering, in a detached way, whether one would prefer drowning to incineration. Of the five hours of storm, during black midnight, when I kept right side up by instruments alone, buffeted about as I never was before. Of much beside, not the least the feeling of fine loneliness and of realization that the machine I rode was doing its best and required from me the best I had.

And one further fact of the flight, which I've not set down in words before. I carried a barograph, an instrument which records on a disc the course of the plane, its rate of ascent and descent, its levels of flight all coordinated with clocked time. My telltale disc could tell a tale. At one point it recorded an almost vertical drop of three thousand feet. It started at an altitude of something over 3,000 feet, and ended—well, something above the water. That happened when the plane suddenly "iced up" and went into a spin. How long we spun I do not know. I do know that I tried my best to do exactly what one should do with a spinning plane, and regained flying control as the warmth of the lower altitude melted the ice. As we righted and held level again, through the blackness below I could see the white-caps too close for comfort.

All that was five full years ago, a long time to recall little things. So I wonder if Bernt Balchen remembers as I do the three words he said to me as I left Harbor Grace. They were: "Okay. So long. Good luck."

NIGHT FLIGHT

ANTOINE DE SAINT-EXUPÉRY

Now the Patagonia mail was entering the storm and Fabien abandoned all idea of circumventing it; it was too widespread for that, he reckoned, for the vista of lightning flashes led far inland, exposing battlement on battlement of clouds. He decided to try passing below it, ready to beat a retreat if things took a bad turn.

He read his altitude, five thousand five hundred feet, and pressed the controls with his palms to bring it down. The engine started thudding violently, setting all the plane aquiver. Fabien corrected the gliding angle approximately, verifying on the map the height of the hills, some sixteen hundred feet. To keep a safety margin he determined to fly at a trifle above two thousand, staking his altitude as a gambler risks his fortune.

An eddy dragged him down, making the plane tremble still more harshly and he felt the threat of unseen avalanches that toppled all about him. He dreamt an instant of retreat and its guerdon of a hundred thousand stars, but did not shift his course by one degree.

Fabien weighed his chances; probably this was just a local storm, as Trelew, the next halt, was signaling a sky only three-quarters overcast. A bare twenty minutes more of solid murk and he would be through with it. Nevertheless the pilot felt uneasy. Leaning to his left, to windward, he sought to catch those vague gleams which, even in darkest nights, flit here and there. But even those vagrant gleams were gone; at most there lingered patches in the mass of shadow where the night seemed less opaque, or was it only that his eyes were growing strained?

The wireless operator handed him a slip of paper. "Where are we?"

Fabien would have given much to know. "Can't say exactly," he answered. "We are flying by compass across a storm."

He leaned down again. The flame from the exhaust was getting on his nerves. There it was, clinging to the motor like a spray of fireflowers, so pale it seemed that moonlight would have quelled it, but, in this nothingness, engulfing all the visible world. He watched it streaming stiffly out into the wind, like a torch flame.

Every thirty seconds Fabien bent down into the cockpit to check the gyroscope and compass. He dared not light the dim red lamps which would have dazzled his eyes for some moments, but the luminous dial hands were ceaselessly emitting their pale and starry radiance. And in all those needles and printed figures the pilot found an illusive reassurance, as in the cabin of a ship swept by the waves. For, like a very sea of strange fatality, the night was rolling up against him with all its rocks and reefs and wreckage.

"Where are we?" the operator asked again.

Fabien drew himself up and, leaning to the left, resumed his tremendous vigil. He had no notion left how many hours more and what efforts would be needed to deliver him from fettering darkness. Would he ever come clear, he wondered, for he was staking his life on this little slip of dirty, crumpled paper, which he unfolded and re-read a thousand times to nurse his hopes: *Trelew. Sky three-quarters overcast. Westerly breeze.* If there still remained a clear patch over Trelew, he would presently glimpse its lights across a cloud rift. Unless . . .

That promise of a faint gleam far ahead beckoned him on; but, to make sure, he scribbled a message to the radio operator. "Don't know if I can get through. Ask if the weather's holding out behind."

The answer appalled him.

"Commodoro reports: Impossible return here. Storm."

He was beginning to measure this unforeseen offensive, launched from the Cordillera toward the sea. Before he could make them the storm would have burst upon the cities.

"Get the San Antonio weather report."

"San Antonio reports: West wind rising. Storm in the west. Sky three-quarters overcast. San Antonio picking up badly on account of interferences. I'm having trouble too. I shall have to pull up the aerial on account of the lightning. Will you turn back? What are your plans?"

"Stow your damned questions! Get Bahia Blanca!"

"Bahia Blanca reports: Violent westerly gale over Bahia Blanca expected in less than twenty minutes."

"Ask Trelew."

"Trelew reports: Westerly gale; a hundred feet per second; rain squalls."

"Inform Buenos Aires: We are cut off on all sides; storm developing over a depth of eight hundred miles; no visibility. What shall we do?"

A shoreless night, the pilot thought, leading to no anchorage (for every port was unattainable, it seemed), nor toward dawn. In an hour and twenty minutes the fuel would run out. Sooner or later he must blindly founder in the sea of darkness. Ah, if only he could have won through to daylight!

Fabien pictured the dawn as a beach of golden sand where a man might get a foothold after this hard night. Beneath him the plains, like friendly shores, would spread their safety. The quiet land would bear its sleeping farms and flocks and hills. And all the flotsam swirling in the shadows would lose its menace. If it were possible, how gladly he would swim toward the strand of daylight! But, well he knew, he was surrounded; for better or for worse the end would come within this murk of darkness . . . Sometimes, indeed, when daybreak came, it seemed like convalescence after illness.

What use to turn his eyes toward the east, home of the sun? Between them lay a gulf of night so deep that he could never clamber up again.

"The Asuncion mail is making good headway; it should be in at about two. The Patagonia mail, however, seems to be in difficulties and we expect it to be much overdue."

"Very good, Monsieur Rivière."

"Quite possibly we won't make the Europe mail wait for it; as soon as Asuncion's in, come for instructions, please. Hold yourself in readiness."

Rivière read again the weather reports from the northern sectors. "Clear sky; full moon; no wind." The mountains of Brazil were standing stark and clear against the moonlit sky, the tangled tresses of their jet-black forests falling sheer into a silver tracery of sea. Upon those forests the moonbeams played and played in vain, tingeing their blackness with no light. Black, too, as drifting wreckage, the islands flecked the sea. But all the outward air route was flooded by that exhaustless fountain of moonlight.

If Rivière now gave orders for the start, the crew of the Europe mail would enter a stable world, softly illuminated all night long. A land which held no threat for the just balance of light and shade, unruffled by the least caress of those cool winds which, when they freshen, can ruin a whole sky in an hour or two.

Facing this wide radiance, like a prospector eyeing a forbidden gold field, Rivière hesitated. What was happening in the south put Rivière, sole protagonist of night flights, in the wrong. His opponents would make such moral capital out of a disaster in Patagonia that all Rivière's faith would henceforth be unavailing. Not that his faith wavered; if, through a fissure in his work, a tragedy had entered in, well, the tragedy might prove the fissure—but it proved nothing else. Perhaps, he thought, it would be well to have look-out posts in the west. That must be seen to. "After all," he said to himself, "my previous arguments hold good as ever and the possibilities of accident are reduced by one, the one tonight has illustrated." The strong are strengthened by reverses; the trouble is that the true meaning of events scores next to nothing in the match we play with men. Appearances decide our gains or losses and the points are trumpery. And a mere semblance of defeat may hopelessly checkmate us.

He summoned an employee. "Still no radio from Bahia Blanca?"

"No."

"Ring up the station on the phone."

Five minutes later he made further inquiries. "Why don't you pass on the messages?"

"We can't hear the mail."

"He's not sending anything?"

"Can't say. Too many storms. Even if he was sending we shouldn't pick it up."

"Can you get Trelew?"

"We can't hear Trelew."

"Telephone."

"We've tried. The line's broken."

"How's the weather your end?"

"Threatening. Very sultry. Lightning in the west and south."

"Wind?"

"Moderate so far. But in ten minutes the storm will break; the lightning's coming up fast."

Silence.

"Hullo, Bhatia Blanca! You hear me? Good. Call me again in ten minutes."

Rivière looked through the telegrams from the southern stations. All alike reported: No message from the plane. Some had ceased by now to answer Buenos Aires and the patch of silent areas was spreading on the map as the cyclone swept upon the little towns and one by one, behind closed doors, each house along the lightless streets grew isolated from the outer world, lonely as a ship on a dark sea. And only dawn would rescue them.

Rivière, poring over the map, still hoped against hope to discover a haven of clear sky, for he had telegraphed to the police at more than thirty up-country police stations and their replies were coming in. And the radio posts over twelve hundred miles of country had orders to advise Buenos Aires within thirty seconds if any message from the plane was picked up, so that Fabien might learn at once whither to fly for refuge.

The employees had been warned to attend at 1 a.m. and were now at their posts. Somehow, mysteriously, a rumor was gaining ground that perhaps the night flights would be suspended in future and the Europe mail would leave by day. They spoke in whispers of Fabien, the cyclone and, above all, of Rivière whom they pictured near at hand and point by point capitulating to this rebuff the elements had dealt.

Their chatter ceased abruptly; Rivière was standing at his door, his overcoat tight-buttoned across his chest, his hat well down upon his eyes, like the incessant traveler he always seemed. Calmly he approached the head clerk.

"It's one ten. Are the papers for the Europe mail in order?"

"I—I thought—"

"Your business is to carry out orders, not to think."

Slowly turning away, he moved toward an open window, his hands clasped behind his back. A clerk came up to him.

"We have very few replies, sir. We hear that a great many telegraph lines in the interior have been destroyed."

"Right!"

Unmoving, Rivière stared out into the night.

Thus each new message boded new peril for the mail. Each town, when a reply could be sent through before the lines were broken, announced the cyclone on its way, like an invading horde. "It's coming up from the Cordillera, sweeping everything before it, toward the sea."

To Rivière the stars seemed over-bright, the air too moist. Strange night indeed! It was rotting away in patches, like the substance of a shining fruit. The stars, in all their host, still looked down on Buenos Aires—an oasis, and not to last. A haven out of Fabien's range, in any case. A night of menace, touched and tainted by an evil wind. A difficult night to conquer.

Somewhere in its depths an airplane was in peril; here, on the margin, they were fighting to rescue it, in vain.

Fabien's wife telephoned.

Each night she calculated the progress of the homing Patagonia mail. "He's leaving Trelew now," she murmured. Then went to sleep again. Presently: "He's getting near San Antonio, he has its lights in view." Then she got out of bed, drew back the curtains and summed up the sky. "All those clouds will worry him." Sometimes the moon was wandering like a shepherd and the young wife was heartened by the faithful moon and stars, the thousand presences that watched her husband. Toward one o'clock she felt him near her. "Not far to go, Buenos Aires is in sight." Then she got up again, prepared a meal for him, a nice steaming cup of coffee. "It's so cold up there!" She always welcomed him as if he had just descended from a snow peak. "You *must* be cold!" "Not a bit." "Well, warm yourself anyhow!" She had everything ready at a quarter past one. Then she telephoned. Tonight she asked the usual question.

"Has Fabien landed?"

The clerk at the other end grew flustered. "Who's speaking?"

"Simone Fabien."

"Ah! A moment, please . . ."

Afraid to answer, he passed the receiver to the head clerk.

"Who's that?"

"Simone Fabien."

"Yes. What can I do for you?"

"Has my husband arrived?"

After a silence which must have baffled her, there came a monosyllable. "No."

"Is he delayed?"

"Yes."

Another silence. "Yes, he is delayed."

"Ah!"

The cry of a wounded creature. A little delay, that's nothing much, but when it lasts, when it lasts . . .

"Yes. And when—when is he expected in?"

"When is he expected? We . . . we don't know exactly . . . "

A solid wall in front of her, a wall of silence, which only gave her back the echo of her questions.

"Do please tell me, where is he now?"

"Where is he? Wait . . ."

This suspense was like a torture. Something was happening there, behind that wall.

At last, a voice! "He left Commodoro at seven-thirty this evening."

"Yes? And then?"

"Then—delayed, seriously delayed by stormy weather."

"Ah! A storm!"

The injustice of it, the sly cruelty of that moon up there, that lazing moon of Buenos Aires! Suddenly she remembered that it took barely two hours to fly from Commodoro to Trelew.

"He's been six hours on the way to Trelew! But surely you've had messages from him. What does he say?"

"What does he say? Well, you see, with weather like that . . . it's only natural . . . we can't hear him."

"Weather like—?"

"You may rest assured, madame, the moment we get news of him, we will ring you up."

"Ah! You've no news."

"Good night, madame."

"No! No! I want to talk to the director."

"I'm sorry, he's very busy just now; he has a meeting on—"

"I can't help that. That doesn't matter. I insist on speaking to him."

The head clerk mopped his forehead. "A moment, please."

He opened Rivière's door.

"Madame Fabien wants to speak to you, sir."

"Here," thought Rivière, "is what I was dreading." The emotional elements of the drama were coming into action. His first impulse was to thrust them aside; mothers and women are not allowed in an operating theater. And all emotion is bidden to hold its peace on a ship in peril; it does not help to save the crew. Nevertheless he yielded.

"Switch on to my phone."

No sooner did he hear that far off, quavering voice, than he knew his inability to answer it. It would be futile for both alike, worse than futile, to meet each other.

"Do not be alarmed, madame, I beg you. In our calling it so often happens that a long while passes without news."

He had reached a point where not the problem of a small personal grief but the very will to act was in itself an issue. Not so much Fabien's wife as another theory of life confronted Rivière now. Hearing that timid voice, he could but pity its infinite distress—and know it for an enemy! For action and individual happiness have no truck with each other; they are eternally at war. This woman, too, was championing a self-coherent world with its own rights and duties, that world where a lamp shines at nightfall on the table, flesh calls to mated flesh, a homely world of love and hopes and memories. She stood up for her happiness and she was right. And Rivière, too, was right, yet he found no words to set against this woman's truth. He was discovering the truth within him, his own inhuman and unutterable truth, by a humble light, the lamplight of a little home!

"Madame . . . !"

She did not hear him. Her hands were bruised with beating on the wall and she lay fallen, or so it seemed to him, almost at his feet.

One day an engineer had remarked to Rivière, as they were bending above a wounded man, beside a bridge that was being erected: "Is the bridge worth a man's crushed face?" Not one of the peasants using the road would ever have wished to mutilate this face so hideously just to save the extra walk to the next bridge. "The welfare of the community," the engineer had continued, "is just the sum of individual welfares and has no right to look beyond them." "And yet," Rivière observed on a subsequent occasion, "even though human life may be the most precious thing on earth, we always behave as if there were something of higher value than human life . . . But what thing?"

Thinking of the lost airmen, Rivière felt his heart sink. All man's activity, even the building of a bridge, involves a toll of suffering and he could no longer evade the issue— "Under what authority?"

These men, he mused, who perhaps are lost, might have led happy lives. He seemed to see as in a golden sanctuary the evening lamplight shine on faces bending side by side. "Under what authority have I taken them from all this?" he wondered. What was his right to rob them of their personal happiness? Did not the highest of all laws ordain that these human joys should be safeguarded? But he destroyed them. And yet one day, inevitably, those golden sanctuaries vanish like mirage. Old age and death, more pitiless than even he, destroy them. There is, perhaps, some other thing, something more lasting, to be saved; and, perhaps, it was to save this part of man that Rivière was working. Otherwise there could be no defense for action. To love, only to love, leads nowhere. Rivière knew a dark sense of duty, greater than that of love. And deep within it there might lie another emotion and a tender one, but worlds away from ordinary feelings. He recalled a phrase that he once had read: "The one thing is to make them everlasting . . . That which you seek within yourself will die." He remembered a temple of the sun god, built by the ancient Incas of Peru. Tall menhirs on a mountain. But for these what would be left of all that mighty civilization which with its massive stones weighs heavy, like a dark regret, on modern man? Under the mandate of what strange love, what ruthlessness, did that primeval leader of men compel his hordes to drag this temple up the mountainside, bidding them raise up their eternity? And now another picture rose in Rivierè's mind; the people of the little towns, strolling by nights around their bandstands. That form of happiness, those shackles . . . he thought. The leader of those ancient races may have had scant compassion for man's sufferings, but he had a boundless pity for his death. Not for his personal death, but pity for his race, doomed to be blotted out beneath a sea of sand. And so he bade his folk set up these stones at least, something the desert never would engulf.

That scrap of folded paper might perhaps save him yet; gritting his teeth, Fabien unfolded it.

"Impossible communicate Buenos Aires. Can't even touch the key, the shocks are numbing my hands."

In his vexation Fabien wanted to reply, but the moment his hands left the controls to write, a vast ground swell seemed to surge up across his body; the eddies lifted him in his five tons of metal and rocked him to and fro. He abandoned the attempt.

Again he clenched his hands upon the tempest and brought it down. Fabien was breathing heavily. If that fellow pulled up the aerial for fear of the storm, Fabien would smash his face in when they landed. At all costs they must get in touch with Buenos Aires—as though across the thousand miles and more a safety line might be flung to rescue them from this abyss! If he could not have one vagrant ray of light, not even the flicker of an inn lamp—of little help indeed, yet shining like a beacon, earnest of the earth—at least let him be given a voice, a single word from that lost world of his. The pilot raised his fist and shook it in the red glow, hoping to make the man behind him understand the tragic truth, but the other was bending down to watch a world in ruins, with its buried cities and dead lights, and did not see him.

Let them shout any order whatever to him and Fabien would obey. If they tell me to go round and round, he thought, I'll turn in circles and if they say I must head due south . . . For somewhere, even now, there still were lands of calm, at peace beneath the wide moon shadows. His comrades down there, omniscient folk like clever scientists, knew all about them, poring upon the maps beneath their hanging lamps, pretty as flower bells. But he, what could he know save squalls and night, this night that buffeted him with its swirling spate of darkness? Surely they could not leave two men to their fate in these whirlwinds and flaming clouds! No, that was unthinkable! They might

order Fabien to set his course at two hundred and forty degrees, and he would do it . . . But he was alone.

It was as if dead matter were infected by his exasperation; at every plunge the engine set up such furious vibra-
tions that all the fuselage seemed convulsed with rage.
Fabien strained all his efforts to control it; crouching in the
cockpit, he kept his eyes fixed on the artificial horizon only,
for the masses of sky and land outside were not to be dis-
tinguished, lost both alike in a welter as of worlds in the
making. But the hands of the flying instruments oscillated
more and more abruptly, grew almost impossible to follow.
Already the pilot, misled by their vagaries, was losing altitude, fighting against odds, while deadly quicksands
sucked him down into the darkness. He read his height, sixteen hundred—just the level of the hills. He guessed their
towering billows hard upon him, for now it seemed that all
these earthen monsters, the least of which could crush him
into nothingness, were breaking loose from their founda-
tions and careering about in a drunken frenzy. A dark tel-
lurian carnival was thronging closer and closer round him.

He made up his mind. He would land no matter where,
even if it meant cracking up! To avoid the hills anyhow, he
launched his only landing flare. It sputtered and spun, illu-
mining a vast plain, then died away; beneath him lay the sea!

His thoughts came quickly. Lost—forty degrees' drift—
yes, I've drifted, sure enough—it's a cyclone—where's
land? He turned due west. Without another flare, he
thought, I'm a goner. Well, it was bound to happen one day.
And that fellow behind there! Sure thing he's pulled up the
aerial . . . But now the pilot's anger had ebbed away. He had
only to unclasp his hands and their lives would slither
through his fingers like a trivial mote of dust. He held the

beating heart of each—his own, his comrade's—in his hands. And suddenly his hands appalled him.

In these squalls that battered on the plane, to counteract the jerks of the wheel, which else would have snapped the control cables, he clung to it with might and main, never relaxing his hold for an instant. But now he could no longer feel his hands, numbed by the strain. He tried to shift his fingers and get some signal they were there, but he could not tell if they obeyed his will. His arms seemed to end in two queer foreign bodies, insentient like flabby rubber pads. "Better try hard to think I'm gripping," he said to himself. But whether his thought carried as far as his hands he could not guess. The tugs upon the wheel were only felt by him as sudden twinges in his shoulders. "I'll let go for sure. My fingers will open." His rashness scared him—that he had dared to even think such words!—for now he fancied that his hands, yielding to the dark suggestion of his thought, were opening slowly, slowly opening in the shadow, to betray him.

He might keep up the struggle, chance his luck; no destiny attacks us from outside. But, within him, man bears his fate and there comes a moment when he knows himself vulnerable; and then, as in a vertigo, blunder upon blunder lures him.

And, at this very moment, there gleamed above his head, across a storm rift, like a fatal lure within a deep abyss, a star or two.

Only too well he knew them for a trap. A man sees a few stars at the issue of a pit and climbs toward them, and then—never can he get down again but stays up there eternally, chewing the stars . . .

But such was his lust for light that he began to climb.

****

He climbed and it grew easier to correct the plunges for the stars gave him his bearings. Their pale magnet drew him up; after that long and bitter quest for light, for nothing in the world would he forego the frailest gleam. If the glimmer of a little inn were all his riches, he would turn around this token of his heart's desire until his death! So now he soared toward the fields of light.

Little by little he spiraled up, out of the dark pit which closed again beneath him. As he rose the clouds began to shed their slime of shadow, flowing past him in cleaner, whiter billows. Fabien rose clear.

And now a wonder seized him; dazzled by that brightness, he had to keep his eyes closed for some seconds. He had never dreamt the night clouds could dazzle thus. But the full moon and all the constellations were changing them to waves of light.

In a flash, the very instant he had risen clear, the pilot found a peace that passed his understanding. Not a ripple tilted the plane but, like a ship that has crossed the bar, it moved across a tranquil anchorage. In an unknown and secret corner of the sky it floated, as in a harbor of the Happy Isles. Below him still the storm was fashioning another world, thridded with squalls and cloudbursts and lightnings, but turning to the stars a face of crystal snow.

Now all grew luminous, his hands, his clothes, the wings, and Fabien thought that he was in a limbo of strange magic; for the light did not come down from the stars but welled up from below, from all that snowy whiteness.

The clouds beneath threw up the flakes the moon was pouring on them; on every hand they loomed like towers of snow. A milky stream of light flowed everywhere, laving the plane and crew. When Fabien turned he saw the wireless operator smile.

"That's better!" he cried.

But his words were drowned by the rumor of the flight; they conversed in smiles. I'm daft, thought Fabien, to be smiling, we're lost.

And yet—at last a myriad dark arms had let him go; those bonds of his were loosed, as of a prisoner whom they let walk a while in liberty amongst the flowers.

"Too beautiful," he thought. Amid the far-flung treasure of the stars he roved, in a world where no life was, no faintest breath of life, save his and his companion's. Like plunderers of fabled cities they seemed, immured in treasure vaults whence there is no escape. Amongst these frozen jewels they were wandering, rich beyond all dreams, but doomed.

One of the wireless operators at the Commodoro Rivadavia station in Patagonia made a startled gesture and all the others keeping helpless vigil there crowded round to read the message.

A harsh light fell upon the blank sheet of paper over which they bent. The operator's hand seemed loath to do its task and his pencil shook. The words to write were prisoned in his hand, but already his fingers twitched.

"Storms?"

He nodded assent; he could hardly hear for interferences. Then he scrawled some illegible signs, then words; then, at last, the text came out.

"Cut off at twelve thousand feet, above the storm. Proceeding due west toward interior; found we had been carried above sea. No visibility below. Impossible to know if still flying over sea. Report if storm extends interior."

By reason of the storms the telegram had to be relayed from post to post to Buenos Aires, bearing its message through the night like balefires lit from tower to tower.

Buenos Aires transmitted a reply. "Storm covers all interior area. How much gasoline left?"

"For thirty minutes." These words sped back from post to post to Buenos Aires.

In under half an hour the plane was doomed to plunge into a cyclone which would crash it to the earth.

Rivière was musing, all hope lost; somewhere this plane would founder in the darkness. A picture rose in his mind of a scene which had impressed him in his boyhood: a pond that was being emptied to find a body. Thus, till this flood of darkness had been drained off the earth and daylight turned toward the plains and cornfields, nothing would be found. Then some humble peasants perhaps would come on two young bodies, their elbows folded on their faces, like children asleep amid the grass and gold of some calm scene. Drowned by the night.

Rivière thought of all the treasure buried in the depths of night, as in deep, legendary seas. Night's apple trees that wait upon the dawn with all their flowers that serve as yet no purpose. Night, perfume-laden, that hides the lambs asleep and flowers that have no color yet.

Little by little the lush tilth, wet woods, and dew-cool meadows, would swing toward the light. But somewhere in the hills, no longer dark with menace, amid the fields and flocks, a world at peace again, two children would seem to sleep. And something would have flowed out of the seen world into that other.

Rivière knew all the tenderness of Fabien's wife, the fears that haunted her; this love seemed only lent her for a while, like a toy to some poor child. He thought of Fabien's hand which, firm on the controls, would hold the balance of his fate some minutes yet; that hand had given caresses and lingered on a breast, wakening a tumult there; a hand of godlike virtue, it had touched a face, transfiguring it. A hand that brought miracles to pass.

Fabien was drifting now in the vast splendor of a sea of clouds, but under him there lay eternity. Among the constellations still he had his being, their only denizen. For yet a while he held the universe in his hand, weighed it at his breast. That wheel he clutched upbore a load of human treasure and desperately, from one star to the other, he trafficked this useless wealth, soon to be his no more.

A single radio post still heard him. The only link between him and the world was a wave of music, a minor modulation. Not a lament, no cry, yet purest of sounds that ever spoke despair.

Robineau broke in upon his thoughts.

"I've been thinking, sir . . . Perhaps we might try—"

He had nothing really to suggest but thus proclaimed his good intentions. A solution, how he would have rejoiced to find it! He went about it as if it were a puzzle to be solved. Solutions were his *forte*, but Rivière would not hear of them. "I tell you, Robineau, in life there are no solutions. There are only motive forces, and our task is to set them acting—then the solutions follow." The only force that Robineau had to activate was one which functioned in the mechanics' shop; a humble force which saved propeller-bosses from rusting.

But this night's happenings found Robineau at fault. His inspectorial mandate could not control the elements, nor yet a phantom ship that, as things were, struggled no longer to win a punctuality bonus but only to evade a penalty which canceled all that Robineau imposed, the penalty of death.

There was no use for Robineau now and he roamed the offices, forlorn.

Rivière was informed that Fabien's wife wished to see him. Tormented by anxiety, she was waiting in the clerks' office till Rivière could receive her. The employees were stealing glances at her face. She felt shy, almost shamefast, and gazed nervously around her; she had no right of presence here. They went about their tasks as usual and to her it was as if they were trampling on a corpse; in their ledgers no human sorrow but dwindled to dross of brittle figures. She looked for something that might speak to her of Fabien; at home all things confessed his absence—the sheets turned back upon the bed, the coffee on the table, a vase of flowers. Here there was nothing of him; all was at war with pity, friendship, memories. The only word she caught (for in her presence they instinctively lowered their voices) was the oath of an employee clamoring for an invoice. "The dynamo account, God blast you! The one we send to Santos." Raising her eyes she gazed toward this man with a look of infinite wonder. Then to the wall where a map hung. Her lips trembled a little, almost imperceptibly.

The realization irked her that in this room she was the envoy of a hostile creed and almost she regretted having come; she would have liked to hide somewhere and, fearful of being remarked, dared neither cough nor weep. She felt her presence here misplaced, indecent, as though she were standing naked before them. But so potent was *her* truth, the truth within her, that furtively their eyes strayed ever and again in her direction, trying to read it on her face. Beauty was hers and she stood for a holy thing, the world of human happiness. She vouched for the sanctity of that material something with which man tampers when he acts. She closed her eyes before their crowded scrutiny, revealing all the peace which in his blindness man is apt to shatter.

Rivière admitted her.

So now she was come to make a timid plea for her flowers, the coffee waiting on the table, her own young body. Again, in this room, colder even than the others, her lips began to quiver. Thus, too, she bore witness to her truth, unutterable in this alien world. All the wild yearning of her love, her heart's devotion, seemed here invested with a selfish, pestering aspect. And again she would have liked to leave this place.

"I am disturbing you—"

"No," said Rivière, "you are not disturbing me. But unfortunately neither you nor I can do anything except—wait."

There was a faint movement of her shoulders and Riviere guessed its meaning. "What is the use of that lamp, the dinner waiting, and the flowers there when I return?" Once a young mother had confided in Rivière. "I've hardly realized my baby's death as yet. It's the little things that are so cruel—when I see the baby clothes I had ready, when I wake up at night and there rises in my heart a tide of love, useless now, like my milk . . . all useless!" And for this woman here, Fabien's death would only just begin tomorrow—in every action, useless now, in trivial objects . . . useless. Little by little Fabien would leave his home. A deep, unuttered pity stirred in Rivière's heart.

"Madame—"

The young wife turned and left him with a weak smile, an almost humble smile, ignoring her own power.

Rivière sat down again rather heavily. "Still she is helping me to discover the thing I'm looking for."

He fingered absent-mindedly the messages from the northern airports. "We do not pray for immortality," he thought, "but only not to see our acts and all things stripped suddenly of all their meaning; for then it is the utter emptiness of everything reveals itself."

His gaze fell on the telegrams. "These are the paths death takes to enter here—messages that have lost their meaning."

He looked at Robineau. Meaningless, too, this fellow who served no purpose now. Rivière addressed him almost gruffly.

"Have I got to tell you what your duties are?"

Then he pushed open the door that led into the Business Office and saw how Fabien's disappearance was recorded there in signs his wife could not have noticed. The slip marked *R.B.903*, Fabien's machine, was already inserted in the wall index of Unavailable Plant. The clerks preparing the papers for the Europe mail were working slackly, knowing it would be delayed. The airport was ringing up for orders respecting the staff on night duty whose presence was no longer necessary. The functions of life were slowing down. That is death! thought Rivière. His work was like a sailing ship becalmed upon the sea.

He heard Robineau speaking. "Sir, they had only been married six weeks."

"Get on with your work!"

Rivière, watching the clerks, seemed to see beyond them the workmen, mechanics, pilots, all who had helped him in his task, with the faith of men who build. He thought of those little cities of old time where men had murmured of the "Indies," built a ship and freighted it with hopes. That men might see their hope outspread its wings across the sea. All of them magnified, lifted above themselves and saved—by a ship! He thought: The goal, perhaps, means nothing, it is the thing done that delivers man from death. By their ship those men will live.

Rivière, too, would be fighting against death when he restored to those telegrams their full meaning, to these men on night duty their unrest and to his pilots their tragic purpose; when life itself would make his work alive again, as winds restore to life a sailing ship upon the sea.

Commodoro Rivadavia could hear nothing now, but twenty seconds later, six hundred miles away, Bahia Blanca picked up a second message.

"Coming down. Entering the clouds . . ."

Then two words of a blurred message were caught at Trelew.

" . . . see nothing . . ."

Short waves are like that; here they can be caught, elsewhere is silence. Then, for no reason, all is changed. This crew, whose position was unknown, made itself heard by living ears, from somewhere out of space and out of time, and at the radio station phantom hands were tracing a word or two on this white paper.

Had the fuel run out already or was the pilot, before catastrophe, playing his last card: to reach the earth again without a crash?

Buenos Aires transmitted an order to Trelew.

"Ask him."

The radio station looked like a laboratory with its nickel and its copper, manometers and sheaves of wires. The operators on duty in their white overalls seemed to be bending silently above some simple experiment. Delicately they touched their instruments, exploring the magnetic sky, dowsers in quest of hidden gold.

"No answer?"

"No answer."

Perhaps they yet might seize upon its way a sound that told of life. If the plane and its lights were soaring up to join the stars, it might be they would hear a sound—a singing star!

The seconds flowed away, like ebbing blood. Were they still in flight? Each second killed a hope. The stream of time was wearing life away. As for twenty centuries it beats against a temple, seeping through the granite, and spreads the fane in ruin, so centuries of wear and tear were thronging in each second, menacing the airmen.

Every second swept something away; Fabien's voice, his laugh, his smile. Silence was gaining ground. Heavier and heavier silence drowned their voices, like a heavy sea.

"One-forty," someone murmured. "They're out of fuel. They can't be flying anymore."

Then silence.

A dry and bitter taste rose on their lips, like the dry savor of a journey's end. Something mysterious, a sickening thing, had come to pass. And all the shining nickel and trellised copper seemed tarnished with the gloom that broods on ruined factories. All this apparatus had grown clumsy, futile, out of use; a tangle of dead twigs.

One thing remained; to wait for daybreak. In a few hours all Argentina would swing toward the sun, and here these men were standing, as on a beach, facing the net that was being slowly, slowly drawn in toward them, none knowing what its take would be.

To Rivière in his office came that quiet aftermath which follows only on great disasters, when destiny has spent its force. He had set the police of the entire country on the alert. He could do no more; only wait.

But even in the house of death order must have its due. Rivière signed to Robineau.

"Circular telegram to the northern airports. *Consider-able delay anticipated Patagonia mail. To avoid undue delay Europe mail, will ship Patagonia traffic on follow-ing Europe mail.*"

He stooped a little forward. Then, with an effort, he called something to mind, something important. Yes, that was it. Better make sure.

"Robineau!"

"Sir."

"Issue an order, please. Pilots forbidden to exceed nineteen hundred revs. They're ruining my engines."

"Very good, sir."

Riviere bowed his head a little more. To be alone—that was his supreme desire.

"That's all, Robineau. Trot off, old chap!" And this, their strange equality before the shades, filled Robineau with awe.

ALL THE BRAVE PROMISES

MARY LEE SETTLE

It took three changes to get from Hereford to Turnbull St. Justin. The trains got smaller each time. Finally I stood on the platform at Turnbull St. Justin and watched the smallest of all, the train to take you nowhere, disappear, my kitbag leaning against my leg, not knowing or caring at that little point how to get out to RAF Turnbull St. Justin. Farther down the platform an RAF officer was looking up the narrow street from the station. He didn't yet fit his uniform. It still carefully fitted him. His wings were new. He seemed as isolated as I felt. The inevitable van drew into the empty parking lot and swung around. It was driven by a WAAF in battle dress.

We were put into the back to be delivered. All along the road winding away behind us the trees were lush even in winter, the blue-green of Gainsborough in the misty light. We both stared at where we'd been, not saying a word. I finally said, "It's lovely."

"Unh?"

"The trees—green in winter . . ."

"It's *ivy.*" His face and voice warmed into anger from his mild stupor. "It's bloody ivy. A bloody blight. Parasite."

For the rest of the way to the station I got a lecture on the dangers of ivy to England. The pilot officer had been a horticulturist.

I said no more about the trees.

We could hear the Oxfords filling the air with that incessant machine buzz which substituted for silence on the station.

RAF Turnbull St. Justin lay out, aurally and physically, in a great circle whose central concentration was the aircraft itself. It was the reason we were there, and the nearer the airman was to his machine, the better was his morale, the more understandable his reason for being.

The rest of RAF Turnbull St. Justin was like the stations I had seen before—flat buildings under a leaden sky, humped oval corrugated iron backs of Nissen huts. But at its center, the blasted space of the airfield blotted out the old Cotswold grazing land in a vast square, crisscrossed by long runways. Huddled near the space, the huge hangars loomed above a few yellow Oxfords, nesting like birds. In the distance, above the other buildings, I could see the top of the flying control tower. It was built like a functional Puritan square, jutting up blindly, covered with brown and green undulations of camouflage, impotent against its unnatural shape.

I first noticed the connection between morale and the machines in the girls who came into the Admin office. Those in touch with them, the mechanics, the "met" girls, the signals operators, carried in with them a verve, a dash from nearer the center. The commanding officer at Turnbull St. Justin recognized this and decided to raise morale by taking the WAAF up for rides. He filled an Anson with WAAF cooks and flew them around the county. They were all sick. It seemed fair. They spent most of their time making us sick.

Those nearer the center suffered the rest of us as a dim necessity; the other women on the station fanned out in a sort of hierarchy of loss. The hierarchy worked on the stations themselves, from "ops"—the operational stations— through the various training commands down to the initial training units.

So when a call for volunteers to signals came into the Admin office, I volunteered, giving up the honor I was supposed to be waiting for, that of being sent into officers' training as an Admin officer. I had already realized that such officers were chosen not for specific skills, but for a mystic hangover from a distant peacetime—a quality called officer material, which usually meant that one's voice was careful, one's bearing "genteel," that one was, at least in form, a "lady"—all of which qualities I was trying to buff off as quickly as possible, like a useless and hampering prehensile tail, unneeded and awkward in the world I was trying to live in. Admin tended to gather together the self-conscious, the reactive, the snobs. Good officers slipped through, in spite of their qualifications, their qualities a mixture of security and strictness and grace.

I could see myself giving the sex lecture, meting out punishments I had no stomach for, dealing with a small army of "Paragraph Elevens." I was drawn away from that hard and human job, seduced toward the center—the machines.

The radio-telephone (R/T) operators sat in the flying control tower connected to the air, human elements like fuse wires, earphones on, plugged into small Marconi transmitter-receiver crystal sets, transmitting orders from the flying control officer, receiving in turn the pilots' recognitions of the ground, complaints, questions, sometimes jokes—all in the terse cut-word code of the RAF, monosyllabic, easy to call, quick to understand, sometimes chosen with the justice of poetry.

In our ears there was a perpetual grumbling of pilots calling to each other thinly down a long sound tunnel of distance. Over it all, striking at the fuse wires, the human element, German jamming was a curtain through which we listened, an undulating carrier wave, maddening and incessant, its efficiency defeating itself for a while because after a few weeks it, like the rumble of the planes, became a part of silence, staying insidiously always in our ears on and off the set, as if it were lodged in our brains, a small, monstrous parody of the hum of the world. To think about it after so long is to hear it again, incessant, like conscience; it has, once heard long enough, a sacred place in one's brain. As with everything else, the loudness of signals heard was categorized into "strengths"—strength five (loud and clear) was the loudest; strength one was the faintest.

On eight-hour duty we learned to point our concentrated hearing through jamming at strength three or four like bird dogs to the tiny strength-one sounds beyond it, answering, transmitting or receiving the clipped English without passion or person or intonation beyond the code sounds themselves, pencils flying through the logbooks before us, logging each fragment of sound, all as impersonal as the color of the station, hearing always through the jamming and the pinpoints of dialogue the urged rumbling of the planes.

Because of this demanded impersonality I had to learn to speak the English of the RAF in one day. The pilots, wary anyway, senses poised in the air, had no time to understand a soft, new voice; annoyed, they called back, clipped out,

"Hello, Nemo. Hello, Nemo [code name for the unknown]. Repeat. Repeat."

I learned to speak in character, "Helleau, *Covey Ninah Fife.* Helleau, *Covey Ninah Fife.*"

I cannot remember the call sign for the central tower at RAF Turnbull St. Justin, but I remember the call signs for the Oxfords—covey—and for one Oxford—*Covey Ninah Fife*—because I have failed in forgetting. *Covey Ninah Fife* was an airplane, and I remember its name though the name of my partner on duty, with whom I shared a room and a watch for months, has been forgotten; for our point of concentration and contact, our preoccupation, was the machine, which had an insane simplicity because we used human terms. We serviced the planes, called to them, lost them (in the cold, calm language of the BBC, "Eight of our aircraft are missing," oh, misplaced, their servant airmen inside, sometimes hosed out). As are all vessels made by man, all carriers, the planes were called "her"; often they were tagged with women's names—cared for, placated, their caprices noticed, and bragged about. *Covey Ninah Fife* was like an impatient, selfish, pouting, demanding woman.

On duty in the daylight, through the wide window which covered nearly the whole of the wall of the signals room, we could see the planes we spoke to coming in to land through the white space above the airdrome. Sometimes on bright days when there was promise in the air, they buzzed the control tower in an excess of freedom. When the flying control officer tried to find out their names to report them, we in contact were suddenly struck a little deaf, unable to hear their call signs.

On those days, coming off duty and out into the sun, into the more immediate roaring of the planes taking off and landing, I would wander down toward the briefing room, drawn toward the machines at work, hoping for the illegal invitation that made my heart flip over and my adrenalin surge.

There the newly graduated pilots, with their shiny embroidered wings, not yet dulled by time and service, waited to fly for pleasure, as boys in love with the planes. None of the student pilots had "tasted" combat, much less been sickened and surfeited. The few instructors I flew with had. Their handling of the machines was calmer, controlled. They knew what they were dealing with and flew warily. The ones who had survived were sad, careful men in their twenties, stripped of arrogance, their uniforms no longer costumes but utilitarian, as rubbed down as their wings and their faces. The student pilots still flirted and called out as I came toward the briefing room, "Want to go for a flip?"

Then I ran toward Equipment for a parachute and ran back, the chute flopping against my legs, the webbing crisscrossed to a metal disk at my breastbone, and climbed into the Oxford, the Miles Magister, the Tiger Club—whatever plane was warming up. Those functional wartime planes uninsulated by upholstery, soft voices, ignorance, were as maneuverable as fine horses. I watched the stick move forward and the ground drop away from us.

England became then, in minutes, an undulating patchwork quilt. Poppies below us, in their season, made some of the fields red, some yellow, some green with white doll houses, and the ancient bones of Cotswold outcroppings, and the gray ruins turned away below us under the free sky. There was no fear, no gravity. We flew, and often, looking up to see familiar abbey ruins as landmarks directly above us, our bodies lunging against the seat belts, our senses accepted the circular vision of the earth.

We went on low-flying exercises, jumping hedges and copses with the greatest sense of speed there can be because the motion was in closest contrast to the steady, known earth. The obstacles whipped behind us as we passed over them low enough to see a steady slipstream of cows bolting and farmers swearing, to see the separation of the grass, the dangerous closeness of the plane to its tossing black shadow.

There was never a more egocentric experience of control than having, with new Phaeton power, the sense that the earth was turning, rolling toward the sky at one's command; still within the plane, one watched, quietly, fingertips as alert as brains, the close ground flow, almost touching-close. Aircraft were then instruments of the arrogance authority tried to curb, of an experience, undigested and unprepared for, of simplicity and power in frames often too frail for it. If I, stealing "flips," was having that experience, so was Tina's pilot officer, taking power into his dangerous mind, and so were the Luftwaffe, so were the other romantics—some sick souls never to grow beyond it, as a first love is sought over and over, more parodied each time. Sometimes, in me, that arrogance would reach the ground for a few minutes after we touched down as I lugged the parachute back to Equipment, and I, still airborne, walked lightly away, forgetting where I was until the voice of an officer would intrude and snap, "Airwoman, step back ten paces and salute."

The day divided itself for the R/T operators into two worlds—that on the set and that off the set. There were two constant watches—the station watch and, even more important and less used, the Darky watch, which blanketed the whole of England with overlapping limited areas of open and waiting reception. On each station, a limited-area Marconi transmitter-receiver was set to the same wavelength, each covering a small area of the open air around its station. It was the safety watch—for the lost planes, those with wounded aboard or crippled wings or knocked-out engines. Whenever a plane needed to come down at the nearest field, the call went out somewhere over England, "Hello, Darky. Hello, Darky," and the answer came, beamed from the nearest sets, "Hello, Nemo. Hello, Nemo," to ask for their identifying call sign. Because of the limited areas of sound around each set, the loudest call came from the nearest field, and the plane would swerve toward the strongest voice.

Sometimes we sat on Darky watch for weeks, waiting until, in the distance, a voice would come ghostlike through the jamming, "Hello, Darky. Hello, Darky," and we would call out safety to the unknown, "Hello, Nemo. Hello, Nemo."

One night an American voice came through at strength one, weak, far away, "Hello, Darky, where the hell are we?" a lost thin whisper. From the overlapping answers, the radio operator in the plane sorted out the faint American lilt left in my disciplined voice. The plane flew toward it like a homing pigeon and landed, and a crew of fourteen homesick airmen from a Flying Fortress piled into the control tower to find the American girl.

The flying control officer was furious at the roar of life breaking into the silence of his night watch. He kept complaining that they had eaten all the eggs in the officers' mess.

On both watches the closeness to the air, to the machine, affected the operators. Some, uninterested in the connections with the air, made the flying control officer the keeper of their duty. When he was gone, responsibility went with him, and they turned down the sets to protect their brains from the jamming, got out knitting or books, unscrewed the "AC's" (batteries) to drop acid on their stockings so they could turn them in to Equipment for new ones.

Flying exercises kept us keyed to the sets and blotted out time with quick, concentrated work. Scrounging flips made me resurge afterward as if I had gone to a well of action, and I found a reason for being there, tied to the earphones. In the vast periods of boredom between, when only jamming could be heard, it was hard for the hand not to reach forward to turn the set down, not to recede from it into the dead areas of animal waiting, waiting for the confinement of the closed signals room, the connection by wavelength, even the sense of floating displacement in the state of war itself to be over.

Only having sought the air, and having heard, loosened in that space, the weak, thin connection with the control tower, stable through the crackling, diffused sound, kept me listening through the months, until there was no chronology of time, only place and the set, waiting before it for the always expected call.

That was the color of day, for day and night, on the set, were split apart by the color against the window. At night the blackout curtain cut us off from sight, and we waited within it through the lonely stretching of the hours toward morning. Time ceased altogether, and only those on their watches were awake in England isolated at live points in the dark.

I sensed the feel, the taste, the smell of space that year in those expanded nights, the other operator nodding, almost asleep, talk long since having ceased; there were no words—only the expansion of the brain and fatigue, dissolving unknowingly into trance. The notes which from long habit I wrote down on any scrap of paper and stuffed into my tunic pocket had, at the time of writing, the certainty of answers; yet later, as in dream answers, they made no sense. They were the only notes I kept of my whole experience in the WAAF, but when I found them later they meant nothing. They had been dredged deep from my unconscious as I floated in night. Once I had written, "We cannot live without love any longer." And again, "The contact is from mast light to mast light to aerial to mast light." Only the crumpled wartime paper, torn from an RAF issue notebook—not the words—brought back the smell, the cold, the space of the night.

We knew that beyond us in the darkness there was nothing, and we floated high in it, in that room; there was no ground, only darkness until the nights of night-flying exercises, when the darkness came alive with sound channeled into our ears.

On those nights we knew that the flare path was stretched away, dimly pinpointing the station in the dark, the faint blue lines of light shaped into a distant funnel for the planes: tiny, confident guide points isolated in an infinite blackout. The winking red eye of the Aldis lamp would be signaling at the flare path's end by the hand of some ground-crew airman huddled in the darkness of the airfield, flashing at the planes as they swooped down through the blackness.

We watched at the same time by listening; urgent, concentrated, seeing nothing but the confines of the room and the logbooks, making of those two elements and the pushing roar of the planes a whole vision of the flyers and the night.

The dark could be controlled, but not the yellow mist which had risen to cover and mute the ancient grazing land for as long as the Celts had run their sheep there and which, from time to time, quickly and silently blotted out RAF Turnbull St. Justin and left us calling and calling impotently through the soft damp blankets of fog.

Because of the quickness of these rising mists, RAF Turnbull St. Justin was known in the language of the RAF as Clamp Hill.

We were told one evening at six o'clock that the ceiling was high enough for night-flying exercises. I saw the first star in the purple sky as I pulled the blackout curtain and we settled into our seats. The flying control officer came in from time to time to stand behind us and talk a little, as he tended to do when we knew there would be the relief of night flying from the monotony of the most disliked watch of all—the four to twelve—when we were aware of the others wandering out to the pubs, going to the "flicks," finding each other in the lowering purple evening after duty was over.

With the visibility infinite, night flying began about eight o'clock. The exercises in taking off and landing we called circuits and bumps. From the flying control officer through us to the planes, the orders clipped out, "Hello, *Covey Eight Foah*, circle at Angels fife. Hello, *Covey Ninah Three*, circle at Angels foah. Hello, *Covey Ninah Two*, circle at Angels two. Hello, *Covey Ninah Fife*, pancake."

We played at control; the planes stacked, circling safely at five, four, three thousand feet, waiting their turn to land, switch off and refuel, take off again to join the circuit in an easy air quadrille.

Then the clamp fell. Within minutes the ceiling dropped to a thousand feet, to five hundred, to three hundred, to the deck. The other R/T operator caught my eye and whispered one word, "Flap!" Flap—panic; we worked faster, carriers for the urgency of the flying control officer and the planes.

There were three down safely, then four. The set was jammed with queries, put off by our voices, "Hello, *Covey Eight Three*, stand by, stand by . . ."

The planes were like air sheep taking their turns at the shambles. The new pilots, their voices crackling with urgency, flew blind, the fog pressed to their windows, their dependable sensuousness in flying no longer possible.

With the concentration of his eyes pinned to the altimeter as the orders came in, *Covey Ninah Fife* flew as the others did, waiting. He heard, "Hello, *Covey Ninah Fife*, circle at Angels four," watched the altometer drop to four thousand feet, calculated the feet above sea level at RAF Turnbull St. Justin as he breathed, slipped his eye to the turn indicator, depending on the balanced bubble of the level, the horizontal position of the tiny red plane at the artificial horizon, as if he were flying it instead of some six thousand pounds of machine; plotting the place of the plane in the darkness, picturing the wings inclining through the swirling darkness to a ground level which could not be seen, but would be felt when, calculations correct, *Covey Ninah Fife* touched down, the jolt of her wheels on the ground the only indication of the agreement of the instruments.

At three thousand feet, *Covey Ninah Fife* reported in and was told to circle and stand by.

We brought down *Covey Eight Three*, concentrating so that we could almost feel her wheels touch and bounce.

Covey Ninah Fife called in, low on fuel. Urging the other planes to stand by, we began bringing her down, all of us, with that blind dependence on orders, instruments and the machines, all of the old dependence on senses channeled to brain and obedience.

We heard the relief in the pilot's voice when he touched down and began to taxi her, guided by the ghost point of the Aldis lamp. We brought down *Covey Ninah Three.*

Through it, *Covey Ninah Fife* had not received orders to switch off. The pilot's voice kept coming in, more and more urgent; he was unable to switch off without the order. *Covey Ninah Fife* idled in the fog, her propellers turning, her grumbling voice interrupting as the other planes called in and were guided down to the flare path, now with lit flares floating, almost invisible, in the eye-tricking, muting fog.

There were two planes still up. With the excess of care engendered by panic, thin-voiced orders went out, dropping them in turn to three, then two, then one thousand feet.

Covey Ninah Fife called in, petulant, annoyed, for orders.

"It's *Covey Ninah Fife*, sir," I told the flying control officer, as urgent as the plane.

"Christ, I thought she was down," he said, forgetting in an hour of flap each separate plane.

"She is. She came down half an hour ago."

"Then for Christ's sake tell her to sign off."

"She . . ."

Covey Eight Three called in for orders to land and reported that she was low on fuel. We were off again, guiding as carefully as if we were setting her down safely on the ground with our own hands.

91

As we worked mechanically within the dependable rotation, so in the darkness did the ground crews, feeling their way through the clamp to the planes, swarming over them, refueling to orders and by habit, though the planes were grounded, the fog grease-slick on their wings. It was drill leaving no room for improvisation, drill drilled in so deeply that circumstances could not change it, drill becoming animal reaction: dependable, certain habit carrying all of us through the natural caprice of the fog. No one was yet experienced enough, or brave enough, or self-reliant enough; we were dulled by training, not yet used to being relit by danger, not capable of knowing when to disobey.

I knew it was midnight by the touch of my relief on my shoulder. We changed places quickly, the earphones still on my ears as she slid into place and got her pencil in hand. I slipped the earphones from my head to hers—even as they went on, her pencil began moving. The last plane was being brought in.

I heard her say, "Hello, *Covey Ninah Fife*," as I stepped back out of the periphery of the set, the panic, and the flying control officer. I put on my greatcoat, not waiting for my partner on duty, whose relief had not yet arrived. I wanted to get out of the atmosphere of urgency, to breathe, even in the thick fog and the blackout, to steal a cigarette while I waited for her so that we could guide each other back to the billet through the fog.

The hall below the control room had only the light from the opening doors of the rooms above to filter down to it. I felt the wall in the dark toward the outside door and opened it. After the blackness of the hall, the fog seemed to carry its own faint light. Somewhere beyond me, the fog obliterating any sense of distance, I could see a dim fuzz of light moving—a blackout torch. There was no sound but the grumbling of the taxiing planes.

I lit a cigarette.

Something, rolling like a football, brushed against my leg, and I reached down toward it to pick it up and give it back toward the sound of steps running toward me.

Someone yelled, "Jesus, it's a WAAF. *Get inside.*"

One of the ground crew reached for me to push me back into the hallway before I saw him. He swept me inside with a flying tackle. For a second we clung together like lovers so that we wouldn't fall. He switched on his torch and his face rose out of the hall darkness above it. His head seemed disembodied in the dark.

"He got up on the wing to refuel *Covey Ninah Fife,*" the airman said, not to me, not to anybody. "He slipped on the wing. He slipped in the fog on the wing. The prop was still going. He lost his head."

For a second I thought he meant panic, then I knew what he meant and I knew what had bounded past my leg and I was sick on the floor.

Covey Ninah Fife had not received her orders to switch off.

THEY SHALL NOT GROW OLD

ROALD DAHL

The two of us sat outside the hangar on wooden boxes.

It was noon. The sun was high and the heat of the sun was like a close fire. It was hotter than hell out there by the hangar. We could feel the hot air touching the inside of our lungs when we breathed and we found it better if we almost closed our lips and breathed in quickly; it was cooler that way. The sun was upon our shoulders and upon our backs, and all the time the sweat seeped out from our skin, trickled down our necks, over our chests and down our stomachs. It collected just where our belts were tight around the tops of our trousers and it filtered under the tightness of our belts where the wet was very uncomfortable and made prickly heat on the skin.

Our two Hurricanes were standing a few yards away, each with that patient, smug look which fighter planes have when the engine is not turning, and beyond them the thin black strip of the runway sloped down toward the beaches and toward the sea. The black surface of the runway and the white grassy sand on the sides of the runway shimmered and shimmered in the sun. The heat haze hung like a vapor over the aerodrome.

The Stag looked at his watch.

"He ought to be back," he said.

The two of us were on readiness, sitting there for orders to take off. The Stag moved his feet on the hot ground.

"He ought to be back," he said.

It was two and a half hours since Fin had gone and he certainly should have come back by now. I looked up into the sky and listened. There was the noise of airmen talking beside the petrol wagon and there was the faint pounding of the sea upon the beaches; but there was no sign of an airplane. We sat a little while longer without speaking.

"It looks as though he's had it," I said.

"Yep," said the Stag. "It looks like it."

The Stag got up and put his hands into the pockets of his khaki shorts. I got up too. We stood looking northward into the clear sky, and we shifted our feet on the ground because of the softness of the tar and because of the heat.

"What was the name of that girl?" said the Stag without turning his head.

"Nikki," I answered.

The Stag sat down again on his wooden box, still with his hands in his pockets and he looked down at the ground between his feet. The Stag was the oldest pilot in the squadron; he was twenty-seven. He had a mass of coarse ginger hair which he never brushed. His face was pale, even after all this time in the sun, and covered with freckles. His mouth was wide and tight closed. He was not tall but his shoulders under his khaki shirt were broad and thick like those of a wrestler. He was a quiet person.

"He'll probably be all right," he said, looking up. "And anyway, I'd like to meet the Vichy Frenchman who can get Fin."

We were in Palestine fighting the Vichy French in Syria. We were at Haifa, and three hours before the Stag, Fin and I had gone on readiness. Fin had flown off in response to an urgent call from the Navy, who had phoned up and said that there were two French destroyers moving out of Beyrouth harbor. Please go at once and see where they are going, said the Navy. Just fly up the coast and have a look and come back quickly and tell us where they are going.

So Fin had flown off in his Hurricane. The time had gone by and he had not returned. We knew that there was no longer much hope. If he hadn't been shot down, he would have run out of petrol some time ago.

I looked down and I saw his blue R.A.F. cap which was lying on the ground where he had thrown it as he ran to his aircraft, and I saw the oil stains on top of the cap and the shabby bent peak. It was difficult now to believe that he had gone. He had been in Egypt, in Libya and in Greece. On the aerodrome and in the mess we had had him with us all of the time. He was gay and tall and full of laughter, this Fin, with black hair and a long straight nose which he used to stroke up and down with the tip of his finger. He had a way of listening to you while you were telling a story, leaning back in his chair with his face to the ceiling but with his eyes looking down on the ground, and it was only last night at supper that he had suddenly said, "You know, I wouldn't mind marrying Nikki. I think she's a good girl."

The Stag was sitting opposite him at the time, eating baked beans.

"You mean just occasionally," he said.

Nikki was in a cabaret in Haifa.

"No," said Fin, "Cabaret girls make fine wives. They are never unfaithful. There is no novelty for them in being unfaithful; that would be like going back to the old job."

The Stag had looked up from his beans. "Don't be such a bloody fool," he said. "You wouldn't really marry Nikki."

"Nikki," said Fin with great seriousness, "comes of a fine family. She is a good girl. She never uses a pillow when she sleeps. Do you know why she never uses a pillow when she sleeps?"

"No."

The others at the table were listening now. Everyone was listening to Fin talking about Nikki.

"Well, when she was very young she was engaged to be married to an officer in the French Navy. She loved him greatly. Then one day when they were sunbathing together on the beach he happened to mention to her that he never used a pillow when he slept. It was just one of those little things which people say to each other for the sake of conversation. But Nikki never forgot it. From that time onward she began to practice sleeping without a pillow. One day the French officer was run over by a truck and killed; but although to her it was very uncomfortable, she still went on sleeping without a pillow to preserve the memory of her lover."

Fin took a mouthful of beans and chewed them slowly. "It is a sad story," he said. "It shows that she is a good girl. I think I would like to marry her."

That was what Fin had said last night at supper. Now he was gone and I wondered what little thing Nikki would do in his memory.

The sun was hot on my back and I turned instinctively in order to take the heat upon the other side of my body. As I turned, I saw Carmel and the town of Haifa. I saw the steep pale-green slope of the mountain as it dropped down toward the sea, and below it I saw the town and the bright colors of the houses shining in the sun. The houses with their whitewashed walls covered the sides of Carmel and the red roofs of the houses were like a rash on the face of the mountain.

Walking slowly toward us from the gray corrugated iron hangar, came the three men who were the next crew on readiness. They had their yellow Mae Wests slung over their shoulders and they came walking slowly toward us, holding their helmets in their hands as they came.

When they were close, the Stag said, "Fin's had it," and they said, "Yes, we know." They sat down on the wooden boxes which we had been using, and immediately the sun was upon their shoulders and upon their backs and they began to sweat. The Stag and I walked away.

The next day was a Sunday and in the morning we flew up the Lebanon valley to ground-strafe an aerodrome called Rayak. We flew past Hermon who had a hat of snow upon his head, and we came down out of the sun onto Rayak and onto the French bombers on the aerodrome and began our strafing. I remember that as we flew past, skimming low over the ground, the doors of the French bombers opened. I remember seeing a whole lot of women in white dresses running out across the aerodrome; I remember particularly their white dresses.

You see, it was a Sunday and the French pilots had asked their ladies out from Beyrouth to look over the bombers. The Vichy pilots had said, come out on Sunday morning and we will show you our airplanes. It was a very Vichy French thing for them to do.

So when we started shooting, they all tumbled out and began to run across the aerodrome in their white Sunday dresses.

I remember hearing Monkey's voice over the radio, saying, "Give them a chance, give them a chance," and the

whole squadron wheeled around and circled the aerodrome once while the women ran over the grass in every direction. One of them stumbled and fell twice and one of
them was limping and being helped by a man, but we gave
them time. I remember watching the small bright flashes
of a machine gun on the ground and thinking that they
should at least have stopped their shooting while we were
waiting for their white-dressed women to get out of the
way.

That was the day after Fin had gone. The next day the
Stag and I sat once more at readiness on the wooden boxes
outside the hangar. Paddy, a big fair-haired boy, had taken
Fin's place and was sitting with us.

It was noon. The sun was high and the heat of the sun
was like a close fire. The sweat ran down our necks, down
inside our shirts, over our chests and stomachs, and we sat
there waiting for the time when we would be relieved. The
Stag was sewing the strap onto his helmet with a needle
and cotton and telling of how he had seen Nikki the night
before in Haifa and of how he had told her about Fin.

Suddenly we heard the noise of an airplane. The Stag
stopped his talking and we all looked up. The noise was
coming from the north, and it grew louder and louder as
the airplane flew closer, and then the Stag said suddenly,
"It's a Hurricane."

The next moment it was circling the aerodrome, lowering its wheels to land.

"Who is it?" said the fair-haired Paddy. "No one's gone
out this morning."

Then, as it glided past us on to the runway, we saw the
number on the tail of the machine, H.4427, and we knew
that it was Fin.

We were standing up now, watching the machine as it taxied toward us, and when it came up close and swung round for parking we saw Fin in the cockpit. He waved his hand at us, grinned and got out. We ran up and shouted at him, "Where've you been?" "Where in the hell have you been?" "Did you force-land and get away again?" "Did you find a woman in Beyrouth?" "Fin, where in the hell have you been?"

Others were coming up and crowding around him now, fitters and riggers and the men who drove the fire tender, and they all waited to hear what Fin would say. He stood there pulling off his helmet, pushing back his black hair with his hand, and he was so astonished at our behavior that at first he merely looked at us and did not speak. Then he laughed and he said, "What in the hell's the matter? What's the matter with all of you?"

"Where have you been?" we shouted. "Where have you been for two days?"

Upon the face of Fin there was a great and enormous astonishment. He looked quickly at his watch.

"Five past twelve," he said. "I left at eleven, one hour and five minutes ago. Don't be a lot of damn fools. I must go and report quickly. The Navy will want to know that those destroyers are still in the harbor at Beyrouth."

He started to walk away; I caught his arm.

"Fin," I said quietly, "you've been away since the day before yesterday. What's the matter with you?"

He looked at me and laughed.

"I've seen you organize much better jokes than this one," he said. "It isn't so funny. It isn't a bit funny." And he walked away.

We stood there, the Stag, Paddy and I, the fitters, the riggers and the men who drove the fire-engine, watching

Fin as he walked away. We looked at each other, not knowing what to say or to think, understanding nothing, knowing nothing except that Fin had been serious when he spoke and that what he said he had believed to be true. We knew this because we knew Fin, and we knew it because when one has been together as we had been together, then there is never any doubting of anything that anyone says when he is talking about his flying; there can only be a doubting of oneself. These men were doubting themselves, standing there in the sun doubting themselves, and the Stag was standing by the wing of Fin's machine peeling off with his fingers little flakes of paint which had dried up and cracked in the sun.

Someone said, "Well, I'll be buggered," and the men turned and started to walk quietly back to their jobs. The next three pilots on readiness came walking slowly toward us from the gray corrugated-iron hangar, walking slowly under the heat of the sun and swinging their helmets in their hands as they came. The Stag, Paddy and I walked over to the pilots' mess to have a drink and lunch.

The mess was a small white wooden building with a veranda. Inside there were two rooms, one a sitting room with armchairs and magazines and a hole in the wall through which you could buy drinks, and the other a dining room with one long wooden table. In the sitting room we found Fin talking to Monkey, our C.O. The other pilots were sitting around listening and everybody was drinking beer. We knew that it was really a serious business in spite of the beer and the armchairs; that Monkey was doing what he had to do and doing it in the only way possible. Monkey was a rare man, tall with a handsome face, an Italian bullet wound in his leg and a casual friendly efficiency. He never laughed out loud, he just choked and grunted deep in his throat.

Fin was saying, "You must go easy, Monkey; you must help me to stop thinking that I've gone mad."

Fin was being serious and sensible, but he was worried as hell.

"I have told you all I know," he said. "That I took off at eleven o'clock, that I climbed up high, that I flew to Beyrouth, saw the two French destroyers and came back, landing at five past twelve. I swear to you that that is all I know."

He looked around at us, at the Stag and me, at Paddy and Johnny and the half-dozen other pilots in the room, and we smiled at him and nodded to show him that we were with him, not against him, and that we believed what he said.

Monkey said, "What in the hell am I going to say to Headquarters at Jerusalem? I reported you missing, now I've got to report your return. They'll insist on knowing where you've been."

The whole thing was getting to be too much for Fin. He was sitting upright, tapping with the fingers of his left hand on the leather arm of his chair, tapping with quick sharp taps, leaning forward, thinking, thinking, fighting to think, tapping on the arm of the chair and then he began tapping the floor with his foot as well. The Stag could stand it no longer.

"Monkey," he said, "Monkey, let's just leave it all for a bit. Let's leave it and perhaps Fin will remember something later on."

Paddy, who was sitting on the arm of the Stag's chair, said, "Yes, and meanwhile we could tell H.Q. that Fin had force-landed in a field in Syria, taken two days to repair his aircraft, then flown home."

Everybody was helping Fin. The pilots were all helping him. In the mind of each of us was the certain knowledge that here was something that concerned us greatly. Fin knew it, although that was all he knew, and the others knew it because one could see it upon their faces. There was a tension, a fine high-drawn tension in the room, because here for the first time was something which was neither bullets nor fire nor the coughing of an engine nor burst tires nor blood in the cockpit nor yesterday nor today, nor even tomorrow. Monkey felt it too, and he said, "Yes, let's have another drink and leave it for a bit. I'll tell H.Q. that you force-landed in Syria and managed to get off again later."

We had some more beer and went in to lunch. Monkey ordered bottles of Palestine white wine with the meal to celebrate Fin's return.

After that no one mentioned the thing at all; we did not even talk about it when Fin wasn't there. But each one of us continued to think about it secretly, knowing for certain that it was something important and that it was not finished. The tension spread quickly through the squadron and it was with all the pilots.

Meanwhile the days went by and the sun shone upon the aerodrome and upon the aircraft and Fin took his place among us flying in the normal way,

Then one day, I think it was about a week later, we did another ground-strafe of Rayak aerodrome. There were six of us, with Monkey leading and Fin flying on his starboard side. We came in low over Rayak and there was plenty of light flak, and as we went in on the first run, Paddy's machine was hit. As we wheeled for the second run we saw his Hurricane wing gently over and dive straight to the ground at the edge of the aerodrome. There was a great billow of white smoke as it hit, then the flames, and as the flames spread the smoke turned from white to black and Paddy was with it. Immediately there was a crackle over the radio and I heard Fin's voice, very excited, shouting into his microphone, "I've remembered it. Hello, Monkey, I've remembered it all," and Monkey's calm slow reply, "OK Fin, OK; don't forget it."

We did our second run and then Monkey led us quickly away, weaving in and out of the valleys, with the bare grey brown hills far above us on either side, and all the way home, all through the half-hour's flight, Fin never stopped shouting over the R.T. First he would call to Monkey and say, "Hello, Monkey, I've remembered it, all of it; every bit of it." Then he would say, "Hello, Stag, I've remembered it; all of it; I can't forget it now." He called me and he called Johnny and he called Wishful; he called us all separately over and over again, and he was so excited that sometimes he shouted too loudly into his mike and we could not hear what he was saying.

When we landed, we dispersed our aircraft and because Fin for some reason had to park his at the far side of the aerodrome, the rest of us were in the Operations room before him.

The Ops room was beside the hangar. It was a bare place with a large table to the middle of the floor on which there was a map of the area. There was another smaller table with a couple of telephones, a few wooden chairs and benches and at one end the floor was stacked with Mae Wests, parachutes, and helmets. We were standing there taking off our flying clothing and throwing it on to the floor at the end of the room when Fin arrived. He came quickly into the doorway and stopped. His black hair was standing up straight and untidy because of the way in which he had pulled off his helmet; his face was shiny with sweat and his khaki shirt was dark and wet. His mouth was open and he was breathing quickly. He looked as though he had been running. He looked like a child who had rushed downstairs into a room full of grown-ups to say that the cat has had kittens in the nursery and who does not know how to begin.

We had all heard him coming because that was what we had been waiting for. Everyone stopped what they were doing and stood still, looking at Fin.

Monkey said, "Hello, Fin," and Fin said, "Monkey, you've got to believe this because it's what happened."

Monkey was standing over by the table with the telephones; the Stag was near him, square short ginger-haired Stag, standing up straight, holding a Mae West in his hand, looking at Fin. The others were at the far end of the room. When Fin spoke, they began to move up quietly until they were closer to him, until they reached the edge of the big map table which they touched with their hands. There they stood, looking at Fin, waiting for him to begin.

He started at once, talking quickly, then calming down and talking more slowly as he got into his story. He told everything, standing there by the door of the Ops room, with his yellow Mae West still on him and with his helmet and oxygen mask in his hand. The others stayed where they were and listened, and as I listened to him, I forgot that it was Fin speaking and that we were in the Ops room at Haifa; I forgot everything and went with him on his journey, and did not come back until he had finished,

"I was flying at about twenty thousand," he said. "I flew over Tyre and Sidon and over the Damour River and then I flew inland over the Lebanon hills, because I intended to approach Beyrouth from the east. Suddenly I flew into cloud, thick white cloud which was so thick and dense that I could see nothing except the inside of my cockpit. I couldn't understand it, because a moment before everything had been clear and blue and there had been no cloud anywhere.

"I started to lose height to get out of the cloud and I went down and down and still I was in it. I knew that I must not go too low because of the hills, but at six thousand the cloud was still around me. It was so thick that I could see nothing, not even the nose of my machine nor the wings, and the cloud condensed on the windshield and little rivers of water ran down the glass and got blown away by the slipstream. I have never seen cloud like that before. It was thick and white right up to the edges of the cockpit. I felt like a man on a magic carpet, sitting there alone in this little glass-topped cockpit, with no wings, no tail, no engine and no airplane.

"I knew that I must get out of this cloud, so I turned and flew west over the sea away from the mountains; then I came down low by my altimeter. I came down to five hundred feet, four hundred, three hundred, two hundred, one hundred, and the cloud was still around me. For a moment I paused. I knew that it was unsafe to go lower. Then, quite suddenly, like a gust of wind, came the feeling that there was nothing below me; no sea nor earth nor anything else and slowly, deliberately, I opened the throttle, pushed the stick hard forward and dived.

"I did not watch the altimeter; I looked straight ahead through the windshield at the whiteness of the cloud and I went on diving. I sat there pressing the stick forward, keeping her in the dive, watching the vast clinging whiteness of the cloud and I never once wondered where I was going. I just went.

"I do not know how long I sat there; it may have been minutes and it may have been hours; I know only that as I sat there and kept her diving, I was certain that what was below me was neither mountains nor rivers nor earth nor sea and I was not afraid.

"Then I was blinded. It was like being half asleep in bed when someone turns on the light.

"I came out of the cloud so suddenly and so quickly that I was blinded. There was no space of time between being in it and being out of it. One moment I was in it and the whiteness was thick around me and in that same moment I was out of it and the light was so bright that I was blinded. I screwed up my eyes and held them tight closed for several seconds.

"When I opened them everything was blue, more blue than anything that I had ever seen. It was not a dark blue, nor was it a bright blue; it was a blue blue, a pure shining color which I had never seen before and which I cannot describe. I looked around. I looked up above me and behind me. I sat up and peered below me through the glass of the cockpit and everywhere it was blue. It was bright and clear, like pleasant sunlight, but there was no sun.

"Then I saw them.

"Far ahead and above I saw a long thin line of aircraft flying across the sky. They were moving forward in a single black line, all at the same speed, all in the same direction, all close up, following one behind the other, and the line stretched across the sky as far as the eye could see. It was the way they moved ahead, the urgent way in which they pressed forward forward forward like ships sailing before a great wind, it was from this that I knew everything. I do not know why or how I knew it, but I knew as I looked at them that these were the pilots and air crews who had been killed in battle, who now, in their own aircraft were making their last flight, their last journey.

"As I flew higher and closer I could recognize the machines themselves. I saw in that long procession nearly every type there was. I saw Lancasters and Dorniers, Halifaxes and Hurricanes, Messerschmitts, Spitfires, Stirlings, Savoia 79s, Junker 88s, Gladiators, Hampdens, Macchi 200s, Blenheims, Focke Wulfs, Beaufighters, Swordfish, and Heinkels. All these and many more I saw, and the moving line reached across the blue sky both to the one side and to the other until it faded from sight.

"I was close to them now and I began to sense that I was being sucked toward them regardless of what I wished to do. There was a wind which took hold of my machine, blew it over and tossed it about like a leaf and I was pulled and sucked as by a giant vortex toward the other airplanes. There was nothing I could do for I was in the vortex and in the arms of the wind. This all happened very quickly, but I remember it clearly. I felt the pull on my aircraft becoming stronger; I was whisked forward faster and faster, and then suddenly I was flying in the procession itself, moving forward with the others, at the same speed and on the same course. Ahead of me, close enough for me to see the color of the paint on its wings, was a Swordfish, an old Fleet Air Arm Swordfish, I could see the heads and helmets of the observer and the pilot as they sat in their cockpits, the one behind the other. Ahead of the Swordfish there was a Dornier, a Flying Pencil, and beyond the Dornier there were others which I could not recognize from where I was.

"We flew on and on. I could not have turned and flown away even if I had wanted to. I do not know why, although it may have been something to do with the vortex and with, the wind, but I knew that it was so. Moreover, I was not really flying my aircraft; it flew itself. There was no maneuvering to reckon with, no speed, no height, no throttle, no stick, no nothing. Once I glanced down at my instruments and saw that they were all dead, just as they are when the machine is sitting on the ground.

"So we flew on. I had no idea how fast we went. There was no sensation of speed and for all I know, it was a million miles an hour. Now I come to think of it, I never once during that time, felt either hot or cold or hungry or thirsty; I felt none of those things. I felt no fear, because I knew nothing of which to be afraid. I felt no worry, because I could remember nothing or think of nothing about which to be worried. I felt no desire to do anything that I was not doing or to have anything that I did not have, because there was nothing that I wished to do and there was nothing that I wished to have. I felt only pleasure at being where I was, at seeing the wonderful light and the beautiful color around me. Once I caught sight of my face in the cockpit mirror and I saw that I was smiling, smiling with my eyes and with my mouth, and when I looked away I knew that I was still smiling, simply because that was the way I felt. Once, the observer in the Swordfish ahead of me turned and waved his hand. I slid back the roof of my cockpit and waved back. I remember that even when I opened the cockpit, there was no rush of air and no rush of cold or heat, nor was there any pressure of the slipstream on my hand. Then I noticed that they were all waving at each other, like children on a roller-coaster and I turned and waved at the man in the Macchi behind me.

"But there was something happening along the line. Far up in front I could see that the airplanes had changed course, were wheeling around to the left and losing height. The whole procession, as it reached a certain point, was banking around and gliding downward in a wide, sweeping circle. Instinctively I glanced down over the cockpit, and there I saw spread out below me a vast green plain. It was green and smooth and beautiful; it reached to the far edges of the horizon where the blue of the sky came down and merged with the green of the plain.

"And there was the light. Over to the left, far away in the distance was a bright white light, shining bright and without any color. It was as though the sun, but something far bigger than the sun, something without shape or form whose light was bright but not blinding, was lying on the far edge of the green plain. The light spread outward from a center of brilliance and it spread far up into the sky and far out over the plain. When I saw it, I could not at first look away from it. I had no desire to go toward it, into it, and almost at once the desire and the longing became so intense that several times I tried to pull my aircraft out of the line and fly straight toward it; but it was not possible and I had to fly with the rest.

"As they banked around and lost height I went with them, and we began to glide down toward the green plain below. Now that I was closer, I could see the great mass of aircraft upon the plain itself. They were everywhere, scattered over the ground like currants upon a green carpet. There were hundreds and hundreds of them, and each minute, each second almost, their numbers grew as those in front of me landed and taxied to a standstill.

"Quickly we lost height. Soon I saw that the ones just in front of me were lowering their wheels and preparing to land. The Dornier next but one to me levelled off and touched down. Then the old Swordfish. The pilot turned a little to the left out of the way of the Dornier and landed beside him. I turned to the left of the Swordfish and levelled off. I looked out of the cockpit at the ground, judging the height, and I saw the green of the ground blurred as it rushed past me and below me.

"I waited for my aircraft to sink and to touch down, It seemed to take a long time. 'Come on,' I said. 'Come on, come on.' I was only about six feet up, but she would not sink. 'Get down,' I shouted, 'please *get down.*' I began to panic, I became frightened. Suddenly I noticed that I was gaining speed. I cut all the switches but it made no difference. The aircraft was gathering speed, going faster and faster, and I looked around and saw behind me the long procession of aircraft dropping down out of the sky and sweeping in to land. I saw the mass of machines upon the ground, scattered far across the plain and away on one side I saw the light, that shining white light which shone so brightly over the great plain and to which I longed to go. I know that had I been able to land, I would have started to run toward that light the moment I got out of my aircraft

"And now I was flying away from it. My fear grew. As I flew faster and farther away, the fear took hold of me until soon I was fighting crazy mad, pulling at the stick, wrestling with the airplane, trying to turn it around, back toward the light. When I saw that it was impossible, I tried to kill myself, I really wanted to kill myself then, I tried to dive the aircraft into the ground, but it flew on straight. I tried to jump out of the cockpit, but there was a hand upon my shoulder which held me down. I tried to bang my head against the sides of the cockpit, but it made no difference and I sat there fighting with my machine and with everything until suddenly I noticed that I was in cloud. I was in the same thick white cloud as before; and I seemed to be climbing. I looked behind me, but the cloud had closed in all round. There was nothing now but this vast impenetrable whiteness. I began to feel sick and giddy, I did not care any longer what happened one way or the other, I just sat there limply, letting the machine fly on by itself.

"It seemed a long time and I am sure that I sat there for many hours. I must have gone to sleep. As I slept, I dreamed. I dreamed not of the things that I had just seen, but of the things of my ordinary life, of the squadron, of Nikki, and of the aerodrome here at Haifa. I dreamed that I was sitting at readiness outside the hangar with two others, that a request came from the Navy for someone to do a quick recco over Beyrouth; and because I was first up, I jumped into my Hurricane and went off. I dreamed that I passed over Tyre and Sidon and over the Damour River, climbing up to twenty thousand as I went. Then I turned inland over the Lebanon hills, swung around and approached Beyrouth from the east. I was above the town, peering over the side of the cockpit, looking for the harbor and trying to find the two French destroyers. Soon I saw them, saw them clearly, tied up close alongside each other by the wharf, and I banked around and dived for home as fast as I could.

"The Navy's wrong, I thought to myself as I flew back. The destroyers are still in the harbor. I looked at my watch. An hour and a half. 'I've been quick,' I said. 'They'll be pleased.' I tried to call up on the radio to give the information, but I couldn't get through.

"Then I came back here. When I landed, you all crowded around me and asked me where I had been for two days, but I could remember nothing. I did not remember anything except the flight to Beyrouth until just now, when I saw Paddy being shot down. As his machine hit the ground, I found myself saying, 'You lucky bastard. You lucky, lucky bastard,' and as I said it, I knew why I was saying it and remembered everything. That was when I shouted to you over the radio. That was when I remembered."

Fin had finished. No one had moved or said anything all the time that he had been talking. Now it was only Monkey who spoke. He shuffled his feet on the floor, turned and looked out of the window and said quietly, almost in a whisper, "Well, I'll be damned," and the rest of us went slowly back to the business of taking off our flying clothing and stacking it in the corner of the room on the floor; all except the Stag, square short Stag, who stood there watching Fin as Fin walked slowly across the room to put away his clothing.

After Fin's story, the squadron returned to normal. The tension, which had been with us for over a week, disappeared. The aerodrome was a happier place in which to be. But no one ever mentioned Fin's journey. We never once spoke about it together, not even when we got drunk in the evening at the Excelsior in Haifa.

The Syrian campaign was coming to an end. Everyone could see that it must finish soon, although the Vichy people were still fighting fiercely south of Beyrouth. We were still flying. We were flying a great deal over the fleet, which was bombarding the coast, for we had the job of protecting them from the Junker 88s which came over from Rhodes. It was on the last one of these flights over the fleet that Fin was killed.

We were flying high above the ships when the Ju-88s came over in force and there was a battle. We had only six Hurricanes in the air; there were many of the Junkers and it was a good fight. I do not remember much about what went on at the time. One never does. But I remember that it was a hectic, chasing fight, with the Junkers diving for the ships, with the ships barking at them, throwing up everything into the air so that the sky was full of white flowers which blossomed quickly and grew and blew away with the wind. I remember the German who blew up in mid-air, quickly, with just a white flash, so that where the bomber had been, there was nothing left except tiny little pieces falling slowly downward. I remember the one that had its rear turret shot away, which flew along with the gunner hanging out of the tail by his straps, struggling to get back into the machine. I remember one, a brave one who stayed up above to fight us while the others went down to dive-bomb. I remember that we shot him up and I remember seeing him turn slowly over on to his back, pale green belly upward like a dead fish, before finally he spun down.

And I remember Fin.

I was close to him when his aircraft caught fire. I could see the flames coming out of the nose of his machine and dancing over the engine cowling. There was black smoke coming from the exhaust of his Hurricane.

I flew up close and I called to him over the R.T. "Hello, Fin," I called, "you'd better jump."

His voice came back, calm and slow. "It's not so easy."

"Jump," I shouted, "jump quickly."

I could see him sitting there under the glass roof of the cockpit. He looked toward me and shook his head,

"It's not so easy," he answered. "I'm a bit shot up. My arms are shot up and I can't undo the straps."

"Get out," I shouted, "For God's sake, get out," but he did not answer. For a moment his aircraft flew on, straight and level, then gently, like a dying eagle, it dipped a wing and dived toward the sea. I watched it as it went; I watched the thin trail of black smoke which it made across the sky, and as I watched, Fin's voice came again over the radio, clear and slow. "I'm a lucky bastard," he was saying. "A lucky, lucky bastard."

THE LOST PILOT

JAMES TATE

FOR MY FATHER, 1922–1944

Your face did not rot
like the others—the co-pilot,
for example, I saw him

yesterday. His face is corn-
mush: his wife and daughter,
the poor ignorant people, stare

as if he will compose soon.
He was more wronged than Job.
But your face did not rot

like the others—it grew dark,
and hard like ebony;
the features progressed in their

distinction. If I could cajole
you to come back for an evening,
down from your compulsive
orbiting, I would touch you,
read your face as Dallas,
your hoodlum gunner, now,

with the blistered eyes, reads
his braille editions. I would
touch your face as a disinterested

scholar touches an original page.
However frightening, I would
discover you, and I would not

turn you in; I would not make
you face your wife, or Dallas,
or the co-pilot, Jim. You

could return to your crazy
orbiting, and I would not try
to fully understand what

it means to you. All I know
is this: when I see you,
as I have seen you at least

once every year of my life,
spin across the wilds of the sky
like a tiny, African god,

I feel dead. I feel as if I were
the residue of a stranger's life,
that I should pursue you.

My head cocked toward the sky,
I cannot get off the ground,
and, you, passing over again,

fast, perfect, and unwilling
to tell me that you are doing
well, or that it was mistake

that placed you in that world,
and me in this; or that misfortune
placed these worlds in us.

CHIEF WHITE HALFOAT

JOSEPH HELLER

Doc Daneeka lived in a splotched gray tent with Chief White Halfoat, whom he feared and despised.

"I can just picture his liver," Doc Daneeka grumbled.

"Picture my liver," Yossarian advised him.

"There's nothing wrong with your liver."

"That shows how much you don't know," Yossarian bluffed, and told Doc Daneeka about the troublesome pain in his liver that had troubled Nurse Duckett and Nurse Cramer and all the doctors in the hospital because it wouldn't become jaundice and wouldn't go away.

Doc Daneeka wasn't interested. "You think you've got troubles?" he wanted to know. "What about me? You should've been in my office the day those newlyweds walked in."

"What newlyweds?"

"Those newlyweds that walked into my office one day. Didn't I ever tell you about them? She was lovely."

So was Doc Daneeka's office. He had decorated his waiting room with goldfish and one of the finest suites of cheap furniture. Whatever he could he bought on credit,

118

even the goldfish. For the rest, he obtained money from greedy relatives in exchange for shares of the profits. His office was in Staten Island in a two-family firetrap just four blocks away from the ferry stop and only one block south of a supermarket, three beauty parlors, and two corrupt druggists. It was a corner location, but nothing helped. Population turnover was small, and people clung through habit to the same physicians they had been doing business with for years. Bills piled up rapidly, and he was soon faced with the loss of his most precious medical instruments: his adding machine was repossessed, and then his typewriter. The goldfish died. Fortunately, just when things were blackest, the war broke out.

"It was a godsend," Doc Daneeka confessed solemnly. "Most of the other doctors were soon in the service, and things picked up overnight. The corner location really started paying off, and I soon found myself handling more patients than I could handle competently. I upped my kick-back fee with those two drugstores. The beauty parlors were good for two, three abortions a week. Things couldn't have been better, and then look what happened. They had to send a guy from the draft board around to look me over. I was Four-F. I had examined myself pretty thoroughly and discovered that I was unfit for military service. You'd think my word would be enough, wouldn't you, since I was a doctor in good standing with my county medical society and with my local Better Business Bureau. But no, it wasn't, and they sent this guy around just to make sure I really did have one leg amputated at the hip and was helplessly bedridden with incurable rheumatoid arthritis. Yossarian, we live in an age of distrust and deteriorating spiritual values. It's a terrible thing," Doc Daneeka protested in a voice quavering with strong emotion. "It's a terrible thing when even the word of a licensed physician is suspected by the country he loves."

Doc Daneeka had been drafted and shipped to Pianosa as a flight surgeon, even though he was terrified of flying.

"I don't have to go looking for trouble in an airplane," he noted, blinking his beady, brown, offended eyes myopically. "It comes looking for me. Like that virgin I'm telling you about that couldn't have a baby."

"What virgin?" Yossarian asked. "I thought you were telling me about some newlyweds."

"That's the virgin I'm telling you about. They were just a couple of young kids, and they'd been married, oh, a little over a year when they came walking into my office without an appointment. You should have seen her. She was so sweet and young and pretty. She even blushed when I asked about her periods. I don't think I'll ever stop loving that girl. She was built like a dream and wore a chain around her neck with a medal of Saint Anthony hanging down inside the most beautiful bosom I never saw. 'It must be a terrible temptation for Saint Anthony,' I joked—just to put her at ease, you know. 'Saint Anthony?' her husband said. 'Who's Saint Anthony?' 'Ask your wife,' I told him. 'She can tell you who Saint Anthony is.' 'Who is Saint Anthony?' he asked her. 'Who?' she wanted to know. 'Saint Anthony,' he told her. 'Saint Anthony?' she said. 'Who's Saint Anthony?' When I got a good look at her inside my examination room I found she was still a virgin. I spoke to her husband alone while she was pulling her girdle back on and hooking it onto her stockings. 'Every night,' he boasted. A real wise guy, you know. 'I never miss a night,' he boasted. He meant it, too. 'I even been puttin' it to her mornings before the breakfasts she makes me before we go to work,' he boasted. There was only one explanation. When I had them both together again I gave them a demonstration of intercourse with the rubber models I've got in my office. I've got these rubber models in my office with all the reproductive organs of both sexes that I keep locked up in separate cabinets to avoid a scandal. I mean I used to have them. I don't have anything any more, not even a practice. The only thing I have now is this low temperature that I'm really starting to worry about. Those two kids I've got working for me in the medical tent aren't worth a damn as diagnosticians. All they know how to do is complain. They think they've got troubles? What about me? They should have been in my office that day with those two newlyweds looking at me as though I were telling them something nobody'd ever heard of before. You never saw anybody so interested. 'You mean like this?' he asked me, and worked the models for himself a while. You know, I can see where a certain type of person might get a big kick out of doing just that. 'That's it,' I told him. 'Now, you go home and try it my way for a few months and see what happens. Okay?' 'Okay,' they said, and paid me in cash without any argument. 'Have a good time,' I told them, and they thanked me and walked out together. He had his arm around her waist as though he couldn't wait to get her home and put it to her again. A few days later he came back all by himself and told my nurse he had to see me right away. As soon as we were alone, he punched me in the nose."

"He did what?"

"He called me a wise guy and punched me in the nose. 'What are you, a wise guy?' he said, and knocked me flat on my ass. Pow! Just like that. I'm not kidding."

"I know you're not kidding," Yossarian said. "But why did he do it?"

"How should I know why he did it?" Doc Daneeka retorted with annoyance.

"Maybe it had something to do with Saint Anthony?"

Doc Daneeka looked at Yossarian blankly. "Saint Anthony?" he asked with astonishment. "Who's Saint Anthony?"

"How should I know?" answered Chief White Halfoat, staggering inside the tent just then with a bottle of whiskey cradled in his arm and sitting himself down pugnaciously between the two of them.

Doc Daneeka rose without a word and moved his chair outside the tent, his back bowed by the compact kit of injustices that was his perpetual burden. He could not bear the company of his roommate.

Chief White Halfoat thought he was crazy. "I don't know what's the matter with that guy," he observed reproachfully. "He's got no brains, that's what's the matter with him. If he had any brains he'd grab a shovel and start digging. Right here in the tent, he'd start digging, right under my cot. He'd strike oil in no time. Don't he know how that enlisted man struck oil with a shovel back in the States? Didn't he ever hear what happened to that kid—what was the name of that rotten rat bastard pimp of a snotnose back in Colorado?"

"Wintergreen."

"Wintergreen."

"He's afraid," Yossarian explained.

"Oh, no. Not Wintergreen." Chief White Halfoat shook his head with undisguised admiration. "That stinking little punk wise guy son of a bitch ain't afraid of nobody."

"Doc Daneeka's afraid. That's what's the matter with him."

"What's he afraid of?"

"He's afraid of you," Yossarian said. "He's afraid you're going to die of pneumonia."

"He'd *better* be afraid," Chief White Halfoat said. A deep, low laugh tumbled through his massive chest. "I will, too, the first chance I get. You just wait and see."

Chief White Halfoat was a handsome, swarthy Indian from Oklahoma with a heavy, hard-boned face and tousled black hair, a half-blooded Creek from Enid who, for occult reasons of his own, had made up his mind to die of pneumonia. He was a glowering, vengeful, disillusioned Indian who hated foreigners with names like Cathcart, Korn, Black, and Havermeyer and wished they'd all go back to where their lousy ancestors had come from.

"You wouldn't believe it, Yossarian," he ruminated, raising his voice deliberately to bait Doc Daneeka, "but this used to be a pretty good country to live in before they loused it up with their goddamn piety."

Chief White Halfoat was out to revenge himself upon the white man. He could barely read or write and had been assigned to Captain Black as assistant intelligence officer.

"How could I learn to read or write?" Chief White Halfoat demanded with simulated belligerence, raising his voice again so that Doc Daneeka would hear. "Every place we pitched our tent, they sank an oil well. Every time they sank a well, they hit oil. And every time they hit oil, they made us pack up our tent and go someplace else. We were human divining rods. Our whole family had a natural affinity for petroleum deposits, and soon every oil company in the world had technicians chasing us around. We were always on the move. It was one hell of a way to bring a child up, I can tell you. I don't think I ever spent more than a week in one place."

His earliest memory was of a geologist.

"Every time another White Halfoat was born," he continued, "the stock market turned bullish. Soon whole drilling crews were following us around with all their equipment just to get the jump on each other. Companies began to merge just so they could cut down on the number of people they had to assign to us. But the crowd in back of us kept growing. We never got a good night's sleep. When we stopped, they stopped. When we moved, they moved, chuckwagons, bulldozers, derricks, generators. We were a walking business boom, and we began to receive invitations from some of the best hotels just for the amount of business we would drag into town with us. Some of those invitations were mighty generous, but we couldn't accept any because we were Indians and all the best hotels that were inviting us wouldn't accept Indians as guests. Racial prejudice is a terrible thing, Yossarian. It really is. It's a terrible thing to treat a decent, loyal Indian like a nigger, kike, wop, or spic." Chief White Halfoat nodded slowly with conviction.

"Then, Yossarian, it finally happened—the beginning of the end. They began to follow us around from in front. They would try to guess where we were going to stop next and would begin drilling before we even got there, so we couldn't even stop. As soon as we'd begin to unroll our blankets, they would kick us off. They had confidence in us. They wouldn't even wait to strike oil before they kicked us off. We were so tired we almost didn't care the day our time ran out. One morning we found ourselves completely surrounded by oilmen waiting for us to come their way so they could kick us off. Everywhere you looked there was an oilman on a ridge, waiting there like Indians getting ready to attack. It was the end. We couldn't stay where we were because we had just been kicked off. And there was no place left for us to go. Only the Army saved me. Luckily, the war broke out just in the nick of time, and a draft board picked me right up out of the middle and put me down safely in Lowery Field, Colorado. I was the only survivor."

Yossarian knew he was lying, but did not interrupt as Chief White Halfoat went on to claim that he had never heard from his parents again. That didn't bother him too much, though, for he had only their word for it that they were his parents, and since they had lied to him about so many other things, they could just as well have been lying to him about that too. He was much better acquainted with the fate of a tribe of first cousins who had wandered away north in a diversionary movement and pushed inadvertently into Canada. When they tried to return, they were stopped at the border by American immigration authorities who would not let them back into the country. They could not come back in because they were red.

It was a horrible joke, but Doc Daneeka didn't laugh until Yossarian came to him one mission later and pleaded again, without any real expectation of success, to be grounded. Doc Daneeka snickered once and was soon immersed in problems of his own, which included Chief White Halfoat, who had been challenging him all that morning to Indian wrestle, and Yossarian, who decided right then and there to go crazy.

"You're wasting your time," Doc Daneeka was forced to tell him.

"Can't you ground someone who's crazy?"

"Oh, sure. I have to. There's a rule saying I have to ground anyone who's crazy."

"Then why don't you ground me? I'm crazy. Ask Clevinger."

JOSEPH HELLER

"Clevinger? Where *is* Clevinger? You find Clevinger and I'll ask him."

"Then ask any of the others. They'll tell you how crazy I am."

"They're crazy."

"Then why don't you ground them?"

"Why don't they ask me to ground them?"

"Because they're crazy, that's why."

"Of course they're crazy," Doc Daneeka replied. "I just told you they're crazy, didn't I? And you can't let crazy people decide whether you're crazy or not, can you?"

Yossarian looked at him soberly and tried another approach. "Is Orr crazy?"

"He sure is," Doc Daneeka said.

"Can you ground him?"

"I sure can. But first he has to ask me to. That's part of the rule."

"Then why doesn't he ask you to?"

"Because he's crazy," Doc Daneeka said. "He has to be crazy to keep flying combat missions after all the close calls he's had. Sure, I can ground Orr. But first he has to ask me to."

"That's all he has to do to be grounded?"

"That's all. Let him ask me."

"And then you can ground him?" Yossarian asked.

"No. Then I can't ground him."

"You mean there's a catch?"

"Sure there's a catch," Doc Daneeka replied. "Catch-22. Anyone who wants to get out of combat duty isn't really crazy."

There was only one catch and that was Catch-22, which specified that a concern for one's own safety in the face of dangers that were real and immediate was the process of a rational mind. Orr was crazy and could be grounded. All he had to do was ask; and as soon as he did, he would no longer be crazy and would have to fly more missions. Orr would be crazy to fly more missions and sane if he didn't, but if he was sane he had to fly them. If he flew them he was crazy and didn't have to; but if he didn't want to he was sane and had to. Yossarian was moved very deeply by the absolute simplicity of this clause of Catch-22 and let out a respectful whistle.

"That's some catch, that Catch-22," he observed.

"It's the best there is," Doc Daneeka agreed.

Yossarian saw it clearly in all its spinning reasonableness. There was an elliptical precision about its perfect pairs of parts that was graceful and shocking, like good modern art, and at times Yossarian wasn't quite sure that he saw it all, just the way he was never quite sure about good modern art or about the flies Orr saw in Appleby's eyes. He had Orr's word to take for the flies in Appleby's eyes.

"Oh, they're there, all right," Orr had assured him about the flies in Appleby's eyes after Yossarian's fist fight with Appleby in the officers' club, "although he probably doesn't even know it. That's why he can't see things as they really are."

"How come he doesn't know it?" inquired Yossarian.

"Because he's got flies in his eyes," Orr explained with exaggerated patience. "How can he see he's got flies in his eyes if he's got flies in his eyes?"

It made as much sense as anything else, and Yossarian was willing to give Orr the benefit of the doubt because Orr was from the wilderness outside New York City and knew so much more about wildlife than Yossarian did, and because Orr, unlike Yossarian's mother, father, sister, brother, aunt, uncle, in-law, teacher, spiritual leader, legislator,

neighbor, and newspaper, had never lied to him about anything crucial before. Yossarian had mulled his newfound
knowledge about Appleby over in private for a day or two
and then decided, as a good deed, to pass the word along
to Appleby himself.

"Appleby, you've got flies in your eyes," he whispered
helpfully as they passed by each other in the doorway of
the parachute tent on the day of the weekly milk run to
Parma.

"What?" Appleby responded sharply, thrown into confusion by the fact that Yossarian had spoken to him at all.

"You've got flies in your eyes," Yossarian repeated.
"That's probably why you can't see them."

Appleby retreated from Yossarian with a look of
loathing bewilderment and sulked in silence until he was in
the jeep with Havermeyer riding down the long, straight
road to the briefing room, where Major Danby, the fidgeting
group operations officer, was waiting to conduct the pre-
liminary briefing with all the lead pilots, bombardiers, and
navigators. Appleby spoke in a soft voice so that he would
not be heard by the driver or by Captain Black, who was
stretched out with his eyes closed in the front seat of the
jeep.

"Havermeyer," he asked hesitantly. "Have I got flies in
my eyes?"

Havermeyer blinked quizzically. "Sties?" he asked.

"No, flies," he was told.

Havermeyer blinked again. "Flies?"

"In my eyes."

"You must be crazy," Havermeyer said.

"No, I'm not crazy. Yossarian's crazy. Just tell me if I've
got flies in my eyes or not. Go ahead. I can take it."

Havermeyer popped another piece of peanut brittle into his mouth and peered very closely into Appleby's eyes.

"I don't see any," he announced.

Appleby heaved an immense sigh of relief. Havermeyer had tiny bits of peanut brittle adhering to his lips, chin, and cheeks.

"You've got peanut brittle crumbs on your face," Appleby remarked to him.

"I'd rather have peanut brittle crumbs on my face than flies in my eyes," Havermeyer retorted.

The officers of the other five planes in each flight arrived in trucks for the general briefing that took place thirty minutes later. The three enlisted men in each crew were not briefed at all, but were carried directly out on the airfield to the separate planes in which they were scheduled to fly that day, where they waited around with the ground crew until the officers with whom they had been scheduled to fly swung off the rattling tailgates of the trucks delivering them and it was time to climb aboard and start up. Engines rolled over disgruntledly on lollipop-shaped hardstands, resisting first, then idling smoothly awhile, and then the planes lumbered around and nosed forward lamely over the pebbled ground like sightless, stupid, crippled things until they taxied into the line at the foot of the landing strip and took off swiftly, one behind the other, in a zooming, rising roar, banking slowly into formation over mottled treetops, and circling the field at even speed until all the flights of six had been formed and then setting course over cerulean water on the first leg of the journey to the target in northern Italy or France. The planes gained altitude steadily and were above nine thousand feet by the time they crossed into enemy territory. One of the surprising things always was the sense of calm and utter silence, broken only by the test rounds fired from the machine guns, by an occasional toneless, terse remark over the intercom, and, at last, by the sobering pronouncement of the bombardier in each plane that they were at the I.P. and about to turn toward the target. There was always sunshine, always a tiny sticking in the throat from the rarefied air.

The B-25s they flew in were stable, dependable, dull-green ships with twin rudders and engines and wide wings. Their single fault, from where Yossarian sat as a bombardier, was the tight crawlway separating the bombardier's compartment in the Plexiglas nose from the nearest escape hatch. The crawlway was a narrow, square, cold tunnel hollowed out beneath the flight controls, and a large man like Yossarian could squeeze through only with difficulty. A chubby, moon-faced navigator with little reptilian eyes and a pipe like Aarfy's had trouble, too, and Yossarian used to chase him back from the nose as they turned toward the target, now minutes away. There was a time of tension then, a time of waiting with nothing to hear and nothing to see and nothing to do but wait as the anti-aircraft guns below took aim and made ready to knock them all sprawling into infinite sleep if they could.

The crawlway was Yossarian's lifeline to outside from a plane about to fall, but Yossarian swore at it with seething antagonism, reviled it as an obstacle put there by providence as part of the plot that would destroy him. There was room for an additional escape hatch right there in the nose of a B-25, but there was no escape hatch. Instead there was the crawlway, and since the mess on the mission over Avignon he had learned to detest every mammoth inch of it, for it slung him seconds and seconds away from his parachute, which was too bulky to be taken up front with him, and seconds and seconds more after that away from the escape hatch on the floor between the rear of the elevated flight deck and the feet of the faceless top turret gunner mounted high above. Yossarian longed to be where Aarfy could be once Yossarian had chased him back from the nose; Yossarian longed to sit on the floor in a huddled ball right on top of the escape hatch inside a sheltering igloo of extra flak suits that he would have been happy to carry along with him, his parachute already hooked to his harness where it belonged, one fist clenching the red-handled rip cord, one fist gripping the emergency hatch release that would spill him earthward into air at the first dreadful squeal of destruction. That was where he wanted to be if he had to be there at all, instead of hung out there in front like some goddamn cantilevered goldfish in some goddamn cantilevered goldfish bowl while the goddamn foul black tiers of flak were bursting and booming and billowing all around and above and below him in a climbing, cracking, staggered, banging, phantasmagorical, cosmological wickedness that jarred and tossed and shivered, clattered and pierced, and threatened to annihilate them all in one splinter of a second in one vast flash of fire.

Aarfy had been no use to Yossarian as a navigator or as anything else, and Yossarian drove him back from the nose vehemently each time so that they would not clutter up each other's way if they had to scramble suddenly for safety. Once Yossarian had driven him back from the nose, Aarfy was free to cower on the floor where Yossarian longed to cower, but he stood bolt upright instead with his stumpy arms resting comfortably on the backs of the pilot's and co-pilot's seats, pipe in hand, making affable small talk to McWatt and whoever happened to be co-pilot and pointing out amusing trivia in the sky to the two men, who were too busy to be interested. McWatt was too busy responding at the controls to Yossarian's strident instructions as Yossarian slipped the plane in on the bomb run and then whipped them all away violently around the ravenous pillars of exploding shells with curt, shrill, obscene commands to McWatt that were much like the anguished, entreating nightmare yelpings of Hungry Joe in the dark. Aarfy would puff reflectively on his pipe throughout the whole chaotic clash, gazing with unruffled curiosity at the war through McWatt's window as though it were a remote disturbance that could not affect him. Aarfy was a dedicated fraternity man who loved cheerleading and class reunions and did not have brains enough to be afraid. Yossarian did have brains enough and was, and the only thing that stopped him from abandoning his post under fire and scurrying back through the crawlway like a yellow-bellied rat was his unwillingness to entrust the evasive action out of the target area to anybody else. There was nobody else in the world he would honor with so great a responsibility. There was nobody else he knew who was as big a coward. Yossarian was the best man in the group at evasive action, but had no idea why.

There was no established procedure for evasive action. All you needed was fear, and Yossarian had plenty of that, more fear than Orr or Hungry Joe, more fear even than Dunbar, who had resigned himself submissively to the idea that he must die someday. Yossarian had not resigned himself to that idea, and he bolted for his life wildly on each mission the instant his bombs were away, hollering, *"Hard, hard, hard, hard, you bastard, hard!"* at McWatt and hating McWatt viciously all the time as though McWatt were to blame for their being up there at all to be rubbed out by strangers, and everybody else in the plane kept off the intercom, except for the pitiful time of the mess on the mission to Avignon when Dobbs went crazy in mid-air and began weeping pathetically for help.

"Help him, help him," Dobbs sobbed. "Help him, help him."

"Help who? Help who?" called back Yossarian, once he had plugged his headset back into the intercom system, after it had been jerked out when Dobbs wrested the controls away from Huple and hurled them all down suddenly into the deafening, paralyzing, horrifying dive which had plastered Yossarian helplessly to the ceiling of the plane by the top of his head and from which Huple had rescued them just in time by seizing the controls back from Dobbs and leveling the ship out almost as suddenly right back in the middle of the buffeting layer of cacophonous flak from which they had escaped successfully only a moment before. *Oh, God! Oh, God, oh, God,* Yossarian had been pleading wordlessly as he dangled from the ceiling of the nose of the ship by the top of his head, unable to move.

"The bombardier, the bombardier," Dobbs answered in a cry when Yossarian spoke. "He doesn't answer, he doesn't answer. Help the bombardier, help the bombardier."

"I'm the bombardier," Yossarian cried back at him. "I'm the bombardier. I'm all right. I'm all right."

"Then help him, help him," Dobbs begged. "Help him, help him."

And Snowden lay dying in back.

BURNING THE DAYS

JAMES SALTER

I flew in the 75th, the 335th in Korea, the 22nd in Germany, and at the end with the 119th Squadron in New Jersey, years of it, like cavalry years, the waiting by empty runways, the barren operations rooms, the apocalyptic sound of engines tremendous and uneven, the idleness and cynicism, the myth.

In those days there was nothing in the world but us. The rarity was fine. There were other squadrons, of course. Some you knew quite well. Ships from all three squadrons in the group and also from other fields came in past the little shack on wheels by the side of the runway. Many times it is you yourself who are returning, coming back beneath the clouds, seeing the long straight runway, or the hangars alongside it blurring in the rain—an incomparable happiness, the joy of coming home.

We had pilots named Homer and Ulysses, country boys unfrivolous by nature who took good care of their cars. Farm boys, for some reason, always seemed the truest men. They were even-tempered and unhurried in the way of someone who will watch a man doing something foolish and not make any comment—the joke will come at the end. They became flyers instead of going to the city though of course it was not the same thing, and they saw the world from a distance—the Grand Canal like a gray thread winding among the barely distinguishable piazzas far below, the unmistakable narrowing spire of Paris rising above the haze. Beneath them passed all the miracles of Europe, few of great interest—their wonders were more elemental, in a room, standing naked with a member like a grazing horse's, in front of a full-length mirror with a German whore. Some married waitresses.

You knew them, that is to say their ability and to an extent their character, but much was hidden. After two or three years you knew little more than at the start, but still you were attached to their silence, the honesty of their thoughts. One night one of them, on a motorcycle, sped into the concrete pillar of a bridge and was in the hospital for weeks, legs broken, jaw bound together with silver wire. Nevertheless when I came into the room he managed to smile. He had a willing nature and the name of an ace, strange and abrupt: Uden. Broad and capable hands, fearless eyes, yet somehow it all came to nothing. Face-to-face for the last time at the noisy farewell party, the blue, farm-country eyes suddenly filled with tears. "I know I've disappointed you."

"That's true."

"I just wanted you to know one thing—I won't do it the next time."

That was true also. There was no next time. A year later someone was describing an accident at Myrtle Beach, a night takeoff with full fuel load, 450-gallon drop tanks, the planes wallowing, the overcast seamlessly black. The join-up was in sky undivided between the darkness of air and water, a sky without top or bottom; in fact there was no sky, only total blackness in which, banking steeply to try and catch up with the lights of the fleeing leader, the number-three man, low in the roaring nightmare, determined to do well, went into the sea. Uden.

The leader of that flight was one of the great war aces, highly visible and bulletproof; there were a number still around. Combat had never really ended for them. The sign on the desk of one read, *The mission of the Air Force is to fly and fight, and don't you ever forget it.* Blakeslee, another, an untamable fighter whose reputation was one of temper and violence, I met only once, in my final year of flying. It was at a dinner dance in Germany and he walked into the bar of the club not in uniform with two or three significant ribbons but dressed like the owner of a 1930s nightclub in an out-of-fashion tuxedo with a stiff shirt. He stood down at the end, a little apart; I would not have known who he was had the bartender not greeted him by name.

A couple of young officers, transients like myself, approached him as he stood waiting for his order. They were F-104 pilots from England. In war it is not like other things, where youth is arrogance. War is terra incognita. The young are usually eager to have the curtain lifted, even slightly, by one of the greats.

"Evening, Colonel," they said.

He looked at them without expression. His power was such that he could destroy the ego of all but the most aggressive.

"Sir," one of them said, "I just wanted to ask you a question. It's something I've never been able to get an answer to. It's about German aces."

Blakeslee, who had been a colonel and then reduced in rank, possibly for cause, so he was now a lieutenant colonel, stood there. He listened without showing the least sign of interest.

"Is it true," the young captain went on, "that the Germans counted their kills by the number of engines and would get four victories for, say, shooting down a B-17?"

Perhaps Blakeslee knew the answer. Perhaps he was weighing the real intent of the question. His face was heavier than it once had been, his body thicker. The electric skies over the Reich with their decks of clouds, shouts on the radio, confusion and vertical descents, those legend skies were gone. Finally he spoke.

"I don't know," he said slowly. He was picking up three or four glasses. "I only know one thing: it's all phony," he said.

They like to say you cannot understand unless you've been there, unless you've lived it. You could not argue with his scorn.

How well one remembers that world, the whiff of jet exhaust, oily and dark, in the morning air as you walk to where the planes are parked out in the mist.

Soon you are up near the sun where the air is burning cold, amid all that is familiar, the scratches on the canopy, the chipped black of the instrument panel, the worn red cloth of the safety streamers stuffed in a pocket down near your shoe. From the tailpipe of the leader's plane comes an occasional dash of smoke, the only sign of motion as it streaks rearward.

Below, the earth has shed its darkness. There is the silver of countless lakes and streams. The greatest things to be seen, the ancients wrote, are sun, stars, water, and clouds. Here among them, of what is one thinking? I cannot remember but probably of nothing, of flying itself, the imperishability of it, the brilliance. You do not think about the fish in the great, winding river, thin as string, miles below, or the frogs in the glinting ponds, nor they of you; they know little of you, though once, just after takeoff, I saw the shadow of my plane skimming the dry grass like the wings of god and passing over, frozen by the noise, a hare two hundred feet below. That lone hare, I, the morning sun, and all that lay beyond it were for an instant joined, like an eclipse.

One night in early spring there were two of us—I was wingman. No one else was flying at the time. We were landing in formation after an instrument approach. It was very dark, it had been raining, and the leader misread the threshold lights. We crossed the end of the runway high and touched down long. In exact imitation I held the nose high, as he did, to slow down, wheels skipping along the concrete like flat stones on a lake. Halfway down we lowered the noses and started to brake. Incredibly we began to go faster. The runway, invisible and black, was covered with the thinnest sheet of ice. Light rain had frozen sometime after sundown and the tower did not know it. We might, at the last moment, have gone around—put on full power and tried to get off again—but it was too close. We were braking in desperation. I stop-cocked my engine—shut it off to provide greater air resistance—and a moment later he called that he was doing the same. We were standing on the brakes and then releasing, hard on and off. The end of the runway was near. The planes were slithering, skidding sideways. I knew we were going off and that we might collide. I had full right rudder in, trying to stay to the side.

We slid off the end of the runway together and went about two hundred feet on the broken earth before we finally stopped. Just ahead of us was the perimeter road and beyond it, lower, some railroad tracks.

When I climbed out of the cockpit I wasn't shaking. I felt almost elated. It could have been so much worse. The duty officer came driving up. He looked at the massive, dark shapes of the planes, awkwardly placed near each other, the long empty highway behind them, the embankment ahead. "Close one, eh?" he said.

This was at Fürstenfeldbruck, the most lavish of the prewar German airfields, near Munich. We came there from our own field, Bitburg, in the north, the Rhineland, to stand alert or fire gunnery close by. Zulu alert, two ships on five-minute, two on fifteen. The long, well-built barracks, the red tile roofs and marble corridors. The stands of pine on the way to the pilots' dining room, where you could eat breakfast in your flying suit and the waitresses knew what you preferred.

We were not far from Dachau, the ash-pit. One of them. I had seen its flat ruins. That Otto Frank, Anne Frank's father, had served as an officer in the German army in the First World War, I may not have known, but I was aware that patriotism and devotion had not saved him or others. They might not save me, though I swore to myself they would. I knew I was different, if nothing else marked by my name. I acted always from two necessities; the first was to be like everyone, and the second—was it foolish?—was to be better than other men. If I was to be despised I wanted it to be by inferiors.

Munich was our city, its great night presence, the bars and clubs, the Isar green and pouring like a faucet through its banks, the Regina Hotel, dancing on Sunday afternoons, faces damp with the heat, the Film Casino Bar, Bei Heinz. All the women, Panas's girlfriend in the low-cut dress, Van Bockel's, who was a secretary and had such an exceptional figure, Cortada's, who smelled like a florist's on a warm day. Munich in the snow, coming back to the field alone on the streetcar.

I flew back to Bitburg with White, one of the two men in the squadron to become famous—Aldrin was the other—on a winter day. It was late in the afternoon, everything blue as metal, the sky, the towns and forests, even the snow. The other ship, silent, constant on your wing. With the happiness of being with someone you like, through it we went together, at thirty-five thousand, the thin froth of contrails fading behind.

White had been the first person I met when I came to the squadron and I knew him well. In the housing area he and his wife lived on our stairway. He had a fair, almost milky, complexion and reddish hair. An athlete, a hurdler; you see his face on many campuses, idealistic, aglow. He was an excellent pilot, acknowledged as such by those implacable judges, the ground crews. They did not revere him as they did the ruffians who might drink with them, discuss the merits of the squadron commander or sexual exploits, but they respected him and his proper, almost studious, ways. God and country—these were the things he had been bred for.

In Paris, a lifetime later, in a hotel room I watched as on screens everywhere he walked dreamily in space, the first American to do so. I was nervous and depressed. My chest ached. My hair had patches of gray. White was turning slowly, upside down, tethered to the spacecraft by a lazy cord. I was sick with envy—he was destroying hope. Whatever I might do, it would not be as overwhelming as this. I felt a kind of loneliness and terror. I wanted to be home, to see my children again before the end, and I was certain it was near the end; I felt suicidal, ready to burst into tears. He did this to me unknowingly, as a beautiful woman crossing the street crushes hearts beneath her heel.

White burned to ashes in the terrible accident on the launching pad at Cape Canaveral in 1967. He died with Virgil Grissom, with whom I had also flown. His funeral was solemn. I attended, feeling out of place. To be killed flying had always been a possibility, but the two of them had somehow moved beyond that. They were already visible in that great photograph of our time, the one called celebrity. Still youthful and, so far as I knew, unspoiled, they were like jockeys moving to the post for an event that would mark the century, the race to the moon. The absolutely unforeseen destroyed them. Aldrin went instead.

White is buried in the same cemetery as my father, not far away. I visit both graves when I am there. White's, though amid others, seems visible from some distance off, just as he himself was if you looked intently at the ranks. You remember the airfields, the first sight of some, the deep familiarity of others.

Apart from those that finally appeared when you were coming in, nose high, in fog or heavy rain, the most beautiful field I ever saw was in Morocco, down toward the south. It was called Boulhaut, a long, flawless black runway built for strategic bombers and never used, the numbers at each end huge and clear—no tire had ever marked them. You could not but marvel at its extraordinary newness.

I liked fields near the sea, Westhampton Beach on Long Island, Myrtle Beach, Langley, Eglin, Alameda, where we landed in the fall, ferrying planes to be shipped to the fighting in Korea, and went on to Vanessi's with the navy pilots' wives. I liked Sidi Slimane for its openness and the German fields, Hahn and Wiesbaden, Fürstenfeldbruck.

There are fields I would like to forget, Polk, where one night, as a rank amateur, I nearly went into the trees, trying clumsily to go around with my flaps down. Later, in the wooden barracks, came another lesson. Two men in flying suits, drab in appearance, paused at the open door of the room where I sat on a bed. "Are you the one flying the P-51? Where are you from?" one asked.

"Andrews," I said. I felt a kind of glamour, being connected with the silvery plane and its slim, aggressive shape, parked by itself on the ramp. It was not hard to deduce that they were lesser figures, transport pilots probably. I told them I was in the Fourth Group rather than going into the less interesting facts—I was actually a graduate student at Georgetown. They did not seem very impressed. "Ever hear of Don Garland?" I said, naming a noted pilot in the Fourth.

"Who's that?"

"One of the best pilots in the Air Force."

"Oh, yeah?"

I offered a few exaggerations I had overheard at one time or another in the Andrews Club. Garland flew the slot position on the acrobatic team, hanging there with his bare teeth, so to speak, the proof of it being the blackened rudder of his ship, stained by the leader's exhaust and as a mark of pride always left that way—no mechanic would dare to rub it clean. He was a wild man, Garland—I could tell them any number of stories.

"What does he look like?"

I gave a vague answer. Was he a decent guy? they wanted to know.

I had almost been in a fight one evening at Andrews, not with Garland but with another member of the team. "Not particularly," I said.

Suddenly one of them began laughing. The other glanced at him. "Shut up," he said.

"Oh, for Christ's sake," the first one said. Then to me, "This is Garland," he said, gesturing.

I was speechless.

"What the hell's your name?" they wanted to know.

I left early in the morning, before they were up.

Later, when I actually joined the Fourth, they were luckily gone by then. There were other Garlands. At Bitburg one of the wing lieutenant colonels used to sit in my office, aimless as a country lawyer, looking at the board on which there were photographs of our pilots—I was squadron operations officer then—and ask, if war broke out, which of them would become aces? We sat examining the faces together. "Emigholz," I said.

"Who else?"

A pause. "Cass, probably. It's hard to say. Minish."

There was no real way of judging. It was their skill but also their personalities, their remorselessness. "Maybe Whitlow," I added. I was trying to match them to the memory of aces or near-aces in Korea. Emigholz was like Billy Dobbs, Cass was like Matson. "And Cortada," I finally said. He was from Puerto Rico, small, excitable, and supremely confident. Not everyone shared his opinion of his ability— his flight commander was certain he would kill himself.

With the instinct that dogs have, you knew where in the order anyone ranked. Experience counted, and day-to-day performance. Pilots with few flying hours, in the early years of their career, were the most dangerous. They were young, in the well-being of ignorance, like flies on a sunny table, unaware of the fate of countless others. As regards flying, they had only a limited idea of the many ways to fail, most of them deadly.

With a lanky, indecisive lieutenant named Kelly, I left Bitburg late one day bound for Marseille. Destination weather was forecast to be scattered clouds and eight miles' visibility. I had put him in the lead. It was important to give pilots the chance to make decisions, gain confidence. The ships in a flight, for whatever reason, might become separated, setting every man on his own, or a leader's radio could go out and force a wingman to take over. In an instant the responsibility for everything could shift.

Over Marseille at thirty-five thousand feet we had just under eighteen hundred pounds of fuel remaining. The field, Marignane, was not visible. It was hidden by a deck of clouds that had moved in unexpectedly from the sea. In addition, neither Marignane nor Marseille Control would answer our calls.

The sun had already set and the earth was dimming. Kelly signaled for speed brakes and we dove toward a corner of the great lagoon that lay east of the field. We leveled out at three hundred feet. Ahead, like a dark reef, were the clouds. Squeezed as we were into a narrow layer of vanishing light and haze—the bottom of the overcast was perhaps a hundred feet above us—we missed the field. Suddenly the ground began to rise; it disappeared in the clouds just ahead, and we pulled up, breaking out on top at two thousand feet. It had grown darker. I looked at the fuel gauge: a thousand pounds. Kelly seemed hesitant and we were at the threshold of real difficulty.

"I've got it," I said. "Get on my wing." I could hear something he could not, the finality of the silence in which we found ourselves, in which the sole sound was that of the Marignane radio beacon—I rechecked the call letters against my let-down book, FNM.

I turned immediately toward the beacon and examined the let-down diagram. The light was dim. The details were complex—I noted only the heading to the field from the beacon, and the distance and time to fly. At 175 knots this was a minute and twenty-seven seconds.

When things do not go as planned and the fuel gauge is slowly going down, there is a feeling of unreality, of hostile earth and sky. There comes a point when the single fuel needle is all you think about, the focus of all concern. The thought of bailing out of two airplanes over Marseille because we could not find the field in low clouds and darkness was making me even more precise. It was the scenario for many accidents. Did I have the right frequency and beacon? I checked again. It was right. A moment later, for the first time, the tower came on the air. I suspected they had been waiting for someone to arrive who could speak English. Talking to them, although they were hard to understand, gave some relief: the field was open; there were lights.

We passed over the beacon at two thousand feet, turned to the reciprocal of the field heading and flew for thirty seconds. It seemed minutes. The world was thundering and pouring out. I was determined to do everything exactly, to make a perfect approach. We began a procedure turn—forty-five degrees to the left, hold for one minute, turn back in. The direction-finding needle was rigid. It began to quiver and then swung completely around as we hit the beacon.

We started to descend. The minimum altitude for the field was eight hundred feet, minimum visibility a mile and a half. At five hundred feet we were still in the clouds. Four hundred. Suddenly the ground was just beneath us. The visibility was poor, less than a mile. I glanced at the fuel gauge: six hundred pounds.

A minute had passed. The second hand of the clock was barely moving. A minute and five seconds. A minute ten. Then ahead, like distant stars, faint lines of them, the lights of the field. Speed brakes out, I signaled. Gear and flaps down. We landed smoothly together in the dark.

A taxi drove us into town. We talked about what had happened, what might have. It was not an incident; it was nothing; routine. One flight among innumerable. We could find no place to eat. We slept in a small hotel on a tree-lined street and left early in the morning.

Once in a great while there was a letter from Horner. He had resigned his commission and was in his father-in-law's business, landscaping. *Dear Fly-boy*, he would write, with a touch of wistfulness it seemed, *I hope you're having a good time in Europe. I used to.*

At one reunion, years later, the rumor spread that he had just been seen driving through the main gate with two chorus girls. It turned out to be untrue. The days of chorus girls were past though we had once gone with two from the Versailles when we were in pursuit of everything except wisdom. *Susie and I were there the other night,* he wrote of another place, *and the violinist came up to our table and asked us where the gentleman was who had been so fond of "Granada." I assumed he was speaking of you, so I told him that you had returned to the front . . .*

There are things that seem insignificant at the time and that turn out to be so. There are others that are like a gun in a bedside drawer, not only serious but unexpectedly fatal.

For Colonel Brischetto, it was not a single detail but a series of them, none of great importance and spread over months. He was the new wing commander at Bitburg who had arrived in August, filled with ambition but having very little jet time. Tom Whitehouse, the old commander, diminutive and gallant, turned over to him a veteran fighter wing. It was like turning over a spirited horse to a new, inexperienced owner who would, of course, attempt to ride.

All wing and group flying officers were attached to one of the squadrons. The wing commander flew with ours, not very frequently, as it happened, and not very well, though there was nothing alarmingly wrong. You could feel his weakness on the radio where he was like an actor fumbling for his lines, and in following instructions in the air there was often a slight, telltale delay.

We went, each year, to North Africa to gunnery camp. The weather was always good there. At Wheelus, a large airfield in Tripoli, we lived in tents for four or five weeks and flew every day. It was essential for all pilots to qualify during that time though there were occasional opportunities for a few planes to go and fire elsewhere. There were fighter wings from all over Europe scheduled into Tripoli throughout the year, nose to tail. Not so much as an extra day there could be begged.

That year we were booked for Wheelus in the very beginning of January. All preparations had been made but we did not go—the weather at Bitburg prevented it. Throughout the holidays there had been freezing rain and low ceilings; the runway was covered with heavy ice. In North Africa the sun was shining and irreplaceable days were passing. At last the rain stopped and the forecast seemed encouraging. All through the final night there were airplanes taxiing slowly up and down the runway, trying to melt the ice with the heat of their exhaust.

At noon the next day the ceiling lifted sufficiently. We were ready. It was six days after our intended departure.

An outwardly calm but impatient Colonel Brischetto was to go in the first flight. He was on the wing of an experienced pilot, a lieutenant, his favorite instructor, in fact, Cass. They were already on the runway when he called that his tailpipe temperature, a critical instrument, was fluctuating wildly, and asked Cass for advice—he had already had some minor difficulties with the ship. Airplanes had their own personalities. They were not mere mechanical objects but possessed temperaments and traits. Some were good in gunnery, others hopeless. Some were always ready to fly, others rarely. Some planes, if not creaking like ships, nevertheless made strange noises. Without minds or hearts, they were somehow not wholly inanimate. An airplane did not belong to one pilot, like a horse, but to all communally. There were no secrets—pilots talked freely about the behavior of planes and in time flew most of them.

When Brischetto asked Cass whether or not he should take off with an erratic indication, he was told that such a decision was up to the pilot. Despite his great anxiety, Brischetto made a prudent choice and aborted. He taxied back to the ramp, was assigned another airplane, and became part of another flight.

Now it was early afternoon. The first planes, Cass and his flight, were well on their way to Rome, where they would refuel before continuing. The clouds at Bitburg were holding at six hundred feet. The bases were ragged, the top of the overcast layered and uncertain; the visibility, threatened by rain, stood at five miles. Brischetto had just forty minutes of actual weather experience in the airplane. He felt, probably correctly, that he would have more difficulty flying on the wing of another plane in these conditions than having another plane flying on his, and he indicated he would like to lead the flight.

The four ships, in elements of two, the colonel leading, taxied out to the runway. The takeoff interval between elements was to be five seconds, and they were to join up, if possible, beneath the clouds so that all four could penetrate together with a single leader and a single voice.

Brischetto read his clearance back to the tower incorrectly. He was obliged to repeat it three times before permission was given to take the runway. He had a very steady pilot, Tracy, who had never flown with him previously, however, on his wing. So, after many delays, some unavoidable, they were ready to depart.

The planes lined up on the runway together. The noise of their engines swelled. With an almost dainty slowness, the first two ships began to roll. Five seconds later, the next two. I was watching with no particular interest, sitting in the cockpit in the squadron area, a flight leader, waiting to start. Very quickly the four planes disappeared into the clouds. They had not—I attached no meaning to it—come together as a flight.

In the air the colonel, as it happened, had responded with a distracted "Roger" to the request to reduce power slightly to allow the second element to catch up after takeoff. He then gave the command to change channels, from tower to departure control. Changing radio channels meant reaching down and back. The indicator was hard to see. It was best done by counting the clicks between numbers— perhaps Brischetto did this, though he was never heard on departure control.

On the ground time passed slowly, slipping by in the small, hesitant movement of the second hand on the instrument panel clock. Though it is hard to imagine, it was passing at different rates, not to be calculated in ordinary seconds, for the colonel and his wingman when they went into the clouds. For Tracy on the left wing it was like the regular, slow beat of a pulse, but for the colonel, in an abstract world of utter whiteness and noise, it had begun to accelerate. He had started a slight turn to the left toward the departure beacon, which became tighter, nearly vertical, his wingman at full power pulling hard to stay in position. Then, suddenly correcting, he began to roll the other way, to the right, going past straight and level, banking steeper and steeper, past the point where Tracy could stay with him, becoming inverted, heading down.

"Cousin Echo," Tracy called, "I've lost you."

Rolling out, on his own instruments then, Tracy managed to stop his descent. He found himself going over five hundred miles an hour. He called his leader a number of times on both channels, tower and departure control, but there was no reply.

The last few seconds, beneath the clouds, must have been a collapse of all reality for the colonel as he burst into the visible world in a nearly vertical dive. Everything he knew and had known was suddenly of no avail. If, even for a moment, he thought of bailing out, it was already too late. As if in a nightmare, in the final second his eyes smashed through surfaces, he entered a new dimension.

The first awareness for us that anything was wrong was the announcement by the tower that the field was closed to all traffic, an emergency was in progress. There was nothing more, no voices on the air, no instructions or calls. Only silence and a few dark birds flying low, near the wintry clouds.

Brischetto was forty-one years old. He had a family, children. In the housing area the telephone must have eventually rung in his apartment. "Colonel Brischetto's quarters," one of them would say.

The aircraft was completely demolished, the accident report read. Cause of death: *injuries multiple extreme.* The body, it was stated, was destroyed beyond recognition. More than that can hardly occur. It was impossible to know with certainty why it all had happened. Most likely the colonel had looked away from his instruments for several seconds, absorbed in trying to read the number on the channel selector, down by his left elbow. That had caused the first unintentional, steep turn. He had corrected that. Perhaps he could not understand why he heard no one on the radio and looked down again. Perhaps when he returned to his instruments he saw chaos beyond his power to decipher.

Subdued, we nevertheless flew to Rome that afternoon and on to Africa where we fired gunnery for weeks over the green, unoccupied sea.

North Africa had its spell. Silent, forgotten cities along the coast, joined by a single empty road. The marble columns from Roman days pillaged over the centuries for European palaces and estates.

On windless mornings we took off early and headed out to sea. The tow plane was already on course, at twenty thousand feet, the slender white target moving serenely some distance behind it.

The first mission of the day. The air has a full, damp quality. Long, holy streamers curve through it, marking our passes. There is a rhythm, like section hands dreamily pounding spikes. In the gunsight the target grows larger, slowly at first and then with a rush, in range for only a second or two. The bullets leave thin traces of smoke as they vanish into the cloth—each plane's have been dipped in a different color paint so they can afterward be counted. To the south, invisible, on the one great road of the kingdom, paralleling the sea, there are arches of palms and thousands upon thousands of stiff, laundered flags to mark the route of the wedding party traveling west from Benghazi. The king had taken a second wife, who was Egyptian.

That night in Tripoli, amid the rancid smell of smoke, a torchlight parade passed along the street through the crowds. I stood outside a tailor shop and watched. The owner, Salvatore Perrucio, stood beside me. "What is it, is the king coming?" I asked.

"Oh, no," Perrucio said. "He wouldn't dare."

"Why not?"

"They kill him," he said.

I laughed at the joke.

"Don't," he warned. "Never laugh. If they see you doing that, they kill you, too. Never laugh at them. Call them anything you want, but never laugh."

It was difficult to know who he was talking about, the mobs in the street, the short dark men in double-breasted suits in the Uaddan Hotel, the wraithlike figures drifting without apparent purpose along the beach, the bare-legged men working in the salt flats near our planes? We knew none of them. They were part of something impenetrable. Together with the buildings and statuary of an ancient colonial world, they went back at least two thousand years, to the days of Leptis Magna and Sabratha. Surviving within them all this time was a seething and unalterable code.

Perrucio made suits, bespoke, for thirty or forty dollars, as I recall. When he was twelve, he told me modestly, he could make a complete suit all by himself. He'd been a prisoner of the English during the war and had made uniforms for them. The time he spent in prison camp was the happiest of his life, he said. "A lovely country. Such beautiful women—and so easy to get. Of course, I was different-looking then. I wasn't like this"—he clasped his wide waist with his hands. He had the full, pleasant face of a man in touch with life. Inside the shop, half concealed by a curtain, a boy sat, two thin legs in shorts and a plum-shaped body, cutting and basting patterns, the very age Perrucio had been.

I flew south one day, a hundred or two hundred miles into the desert, the earth changing from ruggedness to orange dust. There was no life, no roads, no trace of anything. Turning, I began to descend in long, uninquisitive arcs until finally, at fifty or a hundred feet, I was heading back north.

At that height one can see only a few miles ahead. Unexpectedly, things began to appear, occasional lonely shepherds, grazing camels, a low, dark group of tents. Suddenly there were animals scattering before me, children throwing themselves to the ground, the momentary glimpse of women who had hurried to tent doors. In twenty minutes I would be on the ground at Wheelus but I would remain aloft much longer in the minds of these unknown people, crossing their world with furious sound and then gone.

Beyond them, past shale mountains and stretches of sand, came the first faint tincture of civilization: telegraph wires, cultivation, roads. Farther still, hard and gleaming, the sea.

It was from the other side of this sea that Perrucio had come, from the long, rugged peninsula that had been the center of the world. It was easy to see the long throw of his life, Italy, North Africa, the war, and finally North Africa again in unmarked exile, a life begun perhaps ten years earlier than mine and meant from the beginning to be more conventional and unesteemed. I envied its simplicity, the fineness of the suits he so carefully made. The days of pale English roses, probably less well scrubbed than I imagined and coarser voiced, were far behind. He lived among a less exotic species now, his wife, daughter, mother-in-law.

At the Bath Club, dreary and English, there were desiccated copies of *London Illustrated News* spread on the tables and a drink of scotch cost a dime. One night, when her escort had gone off for a few minutes, we invited a watery blonde, the only woman in the club, to come to the base on Saturday night. All right, she said. She wanted to bring along a friend, someone named Emma.

"Who is Emma?"

"You'll like her," she said.

I seem to recall Emma now as being older. Saturday night was always crowded and boisterous. Half-drunk and suddenly remembering the invitation, three of us went to the main gate to meet the women and guide their car to the club. "We're waiting for a couple of visitors," I told the guards.

The road leading to the base was empty. There were no headlights, only alien darkness. Minutes passed.

"What time is it?"

"Eight-thirty."

"What time did we say?"

"I forget."

After a while one of the guards turned his head. He heard someone approaching. "Might be your visitors," he said.

"Couldn't be," I said with assurance. "They'll be in a car," I explained as the shadowy figures of the two demoiselles materialized down the road. They were walking in high heels. It was miles to town. Such was the allure of our pay and wrinkled khaki.

These European women, few as they were, now seem faint pencil marks on the North African page. It was more or less clear why they had come and also that they would find little here. The bargains that could be struck were meager. Perhaps it was exactly this, the injudiciousness, their need for luck, that made one remember them at all.

In Morocco, where we went for good weather in which to fly the new airplanes, F-100s—more powerful and less forgiving—with which we were to be equipped, the air was different. Morocco had been a French colony and bordered another sea. From its coast one could reach England or even the New World. There were boulevards, apartment houses, the elegy of French names.

Fedala was to the south with wide beaches and surf breaking close to shore. It was for off-duty hours, inexplicable blue bulbs in the ceiling of the hotel and a waiter awkwardly pouring the wine. We would sit on the terrace in the evening, the faces around the table slowly becoming indistinct. In the distance the sea, which defined everything, fell endlessly upon itself. Our glory was endless, too. We were great captains all. We sat at ease. The beeves had been slaughtered; the cooks, all in white, stood ready to prepare the meal. The idle hours are passed in drinking, talking, desiring. There are weeks left in the campaign; another follows.

Later there is the Sphinx, named probably for its predecessor in Paris on Boulevard Edgar Quinet. You could see it from the air, iron gates and a gravel driveway. Inside it was tiled, a nightclub: downstairs, blue films and books; upstairs, women. The rooms on the second floor faced the sea. "As many times as you like," she said, speaking French at the bar. At the far end of the room a band was playing. She was from Marseille, skin pale and shining like fruitwood. Her dress was cut low, her breasts smooth and perfectly separated. We danced like a couple, as if we had come there together. She was pressed against me. The black tile pillars slid before my eyes, the mirrors, the trio at the floorside table, two men and a girl with short black hair, the gold of a wedding band on her finger. They were the *haut monde*, come for titillation.

Canadian pilots are entering. The band is playing something I would like to remember. Far away it seems, unmourned, are all the other nights, the unattainable women, nurses, admirals' daughters, the colonel's wife that time unsteadily playing blackjack. "Just give me a little bitty one," she pleaded, "don't give it to me unless it's little." It was dealt. A jack. She stared at it, looked at her hole card, stared again. Her handsome, slurred face. "All right," she announced, "twenty-one." But it was not. The dealer took the money.

The morning light of Africa is brilliant and flat. The empty street, the silence. How was it? they want to know. That, one can embroider, one can tell, but there is a foolish thing one cannot—she came to the gate to say goodbye. She asked if you would write, a postcard from Port Lyautey, addressed simply to Dene, Sphinx, Fedala.

In Tangier the peddlers and guides were outside at all hours, some displaying letters of recommendation. In 1956 you could buy a palace—baths, servants' quarters, patios—for twelve thousand dollars. Like other exotic cities, Tangier reeked of dust, of the endless cycle of living and dying. The market was teeming, hundreds of stalls, chickens with their feet tied lying docilely on the ground, mounds of tomatoes, many misshapen, goats, women nursing babies, bags of grain. It seemed merciless. In the garden of the sultan's palace legions of ants were streaming around a dead sparrow.

I wake from a nap. The city is at its most frightening, most implacable. Day is past and night is falling. Across the avenue two girls at the beach club are hanging up their bathing suits to dry. To be alone here, I think . . . to be improvident or penniless, to feel the darkness on every side.

I am not sure where the terror of North Africa comes from—from its emptiness, I suppose, from all that is unknowable. Life is cheap there, it is only a husk. Perhaps it is the cruelty, the mutilation, the followers of El Glaoui drenched with gasoline and set afire, although, as someone said, it had thoughtfully not been done in front of their children and wives; the British sergeants found with their genitals sewn in their mouths; the man who was in "that square" in Marrakech and turned to bargain with someone—when he turned back, his wife was gone, never seen again. Perhaps it was the trade in sex, the White Horse, where beneath bright lights, as calmly as if undressing backstage, a young Spanish girl, flawless as a statue, steps from her clothes. A heavier girl produces a threatening device and straps it on . . .

We crossed Gibraltar, like a pebble far below, and then brown, hard Spain. We were going home with new airplanes, the first of those that could routinely fly faster than the speed of sound. They landed at high speed, touching down at a hundred and eighty miles an hour. On the luxurious runways and in the smooth air of North Africa this was not a challenge, but our own field was much smaller. We were at thirty-seven thousand feet, and letting down, I felt a nervousness I couldn't get rid of. We entered traffic, dropped gear on the downwind leg, turned onto final. Everything looked all right. Two hundred and twenty on approach, then across the end of the runway, power off, waiting to touch. A faint jolt. The ground is streaming by. As we park, the group and wing commanders hand up cold beer.

In the end I missed North Africa. I missed its desolation and the brilliance of the light. We, too, were nomads there. We traveled and lived in tents; we had our time-worn code, our duties, and nothing more: to fly, to sit in the shade of the canvas and eat a white-bread sandwich with grimy hands, to fly again.

We were equals there, all ranks. "Hit me," the colonel says. "I can't, I'll get court-martialed," Geraghty, who is dealing, squeals. They are drunkenly comparing Rolexes. "What's wrong with yours? It has no calendar, must be experimental," Geraghty says. All these faces, so well known. All these lives, so momentarily intimate.

In formation with Minish one day, coming back from a mission, I on his wing—without a word he pulled up and did an Immelmann, I as close as you can get, then another and another, then some loops and rolls, two or three away from me, all in hot silence, I had not budged a foot, the two of us together, not a word exchanged, like secret lovers in some apartment on a burning afternoon.

****

We went in the autumn, a squadron at a time, to the Gironde, in the southwest of France, for more gunnery. The field there, Cazaux, girlishly white, was beside a lake. A squadron from another wing, one I had for a time flown with, was already there. They were sitting outside the barracks when we arrived, like ranch hands, sucking blades of grass. It often seemed not so much a profession as a way of wasting time, waiting for something to happen, your name to come up on the scheduling board, the scramble phone to ring, the last flights to land. The faces of these others had not changed in the year or two since last seen: Vandenburg, Paul Ingram, Christman, who married a countess, Vandevander, Leach. They greeted us casually. It was as if we had come to graze and they were another clan, peaceful if not friendly, now obliged to share.

We laze through the days. They become the sacred past. The days that Faulkner said were the most exciting of his life. He said that to Sylvester, a major who'd been an information officer stationed in Greenville, Mississippi, not far from Faulkner's home, during the Korean War. A librarian Sylvester knew had offered to introduce him to Faulkner as a favor. At the agreed-upon time, Faulkner appeared. He was drunk. He was wearing a wrinkled planter's suit in the coat pocket of which was a bottle, Sylvester took it to be gin. They talked about flying and the days, Faulkner said, when he had been a flyer in France. He had never been that. He had told it many times, to women, to men. Perhaps he had come to believe it.

There is a feeling Faulkner probably had—I have had it myself—that somewhere the true life is being lived, though not where you are. He may have heard the sound of it in Greenville, the rich, destructive roar not of planes such as he had known but ones far more potent. Something in him responded to that, the same thing most likely that had made him pose as an officer in the Royal Flying Corps, invent combat missions, crashes, a silver plate in his head. He was a small man. He could sit in a chair and his feet sometimes might not touch the floor. His world was small, an illiterate county seat, a backward state, though from it he fashioned something greater, far greater perhaps than even he knew. A writer cannot really grasp what he has written. It is not like a building or a sculpture; it cannot be seen whole. It is only a kind of smoke seized and printed on a page.

One thing about Faulkner I like, apart from the simplicity, on the whole, of his life, was that he wrote on the bedroom walls. That seems to me the true mark of a writer. It is like a pianist practicing in the middle of the night when the whole household is asleep or trying to sleep—the music is greater than any of their lives.

That day in Greenville, Faulkner, ten years from his death, offered to write a story about the Air Force if in exchange he might have a ride in a jet. Sylvester promptly called the base commander, a colonel, who listened to the proposal. At the end his reply was only "Who's Faulkner?"

One Monday, just after the pilots' meeting, the phone rang. It was a clerk in combat operations. Did I know that one of my pilots had bailed out over Chaumont? Chaumont? In France? It must be a mistake—we had nobody flying yet, I said.

Then I remembered the two planes being ferried.

The preceding Friday night, in the camaraderie at the club, someone had suggested that the planes being sent to the depot at Châteauroux for overhaul, since they still had some hours remaining on them before inspection, be released to fly over the weekend. Why not? I thought. Pilots always wanted flying time. I did not check where they had gone. It was of no importance. They were heading for Châteauroux by a roundabout route.

We waited uneasily to hear something more. After a while it came. One pilot, it was reported, had bailed out on the approach. The second had landed; it was Carney. Of De-Shazer, nothing further was known.

It developed that they had gone to Munich, where the ground crew had signed off the planes as fully serviced but failed to check the oil. After the weekend they had left early in the morning for Châteauroux. At thirty-five thousand feet DeShazer had a loss of power. It was the oil-operated main fuel regulator failing. He went over to his emergency fuel system and headed for the nearest field: Chaumont.

They made a long, straight-in final to Chaumont. Carney, flying on DeShazer's wing, saw a burst of flame, brilliant and terrifying, come out of the tailpipe. The bearings had failed. The engine was devouring itself. "Get out, Bill!" he called, but DeShazer anticipated him. The canopy shot away. The seat followed, up and over, tumbling behind the airplane, DeShazer's arms fluttering wildly. All our planes were equipped with a device that opened the safety belt automatically and allowed the pilot and seat to come quickly apart—all planes, it turned out, except one. The seat fell and fell, Carney trying to keep it in sight. Finally the seat and pilot separated. A long white writhing shape streamed out and reached full length but never completely bloomed before going into the trees. The sum of trivialities had reached a certain number—the result was the disappearance of a man.

They looked for him all day. At last, in midafternoon, they found him. He was dead.

Unmarried, homely, balding, with widely spaced teeth
like pickets, he was good-natured. Someone had asked to
borrow money and DeShazer said there was some in the
bureau in his room. It was Kelley, I think, who went there
and found five or six hundred dollars lying loose and un-
counted among the clothes.

After it was over and the reports had been sent in, I
stopped at the club for a drink on the way home. An accident occurring in another squadron seemed a consequence
of some kind; in one's own squadron it was fate, heavy and
humbling. The days became divided, those before and
those to come. DeShazer's name would be taken from the
board on which pilots were listed, the loss probably of his
chief distinction. His personal effects would be packed and
shipped home. The squadron commander, Norman Phillips,
would compose a letter to his parents. In the year to come,
four or five new pilots would arrive in the squadron to
begin their tours, none of them having heard of DeShazer
or prepared to believe in the sudden amazing flare, like the
gust before a magician's act, announcing the unfathomable.

Yet he would not be forgotten. Like others he would
reappear, like the fair-haired, imaginary aces Faulkner
wrote poems about. DeShazer, far more unassuming, with
his wide, cracked-lip smile, would remain in one's life.
Arms flapping, he would tumble endlessly, his parachute,
long and useless, trailing behind.

Not at first, and not until you accept that you are mortal, do you begin to realize that life and death are the same
thing. DeShazer had gone elsewhere. Into the stars.

Munich for the last time, glittering in the darkness, immense—the shops, the avenues, the fine cars. The wingman's ship is out to one side near a crescent moon. The

Arend-Roland comet is visible, its milky tail flying southward for thousands of miles, an inch in the sky. I lean back and gaze at it, my helmet against the padding. I will never see it again or, just this way, all that is below. Some joys exist in retrospect but not this, the serenity, the cities shining in detailed splendor. From the deeps of the sky we look down as if upon our flocks.

The farewell party a few weeks later seems like any other though it is the last; drinking, singing, the end of the tour, and an occasion that fixes everything but that is also something else, not quite animate, an episode in the life of a squadron that will go on without you, without everyone. All will be superseded, all forgotten.

Uden and Tucker have come with German girls. The father of Uden's had been a pilot, a Luftwaffe pilot, she said. He had never returned from his third raid over England. They never had any further news. She had been five or six years old when it happened, a child of the war, handsome now and composed.

For me it is particularly poignant, not her lost father but the evening. At the appropriate time, rising to my feet, I try to say something of what I feel, the allowable portion. I cannot simply say I've liked being in the squadron, I tell them—my life has *been* the squadron, a life, I do not explain, that I am abandoning. A few months earlier, Spry, who had graduated a few classes after me and was in group operations, had told me he was resigning. Almost at that instant—he had somehow given me the freedom, hurled the first stone—I made the decision. It was far from decisive. I discussed it with my wife who, with only a partial understanding of what was involved, did not attempt to change my mind. I had perhaps waited too long, but there was still part of me that existed when I was a schoolboy and had never really died—it was in me like a pathogen—the idea of being a writer and from the great heap of days making something lasting.

The Air Force—I ate and drank it, went in whatever weather on whatever day, talked its endless talk, climbed onto the wing to fuel the ship myself, fell into the wet sand of its beaches with sweaty others and was bitten by its flies, ignored wavering instruments, slept in dreary places, rendered it my heart. I had given up the life into which I had been born and taken up another and was about to leave that, too, only with far greater difficulty.

To those that night, among whom there were some that fate would beckon, I said I would see them again. Good luck.

I was on leave at Langley and drove up to Washington to resign. It was June, the tenth, the day on which I'd been born. It seemed fitting.

All the way, in anguish, I weighed the choices. I had published a book that year, the first, written at night and on weekends, page by unsuspected page. *The Hunters* appeared under a nom de plume. Salter was as distant as possible from my own name. It was essential not to be identified and jeopardize a career—I had heard the sarcastic references to "God Is My Copilot" Scott. I wanted to be admired but not known. I was thirty-two years old and had been in uniform since I was seventeen. I had a wife and child with another coming soon. As I walked into the Pentagon I felt I was walking to my death.

On various floors I stopped and looked at the directories, brigadiers, and major generals one had never heard of, hard at work in their bureaus: Plans, where I used to drop in and talk to Beukema about fighters. Would it be difficult, he wanted to know, for him to make the transition to them? He'd been trained in B-29s.

He had been in my company, a class ahead of me at West Point, outstanding in studies and captain of the hockey team. Superior in every way, charming, unsuperficial, an exceedingly rare type, he had grown up at West Point in an idyllic boyhood, the son of a professor there. He had married General Bradley's daughter and was marked—though not by that—everyone agreed, for greatness. I knew the room in barracks he had lived in, the exact color of his blond hair. I could easily see him as a fighter pilot—it seemed natural.

He was ultimately assigned to Langley and F-84s, a plane with a fine appearance but underpowered and with a long takeoff roll. At thirty thousand feet one day, as squadron commander-designate, he told his flight leader he wanted to try something. He began a shallow dive. It continued and began to steepen, more and more. It was a characteristic of the airplane, which may have come into effect here, that when maximum speed, the red line, was exceeded there was a control reversal, and pulling back on the stick made the nose go further down rather than come up.

He crashed in the water off Langley at high speed. He perished, not from having flown too near the sun—he was the sun's angel—but from taunting the demon of speed.

I sat at a desk in Separations and typed out my letter; then, like the survivor of some wreck, I roamed, carrying it, through the corridors for more than an hour. Finally I saw a colonel I knew, Berg, coming out of a doorway. He worked in Personnel, in charge of promotion boards. Needing the confidence of someone, I told him what I was about to do. He made no effort to dissuade me. He merely nodded. He mentioned several other officers who had recently resigned. I found it of little comfort. Late in the afternoon, feeling almost ill, I handed in the letter. It was the most difficult act of my life.

In thick heat I drove up Connecticut Avenue to an apartment we had the use of. Alone, I began to weep—the emptiness, the long years, all the men, the places. My former wing commander from Bitburg who had come back to Washington some months earlier was in Arlington, in the suburbs. I still felt close to him, one of his own. I called him on the telephone and, in unhappiness, managed to tell him what I had done. "You idiot," he said.

I went there for dinner. Why had I done it? he wanted to know. I had intended to tell the truth but broke off at the last moment knowing it would sound foolish to him and instead, as an apology, brought forth something from the schoolroom. I had done it, I said, because the future looked unpromising to me. As Napoleon had remarked at his coronation, if he had been born under Louis XIV, the most he could have hoped to be was a marshal, like Turenne. I cannot imagine what he thought.

Over and over during the days that followed, with nothing to do, I watched the cars going down the avenue in the morning or looked at the lighted Capitol and the city spread brilliantly around it at night. A baby, my daughter, was crying in the next room. Never another city, over it for the first time, in the lead, the field that you have never landed on far below, dropping down toward it, banking steeply one way, then the other, calling the tower, telling them who you are. Never another sunburned face in Tripoli looking up at you as you taxi to a stop, the expression asking, ship OK? A thumb raised, OK. And the dying whine, like a great sigh, of the engine shutting down, the needles on the gauges collapsing. It is over.

We went back to Langley. A strange, bottomless reaction had set in. With Paula and Leland, in whose house we were staying, I could hardly talk and found it impossible to laugh. Paula said she admired my courage, though what I'd had felt gone. We spent that evening talking about God. They were firm believers. It all seemed unimportant and beside the point.

Dreams remained. For years afterward in nightmares stark as archive footage, I was what I had been. We were in Asia somewhere. Disaster was in the air. We were surrendering and there had been a warning from the enemy, a written warning, that because of the many atrocities we had committed there could be no guarantee of safety. I was standing in a hospital near three or four pilots, one of whom I knew. They were going to try to cross to where their planes were parked, take off, and continue fighting. They started for the field. There was firing, heavy and relentless. Someone came to ask if I would take the fourth plane. An F-100. I hadn't been in one for years . . .

I did fly, however. On weekends I flew with the National Guard and went with them to summer camp in Cape Cod or Virginia. In the fall of 1961 we were placed on active duty—it was the so-called Berlin crisis—and went to France for nearly a year, to Chaumont, where DeShazer had crashed and where my agent, Kenneth Littauer, had flown during the First World War. They had lit bonfires at the corners of the field, he said, to guide planes home after dark.

It was September. We landed in a light rain, the first ones, having flown the planes across the Atlantic, stopping in the Azores and Seville. I asked the crew chief who met me what the town was like. He answered without hesitation, "Looks all right."

That year, I understood quite well, was the close of things. We were reserves—I had looked down upon such as we were now. I wore the uniform still, the colored ribbons, but the genuineness was gone, even when Norstad, the glamorous theater commander, came on a visit and lay sideways in an easy chair in his flying suit, chatting about the outbreak of war and what it would bring as he saw it, or even the brusque appearance of LeMay himself, with a retinue that filled an entire plane. We were able to conduct ourselves well enough if called upon and convincingly say "Sir," but it was only for a time.

This transparency set me free. All that before had been insignificant, unmartial, caught my eye, buildings, country-side, towns, hotels. As a lieutenant colonel I had a room of my own at the head of the stairs. There, late at night, back from a restaurant, back from the bar, I sat writing. I had three lives, one during the day, one at night, and the last in a drawer in my room in a small book of notes.

There were wonderful things in that book, things that I am unable to write or even imagine again. That they were wonderful was not my doing—I merely took the trouble to put them down. They were like the secret notebook of the *chasseur* at Maxim's, without ego or discretion, and the novel woven around them (*A Sport and a Pastime*) owed them everything. The leather-seated car I drove is gone; the house of Lazan and his wife, where we went for Thanks-giving and Christmas dinner, I know is off toward Langres somewhere but I doubt I would be able to find it again; the elegant couple in Paris have divorced; the young girl, the essential element—of course, she cannot change; that is the whole point—went to America and became what you might expect. Ironically, the portrait I made of her she never read.

Much has faded but not the incomparable taste of France, given then so I would always remember it. I know that taste, the yellow headlights flowing along the road at night, the towns by a river, the misty mornings, the thoughts of everything that happened there, the notes that confirmed it and made it imperishable.

In the blue twilight, lightning descends to the dim Texas plains. I can hear it crackling on the radio. The sky is filled with storms, a huge line of them. I am barely on top at forty-two thousand feet; they boil beneath me, shot with lightning like a kind of x-ray, heaving the airplane around. Down there is Frederick, Oklahoma, where we were stationed for a while just after the war. There were shining new planes in rows but no one to maintain them. The bare wooden barracks in which we sat idle grew cold as autumn advanced.

By now it is dark. The radio compass is erratic. I believe I have Tyler but can't be sure. A bit later I try Baton Rouge—nothing. The fuel is just at fifteen hundred pounds. I call for New Orleans destination weather: scattered and ten miles' visibility, they reply, but beneath me it is overcast despite the report. Then, not more than five minutes out, the clouds begin to break, there are lights.

Years when I crossed the country alone, like some replica Philip Nolan, in thousand-mile legs. Taking off from Wright-Patterson in a tremendous rainstorm, unable to even see the end of the runway or the trees. Taking off from McGuire in another downpour—Ritchings with an umbrella walking me out to the ship—taking off at Mobile, taking off at March and Forbes. Taking off at Tyndall, the earth like dust on a mirror, a long, unmoving line of smoke— from the paper mill, was it?—running south as far as the eye could see. Going out early in the morning, hands still numb, the magical silence of the runways, the whole pale scene. Heading for the Gulf under its blue haze, counties and parishes intent and unaware though I know their lives in vast detail, Brookley shining like a coin in the light off Mobile Bay.

Sometimes, because of the light, in the visor there is the moist dark of one's own eye, bigger than a movie poster. Sometimes there is the sun directly ahead making it impossible to read the instruments. The earth below is shadowed. There are mythic serpents of water, lakes, rivers smooth as marble. Empty sky, the rumbling aircraft, the radio overflowing with voices and sounds. Above the yellow horizon, near the vanishing sun, suddenly, a dot. Behind it a faint line, a contrail. By some forgotten reflex I am stunned awake, as in days past when we watched intently, when the body filled with excitement to see it: the enemy!

There were airfields everywhere, left over from the war, relic fields the names of which I knew from stories, Wendover, Pocatello. Leaving them and climbing out, over the alkali, the thin trace of roads, railroad tracks, dust. Not a city, not even a house. Snow on the distant hills, which are slowly sinking as I rise, all else brown. The West. From here it is endless, land that goes on forever. Down there it is the sky that has no end.

One night as I was calling for a letdown near St. Louis, the city jewel-like and clear, a voice in the darkness asked, "Flatfoot Red, is that you?" Flatfoot, our call sign from Bitburg, and Red, the color of the lead flight.

"Yes," I said. "Who's that?"

En route you seldom saw other fighters and almost never recognized a voice.

"Ed White."

The pleasure, the thrill, in fact, the sort that comes from a lingering glance across a room, a knowing nod, or a pair of fingers touched briefly to the brow. We were able to exchange only a few words—How are you? Where are you headed? I looked for him in the blackness, the moving star that would be his plane, but the heavens were littered with stars, the earth strewn with lights. He was on his way to somewhere, the heights, I was sure. I was going in to land.

"See you," he said.

Who could know it would be otherwise and he was one whom I would never see again? We had flown on the acrobatic team together, he the right wing, Whitlow the left, Tracy in the slot.

After his death his widow remarried. Not many years later, she herself died, apparently a suicide. The waters had closed over them both.

I often thought of White and that hail across the darkness I took as a last meeting. I thought of him as I watched a parade in the city one day. It was November, Armistice Day, but there was the heat and fullness of late summer. The dirt was blowing in the streets. I was part of New York myself by then, returned to it. They came along Fifth Avenue, the ranks of the American Legion, the police and high school bands, teenage girls dressed in blazers, ten-year-old colonels wearing sunglasses, fat men, limpers. The drums went by. The sidewalks were crowded with people. Rows of silver trumpets passed. Then the flags. The crowd watched. Not a hat was lifted, not a hand stirred.

Once at a dinner party I was asked by a woman what on earth I had ever seen in military life. I couldn't answer her, of course. I couldn't summon it all, the distant places, the comradeship, the idealism, the youth. I couldn't tell about flying over the islands long ago, seeing them rise in the blue distance wreathed in legend, the ring of white surf around them. Or the cities, Shanghai and Tokyo, Amsterdam and Venice, gunnery camps in North Africa and forgotten colonies of Rome along the shore.

I couldn't describe that, or what it was like waiting to take off on missions in Korea, armed, nervous, singing songs to yourself, or the electric jolt that went through you when the MIGs came up. I couldn't tell about Mahurin being shot down and not a soul seeing him go, or George Davis, or deArmont, who used to jump up on a table in the club and recite "Gunga Din"—the drunken pilots thought he was making it up.

I couldn't tell her about brilliant group commanders or flying with men who later became famous, the days and days of boredom and moments of pure ecstasy, of walking out to the parked planes in the early morning or coming in at dusk when the wind had died to make the last landing of the day and the mobile control officer giving two quick clicks of the mike to confirm: grease job. To fly with the thirty-year-old veterans and finally earn the right to lead yourself, flights, squadrons, a few times the entire group. The great days of youth when you are mispronouncing foreign words and trading dreams.

We came in from the flight line at Giebelstadt or Cazaux, weary, faces marked, unknown, and went into town to drink. Money meant nothing and in a way neither did fame. I couldn't tell any of that or of the roads along the sea in Honolulu, the dances, the last drinks at the bar, or who Harry Thyng was, or Kasler, or the captain's wife.

HOW I MET MY HUSBAND

ALICE MUNRO

We heard the plane come over at noon, roaring through the radio news, and we were sure it was going to hit the house, so we all ran out into the yard. We saw it come in over the treetops, all red and silver, the first close-up plane I ever saw. Mrs. Peebles screamed.

"Crash landing," their little boy said. Joey was his name.

"It's okay," said Dr. Peebles. "He knows what he's doing." Dr. Peebles was only an animal doctor, but had a calming way of talking, like any doctor.

This was my first job—working for Dr. and Mrs. Peebles, who had bought an old house out on the Fifth Line, about five miles out of town. It was just when the trend was starting of town people buying up old farms, not to work them but to live on them.

We watched the plane land across the road, where the fairgrounds used to be. It did make a good landing field, nice and level for the old racetrack, and the barns and display sheds torn down now for scrap lumber so there was nothing in the way. Even the old grandstand boys had burned.

"All right," said Mrs. Peebles, snappy as she always was when she got over her nerves. "Let's go back in the house. Let's not stand here gawking like a set of farmers."

She didn't say that to hurt my feelings. It never occurred to her.

I was just setting the dessert down when Loretta Bird arrived, out of breath, at the screen door.

"I thought it was going to crash into the house and kill youse all!"

She lived on the next place and the Peebles thought she was a countrywoman, they didn't know the difference. She and her husband didn't farm, he worked on the roads and had a bad name for drinking. They had seven children and couldn't get credit at the Hi-Way Grocery. The Peebles made her welcome, not knowing any better, as I say, and offered her dessert.

Dessert was never anything to write home about, at their place. A dish of Jell-O or sliced bananas or fruit out of a tin. "Have a house without a pie, be ashamed until you die," my mother used to say, but Mrs. Peebles operated differently.

Loretta Bird saw me getting the can of peaches.

"Oh, never mind," she said. "I haven't got the right kind of a stomach to trust what comes out of those tins, I can only eat home canning."

I could have slapped her. I bet she never put down fruit in her life.

"I know what he's landed here for," she said. "He's got permission to use the fairgrounds and take people up for rides. It costs a dollar. It's the same fellow who was over at Palmerston last week and was up the lakeshore before that. I wouldn't go up if you paid me."

"I'd jump at the chance," Dr. Peebles said. "I'd like to see this neighborhood from the air."

Mrs. Peebles said she would just as soon see it from the ground. Joey said he wanted to go and Heather did, too. Joey was nine and Heather was seven.

"Would you, Edie?" Heather said.

I said I didn't know. I was scared, but I never admitted that, especially in front of children I was taking care of.

"People are going to be coming out here in their cars raising dust and trampling your property, if I was you I would complain," Loretta said. She hooked her legs around the chair rung and I knew we were in for a lengthy visit. After Dr. Peebles went back to his office or out on his next call and Mrs. Peebles went for her nap, she would hang around me while I was trying to do the dishes. She would pass remarks about the Peebles in their own house.

"She wouldn't find time to lay down in the middle of the day, if she had seven kids like I got."

She asked me did they fight and did they keep things in the dresser drawer not to have babies with. She said it was a sin if they did. I pretended I didn't know what she was talking about.

I was fifteen and away from home for the first time. My parents had made the effort and sent me to high school for a year, but I didn't like it. I was shy of strangers and the work was hard, they didn't make it nice for you or explain the way they do now. At the end of the year the averages were published in the paper, and mine came out at the very bottom, 37 percent. My father said that's enough and I didn't blame him. The last thing I wanted, anyway, was to go on and end up teaching school. It happened the very day the paper came out with my disgrace in it, Dr. Peebles was staying at our place for dinner, having just helped one of our cows have twins, and he said I looked smart to him and his wife was looking for a girl to help. He said she felt tied down, with the two children, out in the country. I guess she would, my mother said, being polite, though I could tell from her face she was wondering what on earth it would be like to have only two children and no barn work, and then to be complaining.

When I went home I would describe to them the work I had to do, and it made everybody laugh. Mrs. Peebles had an automatic washer and dryer, the first I ever saw. I have had those in my own home for such a long time now it's hard to remember how much of a miracle it was to me, not having to struggle with the wringer and hang up and haul down. Let alone not having to heat water. Then there was practically no baking. Mrs. Peebles said she couldn't make pie crust, the most amazing thing I ever heard a woman admit. I could, of course, and I could make light biscuits and a white cake and a dark cake, but they didn't want it, she said they watched their figures. The only thing I didn't like about working there, in fact, was feeling half hungry a lot of the time. I used to bring back a box of doughnuts made out at home, and hide them under my bed. The children found out, and I didn't mind sharing, but I thought I better bind them to secrecy.

The day after the plane landed Mrs. Peebles put both children in the car and drove over to Chesley, to get their hair cut. There was a good woman then at Chesley for doing hair. She got hers done at the same place, Mrs. Peebles did, and that meant they would be gone a good while. She had to pick a day Dr. Peebles wasn't going out into the country, she didn't have her own car. Cars were still in short supply then, after the war.

I loved being left in the house alone, to do my work at leisure. The kitchen was all white and bright yellow, with fluorescent lights. That was before they ever thought of making the appliances all different colors and doing the cupboards like dark old wood and hiding the lighting. I loved light. I loved the double sink. So would anybody new-come from washing dishes in a dishpan with a rag-plugged hole on an oilcloth-covered table by light of a coal-oil lamp. I kept everything shining.

The bathroom too. I had a bath in there once a week. They wouldn't have minded if I took one oftener, but to me it seemed like asking too much, or maybe risking making it less wonderful. The basin and the tub and the toilet were all pink, and there were glass doors with flamingoes painted on them, to shut off the tub. The light had a rosy cast and the mat sank under your feet like snow, except that it was warm. The mirror was three-way. With the mirror all steamed up and the air like a perfume cloud, from things I was allowed to use, I stood up on the side of the tub and admired myself naked, from three directions. Sometimes I thought about the way we lived out at home and the way we lived here and how one way was so hard to imagine when you were living the other way. But I thought it was still a lot easier, living the way we lived at home, to picture something like this, the painted flamingoes and the warmth and the soft mat, than it was for anybody knowing only things like this to picture how it was the other way. And why was that?

I was through my jobs in no time, and had the vegetables peeled for supper and sitting in cold water besides. Then I went into Mrs. Peebles's bedroom. I had been in there plenty of times, cleaning, and I always took a good look in her closet, at the clothes she had hanging there. I wouldn't have looked in her drawers, but a closet is open to anybody. That's a lie. I would have looked in drawers, but I would have felt worse doing it and been more scared she could tell.

Some clothes in her closet she wore all the time, I was quite familiar with them. Others she never put on, they were pushed to the back. I was disappointed to see no wedding dress. But there was one long dress I could just see the skirt of, and I was hungering to see the rest. Now I took note of where it hung and lifted it out. It was satin, a lovely weight on my arm, light bluish-green in color, almost silvery. It had a fitted, pointed waist and a full skirt and an off-the-shoulder fold hiding the little sleeves.

Next thing was easy. I got out of my own things and slipped it on. I was slimmer at fifteen than anybody would believe who knows me now and the fit was beautiful. I didn't, of course, have a strapless bra on, which was what it needed, I just had to slide my straps down my arms under the material. Then I tried pinning up my hair, to get the effect. One thing led to another. I put on rouge and lipstick and eyebrow pencil from her dresser. The heat of the day and the weight of the satin and all the excitement made me thirsty, and I went out to the kitchen, got-up as I was, to get a glass of ginger ale with ice cubes from the refrigerator. The Peebles drank ginger ale, or fruit drinks, all day, like water, and I was getting so I did too. Also there was no limit on ice cubes, which I was so fond of I would even put them in a glass of milk.

I turned from putting the ice tray back and saw a man watching me through the screen. It was the luckiest thing in the world I didn't spill the ginger ale down the front of me then and there.

"I never meant to scare you. I knocked but you were getting the ice out, you didn't hear me."

I couldn't see what he looked like, he was dark the way somebody is pressed up against a screen door with the bright daylight behind them. I only knew he wasn't from around here.

"I'm from the plane over there. My name is Chris Watters and what I was wondering was if I could use that pump."

There was a pump in the yard. That was the way the people used to get their water. Now I noticed he was carrying a pail.

"You're welcome," I said. "I can get it from the tap and save you pumping." I guess I wanted him to know we had piped water, didn't pump ourselves.

"I don't mind the exercise." He didn't move, though, and finally he said, "Were you going to a dance?"

Seeing a stranger there had made me entirely forget how I was dressed.

"Or is that the way ladies around here generally get dressed up in the afternoon?"

I didn't know how to joke back then. I was too embarrassed.

"You live here? Are you the lady of the house?"

"I'm the hired girl."

Some people change when they find that out, their whole way of looking at you and speaking to you changes, but his didn't.

"Well, I just wanted to tell you you look very nice. I was so surprised when I looked in the door and saw you. Just because you looked so nice and beautiful."

I wasn't even old enough then to realize how out of the common it is, for a man to say something like that to a woman, or somebody he is treating like a woman. For a man to say a word like *beautiful*. I wasn't old enough to realize or to say anything back, or in fact to do anything but wish he would go away. Not that I didn't like him, but just that it upset me so, having him look at me, and me trying to think of something to say.

He must have understood. He said goodbye, and thanked me, and went and started filling his pail from the pump. I stood behind the Venetian blinds in the dining room, watching him. When he had gone, I went into the bedroom and took the dress off and put it back in the same place. I dressed in my own clothes and took my hair down and washed my face, wiping it on Kleenex, which I threw in the wastebasket.

The Peebles asked me what kind of man he was. Young, middle-aged, short, tall? I couldn't say.

"Good-looking?" Dr. Peebles teased me.

I couldn't think a thing but that he would be coming to get his water again, he would be talking to Dr. or Mrs. Peebles, making friends with them, and he would mention seeing me that first afternoon, dressed up. Why not mention it? He would think it was funny. And no idea of the trouble it would get me into.

After supper the Peebles drove into town to go to a movie. She wanted to go somewhere with her hair fresh done. I sat in my bright kitchen wondering what to do, knowing I would never sleep. Mrs. Peebles might not fire me, when she found out, but it would give her a different feeling about me altogether. This was the first place I ever worked but I already had picked up things about the way people feel when you are working for them. They like to think you aren't curious. Not just that you aren't dishonest, that isn't enough. They like to feel you don't notice things, that you don't think or wonder about anything but what they liked to eat and how they like things ironed, and so on. I don't mean they weren't kind to me, because they were. They had me eat my meals with them (to tell the truth I expected to, I didn't know there were families who don't) and sometimes they took me along in the car. But all the same.

I went up and checked on the children being asleep and then I went out. I had to do it. I crossed the road and went in the old fairgrounds gate. The plane looked unnatural sitting there and shining with the moon. Off at the far side of the fairgrounds, where the bush was taking over, I saw his tent.

He was sitting outside it smoking a cigarette. He saw me coming.

"Hello, were you looking for a plane ride? I don't start taking people up till tomorrow." Then he looked again and said, "Oh, it's you. I didn't know you without your long dress on."

My heart was knocking away, my tongue was dried up. I had to say something. But I couldn't. My throat was closed and I was like a deaf-and-dumb.

"Did you want a ride? Sit down. Have a cigarette."

I couldn't even shake my head to say no, so he gave me one.

"Put it in your mouth or I can't light it. It's a good thing I'm used to shy ladies."

I did. It wasn't the first time I had smoked a cigarette, actually. My girlfriend out home, Muriel Lower, used to steal them from her brother.

"Look at your hand shaking. Did you just want to have a chat, or what?"

In one burst I said, "I wisht you wouldn't say anything about that dress."

"What dress? Oh, the long dress."

"It's Mrs. Peebles's."

"Whose? Oh, the lady you work for? Is that it? She wasn't home so you got dressed up in her dress, eh? You got dressed up and played queen. I don't blame you. You're not smoking that cigarette right. Don't just puff. Draw it in. Did nobody ever show you how to inhale? Are you scared I'll tell on you? Is that it?"

I was so ashamed at having to ask him to connive this way I couldn't nod. I just looked at him and he saw *yes*.

"Well I won't. I won't in the slightest way mention it or embarrass you. I give you my word of honor."

Then he changed the subject, to help me out, seeing I couldn't even thank him.

"What do you think of this sign?"

It was a board sign lying practically at my feet.

SEE THE WORLD FROM THE SKY. ADULTS $1.00, CHILDREN 50¢. QUALIFIED PILOT.

"My old sign was getting pretty beat up, I thought I'd make a new one. That's what I've been doing with my time today."

The lettering wasn't all that handsome, I thought. I could have done a better one in half an hour.

"I'm not an expert at sign-making."

"It's very good," I said.

"I don't need it for publicity, word of mouth is usually enough. I turned away two carloads tonight. I felt like taking it easy. I didn't tell them ladies were dropping in to visit me."

Now I remembered the children and I was scared again, in case one of them had waked up and called me and I wasn't there.

"Do you have to go so soon?"

I remembered some manners. "Thank you for the cigarette."

"Don't forget. You have my word of honor."

I tore off across the fairgrounds, scared I'd see the car heading home from town. My sense of time was mixed up, I didn't know how long I'd been out of the house. But it was all right, it wasn't late, the children were asleep. I got in bed myself and lay thinking what a lucky end to the day, after all, and among things to be grateful for I could be grateful Loretta Bird hadn't been the one who caught me.

The yard and borders didn't get trampled, it wasn't as bad as that. All the same it seemed very public, around the house. The sign was on the fairgrounds gate. People came mostly after supper but a good many in the afternoon, too. The Bird children all came without fifty cents between them and hung on the gate. We got used to the excitement of the plane coming in and taking off, it wasn't excitement anymore. I never went over, after that one time, but would see him when he came to get his water. I would be out on the steps doing sitting-down work, like preparing vegetables, if I could.

"Why don't you come over? I'll take you up in my plane."

"I'm saving my money," I said, because I couldn't think of anything else.

"For what? For getting married?"

I shook my head.

"I'll take you up for free if you come sometime when it's slack. I thought you would come and have another cigarette."

I made a face to hush him, because you never could tell when the children would be sneaking around the porch, or Mrs. Peebles herself listening in the house. Sometimes she came out and had a conversation with him. He told her things he hadn't bothered to tell me. But then I hadn't thought to ask. He told her he had been in the War, that was where he learned to fly a plane, and now he couldn't settle down to ordinary life, this was what he liked. She said she couldn't imagine anybody liking such a thing. Though sometimes, she said, she was almost bored enough to try anything herself, she wasn't brought up to living in the country. It's all my husband's idea, she said. This was news to me.

"Maybe you ought to give flying lessons," she said.

"Would you take them?"

She just laughed.

Sunday was a busy flying day in spite of it being preached against from two pulpits. We were all sitting out watching. Joey and Heather were over on the fence with the Bird kids. Their father had said they could go, after their mother saying all week they couldn't.

A car came down the road past the parked cars and pulled up right in the drive. It was Loretta Bird who got out, all importance, and on the driver's side another woman got out, more sedately. She was wearing sunglasses.

"This is a lady looking for the man that flies the plane," Loretta Bird said. "I heard her inquire in the hotel coffee shop where I was having a Coke and I brought her out."

"I'm sorry to bother you," the lady said. "I'm Alice Kelling, Mr. Watters' fiancée."

This Alice Kelling had on a pair of brown and white checked slacks and a yellow top. Her bust looked to me rather low and bumpy. She had a worried face. Her hair had had a permanent, but had grown out, and she wore a yellow band to keep it off her face. Nothing in the least pretty or even young-looking about her. But you could tell from how she talked she was from the city, or educated, or both.

Dr. Peebles stood up and introduced himself and his wife and me and asked her to be seated.

"He's up in the air right now, but you're welcome to sit and wait. He gets his water here and he hasn't been yet. He'll probably take his break about five."

"That is him, then?" said Alice Kelling, wrinkling and straining at the sky.

"He's not in the habit of running out on you, taking a different name?" Dr. Peebles laughed. He was the one, not his wife, to offer iced tea. Then she sent me into the kitchen to fix it. She smiled. She was wearing sunglasses too.

"He never mentioned his fiancée," she said.

I loved fixing iced tea with lots of ice and slices of lemon in tall glasses. I ought to have mentioned before, Dr. Peebles was an abstainer, at least around the house, or I wouldn't have been allowed to take the place. I had to fix a glass for Loretta Bird too, though it galled me, and when I went out she had settled in my lawn chair, leaving me the steps.

"I knew you was a nurse when I first heard you in that coffee shop."

"How would you know a thing like that?"

"I get my hunches about people. Was that how you met him, nursing?"

"Chris? Well yes. Yes, it was."

"Oh, were you overseas?" said Mrs. Peebles.

"No, it was before he went overseas. I nursed him when he was stationed at Centralia and had a ruptured appendix. We got engaged and then he went overseas. My, this is refreshing, after a long drive."

"He'll be glad to see you," Dr. Peebles said. "It's a rackety kind of life, isn't it, not staying one place long enough to really make friends."

"Youse've had a long engagement," Loretta Bird said.

Alice Kelling passed that over. "I was going to get a room at the hotel, but when I was offered directions I came on out. Do you think I could phone them?"

"No need," Dr. Peebles said. "You're five miles away from him if you stay at the hotel. Here, you're right across the road. Stay with us. We've got rooms on rooms, look at this big house."

Asking people to stay, just like that, is certainly a country thing, and maybe seemed natural to him now, but not to Mrs. Peebles, from the way she said, oh yes, we have plenty of room. Or to Alice Kelling, who kept protesting, but let herself be worn down. I got the feeling it was a temptation to her, to be that close. I was trying for a look at her ring. Her nails were painted red, her fingers were freckled and wrinkled. It was a tiny stone. Muriel Lowe's cousin had one twice as big.

Chris came to get his water, late in the afternoon just as Dr. Peebles had predicted. He must have recognized the car from a way off. He came smiling.

"Here I am chasing after you to see what you're up to," called Alice Kelling. She got up and went to meet him and they kissed, just touched, in front of us.

"You're going to spend a lot on gas that way," Chris said.

Dr. Peebles invited Chris to stay for supper, since he had already put up the sign that said: NO MORE RIDES TILL 7 P.M. Mrs. Peebles wanted it served in the yard, in spite of bugs. One thing strange to anybody from the country is this eating outside. I had made a potato salad earlier and she had made a jellied salad, that was one thing she could do, so it was just a matter of getting those out, and some sliced meat and cucumbers and fresh leaf lettuce. Loretta Bird hung around for some time saying, "Oh, well, I guess I better get home to those yappers," and, "It's so nice just sitting here, I sure hate to get up," but nobody invited her, I was relieved to see, and finally she had to go.

That night after rides were finished Alice Kelling and Chris went off somewhere in her car. I lay awake till they got back. When I saw the car lights sweep my ceiling I got up to look down on them through the slats of my blind. I don't know what I thought I was going to see. Muriel Lowe and I used to sleep on her front veranda and watch her sister and her sister's boyfriend saying good night. Afterwards we couldn't get to sleep, for longing for somebody to kiss us and rub up against us and we would talk about suppose you were out in a boat with a boy and he wouldn't bring you in to shore unless you did it, or what if somebody got you trapped in a barn, you would have to, wouldn't you, it wouldn't be your fault. Muriel said her two girl cousins used to try with a toilet paper roll that one of them was the boy. We wouldn't do anything like that; just lay and wondered.

All that happened was that Chris got out of the car on one side and she got out on the other and they walked off separately—him toward the fairgrounds and her toward the house. I got back in bed and imagined about me coming home with him, not like that.

Next morning Alice Kelling got up late and I fixed a grapefruit for her the way I had learned and Mrs. Peebles sat down with her to visit and have another cup of coffee. Mrs. Peebles seemed pleased enough now, having company. Alice Kelling said she guessed she better get used to putting in a day just watching Chris take off and come down, and Mrs. Peebles said she didn't know if she should suggest it because Alice Kelling was the one with the car, but the lake was only twenty-five miles away and what a good day for a picnic.

Alice Kelling took her up on the idea and by eleven o'clock they were in the car with Joey and Heather and a sandwich lunch I had made. The only thing was that Chris hadn't come down, and she wanted to tell him where they were going.

"Edie'll go over and tell him," Mrs. Peebles said. "There's no problem."

Alice Kelling wrinkled her face and agreed.

"Be sure and tell him we'll be back by five!"

I didn't see that he would be concerned about knowing this right away, and I thought of him eating whatever he ate over there, alone, cooking on his camp stove, so I got to work and mixed up a crumb cake and baked it, in between the other work I had to do; then, when it was a bit cooled, wrapped it in a tea towel. I didn't do anything to myself but take off my apron and comb my hair. I would like to have put some makeup on, but I was too afraid it would remind him of the way he first saw me, and that would humiliate me all over again.

He had come and put another sign on the gate: NO RIDES THIS P.M. APOLOGIES. I worried that he wasn't feeling well. No sign of him outside and the tent flap was down. I knocked on the pole.

"Come in," he said, in a voice that would just as soon have said *Stay out.*

I lifted the flap.

"Oh, it's you. I'm sorry. I didn't know it was you."

He had been just sitting on the side of the bed, smoking. Why not at least sit and smoke in the fresh air?

"I brought a cake and hope you're not sick," I said.

"Why would I be sick? Oh—that sign. That's all right. I'm just tired of talking to people. I don't mean you. Have a seat." He pinned back the tent flap. "Get some fresh air in here."

I sat on the edge of the bed, there was no place else. It was one of those fold-up cots, really: I remembered and gave him his fiancée's message.

He ate some of the cake. "Good."

"Put the rest away for when you're hungry later."

"I'll tell you a secret. I won't be around here much longer."

"Are you getting married?"

"Ha ha. What time did you say they'd be back?"

"Five o'clock."

"Well, by that time this place will have seen the last of me. A plane can get further than a car." He unwrapped the cake and ate another piece of it, absentmindedly.

"Now you'll be thirsty."

"There's some water in the pail."

"It won't be very cold. I could bring some fresh. I could bring some ice from the refrigerator."

"No," he said. "I don't want you to go. I want a nice long time of saying goodbye to you."

He put the cake away carefully and sat beside me and started those little kisses, so soft, I can't ever let myself think about them, such kindness in his face and lovely kisses, all over my eyelids and neck and ears, all over, then me kissing back as well as I could (I had only kissed a boy on a dare before, and kissed my own arms for practice) and we lay back on the cot and pressed together, just gently, and he did some other things, not bad things or not in a bad way. It was lovely in the tent, that smell of grass and hot tent cloth with the sun beating down on it, and he said, "I wouldn't do you any harm for the world." Once, when he had rolled on top of me and we were sort of rocking together on the cot, he said softly, "Oh, no," and freed himself and jumped up and got the water pail. He splashed some of it on his neck and face, and the little bit left, on me lying there.

"That's to cool us off, Miss."

When we said goodbye I wasn't at all sad, because he held my face and said, "I'm going to write you a letter. I'll tell you where I am and maybe you can come and see me. Would you like that? Okay then. You wait." I was really glad I think to get away from him, it was like he was piling presents on me I couldn't get the pleasure of till I considered them alone.

No consternation at first about the plane being gone. They thought he had taken somebody up, and I didn't enlighten them. Dr. Peebles had phoned he had to go to the country, so there was just us having supper, and then Loretta Bird thrusting her head in the door and saying, "I see he's took off."

"What?" said Alice Kelling, and pushed back her chair.

"The kids come and told me this afternoon he was taking down his tent. Did he think he'd run through all the business there was around here? He didn't take off without letting you know, did he?"

"He'll send me word," Alice Kelling said. "He'll probably phone tonight. He's terribly restless, since the War."

"Edie, he didn't mention to you, did he?" Mrs. Peebles said. "When you took over the message?"

"Yes," I said. So far so true.

"Well why didn't you say?" All of them were looking at me. "Did he say where he was going?"

"He said he might try Bayfield," I said. What made me tell such a lie? I didn't intend it.

"Bayfield, how far is that?" said Alice Kelling.

Mrs. Peebles said, "Thirty, thirty-five miles."

"That's not far. Oh, well, that's really not far at all. It's on the lake, isn't it?"

You'd think I'd be ashamed of myself, setting her on the wrong track. I did it to give him more time, whatever time he needed. I lied for him, and also, I have to admit, for me. Women should stick together and not do things like that. I see that now, but didn't then. I never thought of myself as being in any way like her, or coming to the same troubles, ever.

She hadn't taken her eyes off me. I thought she suspected my lie.

"When did he mention this to you?"

"Earlier."

"When you were over at the plane?"

"Yes."

"You must've stayed and had a chat." She smiled at me, not a nice smile. "You must've stayed and had a little visit with him."

"I took a cake," I said, thinking that telling some truth would spare me telling the rest.

"We didn't have a cake," said Mrs. Peebles rather sharply.

"I baked one."

Alice Kelling said, "That was very friendly of you."

"Did you get permission?" asked Loretta Bird. "You never know what these girls'll do next," she said. "It's not they mean harm so much, as they're ignorant."

"The cake is neither here nor there," Mrs. Peebles broke in. "Edie, I wasn't aware you knew Chris that well."

I didn't know what to say.

"I'm not surprised," Alice Kelling said in a high voice. "I knew by the look of her as soon as I saw her. We get them at the hospital all the time." She looked hard at me with her stretched smile. "Having their babies. We have to put them in a special ward because of their diseases. Little country tramps. Fourteen and fifteen years old. You should see the babies they have, too."

"There was a bad woman here in town had a baby that pus was running out of its eyes," Loretta Bird put in.

"Wait a minute," said Mrs. Peebles. "What is this talk? Edie. What about you and Mr. Watters? Were you intimate with him?"

"Yes," I said. I was thinking of us lying on the cot and kissing, wasn't that intimate? And I would never deny it.

They were all one minute quiet, even Loretta Bird.

"Well," said Mrs. Peebles. "I am surprised. I think I need a cigarette. This is the first of any such tendencies I've seen in her," she said, speaking to Alice Kelling, but Alice Kelling was looking at me.

"Loose little bitch." Tears ran down her face. "Loose little bitch, aren't you? I knew as soon as I saw you. Men despise girls like you. He just made use of you and went off, you know that, don't you? Girls like you are just nothing, they're just public conveniences, just filthy little rags!"

"Oh, now," said Mrs. Peebles.

"Filthy," Alice Kelling sobbed. "Filthy little rag!"

"Don't get yourself upset," Loretta Bird said. She was swollen up with pleasure at being in on this scene. "Men are all the same."

"Edie, I'm very surprised," Mrs. Peebles said. "I thought your parents were so strict. You don't want to have a baby, do you?"

I'm still ashamed of what happened next. I lost control, just like a six-year-old, I started howling. "You don't get a baby from just doing that!"

"You see. Some of them are that ignorant," Loretta Bird said.

But Mrs. Peebles jumped up and caught my arms and shook me.

"Calm down. Don't get hysterical. Calm down. Stop crying. Listen to me. Listen. I'm wondering, if you know what being intimate means. Now tell me. What did you think it meant?"

"Kissing," I howled.

She let go. "Oh, Edie. Stop it. Don't be silly. It's all right. It's all a misunderstanding. Being intimate means a lot more than that. Oh, I *wondered*."

"She's trying to cover up, now," said Alice Kelling. "Yes. She's not so stupid. She sees she got herself in trouble."

"I believe her," Mrs. Peebles said. "This is an awful scene."

"Well there is one way to find out," said Alice Kelling, getting up. "After all, I am a nurse."

Mrs. Peebles drew a breath and said, "No. No. Go to your room, Edie. And stop that noise. That is too disgusting."

I heard the car start in a little while. I tried to stop crying, pulling back each wave as it started over me. Finally I succeeded, and lay heaving on the bed.

Mrs. Peebles came and stood in the doorway.

"She's gone," she said. "That Bird woman too. Of course, you know you should never have gone near that man and that is the cause of all this trouble. I have a headache. As soon as you can, go and wash your face in cold water and get at the dishes and we will not say any more about this."

Nor we didn't. I didn't figure out till years later the extent of what I had been saved from. Mrs. Peebles was not very friendly to me afterwards, but she was fair. Not very friendly is the wrong way of describing what she was. She never had been very friendly. It was just that now she had to see me all the time and it got on her nerves, a little.

As for me, I put it all out of my mind like a bad dream and concentrated on waiting for my letter. The mail came every day except Sunday, between one-thirty and two in the afternoon, a good time for me because Mrs. Peebles was always having her nap. I would get the kitchen all cleaned and then go up to the mailbox and sit in the grass, waiting. I was perfectly happy, waiting, I forgot all about Alice Kelling and her misery and awful talk and Mrs. Peebles and her chilliness and the embarrassment of whether she had told Dr. Peebles and the face of Loretta Bird, getting her fill of other people's troubles. I was always smiling when the mailman got there, and continued smiling even after he gave me the mail and I saw today wasn't the day.

The mailman was a Carmichael. I knew by his face because there are a lot of Carmichaels living out by us and so many of them have a sort of sticking-out top lip. So I asked his name (he was a young man, shy, but good humored, anybody could ask him anything) and then I said, "I knew by your face!" He was pleased by that and always glad to see me and got a little less shy. "You've got the smile I've been waiting on all day!" he used to holler out the car window.

It never crossed my mind for a long time a letter might not come. I believed in it coming just like I believed the sun would rise in the morning. I just put off my hope from day to day, and there was the goldenrod out around the mailbox and the children gone back to school, and the leaves turning, and I was wearing a sweater when I went to wait. One day walking back with the hydro bill stuck in my hand, that was all, looking across at the fairgrounds with the full-blown milkweed and dark teasels, so much like fall, it just struck me: *No letter was ever going to come.* It was an impossible idea to get used to. No, not impossible. If I thought about Chris's face when he said he was going to write to me, it was impossible, but if I forgot that and thought about the actual tin mailbox, empty, it was plain and true. I kept on going to meet the mail, but my heart was heavy now like a lump of lead. I only smiled because I thought of the mailman counting on it, and he didn't have an easy life, with the winter driving ahead.

Till it came to me one day there were women doing this with their lives, all over. There were women just waiting and waiting by mailboxes for one letter or another. I imagined me making this journey day after day and year after year, and my hair starting to go gray, and I thought, I was never made to go on like that. So I stopped meeting the mail. If there were women all through life waiting, and women busy and not waiting, I knew which I had to be. Even though there might be things the second kind of women have to pass up and never know about, it still is better.

I was surprised when the mailman phoned the Peebles's place in the evening and asked for me. He said he missed me. He asked if I would like to go to Goderich where some well-known movie was on, I forget now what. So I said yes, and I went out with him for two years and he asked me to marry him, and we were engaged a year more while I got my things together, and then we did marry. He always tells the children the story of how I went after him by sitting by the mailbox every day, and naturally I laugh and let him, because I like for people to think what pleases them and makes them happy.

THE ANGELS

TOM WOLFE

Within five minutes, or ten minutes, no more than that, three of the others had called her on the telephone to ask her if she had heard that something had happened out there.

"Jane, this is Alice. Listen, I just got a call from Betty, and she said she heard something's happened out there. Have you heard anything?" That was the way they phrased it, call after call. She picked up the telephone and began relaying this same message to some of the others.

"Connie, this is Jane Conrad. Alice just called me, and she says something's happened . . ."

Something was part of the official Wife Lingo for tiptoeing blindfolded around the subject. Being barely twenty-one years old and new around here, Jane Conrad knew very little about this particular subject, since nobody ever talked about it. But the day was young! And what a setting she had for her imminent enlightenment! And what a picture she herself presented! Jane was tall and slender and had rich brown hair and high cheekbones and wide brown eyes. She looked a little like the actress Jean Simmons. Her father was a rancher in southwestern Texas. She had gone

East to college, to Bryn Mawr, and had met her husband, Pete, at a debutante's party at the Gulph Mills Club in Philadelphia, when he was a senior at Princeton. Pete was a short, wiry, blond boy who joked around a lot. At any moment his face was likely to break into a wild grin revealing the gap between his front teeth. The Hickory Kid sort, he was; a Hickory Kid on the deb circuit, however. He had an air of energy, self-confidence, ambition, *joie de vivre*. Jane and Pete were married two days after he graduated from Princeton. Last year Jane gave birth to their first child, Peter. And today, here in Florida, in Jacksonville, in the peaceful year 1955, the sun shines through the pines outside, and the very air takes on the sparkle of the ocean. The ocean and a great mica-white beach are less than a mile away. Anyone driving by will see Jane's little house gleaming like a dream house in the pines. It is a brick house, but Jane and Pete painted the bricks white, so that it gleams in the sun against a great green screen of pine trees with a thousand little places where the sun peeks through. They painted the shutters black, which makes the white walls look even more brilliant. The house has only eleven hundred square feet of floor space, but Jane and Pete designed it themselves and that more than makes up for the size. A friend of theirs was the builder and gave them every possible break, so that it cost only eleven thousand dollars. Outside, the sun shines, and inside, the fever rises by the minute as five, ten, fifteen, and, finally, nearly all twenty of the wives join the circuit, trying to find out what has happened, which, in fact, means: to whose husband.

After thirty minutes on such a circuit—this is not an unusual morning around here—a wife begins to feel that the telephone is no longer located on a table or on the kitchen wall. It is exploding in her solar plexus. Yet it would

be far worse right now to hear the front doorbell. The protocol is strict on that point, although written down
nowhere. No woman is supposed to deliver the final news,
and certainly not on the telephone. The matter mustn't be
bungled!—that's the idea. No, a man should bring the news
when the time comes, a man with some official or moral
authority, a clergyman or a comrade of the newly deceased.
Furthermore, he should bring the bad news in person. He
should turn up at the front door and ring the bell and be
standing there like a pillar of coolness and competence,
bearing the bad news on ice, like a fish. Therefore, all the
telephone calls from the wives were the frantic and porten-
tous beating of the wings of the death angels, as it were.
When the final news came, there would be a ring at the
front door—a wife in this situation finds herself staring at
the front door as if she no longer owns it or controls it—
and outside the door would be a man . . . come to inform
her that unfortunately something has happened out there,
and her husband's body now lies incinerated in the swamps
or the pines or the palmetto grass, "burned beyond recognition," which anyone who had been around an air base for
very long (fortunately Jane had not) realized was quite an
artful euphemism to describe a human body that now
looked like an enormous fowl that has burned up in a
stove, burned a blackish brown all over, greasy and blistered, fried, in a word, with not only the entire face and all
the hair and the ears burned off, not to mention all the
clothing, but also the *hands* and *feet*, with what remains of
the arms and legs bent at the knees and elbows and burned
into absolutely rigid angles, burned a greasy blackish
brown like the bursting body itself, so that this husband,
father, officer, gentleman, this *ornamentum* of some
mother's eye, His Majesty the Baby of just twenty-odd years

back, has been reduced to a charred hulk with wings and shanks sticking out of it.

My own husband—how could this be what they were talking about? Jane had heard the young men, Pete among them, talk about other young men who had "bought it" or "augered in" or "crunched," but it had never been anyone they knew, no one in the squadron. And in any event, the way they talked about it, with such breezy, slangy terminology, was the same way they talked about sports. It was as if they were saying, "He was thrown out stealing second base." And that was all! Not one word, not in print, not in conversation—not in this amputated language!—about an incinerated corpse from which a young man's spirit has vanished in an instant, from which all smiles, gestures, moods, worries, laughter, wiles, shrugs, tenderness, and loving looks—*you, my love!*—have disappeared like a sigh, while the terror consumes a cottage in the woods, and a young woman, sizzling with the fever, awaits her confirmation as the new widow of the day.

The next series of calls greatly increased the possibility that it was Pete to whom something had happened. There were only twenty men in the squadron, and soon nine or ten had been accounted for . . . by the fluttering reports of the death angels. Knowing that the word was out that an accident had occurred, husbands who could get to a telephone were calling home to say *it didn't happen to me.* This news, of course, was immediately fed to the fever. Jane's telephone would ring once more, and one of the wives would be saying:

"Nancy just got a call from Jack. He's at the squadron and he says something's happened, but he doesn't know what. He said he saw Frank D—— take off about ten minutes ago with Greg in back, so they're all right. What have you heard?"

But Jane has heard nothing except that other husbands, and not hers, are safe and accounted for. And thus, on a sunny day in Florida, outside of the Jacksonville Naval Air Station, in a little white cottage, a veritable dream house, another beautiful young woman was about to be apprised of the *quid pro quo* of her husband's line of work, of the trade-off, as one might say, the subparagraphs of a contract written in no visible form. Just as surely as if she had the entire roster in front of her, Jane now realized that only two men in the squadron were unaccounted for. One was a pilot named Bud Jennings; the other was Pete. She picked up the telephone and did something that was much frowned on in a time of emergency. She called the squadron office. The duty officer answered.

"I want to speak to Lieutenant Conrad," said Jane. "This is Mrs. Conrad."

"I'm sorry," the duty officer said—and then his voice cracked. "I'm sorry . . . I . . ." He couldn't find the words! He was about to cry! "I'm—that's—I mean . . . he can't come to the phone!"

He can't come to the phone!

"It's very important!" said Jane.

"I'm sorry—it's impossible—" The duty officer could hardly get the words out because he was so busy gulping back sobs. *Sobs!* "He can't come to the phone."

"Why not? Where is he?"

"I'm sorry—" More sighs, wheezes, snuffling gasps. "I can't tell you that. I—I have to hang up now!"

And the duty officer's voice disappeared in a great surf of emotion and he hung up.

The duty officer! *The very sound of her voice was more than he could take!*

The world froze, congealed, in that moment. Jane could no longer calculate the interval before the front doorbell would ring and some competent long-faced figure would appear, some Friend of Widows and Orphans, who would inform her, officially, that Pete was dead.

Even out in the middle of the swamp, in this rot-bog of pine trunks, scum slicks, dead dodder vines, and mosquito eggs, even out in this great overripe sump, the smell of "burned beyond recognition" obliterated everything else. When airplane fuel exploded, it created a heat so intense that everything but the hardest metals not only *burned*—everything of rubber, plastic, celluloid, wood, leather, cloth, flesh, gristle, calcium, horn, hair, blood, and protoplasm—it not only burned, it gave up the ghost in the form of every stricken putrid gas known to chemistry. One could smell the horror. It came in through the nostrils and burned the rhinal cavities raw and penetrated the liver and permeated the bowels like a black gas until there was nothing in the universe, inside or out, except the stench of the char. As the helicopter came down between the pine trees and settled onto the bogs, the smell hit Pete Conrad even before the hatch was completely open, and they were not even close enough to see the wreckage yet. The rest of the way Conrad and the crewmen had to travel on foot. After a few steps the water was up to their knees, and then it was up to their armpits, and they kept wading through the water and the scum and the vines and the pine trunks, but it was nothing compared to the smell. Conrad, a twenty-five-year-old lieutenant junior grade, happened to be on duty as squadron safety officer that day and was supposed to make the on-site investigation of the crash. The fact was, however, that this squadron was the first duty assignment of his career, and he had never been at a crash site before and had never smelled any such revolting stench or seen anything like what awaited him.

When Conrad finally reached the plane, which was an SNJ, he found the fuselage burned and blistered and dug into the swamp with one wing sheared off and the cockpit canopy smashed. In the front seat was all that was left of his friend Bud Jennings. Bud Jennings, an amiable fellow, a promising young fighter pilot, was now a horrible roasted hulk—with no head. His head was completely gone, apparently torn off the spinal column like a pineapple off a stalk, except that it was nowhere to be found.

Conrad stood there soaking wet in the swamp bog, wondering what the hell to do. It was a struggle to move twenty feet in this freaking muck. Every time he looked up, he was looking into a delirium of limbs, vines, dappled shadows, and a chopped-up white light that came through the tree-tops—the ubiquitous screen of trees with a thousand little places where the sun peeked through. Nevertheless, he started wading back out into the muck and the scum, and the others followed. He kept looking up. Gradually he could make it out. Up in the treetops there was a pattern of broken limbs where the SNJ had come crashing through. It was like a tunnel through the treetops. Conrad and the others began splashing through the swamp, following the strange path ninety or a hundred feet above them. It took a sharp turn. That must have been where the wing broke off. The trail veered to one side and started downward. They kept looking up and wading through the muck. Then they stopped. There was a great green sap wound up there in the middle of a tree trunk. It was odd. Near the huge gash was . . . tree disease . . . some sort of brownish lumpy sac up in the branches, such as you see in trees infested by bagworms, and there were yellowish curds on the branches around it, as if the disease had caused the sap to ooze out and fester and congeal—except that it couldn't be sap because it was streaked with blood. In the next instant—Conrad didn't have to say a word. Each man could see it all. The lumpy sack was the cloth liner of a flight helmet, with the earphones attached to it. The curds were Bud Jennings's brains. The tree trunk had smashed through the cockpit canopy of the SNJ and knocked Bud Jennings's head to pieces like a melon.

In keeping with the protocol, the squadron commander was not going to release Bud Jennings's name until his widow, Loretta, had been located and a competent male death messenger had been dispatched to tell her. But Loretta Jennings was not at home and could not be found. Hence, a delay—and more than enough time for the other wives, the death angels, to burn with panic over the telephone lines. All the pilots were accounted for except the two who were in the woods, Bud Jennings and Pete Conrad. One chance in two, acey-deucey, one finger-two finger, and this was not an unusual day around here.

Loretta Jennings had been out at a shopping center. When she returned home, a certain figure was waiting outside, a man, a solemn Friend of Widows and Orphans, and it was Loretta Jennings who lost the game of odd and even, acey-deucey, and it was Loretta whose child (she was pregnant with a second) would have no father. It was this young woman who went through all the final horrors that Jane Conrad had imagined—*assumed!*—would be hers to endure forever. Yet this grim stroke of fortune brought Jane little relief.

On the day of Bud Jennings's funeral, Pete went into the back of the closet and brought out his bridge coat, per regulations. This was the most stylish item in the Navy officer's wardrobe. Pete had never had occasion to wear his before. It was a double-breasted coat made of navy-blue melton cloth and came down almost to the ankles. It must have weighed ten pounds. It had a double row of gold buttons down the front and loops, for shoulder boards, big beautiful belly-cut collar and lapels, deep turnbacks on the sleeves, a tailored waist, and a center vent in back that ran from the waistline to the bottom of the coat. Never would Pete, or for that matter many other American males in the mid-twentieth century, have an article of clothing quite so impressive and aristocratic as that bridge coat. At the funeral the nineteen little Indians who were left—Navy boys!— lined up manfully in their bridge coats. They looked so young. Their pink, lineless faces with their absolutely clear, lean jawlines popped up bravely, correctly, out of the enormous belly-cut collars of the bridge coats. They sang an old Navy hymn, which slipped into a strange and lugubrious minor key here and there, and included a stanza added especially for aviators. It ended with: "O hear us when we lift our prayer for those in peril in the air."

Three months later another member of the squadron crashed and was burned beyond recognition and Pete hauled out the bridge coat again and Jane saw eighteen little Indians bravely going through the motions at the funeral Not long after that, Pete was transferred from Jacksonville to the Patuxent River Naval Air Station in Maryland. Pete and Jane had barely settled in there when they got word that another member of the Jacksonville squadron, a close friend of theirs, someone they had had over to dinner many times, had died trying to take off from the deck of a carrier in a routine practice session a few miles out in the Atlantic. The catapult that propelled aircraft off the deck lost pressure and his ship just dribbled off the end of the deck, with its engine roaring vainly, and fell sixty feet into the ocean and sank like a brick, and he vanished, *just like that.*

Pete had been transferred to Patuxent River, which was known in Navy vernacular as Pax River, to enter the Navy's new test-pilot school. This was considered a major step up in the career of a young Navy aviator. Now that the Korean War was over and there was no combat flying, all the hot young pilots aimed for flight test. In the military they always said "flight test" and not "test flying." Jet aircraft had been in use for barely ten years at the time, and the Navy was testing new jet fighters continually. Pax River was the Navy's prime test center.

Jane liked the house they bought at Pax River. She didn't like it as much as the little house in Jacksonville, but then she and Pete hadn't designed this one. They lived in a community called North Town Creek, six miles from the base. North Town Creek, like the base, was on a scrub-pine peninsula that stuck out into Chesapeake Bay. They were tucked in amid the pine trees. (Once more!) All around were rhododendron bushes. Pete's classwork and his flying duties were very demanding. Everyone in his flight-test class, Group 20, talked about how difficult it was—and obviously loved it, because in Navy flying this was the big league. The young men in Group 20 and their wives were Pete and Jane's entire social world. They associated with no one else. They constantly invited each other to dinner during the week; there was a Group party at someone's house practically every weekend; and they would go off on outings to fish or waterski in Chesapeake Bay. In a way they could not have associated with anyone else, at least not easily, because the boys could talk only about one thing: their flying. One of the phrases that kept running through the conversation was "pushing the outside of the envelope." The "envelope" was a flight-test term referring to the limits of a particular aircraft's performance, how tight a turn it could make at such and such a speed, and so on. "Pushing the outside," probing the outer limits, of the envelope seemed to be the great challenge and satisfaction of flight test. At first "pushing the outside of the envelope" was not a particularly terrifying phrase to hear. It sounded once more as if the boys were just talking about sports.

Then one sunny day a member of the Group, one of the happy lads they always had dinner with and drank with and went waterskiing with, was coming in for a landing at the base in an A3J attack plane. He let his airspeed fall too low before he extended his flaps, and the ship stalled out, and he crashed and was burned beyond recognition. And they brought out the bridge coats and sang about those in peril in the air and put the bridge coats away, and the Indians who were left talked about the accident after dinner one night. They shook their heads and said it was a damned shame, but he should have known better than to wait so long before lowering the flaps.

Barely a week had gone by before another member of the Group was coming in for a landing in the same type of aircraft, the A3J, making a ninety-degree turn to his final approach, and something went wrong with the controls, and he ended up with one rear stabilizer wing up and the other one down, and his ship rolled in like a corkscrew from eight hundred feet up and crashed, and he was burned beyond recognition. And the bridge coats came out and they sang about those in peril in the air and then they put the bridge coats away and after dinner one night they mentioned that the departed had been a good man but was inexperienced, and when the malfunction in the controls put him in that bad corner, he didn't know how to get out of it.

Every wife wanted to cry out: "Well, my God! The *machine* broke! What makes *any* of you think you would have come out of it any better!" Yet intuitively Jane and the rest of them knew it wasn't right even to suggest that. Pete never indicated for a moment that he thought any such thing could possibly happen to him. It seemed not only wrong but dangerous to challenge a young pilot's confidence by posing the question. And that, too, was part of the unofficial protocol for the Officer's Wife. From now on every time Pete was late coming in from the flight line, she would worry. She began to wonder if—no! *assume!*—he had found his way into one of those corners they all talked about so spiritedly, one of those little dead ends that so enlivened conversation around here.

Not long after that, another good friend of theirs went up in an F-4, the Navy's newest and hottest fighter plane, known as the Phantom. He reached twenty thousand feet and then nosed over and dove straight into Chesapeake Bay. It turned out that a hose connection was missing in his oxygen system and he had suffered hypoxia and passed out at the high altitude. And the bridge coats came out and they lifted a prayer about those in peril in the air and the bridge coats were put away and the little Indians were incredulous. How could anybody fail to check his hose connections? And how could anybody be in such poor condition as to pass out *that quickly* from hypoxia?

A couple of days later Jane was standing at the window of her house in North Town Creek. She saw some smoke rise above the pines from over in the direction of the flight line. Just that, a column of smoke; no explosion or sirens or any other sound. She went to another room, so as not to have to think about it, but there was no explanation for the smoke. She went back to the window. In the yard of a house across the street she saw a group of people . . . standing there and looking at her house, as if trying to decide what to do. Jane looked away—but she couldn't keep from looking out again. She caught a glimpse of *a certain figure* coming up the walkway toward her front door. She knew exactly who it was. She had had nightmares like this. And yet this was no dream. She was wide awake and alert. Never more alert in her entire life! Frozen, completely defeated by the sight, she simply waited for the bell to ring. She waited, but there was not a sound. Finally she could stand it no more. In real life, unlike her dream life, Jane was both too self-possessed and too polite to scream through the door: "Go away!" So she opened it. There was no one there, no one at all. There was no group of people on the lawn across the way and no one to be seen for a hundred yards in any direction along the lawns and leafy rhododendron roads of North Town Creek.

Then began a cycle in which she had both the nightmares and the hallucinations, continually. Anything could touch off an hallucination: a ball of smoke, a telephone ring that stopped before she could answer it, the sound of a siren, even the sound of trucks starting up (crash trucks!). Then she would glance out the window, and a certain figure would be coming up the walk, and she would wait for the bell. The only difference between the dreams and the hallucinations was that the scene of the dreams was always the little white house in Jacksonville. In both cases, the feeling that *this time it has happened* was quite real.

The star pilot in the class behind Pete's, a young man who was the main rival of their good friend Al Bean, went up in a fighter to do some power-dive tests. One of the most demanding disciplines in flight test was to accustom yourself to making precise readings from the control panel in the same moment that you were pushing the outside of the envelope. This young man put his ship into the test dive and was still reading out the figures, with diligence and precision and great discipline, when he augered straight into the oyster flats and was burned beyond recognition. And the bridge coats came out and they sang about those in peril in the air and the bridge coats were put away, and the little Indians remarked that the departed was a swell guy and a brilliant student of flying; a little too *much* of a student, in fact; he hadn't bothered to look out the window at the real world soon enough. Beano—Al Bean—wasn't quite so brilliant; on the other hand, he was still here.

Like many other wives in Group 20 Jane wanted to talk about the whole situation, the incredible series of fatal accidents, with her husband and the other members of the Group, to find out how they were taking it. But somehow the unwritten protocol forbade discussions of this subject, which was the fear of death. Nor could Jane or any of the rest of them talk, really *have a talk*, with anyone around the base. You could talk to another wife about being worried. But what good did it do? Who *wasn't* worried? You were likely to get a look that said: *"Why dwell on it?"* Jane might have gotten away with divulging the matter of the nightmares. But *hallucinations?* There was no room in Navy life for any such anomalous tendency as that.

By now the bad string had reached ten in all, and almost all of the dead had been close friends of Pete and Jane, young men who had been in their house many times, young men who had sat across from Jane and chattered like the rest of them about the grand adventure of military flying. And the survivors still sat around *as before*—with the same inexplicable exhilaration! Jane kept watching Pete for some sign that his spirit was cracking, but she saw none. He talked a mile a minute, kidded and joked, laughed with his Hickory Kid cackle. He always had. He still enjoyed the company of members of the group like Wally Schirra and Jim Lovell. Many young pilots were taciturn and cut loose with the strange fervor of this business only in the air. But Pete and Wally and Jim were not reticent; not in any situation. They loved to kid around. Pete called Jim Lovell "Shaky," because it was the last thing a pilot would want to be called. Wally Schirra was outgoing to the point of hearty; he loved practical jokes and dreadful puns, and so on. The three of them—even *in the midst of this bad string!*—would love to get on a subject such as accident-prone Mitch Johnson. Accident-prone Mitch Johnson, it seemed, was a Navy pilot whose life was in the hands of two angels, one of them bad and the other one good. The bad angel would put him into accidents that would have annihilated any ordinary pilot, and the good angel would bring him out of them without a scratch. Just the other day—this was the sort of story Jane would hear them tell— Mitch Johnson was coming in to land on a carrier. But he came in short, missed the flight deck, and crashed into the fantail, below the deck. There was a tremendous explosion, and the rear half of the plane fell into the water in flames. Everyone on the flight deck said, "Poor Johnson. The good angel was off duty." They were still debating how to remove the debris and his mortal remains when a phone rang on the bridge. A somewhat dopey voice said, "This is Johnson. Say, listen, I'm down here in the supply hold and the hatch is locked and I can't find the lights and I can't see a god-damned thing and I tripped over a cable and I think I hurt my leg." The officer on the bridge slammed the phone down, then vowed to find out what morbid sonofabitch could pull a phone prank at a time like this. Then the phone rang again, and the man with the dopey voice managed to establish the fact that he was, indeed, Mitch Johnson. The good angel had not left his side. When he smashed into the fantail, he hit some empty ammunition drums, and they cushioned the impact, leaving him groggy but not seriously hurt. The fuselage had blown to pieces; so he just stepped out onto the fantail and opened a hatch that led into the supply hold. It was pitch black in there, and there were cables all across the floor, holding down spare aircraft engines. Accident-prone Mitch Johnson kept tripping over these cables until he found a telephone. Sure enough, the one injury he had was a bruised shin from tripping over a cable. The man was accident-prone! Pete and Wally and Jim absolutely cracked up over stories like this. It was amazing. Great sports yarns! Nothing more than that.

A few days later Jane was out shopping at the Pax River commissary on Saunders Road, near the main gate to the base. She heard the sirens go off at the field, and then she heard the engines of the crash trucks start up. This time Jane was determined to keep calm. Every instinct made her want to rush home, but she forced herself to stay in the commissary and continue shopping. For thirty minutes she went through the motions of completing her shopping list. Then she drove home to North Town Creek. As she reached the house, she saw a figure going up the sidewalk. It was a man. Even from the back there was no question as to who he was. He had on a black suit, and there was a white band around his neck. It was her minister, from the Episcopal Church. She stared, and this vision did not come and go. The figure kept on walking up the front walk. She was not asleep now, and she was not inside her house glancing out the front window. She was outside in her car in front of her house. She was not dreaming, and she was not hallucinating, and the figure kept walking up toward her front door.

The commotion at the field was over one of the most extraordinary things that even veteran pilots had ever seen at Pax River. And they had all seen it, because practically the entire flight line had gathered out on the field for it, as if it had been an air show.

Conrad's friend Ted Whelan had taken a fighter up, and on takeoff there had been a structural failure that caused a hydraulic leak. A red warning light showed up on Whelan's panel, and he had a talk with the ground. It was obvious that the leak would cripple the controls before he could get the ship back down to the field for a landing. He would have to bail out; the only question was where and when, and so they had a talk about that. They decided that he should jump at 8,100 feet at such-and-such a speed, directly over the field. The plane would crash into the Chesapeake Bay, and he would float down to the field. Just as coolly as anyone could have asked for it, Ted Whelan lined the ship up to come across the field at 8,100 feet precisely and he punched out, ejected.

Down on the field they all had their faces turned up to the sky. They saw Whelan pop out of the cockpit. With his Martin-Baker seat-parachute rig strapped on, he looked like a little black geometric lump a mile and a half up in the blue. They watched him as he started dropping. Everyone waited for the parachute to open. They waited a few more seconds, and then they waited some more. The little shape was getting bigger and bigger and picking up tremendous speed. Then there came an unspeakable instant at which everyone on the field who knew anything about parachute jumps knew what was going to happen. Yet even for them it was an unearthly feeling, for no one had ever seen any such thing happen so close up, from start to finish, from what amounted to a grandstand seat. Now the shape was going so fast and coming so close it began to play tricks on the eyes. It seemed to stretch out. It became much bigger and hurtled toward them at a terrific speed, until they couldn't make out its actual outlines at all. Finally there was just a streaking black blur before their eyes, followed by what seemed like an explosion. Except that it was not an explosion; it was the tremendous *crack* of Ted Whelan, his helmet, his pressure suit, and his seat-parachute rig smashing into the center of the runway, precisely on target, right in front of the crowd; an absolute bull's-eye. Ted Whelan had no doubt been alive until the instant of impact. He had had about thirty seconds to watch the Pax River base and the peninsula and Baltimore County and continental America and the entire comprehensible world rise up to smash him. When they lifted his body up off the concrete, it was like a sack of fertilizer.

Pete took out the bridge coat again and he and Jane and all the little Indians went to the funeral for Ted Whelan. That it hadn't been Pete was not solace enough for Jane. That the preacher had not, in fact, come to her front door as the Solemn Friend of Widows and Orphans, but merely for a church call . . . had not brought peace and relief. That

Pete still didn't show the slightest indication of thinking that any unkind fate awaited him no longer lent her even a moment's courage. The next dream and the next hallucination, and the next and the next, merely seemed more real. For she now *knew*. She now knew the subject and the essence of this enterprise, even though not a word of it had passed anybody's lips. She even knew why Pete—the Princeton boy she met at a deb party at the Gulph Mills Club!—would never quit, never withdraw from this grim business, unless in a coffin. And God knew, and she knew, there was a coffin waiting for each little Indian.

Seven years later, when a reporter and a photographer from *Life* magazine actually stood near her in her living room and watched her face, while outside, on the lawn, a crowd of television crewmen and newspaper reporters waited for a word, an indication, anything—perhaps a glimpse through a part in a curtain!—waited for some sign of what she felt—when one and all asked with their ravenous eyes and, occasionally, in so many words: "How do you feel?" and "Are you scared?"—America wants to know!— it made Jane want to laugh, but in fact she couldn't even manage a smile.

"Why ask *now?*" she wanted to say. But they wouldn't have had the faintest notion of what she was talking about.

THE AGE OF LOVE

JERRY STAHL

Her husband invented panty shields.

"They're going to be very big," she told me. "Bob used to say, 'Create a need, then push the solution.'"

This was 1969. I was fourteen years old. We were sitting next to each other on a plane from Pittsburgh to San Francisco. I had no idea what she was talking about.

Doris later told me she was forty. But I couldn't tell. When I first saw her, in the airport lounge, it was from the back. She was bent over a lady in a wheelchair, giving her a goodbye kiss. By chance I gazed over at this tableau. I was instantly entranced by the view under her rising hem. My eyes followed hungrily up over the backs of her thighs, under her girdle to a thrilling darkness the mere thought of which had me craning my head right and left to see if any other passengers saw me peeking.

At fourteen, a virgin and chronic masturbator, I knew I could file away this glimpse and call up the memory of those mysterious creamy thighs for unlimited sessions of self-abuse in the months and years to come. At that age, I don't know that I expected to ever even have sex. It was enough, really, just to have actually, almost, gotten a peek of the exalted area. Which may explain my alarm when the woman stood up, looked my way, and turned out to be my mother's age.

I wasn't sure whether I should still be excited. Or if the lines in her face should somehow cancel out the thrill I felt at nearly seeing between her legs. She wore butterfly glasses, another Mom-like detail, and a neck scarf printed over with little penguins. It was all very confusing. I felt my face flush into hot red blotches. For the first time in my life I wondered if I might be perverted. Though I wasn't entirely sure what a pervert was.

To disguise my discomfort, I pretended to read my hardback copy of *The Call of the Wild*. It was a Bar Mitzvah gift from my grandmother. By now I was convinced the entire waiting room was staring at me, that everyone in the immediate vicinity was whispering about the young boy who got a boner looking up a skirt that might have been his mom's.

It would not have surprised me, at that moment, if some kind of Erection Police swooped into gate number four, guns drawn, led by some burly old veteran with a bullhorn who broadcast the situation to the folks on hand. "It's all right, ladies and gentlemen. It's all right . . . We've got a lad here who seems to be aroused by the sight of a heinie that could belong to his mother . . . We'll take care of it, folks. We've seen a thousand punks like him."

When I ventured to glance up again, I noticed that she'd been joined by a couple her age. I knew at once that the woman was her sister, and the man probably her brother-in-law. Both ladies wore their reddish hair brushed up in the back and down in the front, like Lucille Ball. The husband, who seemed to be a real joker, sported a short-sleeve Steelers shirt and arms so dense with hair I could see it from my seat. I wondered, for the millionth time, when *my* arms would start sprouting such a crop. Until recently, I hadn't been hairy anywhere, and it tormented me.

The husband leaned down to the old lady and made a face—bug-eyed, tongue-wagging—and both his wife and the lady I'd peeked at broke into gales of helpless, showy laughter. Except that my lady, as I'd already begun to call her, did not really seem to be enjoying herself. She chain-smoked, she kept looking all over the place, and her two hands never stopped touching, as if the one had to constantly remind the other that it was not alone.

When our glances met, for the briefest second, there was a nervous, almost hysterical quality to her grin. Her lips made a show of mirth, but her eyes glimmered with a desperation I could recognize. It was all so clear.

She's not married. They're sorry for her. She's joking around to hide how bad she feels.

Of course, I knew that feeling. That's how I felt all the time. As I sat there, pretending to read Jack London, spying on Mr. and Mrs. Hairy Arms, on old Moms in the wheelchair, and on my secret soul mate, the Unhappy Girdle Woman, this sense of knowing exactly how she felt—how different, how ashamed, how uncomfortable—was absolutely overwhelming.

I didn't even realize I was staring until *The Call of the Wild* clattered to the floor.

There were a few reasons my parents wanted to send me to California. But only one that the three of us could actually speak about. My sister Trudy had moved to Berkeley the previous year with her husband, Vance, and everybody thought it would be nice if I went for a couple weeks to visit.

The truth behind this sentiment was not so nice. My parents hated their son-in-law. "Vance!" my mother had spit right up to the minute of their wedding. "What kind of name is Vance?"

It was her habit, when she loathed someone—which she did with alarming frequency—to find some innocuous detail and rant about it as the source of her boundless repulsion. "Forget that the boy looks like a sneak-thief with those little eyes of his," she'd holler from the bedroom. "Forget that he said *from day one* that he had no intention of getting a job. Forget that it broke your father's heart the day *that thing* married your sister . . . *What kind of a name is Vance?*"

My sister had upped and married him, at twenty, after a two-year engagement to Larry, a brilliant, suit-wearing pre-law student from Syracuse my parents both adored. Larry was perfect son-in-law material.

In my twelve-year-old naïveté, even I did not understand what Trudy was thinking. Until one day, during one of our long-distance chats, she told me she broke it off when she realized Larry's hair was thinning. "I just didn't want to wake up beside a bald man in a suit," she said. "Would you?" I said that I wouldn't. Vance wore a Che Guevara T-shirt and holey bell-bottoms every day. He also supported an enormous ball of frizzy hair he called his "Jew-fro," and refused to cut it off for their wedding until my father gave him five hundred dollars. Over the years, the "haircut deal" proved another perennial in my mother's boudoir-shouting repertoire.

The truth is, my mother's bedroom habits were another reason for this trip. Along with the reconnaissance aspect—my parents refused to visit my sister now that she'd married Vance, and wanted to send me out to check up on them—was the fact that my mother had started "staying in" again.

"Staying in" was family code for not getting out of bed. For not washing up or getting dressed or doing much of anything but staying horizontal and shouting out peculiar comments or requests for food. My mother would lie in the dark for days at a time. After a while the room grew thick with her scent, a close, private muskiness that drove my father, if he was in town, to sleep downstairs on the couch. When he was on the road—he sold novelty items, supplying "Joke & Gag" stores as far away as Duluth or Buffalo—it was just me and Mom.

No matter what, during daylight hours, it fell to me to do bedroom duty. "Bring me a peach!" she'd croak from the pungent dark. If I had a friend over after school, I'd smart from embarrassment at having to stop playing and hop to for this creepy, disembodied voice. Upstairs, with the drapes shut against the afternoon sun, she would throw back the blankets, instantly filling the air with great gusts of Momness. "Wanna cuddle? Wanna play Mommy's little boy like we used to?"

"I didn't know anybody else was home," the friend would say when I came back down. Then he'd look at me in that way people look at you when something's off, when something's wrong in a way that you don't want to talk about. "Is that your mother? Is she sick, is that why it smells?" And whatever I'd say, whatever I'd come up with as a cover, they'd always treat me a little differently the next day in school. I didn't have a lot of friends.

Sometimes a whole year went by without my mother "staying in." But now she was doing it again. And it was worse than ever. My father told me she'd be going "on vacation" soon. Which meant another visit to Western Psychiatric. This seemed like a good time to get on a plane and visit Trudy in California.

When we finally boarded, it didn't even surprise me that she was 21-F and I was 21-E. She had the window and I had the aisle. Long before we took off, the heat from her leg was so intense that I leaned her way, feigning boyish fascination in the weedy runway, just to see if I was imagining the oven-like warmth or if she were really burning. What I felt, when I let my right thigh graze accidentally against her left, was an even higher centigrade than I had imagined.

My seatmate pressed back at once. As possessed as I was by sudden interest in runway activities, she edged against me and craned her neck to take in the cart piled high with Samsonite. Still not speaking, we both pretended utter absorption in the sluggish hand-to-hand loading of each suitcase into the hold.

I could hardly believe what was happening. My whole body shook with excitement. I had to clamp my jaw shut to keep my teeth from chattering. Drawing on some heretofore undreamed of reservoir of nerve, a reserve of untested manliness, I risked still more pressure.

This time my maneuver was blatant. I not only jammed my limb lengthwise against hers, I let my hand dip casually off the armrest, until my little finger dangled against her thigh. To my astonishment, her response was just as bold. The flesh of her hip under her drip-dry dress seemed to stream right through my stiff white Levi's. But that was nothing. Still facing the porthole—baggage-handling was just so fascinating!—she settled her left hand atop my right, pushing downward, so that my initial, timid exploration was hurtled instantly into another dimension.

For a moment, I had to hold my breath to fight off the excited tremors that threatened to slide me out of my seat in a complete swoon. My neck was so stiff I thought it would snap. I had my hand up her wash 'n' wear dress. Clamped between her warm, thin thighs, my fingers jammed against what felt like a moist slice of toast. Toast wrapped in nylon.

To counter this dizzy arousal, I drew back from the window and studied the unlikely object of my desire. Up close, I noticed, her scalp was visible through her auburn hair. I didn't think that women could go bald, yet had to wonder if she might be even older than I suspected. Her hands, too, were less than pretty, the backs showing raised veins that looked puffy and a little blue. Yet even if there was something old ladyish about her, it didn't matter. I'd never been so close to touching a girl—let alone a grown woman—"down there" as I was now. A state of affairs made all the more tempestuous by the fact neither of us acknowledged what we were doing.

Our limbs now jammed together from flank to ankle, I took the liberty of canting my face still nearer, until I could breathe her heat, the way you would a humidifier placed in the room to fend off croup. She smelled vaguely of camphor, an odor I recognized from having to rub Bag Balm on my schnauzer's teats after she'd suckled puppies. Camphor was Bag Balm's main ingredient, and I found myself stirred anew at the prospect of rubbing the pungent emollient on my neighbor at first sign of a flare-up. If the truth be told, I'd even been a little aroused at rubbing the stuff on Queenie. But this was better. This was a thousand times better, and we hadn't even taken off yet.

By takeoff, I'd managed to hook a finger over the elastic lip of her girdle, somewhere in the waist area, engaging a patch of skin that felt taut and fiery.

It was then I noticed that I had an audience.

One row up, across the aisle, a heavyset old man in bifocals was twisted completely around in his seat. He stared back at us, horrified. Unable to peel his eyes from my seatmate's parted knees. You could tell he wanted to say something, but didn't know what. He kept opening his mouth, then closing it again, like a goldfish.

I decided to look nonchalant. As nonchalant as any fourteen-year-old with half his arm up the dress of a woman old enough to be his mother could. This just made the old guy more furious. He tore off his glasses and scowled. He began clearing his throat, very loudly, all the while keeping his irate gaze fixed on my offending paw. I began to fear someone else would notice. I imagined how they'd turn around, somebody would see them, then *they'd* start staring, and so on, until finally the whole plane was shouting and pointing. For all I knew, the stewardess could arrest me, the captain could drag me off to some secret airplane cell, maybe behind the toilet, where I'd stay locked up until we landed in San Francisco and the FBI scooped me up to ship me back to Pittsburgh. I could already hear my mother, barking down from the bedroom to my Dad when she saw me on the news. *"Herman, I always knew that boy was sick!"*

To my infinite relief, the gaping senior finally turned away. But no sooner did I relax than he spun back around, this time accompanied by the apple-cheeked crone to his right. Side by side, they looked like the Wilsons, the next-door neighbors on *Dennis the Menace*. If Mr. and Mrs. Wilson had caught Dennis the Menace masturbating, I was sure, they'd have worn the same looks of shock and disappointment.

As I stared back, I felt like two different people—cracked by the opposing entities that had slugged it out inside me my whole life. The split was clearest in school. From first grade on, straight As were matched by straight Fs in discipline. Watching the shocked old man and his wife, the A-making half of me was mortified. But the F-half would have liked nothing better than to cause a couple of heart attacks.

"Bob never cared," she said.

"What?"

I was so stunned to hear her speak that my hand popped free. For a second I just sat there, staring at the thin red band where the elastic had bit into my wrist. Then I eased under her dress again, like a small animal heading for its burrow.

She turned from the window with a little smile. Her tone had been matter of fact. But when she looked at me she seemed to get nervous again. Her face broke into the expression she had worn with the people at the airport, like she was just about to laugh or scream and had no idea which it would be.

"Oh sorry," she said. "Bob was the husband. I'm Doris."

"Doris," I repeated, like a man mouthing an unfamiliar language. Up close her eyes were a startling blue. "I'm, uh, Larry," I lied, and for some reason her face relaxed.

I glanced back at the fuming seniors, but, to my relief, they'd turned toward the front again.

Doris checked, too, then aimed those strange eyes back at me.

"What I'm saying, Bob never cared," she began again. "About people, whatever, what they thought. Like when he went to see his project supervisor at Johnson & Johnson to pitch them on shields. Bob invented them, you know. Panty shields were his baby all the way."

She stopped, awaiting my reaction, though I was still fuzzy on the particulars. I pictured something like gladiators used to fend off spears, only smaller, and lodged somewhere south of the border. Then my fingers made their way back to the toast-barrier, and Doris smiled.

"That's right. That's one of the originals. I still have all the prototypes. It's my way of keeping him here, with me. I think he would have wanted it that way."

Again she awaited my reaction, again I was afraid I came up short. "That's . . . that's beautiful," I said. It seemed like the right time to quote Rod McKuen or something. My sister'd given me one of his books for my last birthday, but all I could remember was the title. "*Listen to the Warm*," I said.

It was the most grown-up thing I'd ever uttered. Doris shook her head and smiled gratefully. She was old, maybe older than my mother, but at the same time there was something young about her. I noticed for the first time the way her lipstick formed a kind of ready-made kiss on her mouth.

Doris pressed her legs together, and once again I was shocked by the heat against my flattened palm, and that faint whiff of camphor. I got an erection again, but there was something different about it. I felt all kinds of things at once. For all I knew I was falling in love. My face blotched up red again, but she didn't say anything.

"The J&J guys looked at him like he was nuts." Her voice had gone a little husky. "Some of them were actually mad. *Off-ended.*"

She paused, resting her head of Lucille Ball hair against the airplane window, and I ventured an exploratory probe in an untried direction, toward her thigh, away from Bob's prototype. I soon found myself yanking back a rugged strand of elastic and feeling something I'd never felt before. Something I'd only dreamed about feeling. Feeling *hair.*

"Mmmph," sighed Doris, shifting slightly, guiding my arm with her thighs. "Ten little men in pinstripe suits at a teak table the size of Guam. And you know what he said? 'If you boys don't know why this product is gonna make you a million dollars, I feel sorry for you. You've obviously got some very unhappy gals back at the ranch.' Do you believe it?"

I said I did, though this wasn't exactly true. I'd missed something, even though I'd heard everything she said. I felt fourteen again. On top of which I was getting really turned on from where she'd steered my hand—and the fact that she was the one who steered it there. Try as I might, I could only picture the shield as a kind of sewer lid, and I knew that wasn't right either. I wondered if they were hand painted, maybe even tie-dyed. As I was thinking, I felt my way along the side of the shield, past that tingly patch of fur, to what felt like a ridge of warm meringue.

I'd never done this before. I didn't know what happened to women when they got aroused. I'd never aroused one. I didn't know they got wet. Or if that was some kind of a problem. My fourteen-year-old mind was trying to wrap itself around things it pretended to comprehend and didn't.

As I listened for clues, I kept my fingers moving. I felt like a man doing an appendectomy out of a textbook.

Doris got a dreamy look as she talked. The plane had hit some kind of turbulence but I barely noticed. "It was important to Bob, see, that this was a positive product. Not, you know, something girls are going to buy because they've got some discharge. That's what the Board didn't get. They thought it was just for girls to handle their flow. Girls who didn't want the bulk of a heavy napkin. Girls with some condition that requires insulation!"

"Insulation," I repeated, when I realized she was waiting for a reply. My father, the novelty marketeer, had been passing along tips on What Makes a Top Salesman since I was three. One of his favorites was, "If you don't know what to say next, repeat what the other fellow just said." Until this, I'd never had occasion to use any of his advice. We weren't very close. But now that I'd taken a tip, and it worked, I wished I could call him up and thank him. "Insulation," I marched out again, adding *"huh!"* this time. Doris ate it up.

"Exactly!" she cried, absolutely beaming. When she beamed she didn't look old at all. It was confusing. "Exactly," she yelped again, pronouncing it "egg-ZACK-ly" this time. Her voice was getting louder, and I had to fight the urge to shush her. I had a thing about public scenes, since my mother was always making them. The first emotion I remember having is embarrassment—if that's an emotion. But Doris preached on, oblivious. "Arousal is not some kind of condition a girl has to treat—it's a treat a girl has to condition! That's what Bob said. That's what panty shields are all about!"

In the middle of this, I caught the head of the man in front of us tilt to the side. As I hitched my seat belt, *The Call of the Wild* had slipped off my lap and landed up the aisle, beside his brogans. This was before Doris had plunked down. He made a show of reading the title, then smacked a thick red hand off the cover. "Good book, son. Good clean book." That's when I saw the priest collar.

The priest's face, I noticed, was almost as red as his hand. Especially the nose, which close-up was pocked and dotted with tiny hairs, like a large strawberry. I said I like the book, too, though in fact I hadn't got past page one. *That* I read about forty times, unable to concentrate after my secret undie peek.

"More young people your age should read good books like this."

"Yes, Father," I said. I'd never called anybody "Father" in my life, including my own father, who was always "Dad." But I wanted the priest to think I was Catholic. I wanted him to like me, though I wasn't sure why.

"And you," he announced, as if he'd given the matter serious thought and come to this lofty conclusion, "are a fine young boy. A fine young boy." He gave my hand a little squeeze and handed over the book. "Aren't you?"

"Well, yeah. I mean SURE!" I blurted, half-shouting though he was only inches away. I did not feel like a fine boy. I felt like some kind of sex criminal. But I didn't tell that to the priest.

THE AGE OF LOVE

He nodded, despite my sputtering response, and tapped me on the head, gently mussing my Brylcreemed-but-still-frizzy hair. Now here I was, a mere hour or so later, shattering my good-boy image, chatting about panty apparatus with a strange female. I watched the priest's skull rotate slowly to the right, like some hairy radar device, until his ear was aimed at us.

I don't know how I fell asleep. I had a dream that Queenie gave birth to pups on my lap. Except that the puppies kept sneaking back in. I had to search around inside her to try and find them. My hand was soaking. I was scared. But whenever I looked down, there was Queenie, gazing up at me with her grateful schnauzer eyes, her little pink tongue hanging out, panting away. Instead of a collar, she had a penguin scarf around her neck. I remember thinking, in the dream, *I really love this dog. I love her more than my parents.* But then something happened. I couldn't get in. There was a shield, but it was invisible, like in the Johnson's Wax commercials. "Bullets bounce off!" said the announcer. And suddenly my arms were empty.

I woke up hugging Doris. More than hugging, holding onto her. Squeezing, the way my mother used to when she wanted me to play "cuddle boy." When she was staying in, and it was afternoon forever, and I had to lie in her seething bed, my face in the hollow of her throat, cheek mashed to her bosom, gulping hot, under-the-blanket fumes until my eyes watered and I pretended I had to go to the bathroom and ran away.

"I'm going to call you 'Dreamy,'" Doris laughed when I blinked up at her. Something was different. I tried to disengage myself but she said she wouldn't let me. She

229

wrapped her arms around mine, so that I looked up at her at an angle, from under her chin.

Finally I realized. "You did something. Your hair . . . it's—"

"Step aside Judy Collins!"

"Judy Collins," I repeated dumbly, eyeing the glossy tresses that now fell over her shoulders. When you don't know what to say, say the last thing they said.

"Like it?" she asked.

"Well . . . yeah! I really do!" Of course, I would have lied to make her feel good. But I didn't have to. Even though I remembered my mother once carping that women should not have long hair after forty unless they were witches. Mom was full of these rules, just like Dad had a million tips. But Mom had never met Doris—the mere thought made me shrink. The Judy Collins look was perfect.

I had to lean back and rub my eyes. For a second or two I couldn't take her in. Along with the folksinger hairdo, she'd managed to slip on a flower-print peasant dress, granny glasses, and love beads. There was even a peace-sign decal on her forearm. She looked like she could be her own freaky daughter.

"Wow!" was all I could say. Somewhere under there was the nervous, unhappy, chain-smoking woman I'd spotted bent over a wheelchair at the Greater Pittsburgh Airport. But she was buried pretty far down.

"Are you, like, from San Francisco?" I asked.

"I am now," she said, a little loopily. This was when I noticed the trio of mini–Southern Comfort bottles peeking out of the magazine slot in front of her. "Bob would have wanted it that way." A chiffon hanky appeared in her hand, dabbing away tears. "I swear"—she pronounced it, lurching toward me for emphasis, "shwear"—"that man died of a broken spirit."

Doris, it turned out, had just come from her husband's funeral. The woman with the matching Lucille Ball hair was indeed her sister. But more than that, the jokey guy was Bob's baby brother, Bo. Bob and Bo had married Doris and Dot in a ceremony that got them national attention. Allen Funt, of *Candid Camera*, actually filmed the ceremony for an episode of his own short-lived *Candid* spin-off, *You Won't Believe This!* But the show, she said, was canceled before their double wedding made it on the air.

"Story of our life," she sighed, reaching for the third of her Southern Comforts to pour into her glass of Coke. "I used to tease Bob that we should change our last name to Almost, 'cause of all the stuff that almost happened. And all the stuff that did happen that almost didn't."

She stopped talking then and looked at me a little tearily. Everybody else on the plane seemed to be asleep or numb. The only overhead lights left on were hers and mine. Even the priest appeared to have given up his eavesdropping, having nodded off with his head still askew, his hairy ear positioned for maximum intake.

There was no sound but the hum of the engines that carried us through the night. The plastic glass was in her hand but she wasn't drinking any.

"Could I have some of that?" I asked, before I knew I was going to.

Doris gave a chuckle. Even her laugh seemed different in her hippie get-up. "Are you a juvenile delinquent? How old are you?"

"Almost old enough."

"Well, why not?" she said, offering the drink with two hands, to keep it steady. "What I've just been through, I should get everybody on this tin trap drunk. Including the pilot!"

With this she grabbed the glass back and took a swig.

"First the bastards didn't want the thing, then they stole the patent. They made him jump through hoops, then they shot him in midair. Murder in the boardroom, baby. If old Bob had a shield over his heart, he might still be alive."

Doris let out a long sigh and handed me the drink again. There was almost enough left for a whole gulp.

"I thought it was 'The Summer of Love,'" I said. "That's what they called it in *Newsweek*."

"Don't think small," said Doris. "It's the whole damn age. Howzabout I teach you how to love right now so you'll be ready for it? So you won't have to do any catching up later?"

"That sounds all right."

"Well, don't fall off your seat or anything."

"It sounds great, really. I think everybody else is asleep."

"Pretending," she mumbled, and slowly raised her arms for me to come closer. "Everybody's probably watching right now and wishing they were you."

"Well, jeez . . ."

I felt my throat go dry and couldn't think of anything else to say. I hoped it was too dark for her to see my face flush up. I was already beginning to shake a little. I wondered if my whole life I'd start to twitch whenever things got exciting with a woman. But then, I figured, they'd probably never get this exciting again.

EN ROUTE TO THE CONGRESS OF DREAMS OR THE ZIPLESS FUCK

ERICA JONG

There were 117 psychoanalysts on the Pan Am flight to Vienna and I'd been treated by at least six of them. And married a seventh. God knows it was a tribute either to the shrinks' ineptitude or my own glorious unanalyzability that I was now, if anything, more scared of flying than when I began my analytic adventures some thirteen years earlier.

My husband grabbed my hand therapeutically at the moment of takeoff.

"Christ—it's like ice," he said. He ought to know the symptoms by now since he's held my hand on lots of other flights. My fingers (and toes) turn to ice, my stomach leaps upward into my rib cage, the temperature in the tip of my nose drops to the same level as the temperature in my fingers, my nipples stand up and salute the inside of my bra (or in this case, dress—since I'm not wearing a bra), and for one screaming minute my heart and the engines correspond as we attempt to prove again that the laws of aerodynamics are not the flimsy superstitions which, in my

heart of hearts, I *know* they are. Never mind the diabolical
INFORMATION TO PASSENGERS, I happen to be convinced that
only my own concentration (and that of my mother—who
always seems to *expect* her children to die in a plane crash)
keeps this bird aloft. I congratulate myself on every successful takeoff, but not too enthusiastically because it's
also part of my personal religion that the minute you grow
overconfident and really *relax* about the flight, the plane
crashes instantly. Constant vigilance, that's my motto. A
mood of cautious optimism should prevail. But actually my
mood is better described as cautious pessimism. OK, I tell
myself, we *seem* to be off the ground and into the clouds
but the danger isn't past. This is, in fact, the most perilous
patch of air. Right here over Jamaica Bay where the plane
banks and turns and the "No Smoking" sign goes off. This
may well be where we go screaming down in thousands of
flaming pieces. So I keep concentrating very hard, helping
the pilot (a reassuringly midwestern voice named Don-
nelly) fly the 250-passenger motherfucker. Thank God for
his crew cut and middle-America diction. New Yorker that
I am, I would never trust a pilot with a New York accent.

As soon as the seat-belt sign goes off and people begin
moving about the cabin, I glance around nervously to see
who's on board. There's a big-breasted mama-analyst
named Rose Schwamm-Lipkin with whom I recently had a
consultation about whether or not I should leave my current analyst (who isn't, mercifully, in evidence). There's Dr.
Thomas Frommer, the harshly Teutonic expert on anorexia
nervosa, who was my husband's first analyst. There's
kindly, rotund Dr. Arthur Feet, Jr., who was the third (and
last) analyst of my friend Pia. There's compulsive little Dr.
Raymond Schrift, who is hailing a blonde stewardess
(named "Nanci") as if she were a taxi. (I saw Dr. Schrift for

one memorable year when I was fourteen and starving my-self to death in penance for having finger-fucked on my par-ents' living-room couch. He kept insisting that the horse I was dreaming about was my father and that my periods would return if only I would "ackzept being a vohman.") There's smiling, bald Dr. Harvey Smucker, whom I saw in consultation when my first husband decided he was Jesus Christ and began threatening to walk on the water in Cen-tral Park Lake. There's foppish, hand-tailored Dr. Ernest Klumpner, the supposedly "brilliant theoretician" whose latest book is a psychoanalytic study of John Knox. There's black-bearded Dr. Stanton Rappoport-Rosen, who recently gained notoriety in New York analytic circles when he moved to Denver and branched out into something called "Cross-Country Group Ski-Therapy." There's Dr. Arnold Aaronson pretending to play chess on a magnetic board with his new wife (who was his patient until last year), the singer Judy Rose. Both of them are surreptitiously looking around to see who is looking at them—and for one moment my eyes and Judy Rose's meet. Judy Rose became famous in the fifties for recording a series of satirical ballads about pseudo-intellectual life in New York. In a whiny and delib-erately unmusical voice, she sang the saga of a Jewish girl who takes courses at the New School, reads the Bible for its prose, discusses Martin Buber in bed, and falls in love with her analyst. She has now become one with the role she created.

Besides the analysts, their wives, the crew, and a few poor outnumbered laymen, there were some children of analysts who'd come along for the ride. The sons were mostly sullen-faced adolescents in bell-bottoms and shoul-der-length hair who looked at their parents with a degree of cynicism and scorn which was almost palpable. I remembered myself traveling abroad with my parents as a teen-ager and always trying to pretend they weren't with me. I tried to lose them in the Louvre! To avoid them in the Uffizi! To moon alone over a Coke in a Paris café and pretend that those loud people at the next table were not—though clearly they were— my parents. (I was pretending, you see, to be a Lost Generation exile with my parents sitting three feet away.) And here I was back in my own past, or in a bad dream or a bad movie: *Analyst* and *Son of Analyst. A* planeload of shrinks and my adolescence all around me. Stranded in midair over the Atlantic with 117 analysts, many of whom had heard my long, sad story and none of whom remembered it. An ideal beginning for the nightmare the trip was going to become.

We were bound for Vienna and the occasion was his-toric. Centuries ago, wars ago, in 1938, Freud fled his fa-mous consulting room on the Berggasse when the Nazis threatened his family. During the years of the Third Reich any mention of his name was banned in Germany, and an-alysts were expelled (if they were lucky) or gassed (if they were not). Now, with great ceremony, Vienna was welcom-ing the analysts back. They were even opening a museum to Freud in his old consulting room. The mayor of Vienna was going to greet them and a reception was to be held in Vienna's pseudo-Gothic Rathaus. The enticements included free food, free Schnapps, cruises on the Danube, excursions to vineyards, singing, dancing, shenanigans, learned papers and speeches, and a tax-deductible trip to Europe. Most of all, there was to be lots of good old Austrian *Gemütlichkeit.* The people who invented *schmaltz* (and crematoria) were going to show the analysts how welcome back they were.

Welcome back! Welcome back! At least those of you who survived Auschwitz, Belsen, the London Blitz, and the co-optation of America. *Willkommen!* Austrians are nothing if not charming.

Holding the Congress in Vienna had been a hotly debated issue for years, and many of the analysts had come only reluctantly. Anti-Semitism was part of the problem, but there was also the possibility that radical students at the University of Vienna would decide to stage demonstrations. Psychoanalysis was out of favor with New Left members for being "too individualistic." It did nothing, they said, to further "the worldwide struggle toward communism."

I had been asked by a new magazine to observe all the fun and games of the Congress closely and to do a satirical article on it. I began my research by approaching Dr. Smucker near the galley, where he was being served coffee by one of the stewardesses. He looked at me with barely a glimmer of recognition.

"How do you feel about psychoanalysis returning to Vienna?" I asked in my most cheerful lady-interviewer voice. Dr. Smucker seemed taken aback by the shocking intimacy of the question. He looked at me long and searchingly.

"I'm writing an article for a new magazine called *Voyeur*," I said. I figured he'd at least have to crack a smile at the name.

"Well then," Smucker said stolidly, "how do *you* feel about it?" And he waddled off toward his short bleached-blonde wife in the blue knit dress with a tiny green alligator above her (blue) right breast.

I should have known. Why do analysts always answer a question with a question? And why should this night be different from any other night—despite the fact that we are flying in a 747 and eating unkosher food?

"The Jewish science," as anti-Semites call it. Turn every question upside down and shove it up the asker's ass. Analysts all seem to be Talmudists who flunked out of seminary in the first year. I was reminded of one of my grandfather's favorite gags:

Q: "Why does a Jew always answer a question with a question?"

A: "And why should a Jew *not* answer a question with a question?"

Ultimately, though, it was the unimaginativeness of most analysts which got me down. OK, I'd been helped a lot by my first one—the German who was going to give a paper in Vienna—but he was a rare breed: witty, self-mocking, unpretentious. He had none of the flat-footed literal-mindedness which makes even the most brilliant psychoanalysts sound so pompous. But the others I'd gone to—they were so astonishingly literal-minded. The horse you are dreaming about is your father. The kitchen stove you are dreaming about is your mother. The piles of bullshit you are dreaming about are, in reality, your analyst. This is called the *transference*. No?

You dream about breaking your leg on the ski slope. You have, in fact, just broken your leg on the ski slope and you are lying on the couch wearing a ten-pound plaster cast which has had you housebound for weeks, but has also given you a beautiful new appreciation of your toes and the civil rights of paraplegics. But the broken leg in the dream represents your own "mutilated genital." You always wanted to have a penis and now you feel guilty that you have *deliberately* broken your leg so that you can have the pleasure of the cast, no?

No!

OK, let's put the "mutilated genital" question aside. It's a dead horse, anyway. And forget about your mother the oven and your analyst the pile of shit. What do we have left except the smell? I'm not talking about the first years of analysis when you're hard at work discovering your own craziness so that you can get some work done instead of devoting your *entire* life to your neurosis. I'm talking about when both you and your husband have been in analysis as long as you can remember and it's gotten to the point where no decision, no matter how small, can be made without both analysts having an imaginary caucus on a cloud above your head. You feel rather like the Trojan warriors in the *Iliad* with Zeus and Hera fighting above them. I'm talking about the time when your marriage has become a *menage à quatre*. You, him, your analyst, his analyst. Four in a bed. This picture is definitely rated X.

We had been in this state for at least the past year. Every decision was referred to the shrink, or the shrinking process. Should we move into a bigger apartment? "Better see what's going on first." (Bennett's euphemism for: back to the couch.) Should we have a baby? "Better work things through first." Should we join a new tennis club? "Better see what's going on first." Should we get a divorce? "Better work through the *unconscious meaning* of divorce first."

Because the fact was that we'd reached that crucial time in a marriage (five years and the sheets you got as wedding presents have just about worn thin) when it's time to decide whether to buy new sheets, have a baby perhaps, and live with each other's lunacy ever after—or else give up the ghost of the marriage (throw out the sheets) and start playing musical beds all over again.

The decision was, of course, further complicated by analysis—the basic assumption of analysis being (and never mind all the evidence to the contrary) that you're getting better all the time. The refrain goes something like this:

"Oh-I-was-self-destructive-when-I-married-you-baby-but-I'm-so-much-more-healthy-now-ow-ow-ow."

(Implying that you might just choose someone better, sweeter, handsomer, smarter, and maybe even luckier in the stock market.)

To which he might reply:

"Oh-I-hated-all-women-when-I-fell-for-you-baby-but-I'm-so-much-more-healthy-now-ow-ow-ow."

(Implying that *he* might just find someone sweeter, prettier, smarter, a better cook, and maybe even due to inherit piles of bread from her father.)

"Wise up Bennett, old boy," I'd say (whenever I suspected him of thinking those thoughts), "you'd probably marry someone even more phallic, castrating, and narcissistic than I am." (First technique of being a shrink's wife is knowing how to hurl all their jargon back at them, at carefully chosen moments.)

But I was having those thoughts myself and if Bennett knew, he didn't let on. Something seemed very wrong in our marriage. Our lives ran parallel like railroad tracks. Bennett spent the day at his office, his hospital, his analyst, and then evenings at his office again, usually until nine or ten. I taught a couple of days a week and wrote the rest of the time. My teaching schedule was light, the writing was exhausting, and by the time Bennett came home, I was ready to go out and break loose. I had had plenty of solitude, plenty of long hours alone with my typewriter and my fantasies. And I seemed to meet men everywhere. The world seemed crammed with available, interesting men in a way it never had been before I was married.

What *was* it about marriage anyway? Even if you loved your husband, there came that inevitable year when fucking him turned as bland as Velveeta cheese: filling, fattening even, but no thrill to the taste buds, no bittersweet edge, no danger. And you longed for an overripe Camembert, a rare goat cheese: luscious, creamy, cloven-hoofed.

I was not against marriage. I believed in it in fact. It was necessary to have one best friend in a hostile world, one person you'd be loyal to no matter what, one person who'd always be loyal to you. But what about all those other longings which after a while marriage did nothing much to appease? The restlessness, the hunger, the thump in the gut, the thump in the cunt, the longing to be filled up, to be fucked through every hole, the yearning for dry champagne and wet kisses, for the smell of peonies in a penthouse on a June night, for the light at the end of the pier in *Gatsby* . . . Not those *things* really—because you knew that the very rich were duller than you and me—but what those things *evoked*. The sardonic, bittersweet vocabulary of Cole Porter love songs, the sad sentimental Rogers and Hart lyrics, all the romantic nonsense you yearned for with half your heart and mocked bitterly with the other half.

Growing up female in America. What a liability! You grew up with your ears full of cosmetic ads, love songs, advice columns, whoreoscopes, Hollywood gossip, and moral dilemmas on the level of TV soap operas. What litanies the advertisers of the good life chanted at you! What curious catechisms!

"Be kind to your behind." "Blush like you mean it." "Love your hair." "Want a better body? Well rearrange the one you've got." "That shine on your face should come from him, not from your skin." "You've come a long way, baby." "How to score with every male in the zodiac." "The stars and sensual you." "To a man they say Cutty Sark." "A diamond is forever." "If you're concerned about douching . . ." "Length and coolness come together." "How I solved my intimate odor problem." "Lady be cool." "Every woman alive loves Chanel No. 5." "What makes a shy girl get intimate?" *"Femme,* we named it after you."

What all the ads and all the whoreoscopes seemed to imply was that if only you were narcissistic *enough,* if only you took proper care of your smells, your hair, your boobs, your eyelashes, your armpits, your crotch, your stars, your scars, and your choice of scotch in bars—you would meet a beautiful, powerful, potent, and rich man who would satisfy every longing, fill every hole, make your heart skip a beat (or stand still), make you misty, and fly you to the moon (preferably on gossamer wings), where you would live totally satisfied forever.

And the crazy part of it was that even if you were *clever,* even if you spent your adolescence reading John Donne and Shaw, even if you studied history or zoology or physics and hoped to spend your life pursuing some difficult and challenging career—you *still* had a mind full of all the soupy longings that every high-school girl was awash in. It didn't matter, you see, whether you had an IQ of 170 or an IQ of 70, you were brainwashed all the same. Only the surface trappings were different. Only the *talk* was a little more sophisticated. Underneath it all, you longed to be annihilated by love, to be swept off your feet, to be filled up by a giant prick spouting sperm, soapsuds, silks and satins, and of course, money. Nobody bothered to tell you what marriage was really about. You weren't even provided, like European girls, with a philosophy of cynicism and practicality. You expected *not* to desire any other men after marriage. And you expected your husband not to desire any other women. Then the desires came and you were thrown into a panic of self-hatred. What an evil woman you were! How could you keep being infatuated with strange men? How could you study their bulging trousers like that? How could you sit at a meeting imagining how every man in the room would screw? How could you sit on a train fucking total strangers with your eyes? How could you *do* *that* to your husband? Did anyone ever tell you that maybe it had nothing whatever to do with your husband?

And what about those other longings which marriage stifled? Those longings to hit the open road from time to time, to discover whether you could still live alone inside your own head, to discover whether you could manage to survive in a cabin in the woods without going mad; to discover, in short, whether you were still whole after so many years of being half of something (like the back two legs of a horse outfit on the vaudeville stage).

Five years of marriage had made me itchy for all those things: itchy for men, and itchy for solitude. Itchy for sex and itchy for the life of a recluse. I knew my itches were contradictory—and that made things even worse. I knew my itches were un-American—and that made things *still* worse. It is heresy in America to embrace any way of life except as half of a couple. Solitude is un-American. It may be condoned in a man—especially if he is a "glamorous bachelor" who "dates starlets" during a brief interval between marriages. But a woman is always presumed to be alone as a result of abandonment, not choice. And she is treated that way: as a pariah. There is simply no dignified way for a woman to live alone. Oh, she can get along financially perhaps (though not nearly as well as a man), but emotionally she is never left in peace. Her friends, her family, her fellow workers never let her forget that her husbandlessness, her childlessness—her *selfishness*, in short—is a reproach to the American way of life.

243

Even more to the point: the woman (unhappy though she knows her married friends to be) can never let *herself* alone. She lives as if she were constantly on the brink of some great fulfillment. As if she were waiting for Prince Charming to take her away "from all this." All what? The solitude of living inside her own soul? The certainty of being herself instead of half of something else?

My response to all this was not (not yet) to have an affair and not (not yet) to hit the open road, but to evolve my fantasy of the Zipless Fuck. The zipless fuck was more than a fuck. It was a platonic ideal. Zipless because when you came together zippers fell away like rose petals, underwear blew off in one breath like dandelion fluff. Tongues intertwined and turned liquid. Your whole soul flowed out through your tongue and into the mouth of your lover.

For the true, ultimate zipless A-1 fuck, it was necessary that you never get to know the man very well. I had noticed, for example, how all my infatuations dissolved as soon as I really became friends with a man, became sympathetic to his problems, listened to him *kvetch* about his wife, or ex-wives, his mother, his children. After that I would like him, perhaps even love him—but without passion. And it was passion that I wanted. I had also learned that a sure way to exorcise an infatuation was to write about someone, to observe his tics and twitches, to anatomize his personality in type. After that he was an insect on a pin, a newspaper clipping laminated in plastic. I might enjoy his company, even admire him at moments, but he no longer had the power to make me wake up trembling in the middle of the night. I no longer dreamed about him. He had a face.

So another condition for the zipless fuck was brevity. And anonymity made it even better.

During the time I lived in Heidelberg I commuted to Frankfurt four times a week to see my analyst. The ride took an hour each way and trains became an important part of my fantasy life. I kept meeting beautiful men on the train, men who scarcely spoke English, men whose clichés and banalities were hidden by my ignorance of French, or Italian, or even German. Much as I hate to admit it, there are *some* beautiful men in Germany.

One scenario of the zipless fuck was perhaps inspired by an Italian movie I saw years ago. As time went by, I embellished it to suit my head. It used to play over and over again as I shuttled back and forth from Heidelberg to Frankfurt, from Frankfurt to Heidelberg:

A grimy European train compartment (Second Class). The seats are leatherette and hard. There is a sliding door to the corridor outside. Olive trees rush by the window. Two Sicilian peasant women sit together on one side with a child between them. They appear to be mother and grandmother and granddaughter. Both women vie with each other to stuff the little girl's mouth with food. Across the way (in the window seat) is a pretty young widow in a heavy black veil and tight black dress which reveals her voluptuous figure. She is sweating profusely and her eyes are puffy. The middle seat is empty. The corridor seat is occupied by an enormously fat woman with a moustache. Her huge haunches cause her to occupy almost half of the vacant center seat. She is reading a pulp romance in which the characters are photographed models and the dialogue appears in little puffs of smoke above their heads.

This fivesome bounces along for a while, the widow and the fat woman keeping silent, the mother and grandmother talking to the child and each other about the food. And then the train screeches to a halt in a town called (perhaps) CORLEONE. A tall languid-looking soldier, unshaven, but with a beautiful mop of hair, a cleft chin, and somewhat devilish, lazy eyes, enters the compartment, looks insolently around, sees the empty half-seat between the fat woman and the widow, and, with many flirtatious apologies, sits down. He is sweaty and disheveled but basically a gorgeous hunk of flesh, only slightly rancid from the heat. The train screeches out of the station.

Then we become aware only of the bouncing of the train and the rhythmic way the soldier's thighs are rubbing against the thighs of the widow. Of course, he is also rubbing against the haunches of the fat lady—and she is trying to move away from him—which is quite unnecessary because he is unaware of her haunches. He is watching the large gold cross between the widow's breasts swing back and forth in her deep cleavage. Bump. Pause. Bump. It hits one moist breast and then the other. It seems to hesitate in between as if paralyzed between two repelling magnets. The pit and the pendulum. He is hypnotized. She stares out the window, looking at each olive tree as if she had never seen olive trees before. He rises awkwardly, half-bows to the ladies, and struggles to open the window. When he sits down again his arm accidentally grazes the widow's belly. She appears not to notice. He rests his left hand on the seat between his thigh and hers and begins to wind rubber fingers around and under the soft flesh of her thigh. She continues staring at each olive tree as if she were God and had just made them and were wondering what to call them.

Meanwhile the enormously fat lady is packing away her pulp romance in an iridescent green plastic string bag full of smelly cheeses and blackening bananas. And the grandmother is rolling ends of salami in greasy newspaper. The mother is putting on the little girl's sweater and wiping her face with a handkerchief, lovingly moistened with maternal spittle. The train screeches to a stop in a town called (perhaps) PRIZZI, and the fat lady, the mother, the grandmother, and the little girl leave the compartment. Then the train begins to move again. The gold cross begins to bump, pause, bump between the widow's moist breasts, the fingers begin to curl under the widow's thighs, the widow continues to stare at the olive trees. Then the fingers are sliding between her thighs and they are parting her thighs, and they are moving upward into the fleshy gap between her heavy black stockings and her garters, and they are sliding up under her garters into the damp unpantied place between her legs.

The train enters a *galleria*, or tunnel, and in the semi-darkness the symbolism is consummated. There is the soldier's boot in the air and the dark walls of the tunnel and the hypnotic rocking of the train and the long high whistle as it finally emerges.

Wordlessly, she gets off at a town called, perhaps, BIVONA. She crosses the tracks, stepping carefully over them in her narrow black shoes and heavy black stockings. He stares after her as if he were

Adam wondering what to name her. Then he jumps up and dashes out of the train in pursuit of her. At that very moment a long freight train pulls through the parallel track obscuring his view and blocking his way. Twenty-five freight cars later, she has vanished forever.

One scenario of the zipless fuck.

Zipless, you see, *not* because European men have button-flies rather than zipper-flies, and not because the participants are so devastatingly attractive, but because the incident has all the swift compression of a dream and is seemingly free of all remorse and guilt; because there is no talk of her late husband or of his fiancée; because there is no rationalizing; because there is no talk at *all*. The zipless fuck is absolutely pure. It is free of ulterior motives. There is no power game. The man is not "taking" and the woman is not "giving." No one is attempting to cuckold a husband or humiliate a wife. No one is trying to prove anything or get anything out of anyone. The zipless fuck is the purest thing there is. And it is rarer than the unicorn. And I have never had one. Whenever it seemed I was close, I discovered a horse with a papier-mâché horn, or two clowns in a unicorn suit. Alessandro, my Florentine friend, came close. But he was, after all, one clown in a unicorn suit.

Consider this tapestry, my life.

FLYBOYS

TOBIAS WOLFF

My friend Clark and I decided to build a jet plane. We spent weeks perfecting our design at the draftsman's table in his bedroom. Sometimes Clark let me put on the green eyeshade and wield the compasses and calipers, but never for long. I drew like a lip-reader reads; watching me was torture for him. When he couldn't take it anymore he'd bump me aside, leaving me free to fool with his things—the samurai sword, the Webley pistol with the plugged barrel—and wander the house.

Clark's mom was usually out somewhere. I formed the habit of making myself a sandwich and settling back in the leather chair in the den, where I listened to old records and studied the family photo albums. They were lucky people, Clark's parents, lucky and unsurprised by their luck. You could see in the pictures that they took it all in stride, the big spreads behind them, the boats and cars, and their relaxed, handsome families who, it was clear, did not get laid off, or come down with migraines, or lock each other out of the house. I pondered each picture as if it were a door I might enter, until something turned in me and I grew irritable. Then I put the albums away, and went back to Clark's room to inspect his work and demand revisions.

Sure and commanding in everything but this, Clark took most of my ideas to heart, which made a tyrant of me. The more attentive he was, the more I bullied him. His own proposals I laughed off as moronic jokes. Clark cared more for the perfection of the plane than for his own vanity; he thought nothing of crumpling a page he'd spent hours on and starting over because of some brainstorm I'd had. This wasn't humility, but an assurance that ran to imperturbable depths and rendered him deaf to any appeal when he rejected one of my inspirations. There were times—many times—when I contemplated that squarish head of his as I hefted the samurai sword, and imagined the stroke that would drop it to the floor like a ripe melon.

Clark was stubborn but there was no meanness in him. He wouldn't turn on you; he was the same one day as the next, earnest and practical. Though the family had money and spent it freely, he wasn't spoiled or interested in possessions except as instruments of his projects. In the eight or nine months we'd been friends we had shot two horror movies with his dad's 8-mm camera, built a catapult that worked so well his parents made us take it apart, and fashioned a monstrous, unsteerable sled out of a bedframe and five wooden skis we found in his neighbor's trash. We also wrote a radio mystery for a competition one of the local stations put on every year, Clark patiently retyping the script as I improvised more tortuous plot twists and high-falutin dialogue ("My dear Carstairs, it was really most astute of you to notice the mud on my smoking jacket. How unfortunate that you failed to decry the derringer in my pocket!"). We were flabbergasted that we didn't win.

I supplied the genius, or so I believed. But I understood even then that Clark gave it form and did all the work. His drawings of our plane were crisp and minutely detailed, like real blueprints that a spy would cut somebody's throat for. As I pondered them at the end of the day (frontal and side views, views from above and behind and below), the separate designs locked together like a puzzle and lifted away from the flatness of the page. They became an airplane, a jet—my jet. And through all the long run home I was in the cockpit of my jet, skimming sawtooth peaks, weaving through steep valleys, buzzing fishermen in the sound and tearing over the city in such a storm of flash and thunder that football games stopped in mid-play, cheerleaders gaping up at me, legs still flexed under their plaid skirts. A barrel roll, a waggle of the wings and I was gone, racing up through the clouds. I could feel the Gs in my arms, my chest, my face. The skin pulled back from my cheeks. Tears streaked from my eyes. The plane shook like crazy. When I couldn't go any higher, I went higher. Sweet Jesus, I did some flying!

Clark and I hadn't talked much about the actual construction of the jet. We let that question hang while we fine-tuned the plans. But the plans couldn't be worked on forever; we were getting bored and stale. And then Clark came up to me at recess one day and said he knew where we could get a canopy. When I asked him where, he looked over at the guy I'd been shooting baskets with and pushed his lips together. Clark had long ago decided that I was a security risk. "You'll see," he said, and walked off.

All afternoon I nagged him to tell me where the canopy was, who we were getting it from. He wouldn't say a thing. I wanted to tear him apart.

Instead of heading toward his place after school, Clark led me down the avenue past the post office and Safeway and the line of drive-ins and pinball joints where the high-school kids hung out. Clark had long legs and never looked to the right or left, he just flat-out marched, so I had to hustle to keep up. I resented being at his heels, sweaty and short of breath and ignorant of our destination, and most of all I resented his knowing that I would follow him anyway.

We turned down the alley beside the Odd Fellows hall and skirted a big lot full of school buses, then cut through a construction site that gave onto a park where I'd once been chased by some older boys. On the other side of the park we crossed the bridge over Flint Creek, swollen with a week's heavy rain. Beyond the bridge the road turned into a series of mudholes bordered by small, soggy-looking houses overhung by dripping trees. By then I'd stopped asking where we were going, because I knew. I had been this way before, many times.

"I don't remember Freddy having any airplane canopies around," I said.

"He's got a whole barnful of stuff."

"I know, I've seen it, but I didn't see any canopies."

"Maybe he just got it."

"That's a big fat maybe."

Clark picked up the pace.

I said, "So, Mr. Top Secret, how come you told Freddy about the plane?"

"I didn't. Sandra told him."

I let that ride, since I'd told Sandra.

Freddy lived at the dead end of the street. As Clark and I got closer I could hear the snarl of a chain saw from the woods behind the house. Freddy and I used to lose ourselves all day in there. I hung back while Clark went up to the house and knocked. Freddy's mother opened the door. She let Clark in and waited as I crossed the yard and mounted the steps. "Well, aren't you a sight for sore eyes," she said, not as a reproach, though I felt it that way. She ruffled my hair as I went past. "You've grown a few inches."

"Yes, ma'am."

"Freddy's in the kitchen."

Freddy closed his book and stood up from the table. He smiled shyly. "Hi," he said, and I said "Hi" back. It came hard. We hadn't spoken in almost a year, since he went into the hospital. Freddy's mother came in behind us and said, "Sit down, boys. Take off your coats. Freddy, put some of those cookies on a plate."

"I can't stay long," Clark said, but nobody answered him and he finally hung his jacket on a chair and pulled up to the table. It was a round table that took up most of the kitchen. Freddy's brother, Tanker, had carved pictures all over the tabletop, *Field and Stream*–type depictions of noble stags and leaping fish, eagles with rabbits in their talons, cougars crouched above mountain goats. He always kept his Barlow knife busy while he drank Olympia and told his stories. Like the stories, the pictures all ran together. They would've covered the whole table by now if Tanker hadn't been killed.

The air smelled like laundry, and the windows were misted up. Freddy shook some Oreos onto a plate and handed it to me. I passed it on to Clark without taking any. The plate was dingy. Not encrusted, no major food groups in evidence—just dingy. Business as usual. I never ate at Freddy's unless I was starving. Clark didn't seem to notice. He grabbed a handful, and after a show of indecision Freddy's mother took one. She was a thin woman with shoulder blades that stuck out like wings when she hunched over, as she did now, nibbling at her Oreo. She turned to me, her eyes so sad I had to force myself not to look away. "I can't get over how you've grown," she said. "Freddy, hasn't he grown?"

"Like a weed," Freddy said.

"By leaps and bounds," I said, falling into our old game in spite of myself.

Clark looked back and forth between us.

Freddy's mother said, "I understand you boys are building an airplane."

"We're just getting started," Clark said.

"Well, that's just wonderful," Freddy's mother said. "An airplane. Think of that."

"Right now we're looking for a canopy," Clark said.

Nobody spoke for a while. Freddy's mother crossed her arms over her chest and bent down even farther. Then she said, "Freddy, you should tell your friends what you were telling me about that fellow in your book."

"That's okay," Freddy said. "Maybe later."

"About the mountains of skulls."

"Human skulls?" I said.

"Mountains of them," Freddy's mother said.

"Tamerlane," Freddy said. And without further delay he began to describe Tamerlane's revenge on the Persian cities that had resisted his progress. It was grisly stuff, but he did not scrimp on details or try to hide his pleasure in them, or in the starchy phrases he'd picked up from whatever book he was reading. That was Freddy for you. Gentle as a lamb, but very big on the Vikings and Aztecs and Genghis Khan and the Crusaders, all the great old disembowelers and eyeball-gougers. So was I. It was an interest we shared. Clark listened, looking a little stunned.

I never found out exactly how Tanker got killed; it was a motorcycle accident outside Spokane, that was all Freddy told me. You had to know Tanker to know what that meant. This was a very unlucky family. Bats took over their attic. Their cars laid transmissions like eggs. They got caught switching license plates and dumping garbage illegally and owing back taxes, or at least Ivan did. Ivan was Freddy's stepfather and a world of bad luck all by himself.

He wasn't vicious or evil, but full of cute ideas that got him in trouble and made things even worse than they already were, like not paying property taxes on the basis of some veterans' exemption he'd heard about but didn't bother to read up on, and that turned out not to apply to him. That brilliant stroke almost cost them the house, which Freddy's father had left free and clear when he died. Tanker was the only one in the family who could stand up to Ivan, and not just because he was bigger and more competent. Ivan had a soft spot for him. After the accident he took to his bed for almost a week straight, then vanished.

When Tanker was home everybody'd be in the kitchen, sitting around the table and cracking up at his stories. He told stories about himself that I would've locked away for good, like the time his bike broke down in the middle of nowhere and a car stopped but instead of giving him a lift the guys inside hit him over the head with a lunch bag full of fresh shit. Then a patrolman arrested him and made him ride to the station in his trunk—all in the middle of a snowstorm. Tanker told that story as if it was the most precious thing that ever happened to him, tears glistening in his eyes. He had lots of friends, wise guys in creaking leather jackets, and he filled the house with them. He could fix anything—plumbing, engines, leaky roofs, you name it. He took Freddy and me on fishing trips in his rattletrap truck, and gave us Indian names. I was Hard-to-Camp-With, because I complained and snored. Freddy was Cheap-to-Feed.

After Tanker got killed everything changed at Freddy's. The house had the frozen, echoey quiet of abandonment. Ivan finally came back from wherever he'd disappeared to, but he spent most of his time away on some new enterprise. When Freddy and I got to the house after school it was always dim and still. His mother kept to herself in the back bedroom. Sometimes she came out to offer us a sandwich and ask us questions about our day, but I wished she wouldn't. I had never seen such sorrow; it appalled me. And I was even more appalled by her attempts to overcome it, because they so plainly, pathetically failed, and in failing opened up the view of a world I had only begun to suspect, where wounds did not heal, and things did not work out for the best.

One day Freddy and I were shooting baskets in the driveway when his mother called him inside. We'd been playing horse, and I took advantage of his absence to practice my hook shot. My hook had Freddy jinxed; he couldn't even hit the backboard with it. I dribbled and shot, dribbled and shot, ten, twenty times; fifty times. Freddy still didn't come back. It was very quiet. The only sound was the ball hitting the backboard, the rim, the asphalt. I stopped shooting after a while and stood there, waiting, bouncing the ball. The ball was overinflated and rose fast to the hand, making a hollow whang shadowed by a high ringing note that lingered in the silence. It began to give me the creeps. But I kept bouncing the ball, somehow unable to break the rhythm I'd fallen into. My hand moved by itself, lightly palming the pebbled skin and pushing the ball down just hard enough to bring it back. The sound grew louder and larger and emptier, the sound of emptiness it-self, emptiness throbbing like a headache. Spooked, I caught the ball and held it. I looked at the house. Nothing moved there. I thought of the woman closed up inside, and Freddy, closed up with her, swallowed by misery. In its still-ness the house seemed conscious, expectant. It seemed to be waiting. I put the ball down and walked to the end of the driveway, then broke into a run. I was still running when I reached the park. That was the day the older boys chased me, their blood roused by the spectacle of my rab-bity flight. They kept after me for a hundred yards or so and then fell back, though they could've caught me if they'd had their hearts in it. But they were running for sport; the seriousness of my panic confused them, put them off their stride.

Such panic . . . where did it come from? It couldn't have been just the situation at Freddy's. The shakiness of my own family was becoming more and more apparent. At the time I didn't admit to this knowledge, not for a moment, but it was always there, waiting in the gut: a sourness of foreboding, a cramp of alarm at any sign of misfortune or weakness in others, as if such things were catching.

Freddy had asthma. Not long after I ran away from his house he suffered a severe attack and went into the hospi-tal. Our teacher told the class about it. She had everyone write get-well notes, and handed out mimeographed sheets with the address of the hospital and the visiting hours. It was an easy walk. I knew I should go, and I thought about it so much that whatever else I did that week seemed mainly to be *not going*, but I couldn't make myself do it. When Freddy came back to school I was unable to speak to him or even face him. I went straight home after the bell rang, using the main entrance instead of the side door where we used to meet. And then I saw that he was avoiding me, too. He ate at the opposite end of the cafeteria; when we passed in the hallway he blushed and stared at the floor. He acted as if he had done me some wrong, and the shame I felt at this made me even more skittish. I was very lonely for a time, then Clark and I became friends. This was my first visit to Freddy's since the day I bolted.

Clark worked his way through the Oreos as Freddy told his gruesome tale, and when he came to the end I started one of my own from a book my brother had given me about Quantrill's Raiders. It was a truly terrible story, a cruel, mortifying story—the star sociopath was a man named "Bloody Bill." I was aware of Freddy watching me with something like rapture. Freddy's mother shook her head when the going got rough and made exclamations of shock and dismay—"No! He never!"—just like she used to do back when the three of us watched *Queen for a Day* every afternoon, drooling shamelessly over the weird, woeful narratives sobbed out by the competing wretches. Clark watched me without joy. He was impatient for business, and too sane for all this ghoulish stuff. I knew that he was seeing me in a different way, a way he probably didn't like, but I kept piling it on. I couldn't let go of the old pleasure, almost forgotten, of having Freddy on my hook, and feeling his own pleasure thrumming through the line.

And then the back door swung open and Ivan leaned his head into the kitchen. His face was even bigger and whiter than I remembered, and as if to confirm my memory he wore a red hunting cap that was too small and sat his head like a party hat. Black mud encased his pant legs almost to his knees. He looked at me and said, "Hey, by gum! Long time no see!" One of the lenses of his spectacles had a daub of mud in the middle, like an eyeball on a pair of joke glasses. He looked at Clark, then at Freddy's mother. "Hon, you aren't gonna believe this—that darn truck got stuck again."

A damp wind was blowing. Freddy and Clark and I stood with shoulders hunched, hands in our pockets, and looked on as Ivan circled Tanker's old pickup and explained why it wasn't his fault the tires were mired almost to the axle. "The truth is, the old gal just can't pull her weight anymore." He gave the fender a rub. "Past her prime—has been for years."

"Yessir," Freddy said. "She's long in the tooth and that's a fact."

"There you go," Ivan said.

"Ready for the pasture," I said.

"Over the hill," Freddy said.

"That's it exactly," Ivan said. "I just can't bring myself to sell her." And then his jaw started quaking and I thought with horror that he was about to cry. But he didn't. He caught his lower lip under his teeth, sucked it musingly, and pushed it out again. His lips were full and expressive. I tended to watch them for signs of mood rather than his eyes, which he kept buried in a cunning squint.

"So. Gotta get the wood out. You fellows ready to use some of those muscles?"

Freddy and I looked at each other.

Clark was staring at the truck. "You want us to unload all of that?"

"Won't take an hour, strapping boys like you," Ivan said. "Maybe an hour by the time you load her up again," he added.

The truck bed was filled with logs, stacked as high as the sides and heaped to a peak in the middle. Ivan had been clearing out the woods behind the house. Most of it was gone by now, nearly an acre of trees turned into a stumpy bog crisscrossed by tire ruts filled with black water. Behind the bog stood the house of a family whose pale, stringy daughters quarreled incessantly with their mother, screaming as they ran out the door, screaming as they jumped into the souped-up cars of their boyfriends. The father and son also drove hot rods, maintaining them on parts cannibalized from the collection of wrecks in their backyard. They came out during the afternoons and weekends to crawl under the cars and shout at each other over the clanging of their wrenches. Freddy and I used to spy on the family from the trees, our faces darkened, twigs stuck in our hair. He wouldn't have to steal up on them now; they'd be in plain view all the time.

Ivan had been hard at work, turning trees into firewood. Firewood was cheap. Whatever he got wouldn't be worth it, worth all the green and the birds and the scolding squirrels, the coolness in summer, the long shafts of afternoon light. This place had been Iroquois wilderness to me, English forest and African jungle. It had been Mars. Gone, all of them. I was a boy who didn't know he would never build a jet, but I knew that this lake of mud was the work of a fool.

"I'll bet you can drive it out without unloading," Clark said.

"Already tried." Ivan lowered himself onto a stump and looked around with a satisfied air. "Sooner you fellows get started, sooner you'll be done."

"A stitch in time saves nine," I said.

"No time like the present," Freddy said.

"There you go," Ivan said.

Clark had been standing on a web of roots. He stepped off and walked toward the truck. As he got closer the ground turned soupy and he went up on tiptoe, then began hopping from foot to foot, but there was no firm place to land and every time he jumped he went in deeper. When he sank past his ankles he gave up and mucked ahead, his sneakers slurping, picking up more goop with each step. By the time he reached the truck they looked like medicine balls. He crouched by one rear tire, then the other.

"We can put down corduroy tracks," he said.

Ivan winked in our direction. "Corduroy tracks, you say!"

"That's what they used to do when covered wagons got stuck," Clark said. "Put logs down."

"Son, does that look like a covered wagon to you?"

"Also artillery pieces. In the Civil War."

"Maybe we should just unload the truck," I said.

"Hold your horses." Ivan put his hands on his knees. He studied Clark. "I like a boy with ideas," he said. "Go on, give it a stab."

"Never hurts to try," Freddy said.

"That's it exactly," Ivan said.

Freddy and I walked up to the barn for a couple of shovels. We cut wide of the ruts and puddles but the mud still sucked at our shoes. Once we were alone, I kept thinking how thin he'd gotten. I couldn't come up with anything to say. He didn't speak either.

I waited while Freddy went into the barn, and when he came back outside I said, "We're going to move." No one had told me any such thing, but those words came to mind and it felt right to say them.

Freddy handed me a shovel. "Where to?"

"I don't know."

"When."

"I'm not sure."

We started back.

"I hope you don't move," Freddy said.

"Maybe we won't," I said. "Maybe we'll end up staying."

"That would be great, if you stayed."

"There's no place like home."

"Home is where the heart is," Freddy said, but he was looking at the ground just ahead of him and didn't smile back at me.

We took turns digging out the wheels, one resting while the other two worked. Ivan laughed whenever we slipped into the mud, but otherwise watched in silence. It was impossible to dig and keep your feet, especially as we got deeper. Finally I gave up and knelt as I worked—you had more leverage that way—and Clark and Freddy followed suit. I was sheathed in mud up to my waist and elbows. My condition was hopeless, so I stopped trying to spare myself and just let go. I surrendered to the spirit of the mud. It's fair to say I wallowed.

What we did, under Clark's direction, was cut a wide trench from the bottom of each tire forward about five feet, sloping up like a ramp. We jammed cordwood under the tires and then lined the ramps with more logs as we dug. We were about finished when the walls started to collapse. Clark took it personally. "Fudge!" he kept saying, and Ivan laughed and swayed back and forth on the stump. Clark yelled at Freddy and me to *dig! dig! dig!* and stretched flat on his stomach and scooped the sliding mud out with his hands. I could hear Freddy laboring for breath, but he didn't let up, and neither did I. We burrowed like moles and then came a moment when the tracks were clear and the walls holding, and Clark told Ivan to move the truck. Clark was excited and barked at him as he'd been barking at us. Ivan sat there blinking. Clark pitched some spare logs back into the truck. "Come on, guys," he said. "We'll push."

Ivan stood and brushed off his hands and walked over to the truck, still watching Clark. Before he climbed into the cab, he said, "Young fellow, if you ever need a job, call me."

Clark and Freddy and I braced ourselves against the tailgate as Ivan cranked the engine and put it in gear. The rear wheels started to spin, churning back geysers of mud. I was in the middle so I didn't catch much of it, but Freddy and Clark got plastered. Freddy turned away and then leaned forward again and started pushing with Clark and me. Ivan was rocking the truck to and fro, trying to get it onto the logs. It rose a little, hesitated, then slipped and spewed back another blast of mud. Clark and Freddy looked like they'd been stuccoed. They moved in closer beside me as Ivan got the truck rocking again. I held my breath against the heavy black exhaust. My eyes burned. The truck rocked and rose again, hung on the lip. Clark grunted, again and again and again. I picked up his rhythm and pushed for all I was worth, and then my feet slid and I fell flat out as the truck jerked forward. The tires screamed on the wood. A log shot back and flipped past Clark's head. He didn't seem to notice. He was watching the truck. It gathered speed on the track we'd made and hit the mud again and somehow slithered on, languidly, noisily, rear end sashaying, two great plumes of mud arcing off the back wheels. The wheels spun wildly, the engine shrieked, logs tumbled off the sides. The truck slewed and swayed across the bog and rose abruptly, shedding skirts of mud, as it gained the broken asphalt in front of the barn. Ivan shifted gears, beeped merrily, and drove away.

"You all right?" Clark said.

Freddy was bent double, head almost between his knees. He held up a hand but went on panting. The truck had left behind an exaggerated silence in which I could hear the clutch and rasp of every breath he took. It sounded like hard work, hard and lonely. When I moved toward him he waved me off. Clark picked up a stick and began scraping his sneakers. This seemed an optimistic project, caked as he was to the eyeballs, but he went about it with method and gravity. Freddy straightened up. His face was pallid, his chest rose and fell like a bird's. He stood there a while, watching Clark wield the stick. "We can get cleaned up at the house," he said.

"If it's okay with you," Clark said, "I'd like to take a look at that canopy."

I'd been hoping all afternoon that Clark would drop the subject of the canopy, because I knew as a matter of absolute fact that Freddy didn't have one. But he did. It was in the loft of the barn, where Freddy's father had stored items of special interest from the salvage yard he'd owned. In all the rainy afternoons we'd spent fooling around up there I must have seen it a hundred times, but having no use for it, not even recognizing what it was, I'd never taken note. The canopy was smaller than our plans specified, but the plans could be changed; this was the genuine article. Freddy played the flashlight slowly up and down the length of it. He must have prepared for this moment, because unlike everything else up there the canopy was free of dust— polished, even, from the look of it. The light picked up a few scratches. Otherwise it was perfect: clear, unbroken, complete with flashing. Simple, but technical too. Real.

If I'd had any doubts, they left me. It was obvious that our jet was not only possible but as good as built. All we had to do was keep having days like this and soon the pieces would all come together, and we'd be flying.

Clark asked Freddy what he wanted for it.

"Nothing. It's just sitting here."

We poked around a while and went back to the house, where Freddy's mother declared shock at our condition and ordered us to strip and hose off. Clark wouldn't do it, he just washed his face and hands, but I took a long shower and then Freddy's mother gave me some of Tanker's clothes to wear home and wrapped my own dismal duds in a butcher-paper parcel tied off with a string handle, like a mess of gizzards. Freddy walked us to the end of the street. The light was failing. I looked back once and saw him still standing there. When I looked again he was gone.

We stopped on the bridge over Flint Creek and threw rocks at a bottle caught in some weeds. I was all pumped up from getting the truck out and seeing the canopy, plus Freddy's mother had lent me Tanker's motorcycle jacket, which, though it hung to my fingertips, filled me with a conviction of my own powers that verged on madness. I was half hoping we'd run into those older boys in the park so I could whip their asses for them.

I leaned over the railing, spat into the water.

"Freddy wants in," Clark said.

"He said that? He didn't tell me."

"You were in the shower."

"So what did he say?"

"Just that he wished he could come in with us, on the plane."

"What, or he takes the canopy back?"

"No. He just asked."

"We'd have to redesign the whole cockpit. It would change everything."

Clark had a rock in his hand. He looked at it with some interest, then flipped it into the creek.

"What did you tell him?"

"I said we'd let him know."

"What do you think?"

"He seems okay. You know him better than I do."

"Freddy's great, it's just . . ."

Clark waited for me to finish. When it was clear that I wasn't going to, he said, "Whatever you want."

I told him that all things considered, I'd just as soon keep it to the two of us.

As we crossed the park he asked me to have dinner at his place so he wouldn't get skinned alive about the clothes. His dad was still in Portland, he said, as if that explained something. Clark took his time on the walk home, looking in shop windows and inspecting cars in the lots we passed. When we finally got to the house it was all lit up and music was playing. Even with the windows closed we could hear strains of it from the bottom of the sidewalk. Clark stopped. He stood there, listening.

"Strauss," he said. "Good. She's happy."

TESTIMONY OF PILOT

BARRY HANNAH

When I was ten, eleven, and twelve, I did a good bit of my
play in the backyard of a three-story wooden house my
father had bought and rented out, his first venture into real
estate. We lived right across the street from it, but over here
was the place to do your real play. Here there was a harrowed but overgrown garden, a vine-swallowed fence at
the back end, and beyond the fence a cornfield, which belonged to someone else. This was not the country. This was
the town, Clinton, Mississippi, between Jackson on the east
and Vicksburg on the west. On this lot stood a few water
oaks, a few plum bushes, and much overgrowth of honey-
suckle vine. At the very back end, at the fence, stood three
strong nude chinaberry trees.

In Mississippi it is difficult to achieve a vista. But my
friends and I had one here at the back corner of the garden.
We could see across the cornfield, see the one lone tin-
roofed house this side of the railroad tracks, then on across
the tracks many other bleaker houses with rustier tin roofs,
smoke coming out of the chimneys in the late fall. This was
niggertown. We had binoculars and could see the colored
children hustling about and perhaps a hopeless sow or two

267

with her brood enclosed in a tiny boarded-up area. Through the binoculars one afternoon in October we watched some men corner and beat a large hog on the brain. They used an ax and the thing kept running around, head leaning toward the ground, for several minutes before it lay down. I thought I saw the men laughing when it finally did. One of them was staggering, plainly drunk to my sight from three hundred yards away. He had the long knife. Because of that scene I considered Negroes savage cowards for a good five more years of my life. Our maid brought some sausage to my mother and when it was put in the pan to fry, I made a point of running out of the house.

I went directly across the street and to the back end of the garden behind the apartment house we owned, without my breakfast. That was Saturday. Eventually, Radcleve saw me. His parents had him mowing the yard that ran alongside my dad's property. He clicked off the power mower and I went over to his fence, which was storm wire. His mother maintained handsome flowery grounds at all costs; she had a leaf-mold bin and St. Augustine grass as solid as a rug.

Radcleve himself was a violent experimental chemist. When Radcleve was eight, he threw a whole package of .22 shells against the sidewalk in front of his house until one of them went off, driving lead fragments into his calf, most of them still deep in there where the surgeons never dared tamper. Radcleve knew about the sulfur, potassium nitrate, and charcoal mixture for gunpowder when he was ten. He bought things through the mail when he ran out of ingredients in his chemistry sets. When he was an infant, his father, a quiet man who owned the Chevrolet agency in town, bought an entire bankrupt sporting-goods store, and in the middle of their backyard he built a house, plain-painted and neat, one room and a heater, where Radcleve's redundant toys forevermore were kept—all the possible toys he would need for boyhood. There were things in there that Radcleve and I were not mature enough for and did not know the real use of. When we were eleven, we uncrated the new Dunlop golf balls and went on up a shelf for the tennis rackets, went out in the middle of his yard, and served new golf ball after new golf ball with blasts of the rackets over into the cornfield, out of sight. When the strings busted we just went in and got another racket. We were absorbed by how a good smack would set the heavy little pills on an endless flight. Then Radcleve's father came down. He simply dismissed me. He took Radcleve into the house and covered his whole body with a belt. But within the week Radcleve had invented the mortar. It was a steel pipe into which a flashlight battery fit perfectly, like a bullet into a muzzle. He had drilled a hole for the fuse of an M-80 firecracker at the base, for the charge. It was a grand cannon, set up on a stack of bricks at the back of my dad's property, which was the free place to play. When it shot, it would back up violently with thick smoke and you could hear the flashlight battery whistling off. So that morning when I ran out of the house protesting the hog sausage, I told Radcleve to bring over the mortar. His ma and dad were in Jackson for the day, and he came right over with the pipe, the batteries, and the M-80 explosives. He had two gross of them.

Before, we'd shot off toward the woods to the right of niggertown. I turned the bricks to the left; I made us a very fine cannon carriage pointing toward niggertown. When Radcleve appeared, he had two pairs of binoculars around his neck, one pair a newly plundered German unit as big as a brace of whiskey bottles. I told him I wanted to shoot for that house where we saw them killing the pig. Radcleve loved the idea. We singled out the house with heavy use of the binoculars.

There were children in the yard. Then they all went in. Two men came out of the back door. I thought I recognized the drunkard from the other afternoon. I helped Radcleve fix the direction of the cannon. We estimated the altitude we needed to get down there. Radcleve put the M-80 in the breech with its fuse standing out of the hole. I dropped the flashlight battery in. I lit the fuse. We backed off. The M-80 blasted off deafeningly, smoke rose, but my concentration was on that particular house over there. I brought the binoculars up. We waited six or seven seconds. I heard a great joyful wallop on tin. "We've hit him on the first try, the first try!" I yelled. Radcleve was ecstatic. "Right on his roof!" We bolstered up the brick carriage. Radcleve remembered the correct height of the cannon exactly. So we fixed it, loaded it, lit it and backed off. The battery landed on the roof, blat, again, louder. I looked to see if there wasn't a great dent or hole in the roof. I could not understand why niggers weren't pouring out distraught from that house. We shot the mortar again and again, and always our battery hit the tin roof. Sometimes there was only a dull thud, but other times there was a wild distress of tin. I was still looking through the binoculars, amazed that the niggers wouldn't even come out of their house to see what was hitting their roof. Radcleve was on to it better than me. I looked over at him and he had the huge German binocs much lower than I did. He was looking straight through the cornfield, which was all bare and open, with nothing left but rotten stalks. "What we've been hitting is the roof of that house just this side of the tracks. White people live in there," he said.

I took up my binoculars again. I looked around the yard of that white wooden house on this side of the tracks, almost next to the railroad. When I found the tin roof, I saw four significant dents in it. I saw one of our batteries lying in the middle of a sort of crater. I took the binoculars down into the yard and saw a blonde middle-aged woman looking our way.

"Somebody's coming up toward us. He's from that house and he's got, I think, some sort of fancy gun with him. It might be an automatic weapon."

I ran my binoculars all over the cornfield. Then, in a line with the house, I saw him. He was coming our way but having some trouble with the rows and dead stalks of the cornfield.

"That is just a boy like us. All he's got is a saxophone with him," I told Radcleve. I had recently got in the school band, playing drums, and had seen all the weird horns that made up a band.

I watched this boy with the saxophone through the binoculars until he was ten feet from us. This was Quadberry. His name was Ard, short for Arden. His shoes were foot-square wads of mud from the cornfield. When he saw us across the fence and above him, he stuck out his arm in my direction.

"My dad says stop it!"

"We weren't doing anything," says Radcleve.

"Mother saw the smoke puff up from here. Dad has a hangover."

"A what?"

"It's a headache from indiscretion. You're lucky he does. He's picked up the poker to rap on you, but he can't move further the way his head is."

"What's your name? You're not in the band," I said, focusing on the saxophone.

"It's Ard Quadberry. Why do you keep looking at me through the binoculars?"

It was because he was odd, with his hair and its white ends, and his Arab nose, and now his name. Add to that the saxophone.

"My dad's a doctor at the college. Mother's a musician. You better quit what you're doing . . . I was out practicing in the garage. I saw one of those flashlight batteries roll off the roof. Could I see what you shoot 'em with?"

"No," said Radcleve. Then he said: "If you'll play that horn."

Quadberry stood out there ten feet below us in the field, skinny, feet and pants booted with black mud, and at his chest the slung-on, very complex, radiant horn.

Quadberry began sucking and licking the reed. I didn't care much for this act, and there was too much desperate oralness in his face when he began playing. That was why I chose the drums. One had to engage himself like suck's revenge with a horn. But what Quadberry was playing was pleasant and intricate. I was sure it was advanced, and there was no squawking, as from the other eleven-year-olds on sax in the band room. He made the end with a clean upward riff, holding the final note high, pure and unwavering.

"Good!" I called to him.

Quadberry was trying to move out of the sunken row toward us, but his heavy shoes were impeding him.

"Sounded like a duck. Sounded like a girl duck," said Radcleve, who was kneeling down and packing a mudball around one of the M-80s. I saw and I was an accomplice, because I did nothing. Radcleve lit the fuse and heaved the mudball over the fence. An M-80 is a very serious firecracker; it is like the charge they use to shoot up those sprays six hundred feet on July Fourth at country clubs. It went off, this one, even bigger than most M-80s.

When we looked over the fence, we saw Quadberry all muck specks and fragments of stalks. He was covering the mouthpiece of his horn with both hands. Then I saw there was blood pouring out of, it seemed, his right eye. I thought he was bleeding directly out of his eye.

"Quadberry?" I called.

He turned around and never said a word to me until I was eighteen. He walked back holding his eye and staggering through the cornstalks. Radcleve had him in the binoculars. Radcleve was trembling . . . but intrigued.

"His mother just screamed. She's running out in the field to get him."

I thought we'd blinded him, but we hadn't. I thought the Quadberrys would get the police or call my father, but they didn't. The upshot of this is that Quadberry had a permanent white space next to his right eye, a spot that looked like a tiny upset crown.

I went from sixth through half of twelfth grade ignoring him and that wound. I was coming on as a drummer and a lover, but if Quadberry happened to appear within fifty feet of me and my most tender, intimate sweetheart, I would duck out. Quadberry grew up just like the rest of us. His father was still a doctor—professor of history—at the town college; his mother was still blonde, and a musician. She was organist at an Episcopalian church in Jackson, the big capital city ten miles east of us.

As for Radcleve, he still had no ear for music, but he was there, my buddy. He was repentant about Quadberry, although not so much as I. He'd thrown the mud grenade over the fence only to see what would happen. He had not really wanted to maim. Quadberry had played his tune on the sax, Radcleve had played his tune on the mud grenade. It was just a shame they happened to cross talents.

Radcleve went into a long period of nearly nothing after he gave up violent explosives. Then he trained himself to copy the comic strips, *Steve Canyon* to *Major Hoople*, until he became quite a versatile cartoonist with some very provocative new faces and bodies that were gesturing intriguingly. He could never fill in the speech balloons with the smart words they needed. Sometimes he would pencil in "Err" or "What?" in the empty speech places. I saw him a great deal. Radcleve was not spooked by Quadberry. He even once asked Quadberry what his opinion was of his future as a cartoonist. Quadberry told Radcleve that if he took all his cartoons and stuffed himself with them, he would make an interesting dead man. After that, Radcleve was shy of him too.

When I was a senior we had an extraordinary band. Word was we had outplayed all the big A.A.A. division bands last April in the state contest. Then came news that a new blazing saxophone player was coming into the band as first chair. This person had spent summers in Vermont in music camps, and he was coming in with us for the concert season. Our director, a lovable aesthete named Richard Prender, announced to us in a proud silent moment that the boy was joining us tomorrow night. The effect was that everybody should push over a seat or two and make room for this boy and his talent. I was annoyed. Here I'd been with the band and had kept hold of the taste among the whole percussion section. I could play rock and jazz drum and didn't even really need to be here. I could be in Vermont too, give me a piano and a bass. I looked at the kid on first sax, who was going to be supplanted tomorrow. For two years he had thought he was the star, then suddenly enters this boy who's three times better.

The new boy was Quadberry. He came in, but he was meek, and when he tuned up he put his head almost on the floor, bending over trying to be inconspicuous. The girls in the band had wanted him to be handsome, but Quadberry refused and kept himself in such hiding among the sax section that he was neither handsome, ugly, cute or anything. What he was was pretty near invisible, except for the bell of his horn, the all-but-closed eyes, the Arabian nose, the brown hair with its halo of white ends, the desperate oralness, the giant reed punched into his face, and hazy Quadberry, loving the wound in a private dignified ecstasy.

I say dignified because of what came out of the end of his horn. He was more than what Prender had told us he would be. Because of Quadberry, we could take the band arrangement of Ravel's *Bolero* with us to the state contest. Quadberry would do the saxophone solo. He would switch to alto sax, he would do the sly Moorish ride. When he played, I heard the sweetness, I heard the horn which finally brought human *talk* into the realm of music. It could sound like the mutterings of a field nigger, and then it could get up into inhumanly careless beauty, it could get among mutinous helium bursts around Saturn. I already loved *Bolero* for the constant drum part. The percussion was always there, driving along with the subtly increasing triplets, insistent, insistent, at last outraged and trying to steal the whole show from the horns and the others. I knew a large boy with dirty blond hair, name of Wyatt, who played viola in the Jackson Symphony and sousaphone in our band—one of the rare closet transmutations of my time—who was forever claiming to have discovered the

275

central *Bolero* one Sunday afternoon over FM radio as he had seven distinct sexual moments with a certain B., girl flutist with black bangs and skin like mayonnaise, while the drums of Ravel carried them on and on in a ceremony of Spanish sex. It was agreed by all the canny in the band that *Bolero* was exactly the piece to make the band soar—now especially as we had Quadberry, who made his walk into the piece like an actual lean Spanish bandit. This boy could blow his horn. He was, as I had suspected, a genius. His solo was not quite the same as the New York Phil's saxophonist's, but it was better. It came in and was with us. It entered my spine and, I am sure, went up the skirts of the girls. I had almost deafened myself playing drums in the most famous rock and jazz band in the state, but I could hear the voice that went through and out that horn. It sounded like a very troubled forty-year-old man, a man who had had his brow in his hands a long time.

The next time I saw Quadberry up close, in fact the first time I had seen him up close since we were eleven and he was bleeding in the cornfield, was in late February. I had only three classes this last semester, and went up to the band room often, to loaf and complain and keep up my touch on the drums. Prender let me keep my set in one of the instrument rooms, with a tarpaulin thrown over it, and I would drag it out to the practice room and whale away. Sometimes a group of sophomores would come up and I would make them marvel, whaling away as if not only deaf but blind to them, although I wasn't at all. If I saw a sophomore girl with exceptional bod or face, I would do miracles of technique I never knew were in me. I would amaze myself. I would be threatening Buddy Rich and Sam Morello. But this time when I went into the instrument room, there was Quadberry on one side, and, back in a dark corner, a small ninth-grade euphonium player whose face was all red. The little boy was weeping and grinning at the same time.

"Queerberry," the boy said softly.

Quadberry flew upon him like a demon. He grabbed the boy's collar, slapped his face, and yanked his arm behind him in a merciless wrestler's grip, the one that made them bawl on TV. Then the boy broke it and slugged Quadberry in the lips and ran across to my side of the room. He said "Queerberry" softly again and jumped for the door. Quadberry plunged across the room and tackled him on the threshold.

Now that the boy was under him, Quadberry pounded the top of his head with his fist made like a mallet. The boy kept calling him "Queerberry" throughout this. He had not learned his lesson. The boy seemed to be going into concussion, so I stepped over and touched Quadberry, telling him to quit. Quadberry obeyed and stood up off the boy, who crawled on out into the band room. But once more the boy looked back with a bruised grin, saying "Queerberry." Quadberry made a move toward him, but I blocked it.

"Why are you beating up on this little guy?" I said. Quadberry was sweating and his eyes were wild with hate; he was a big fellow now, though lean. He was, at six feet tall, bigger than me.

"He kept calling me Queerberry."

"What do you care?" I asked.

"I care," Quadberry said, and left me standing there.

We were to play at Millsaps College Auditorium for the concert. It was April. We got on the buses, a few took their cars, and were a big tense crowd getting over there. To

Jackson was only a twenty-minute trip. The director, Prender, followed the bus in his Volkswagen. There was a thick fog. A flashing ambulance, snaking the lanes, piled into him head on. Prender, who I would imagine was thinking of *Bolero* and hearing the young horn voices in his band—perhaps he was dwelling on Quadberry's spectacular gypsy entrance, or perhaps he was meditating on the percussion section, of which I was the king—passed into the airs of band-director heaven. We were told by the student director as we set up on the stage. The student director was a senior from the town college, very much afflicted, almost to the point of drooling, by a love and respect for Dick Prender, and now afflicted by a heartbreaking esteem for his ghost. As were we all.

I loved the tough and tender director awesomely and never knew it until I found myself bawling along with all the rest of the boys of the percussion. I told them to keep setting up, keep tuning, keep screwing the stands together, keep hauling in the kettledrums. To just quit and bawl seemed a betrayal to Prender. I caught some girl clarinetists trying to flee the stage and go have their cry. I told them to get the hell back to their section. They obeyed me. Then I found the student director. I had to have my say.

"Look. I say we just play *Bolero* and junk the rest. That's our horse. We can't play *Brighton Beach* and *Neptune's Daughter.* We'll never make it through them. And they're too happy."

"We aren't going to play anything," he said. "Man, to play is filthy. Did you ever hear Prender play piano? Do you know what a cool man he was in all things?"

"We play. He got us ready, and we play."

"Man, you can't play any more than I can direct. You're bawling your face off. Look out there at the rest of them. Man, it's a herd, it's a weeping herd."

"What's wrong? Why aren't you pulling this crowd together?" This was Quadberry, who had come up urgently. "I got those little brats in my section sitting down, but we've got people abandoning the stage, tearful little finks throwing their horns on the floor."

"I'm not directing," said the mustached college man.

"Then get out of here. You're weak, weak!"

"Man, we've got teenagers in ruin here, we got sorrowville. Nobody can—"

"Go ahead. Do your number. Weak out on us."

"Man, I—"

Quadberry was already up on the podium, shaking his arms.

"We're right here! The band is right here! Tell your friends to get back in their seats. We're doing *Bolero*. Just put *Bolero* up and start tuning. *I'm* directing. I'll be right here in front of you. You look at *me!* Don't you dare quit on Prender. Don't you dare quit on me. You've got to be heard. *I've* got to be heard. Prender wanted me to be heard. I am the star, and I say we sit down and blow."

And so we did. We all tuned and were burning low for the advent into *Bolero*, though we couldn't believe that Quadberry was going to remain with his saxophone strapped to him and conduct us as well as play his solo. The judges, who apparently hadn't heard about Prender's death, walked down to their balcony desks.

One of them called out "Ready" and Quadberry's hand was instantly up in the air, his fingers hard as if around the stem of something like a torch. This was not Prender's way, but it had to do. We went into the number cleanly and

Quadberry one-armed it in the conducting. He kept his face, this look of hostility, at the reeds and the trumpets. I was glad he did not look toward me and the percussion boys like that. But he must have known we would be constant and tasteful because I was the king there. As for the others, the soloists especially, he was scaring them into excellence. Prender had never got quite this from them. Boys became men and girls became women as Quadberry directed us through *Bolero*. I even became a bit better of a man myself, though Quadberry did not look my way. When he turned around toward the people in the auditorium to enter on his solo, I knew it was my baby. I and the drums were the metronome. That was no trouble. It was talent to keep the metronome ticking amidst any given chaos of sound.

But this keeps one's mind occupied and I have no idea what Quadberry sounded like on his sax ride. All I know is that he looked grief-stricken and pale, and small. Sweat had popped out on his forehead. He bent over extremely. He was wearing the red brass-button jacket and black pants, black bow tie at the throat, just like the rest of us. In this outfit he bent over his horn almost out of sight. For a moment, before I caught the glint of his horn through the music stands, I thought he had pitched forward off the stage. He went down so far to do his deep oral thing, his conducting arm had disappeared so quickly, I didn't know but what he was having a seizure.

When *Bolero* was over, the audience stood up and made meat out of their hands applauding. The judges themselves applauded. The band stood up, bawling again, for Prender and because we had done so well. The student director rushed out crying to embrace Quadberry, who eluded him with his dipping shoulders. The crowd was still clapping insanely. I wanted to see Quadberry myself. I waded through the red backs, through the bow ties, over the white bucks. Here was the first-chair clarinetist, who had done his bit like an angel; he sat close to the podium and could hear Quadberry.

"Was Quadberry good?" I asked him.

"Are you kidding? These tears in my eyes, they're for how good he was. He was too good. I'll never touch my clarinet again." The clarinetist slung the pieces of his horn into their case like underwear and a toothbrush.

I found Quadberry fitting the sections of his alto in the velvet holds of his case.

"Hooray," I said. "Hip damn hooray for you."

Arden was smiling too, showing a lot of teeth I had never seen. His smile was sly. He knew he had pulled off a monster unlikelihood.

"Hip hip hooray for me," he said. "Look at her. I had the bell of the horn almost smack in her face."

There was a woman of about thirty sitting in the front row of the auditorium. She wore a sundress with a drastic cleavage up front; looked like something that hung around New Orleans and kneaded your heart to death with her feet. She was still mesmerized by Quadberry. She bore on him with a stare and there was moisture in her cleavage.

"You played well."

"Well? Play well? Yes."

He was trying not to look at her directly. Look at *me*, I beckoned to her with full face: I was the *drums*. She arose and left.

"I was walking downhill in a valley, is all I was doing," said Quadberry. "Another man, a wizard, was playing my horn." He locked his sax case. "I feel nasty for not being

281

able to cry like the rest of them. Look at them. Look at them crying."

True, the children of the band were still weeping, standing around the stage. Several moms and dads had come up among them, and they were misty-eyed too. The mixture of grief and superb music had been unbearable.

A girl in tears appeared next to Quadberry. She was a majorette in football season and played third-chair sax during the concert season. Not even her violent sorrow could take the beauty out of the face of this girl. I had watched her for a number of years—her alertness to her own beauty, the pride of her legs in the majorette outfit—and had taken out her younger sister, a second-rate version of her and a wayward overcompensating nymphomaniac whom several of us made a hobby out of pitying. Well, here was Lilian herself crying in Quadberry's face. She told him that she'd run off the stage when she heard about Prender, dropped her horn and everything, and had thrown herself into a tavern across the street and drunk two beers quickly for some kind of relief. But she had come back through the front doors of the auditorium and sat down, dizzy with beer, and seen Quadberry, the miraculous way he had gone on with *Bolero*. And now she was eaten up by feelings of guilt, weakness, cowardice.

"We didn't miss you," said Quadberry.

"Please forgive me. Tell me to do something to make up for it."

"Don't breathe my way, then. You've got beer all over your breath."

"I want to talk to you."

"Take my horn case and go out, get in my car, and wait for me. It's the ugly Plymouth in front of the school bus."

"I know," she said.

Lilian Field, this lovely teary thing, with the rather pious grace of her carriage, with the voice full of imminent swoon, picked up Quadberry's horn case and her own and walked off the stage.

I told the percussion boys to wrap up the packing. Into my suitcase I put my own gear and also managed to steal drum keys, two pairs of brushes, a twenty-inch Turkish cymbal, a Gretsch snare drum that I desired for my collection, a wood block, kettledrum mallets, a tuning harp and a score sheet of *Bolero* full of marginal notes I'd written down straight from the mouth of Dick Prender, thinking I might want to look at the score sheet sometime in the future when I was having a fit of nostalgia such as I am having right now as I write this. I had never done any serious stealing before, and I was stealing for my art. Prender was dead, the band had done its last thing of the year, I was a senior. Things were finished at the high school. I was just looting a sinking ship. I could hardly lift the suitcase. As I was pushing it across the stage, Quadberry was there again.

"You can ride back with me if you want to."

"But you've got Lilian."

"Please ride back with me . . . us. Please."

"Why?"

"To help me get rid of her. Her breath is full of beer. My father always had that breath. Every time he was friendly, he had that breath. And she looks a great deal like my mother." We were interrupted by the Tupelo band director. He put his baton against Quadberry's arm.

"You were big with *Bolero*, son, but that doesn't mean you own the stage."

Quadberry caught the end of the suitcase and helped me with it out to the steps behind the auditorium. The buses were gone. There sat his ugly ocher Plymouth; it was a failed, gay, experimental shade from the Chrysler people. Lilian was sitting in the front seat wearing her shirt and bow tie, her coat off.

"Are you going to ride back with me?" Quadberry said to me.

"I think I would spoil something. You never saw her when she was a majorette. She's not stupid, either. She likes to show off a little, but she's not stupid. She's in the History Club."

"My father has a doctorate in history. She smells of beer."

I said, "She drank two cans of beer when she heard about Prender."

"There are a lot of other things to do when you hear about death. What I did, for example. She ran away. She fell to pieces."

"She's waiting for us," I said.

"One damned thing I am never going to do is drink."

"I've never seen your mother up close, but Lilian doesn't look like your mother. She doesn't look like any-body's mother."

I rode with them silently to Clinton. Lilian made no bones about being disappointed I was in the car, though she said nothing. I knew it would be like this and I hated it. Other girls in town would not be so unhappy that I was in the car with them. I looked for flaws in Lilian's face and neck and hair, but there weren't any. Couldn't there be a mole, an enlarged pore, too much gum on a tooth, a single awkward hair around the ear? No. Memory, the whole lying opera of it, is killing me now. Lilian was faultless beauty, even sweating, even and especially in the white man's shirt and the bow tie clamping together her collar, when one knew her uncomfortable bosoms, her poor nipples. . . .

"Don't take me back to the band room. Turn off here and let me off at my house," I said to Quadberry. He didn't turn off.

"Don't tell Arden what to do. He can do what he wants to," said Lilian, ignoring me and speaking to me at the same time. I couldn't bear her hatred. I asked Quadberry to please just stop the car and let me out here, wherever he was: this front yard of the mobile home would do. I was so earnest that he stopped the car. He handed back the keys and I dragged my suitcase out of the trunk, then flung the keys back at him and kicked the car to get it going again.

My band came together in the summer. We were the Bop Fiends . . . that was our name. Two of them were from Ole Miss, our bass player was from Memphis State, but when we got together this time, I didn't call the tenor sax, who went to Mississippi Southern, because Quadberry wanted to play with us. During the school year the college boys and I fell into minor groups to pick up twenty dollars on a weekend, playing dances for the Moose Lodge, medical-student fraternities in Jackson, teenage recreation centers in Greenwood, and such as that. But come summer we were the Bop Fiends again, and the price for us went up to twelve hundred dollars a gig. Where they wanted the best rock and bop and they had some bread, we were called, The summer after I was a senior, we played in Alabama, Louisiana and Arkansas. Our fame was getting out there on the interstate route.

This was the summer that I made myself deaf.

Years ago Prender had invited down an old friend from a high school in Michigan. He asked me over to meet the friend, who had been a drummer with Stan Kenton at one time and was now a band director just like Prender. This fellow was almost totally deaf and he warned me very sin-

cerely about deafing myself. He said there would come a
point when you had to lean over and concentrate all your
hearing on what the band was doing and that was the time
to quit for a while, because if you didn't you would be irrevocably deaf like him in a month or two. I listened to him
but could not take him seriously. Here was an oldish man
who had his problems. My ears had ages of hearing left.
Not so. I played the drums so loud the summer after I graduated from high school that I made myself, eventually,
stone deaf.

We were at, say, the National Guard Armory in Lake
Village, Arkansas, Quadberry out in front of us on the stage
they'd built. Down on the floor were hundreds of sweaty
teenagers. Four girls in sundresses, showing what they
could, were leaning on the stage with broad ignorant lust
on their minds. I'd play so loud for one particular chick, I'd
get absolutely out of control. The guitar boys would have
to turn the volume up full blast to compensate. Thus I went
deaf. Anyhow, the dramatic idea was to release Quadberry
on a very soft sweet ballad right in the middle of a long ear-
piercing run of rock-and-roll tunes. I'd get out the brushes
and we would astonish the crowd with our tenderness. By
August, I was so deaf I had to watch Quadberry's fingers
changing notes on the saxophone, had to use my eyes to
keep time. The other members of the Bop Fiends told me I
was hitting out of time. I pretended I was trying to do experimental things with rhythm when the truth was I simply
could no longer hear. I was no longer a tasteful drummer,
either. I had become deaf through lack of taste.

Which was—taste—exactly the quality that made
Quadberry wicked on the saxophone. During the howling,
during the churning, Quadberry had taste. The noise did
not affect his personality; he was solid as a brick. He could

blend. Oh, he could hoot through his horn when the right time came, but he could do supporting roles for an hour. Then, when we brought him out front for his solo on something like "Take Five," he would play with such light blissful technique that he even eclipsed Paul Desmond. The girls around the stage did not cause him to enter into excessive loudness or vibrato.

Quadberry had his own girlfriend now, Lilian back at Clinton, who put all the sundressed things around the stage in the shade. In my mind I had congratulated him for getting up next to this beauty, but in June and July, when I was still hearing things a little, he never said a word about her. It was one night in August, when I could hear nothing and was driving him to his house, that he asked me to turn on the inside light and spoke in a retarded deliberate way. He knew I was deaf and counted on my being able to read lips.

"Don't . . . make . . . fun . . . of her . . . or me. . . . We . . . think . . . she . . . is . . . in trouble."

I wagged my head. Never would I make fun of him or her. She detested me because I had taken out her helpless little sister for a few weeks, but I would never think there was anything funny about Lilian, for all her haughtiness. I only thought of this event as monumentally curious.

"No one except you knows," he said.

"Why did you tell me?"

"Because I'm going away and you have to take care of her. I wouldn't trust her with anybody but you."

"She hates the sight of my face. Where are you going?"

"Annapolis."

"You aren't going to any damned Annapolis."

"That was the only school that wanted me."

"You're going to play your saxophone on a boat?"

"I don't know what I'm going to do."

"How . . . how can you just leave her?"

"She wants me to. She's very excited about me at Annapolis. William [this is my name], there is no girl I could imagine who has more inner sweetness than Lilian."

I entered the town college, as did Lilian. She was in the same chemistry class I was. But she was rows away. It was difficult to learn anything, being deaf. The professor wasn't a pantomimer—but finally he went to the blackboard with the formulas and the algebra of problems, to my happiness. I hung in and made a B. At the end of the semester I was swaggering around the grade sheet he'd posted. I happened to see Lilian's grade. She'd only made a C. Beautiful Lilian got only a C while I, with my handicap, had made a B.

It had been a very difficult chemistry class. I had watched Lilian's stomach the whole way through. It was not growing. I wanted to see her look like a watermelon, make herself an amazing mother shape.

When I made the B and Lilian made the C, I got up my courage and finally went by to see her. She answered the door. Her parents weren't home. I'd never wanted this office of watching over her as Quadberry wanted me to, and this is what I told her. She asked me into the house. The rooms smelled of nail polish and pipe smoke. I was hoping her little sister wasn't in the house, and my wish came true. We were alone.

"You can quit watching over me."

"Are you pregnant?"

"No." Then she started crying. "I wanted to be. But I'm not."

"What do you hear from Quadberry?"

She said something, but she had her back to me. She looked to me for an answer, but I had nothing to say. I knew she'd said something, but I hadn't heard it.

"He doesn't play the saxophone anymore," she said.

This made me angry.

"Why not?"

"Too much math and science and navigation. He wants to fly. That's what his dream is now. He wants to get into an F-something jet."

I asked her to say this over and she did. Lilian really was full of inner sweetness, as Quadberry had said. She understood that I was deaf. Perhaps Quadberry had told her. The rest of the time in her house I simply witnessed her beauty and her mouth moving.

I went through college. To me it is interesting that I kept a B average and did it all deaf, though I know this isn't interesting to people who aren't deaf. I loved music, and never heard it. I loved poetry, and never heard a word that came out of the mouths of the visiting poets who read at the campus. I loved my mother and dad, but never heard a sound they made. One Christmas Eve, Radcleve was back from Ole Miss and threw an M-80 out in the street for old times' sake. I saw it explode, but there was only a pressure in my ears. I was at parties when lusts were raging and I went home with two girls (I am medium handsome) who lived in apartments of the old two-story 1920 vintage, and I took my shirt off and made love to them. But I have no real idea what their reaction was. They were stunned and all smiles when I got up, but I have no idea whether I gave them the last pleasure or not. I hope I did. I've always been partial to women and have always wanted to see them satisfied till their eyes popped out.

Through Lilian I got the word that Quadberry was out of Annapolis and now flying jets off the *Bonhomme Richard*, an aircraft carrier headed for Vietnam. He telegrammed her that he would set down at the Jackson airport at ten o'clock one night. So Lilian and I were out there waiting. It was a familiar place to her. She was a stewardess and her loops were mainly in the South. She wore a beige raincoat, had red sandals on her feet; I was in a black turtleneck and corduroy jacket, feeling significant, so significant I could barely stand it. I'd already made myself the lead writer at Gordon-Marx Advertising in Jackson. I hadn't seen Lilian in a year. Her eyes were strained, no longer the bright blue things they were when she was a pious beauty. We drank coffee together. I loved her. As far as I knew, she'd been faithful to Quadberry.

He came down in an F-something Navy jet right on the dot of ten. She ran out on the airport pavement to meet him. I saw her crawl up the ladder. Quadberry never got out of the plane. I could see him in his blue helmet. Lilian backed down the ladder. Then Quadberry had the cockpit cover him again. He turned the plane around so its flaming red end was at us. He took it down the runway. We saw him leap out into the night at the middle of the runway going west, toward San Diego and the *Bonhomme Richard*. Lilian was crying.

"What did he say?" I asked.

"He said, 'I am a dragon. America the beautiful, like you will never know.' He wanted to give you a message. He was glad you were here."

"What was the message?"

"The same thing. 'I am a dragon. America the beautiful, like you will never know.' "

"Did he say anything else?"

"Not a thing."

"Did he express any love toward you?"

"He wasn't Ard. He was somebody with a sneer in a helmet."

"He's going to war, Lilian."

"I asked him to kiss me and he told me to get off the plane, he was firing up and it was dangerous."

"Arden is going to war. He's just on his way to Vietnam and he wanted us to know that. It wasn't just him he wanted us to see. It was him in the jet he wanted us to see. He *is* that black jet. You can't kiss an airplane."

"And what are we supposed to do?" cried sweet Lilian.

"We've just got to hang around. He didn't have to lift off and disappear straight up like that. That was to tell us how he isn't with us anymore."

Lilian asked me what she was supposed to do now. I told her she was supposed to come with me to my apartment in the old 1920 Clinton place where I was. I was supposed to take care of her. Quadberry had said so. His six-year-old directive was still working.

She slept on the fold-out bed of the sofa for a while. This was the only bed in my place. I stood in the dark in the kitchen and drank a quarter bottle of gin on ice. I would not turn on the light and spoil her sleep. The prospect of Lilian asleep in my apartment made me feel like a chaplain on a visit to the Holy Land; I stood there getting drunk, biting my tongue when dreams of lust burst on me. That black jet Quadberry wanted us to see him in, its flaming rear end, his blasting straight up into the night at mid-runway—what precisely was he wanting to say in this stunt? Was he saying remember him forever or forget him forever? But I had my own life and was neither going to mother-hen it over his memory nor his old sweetheart. What did he mean, *America the beautiful, like you will never know?* I, William

Howly, knew a goddamn good bit about America the beautiful, even as a deaf man. Being deaf had brought me up closer to people. There were only about five I knew, but I knew their mouth movements, the perspiration under their noses, their tongues moving over the crowns of their teeth, their fingers on their lips. Quadberry, I said, you don't have to get up next to the stars in your black jet to see America the beautiful.

I was deciding to lie down on the kitchen floor and sleep the night, when Lilian turned on the light and appeared in her panties and bra. Her body was perfect except for a tiny bit of fat on her upper thighs. She'd sunbathed herself so her limbs were brown, and her stomach, and the instinct was to rip off the white underwear and lick, suck, say something terrific into the flesh that you discovered.

She was moving her mouth.

"Say it again slowly."

"I'm lonely. When he took off in his jet, I think it meant he wasn't ever going to see me again. I think it meant he was laughing at both of us. He's an astronaut and he spits on us."

"You want me on the bed with you?" I asked.

"I know you're an intellectual. We could keep on the lights so you'd know what I said."

"You want to say things? This isn't going to be just sex?"

"It could never be just sex."

"I agree. Go to sleep. Let me make up my mind whether to come in there. Turn out the lights."

Again the dark, and I thought I would cheat not only Quadberry but the entire Quadberry family if I did what was natural.

I fell asleep.

****

Quadberry escorted B-52s on bombing missions into North Vietnam. He was catapulted off the *Bonhomme Richard* in his suit at 100 degrees temperature, often at night, and put the F-8 on all it could get—the tiny cockpit, the immense long two-million-dollar fuselage, wings, tail, and jet engine, Quadberry, the genius master of his dragon, going up to twenty thousand feet to be cool. He'd meet with the big B-52 turtle of the air and get in a position, his cockpit glowing with green and orange lights, and turn on his transistor radio. There was only one really good band, never mind the old American rock-and-roll from Cambodia, and that was Red Chinese opera. Quadberry loved it. He loved the nasal horde in the finale, when the peasants won over the old fat dilettante mayor. Then he'd turn the jet around when he saw the squatty abrupt little fires way down there after the B-52s had dropped their diet. It was a seven-hour trip. Sometimes he slept, but his body knew when to wake up. Another thirty minutes and there was his ship waiting for him out in the waves.

All his trips weren't this easy. He'd have to blast out in daytime and get with the B-52s, and a SAM missile would come up among them. Two of his mates were taken down by these missiles. But Quadberry, as on saxophone, had endless learned technique. He'd put his jet perpendicular in the air and make the SAMs look silly. He even shot down two of them. Then, one day in daylight, a MIG came floating up level with him and his squadron. Quadberry couldn't believe it. Others in the squadron were shy, but Quadberry knew where and how the MIG could shoot. He flew below the cannons and then came in behind it. He knew the MIG wanted one of the B-52s and not mainly him. The MIG was so concentrated on the fat B-52 that he forgot about Quadberry. It was really an amateur suicide pilot in the MIG.

Quadberry got on top of him and let down a missile, rising out of the way of it. The missile blew off the tail of the MIG. But then Quadberry wanted to see if the man got safely out of the cockpit. He thought it would be pleasant if the fellow got out with his parachute working. Then Quadberry saw that the fellow wanted to collide his wreckage with the B-52, so Quadberry turned himself over and cannoned, evaporated the pilot and cockpit. It was the first man he'd killed.

The next trip out, Quadberry was hit by a ground missile. But his jet kept flying. He flew it a hundred miles and got to the sea. There was the *Bonhomme Richard*, so he ejected.

His back was snapped but, by God, he landed right on the deck. His mates caught him in their arms and cut the parachute off him. His back hurt for weeks, but he was all right. He rested and recuperated in Hawaii for a month.

Then he went off the front of the ship. Just like that, his F-6 plopped in the ocean and sank like a rock. Quadberry saw the ship go over him. He knew he shouldn't eject just yet. If he ejected now he'd knock his head on the bottom and get chewed up in the motor blades. So Quadberry waited. His plane was sinking in the green and he could see the hull of the aircraft carrier getting smaller, but he had oxygen through his mask and it didn't seem that urgent a decision. Just let the big ship get over. Down what later proved to be sixty feet, he pushed the ejection button. It fired him away, bless it, and he woke up ten feet under the surface swimming against an almost overwhelming body of underwater parachute. But two of his mates were in a helicopter, one of them on the ladder to lift him out.

Now Quadberry's back was really hurt. He was out of this war and all wars for good.

****

Lilian, the stewardess, was killed in a crash. Her jet exploded with a hijacker's bomb, an inept bomb which wasn't supposed to go off, fifteen miles out of Havana; the poor pilot, the poor passengers, the poor stewardesses were all splattered like flesh sparklers over the water just out of Cuba. A fisherman found one seat of the airplane. Castro expressed regrets.

Quadberry came back to Clinton two weeks after Lilian and the others bound for Tampa were dead. He hadn't heard about her. So I told him Lilian was dead when I met him at the airport. Quadberry was thin and rather meek in his civvies—a gray suit and an out-of-style tie. The white ends of his hair were not there—the halo had disappeared—because his hair was cut short. The Arab nose seemed a pitiable defect in an ash-whiskered face that was beyond anemic now. He looked shorter, stooped. The truth was he was sick, his back was killing him. His breath was heavy-laden with airplane martinis and in his limp right hand he held a wet cigar. I told him about Lilian. He mumbled something sideways that I could not possibly make out.

"You've got to speak right at me, remember? Remember me, Quadberry?"

"Mom and Dad of course aren't here."

"No. Why aren't they?"

"He wrote me a letter after we bombed Hué. Said he hadn't sent me to Annapolis to bomb the architecture of Hué. He had been there once and had some important experience—French-kissed the queen of Hué or the like. Anyway, he said I'd have to do a hell of a lot of repentance for that. But he and Mom are separate people. Why isn't *she* here?"

"I don't know."

"I'm not asking you the question. The question is to God."

He shook his head. Then he sat down on the floor of the terminal. People had to walk around. I asked him to get up.

"No. How is old Clinton?"

"Horrible. Aluminum subdivisions, cigar boxes with four thin columns in front, thick as a hive. We got a turquoise water tank; got a shopping center, a monster Jitney Jungle, fifth-rate teenyboppers covering the place like ants." Why was I being so frank just now, as Quadberry sat on the floor downcast, drooped over like a long weak candle? "It's not our town anymore, Ard. It's going to hurt to drive back into it. Hurts me every day. Please get up."

"And Lilian's not even over there now."

"No. She's a cloud over the Gulf of Mexico. You flew out of Pensacola once. You know what beauty those pink and blue clouds are. That's how I think of her."

"Was there a funeral?"

"Oh, yes. Her Methodist preacher and a big crowd over at Wright Ferguson funeral home. Your mother and father were there. Your father shouldn't have come. He could barely walk. Please get up."

"Why? What am I going to do, where am I going?"

"You've got your saxophone."

"Was there a coffin? Did you all go by and see the pink or blue cloud in it?" He was sneering now as he had done when he was eleven and fourteen and seventeen.

"Yes, they had a very ornate coffin."

"Lilian was the Unknown Stewardess. I'm not getting up."

"I said you still have your saxophone."

"No, I don't. I tried to play it on the ship after the last time I hurt my back. No go. I can't bend my neck or spine to play it. The pain kills me."

"Well, *don't* get up, then. Why am I asking you to get up? I'm just a deaf drummer, too vain to buy a hearing aid. Can't stand to write the ad copy I do. Wasn't I a good drummer?"

"Superb."

"But we can't be in this condition forever. The police are going to come and make you get up if we do it much longer."

The police didn't come. It was Quadberry's mother who came. She looked me in the face and grabbed my shoulders before she saw Ard on the floor. When she saw him she yanked him off the floor, hugging him passionately. She was shaking with sobs. Quadberry was gathered to her as if he were a rope she was trying to wrap around herself. Her mouth was all over him. Quadberry's mother was a good-looking woman of fifty. I simply held her purse. He cried out that his back was hurting. At last she let him go.

"So now we walk," I said.

"Dad's in the car trying to quit crying," said his mother.

"This is nice," Quadberry said. "I thought everything and everybody was dead around here." He put his arms around his mother. "Let's all go off and kill some time together." His mother's hair was on his lips. "You?" he asked me.

"Murder the devil out of it," I said.

I pretended to follow their car back to their house in Clinton. But when we were going through Jackson, I took the North 55 exit and disappeared from them, exhibiting a great amount of taste, I thought. I would get in their way in this reunion. I had an unimprovable apartment on Old Canton Road in a huge plaster house, Spanish style, with a terrace and ferns and yucca plants, and a green door where I went in. When I woke up I didn't have to make my coffee or fry my egg. The girl who slept in my bed did that. She was Lilian's little sister, Esther Field. Esther was pretty in a minor way and I was proud how I had tamed her to clean and cook around the place. The Field family would appreciate how I lived with her. I showed her the broom and the skillet, and she loved them. She also learned to speak very slowly when she had to say something.

Esther answered the phone when Quadberry called me seven months later. She gave me his message. He wanted to know my opinion on a decision he had to make. There was this Dr. Gordon, a surgeon at Emory Hospital in Atlanta, who said he could cure Quadberry's back problem. Quadberry's back was killing him. He was in torture even holding up the phone to say this. The surgeon said there was a seventy-five/twenty-five chance. Seventy-five that it would be successful, twenty-five that it would be fatal. Esther waited for my opinion. I told her to tell Quadberry to go over to Emory. He'd got through with luck in Vietnam, and now he should ride it out in this petty back operation.

Esther delivered the message and hung up.

"He said the surgeon's just his age; he's some genius from Johns Hopkins Hospital. He said this Gordon guy has published a lot of articles on spinal operations," said Esther.

"Fine and good. All is happy. Come to bed."

I felt her mouth and her voice on my ears, but I could hear only a sort of loud pulse from the girl. All I could do was move toward moisture and nipples and hair.

Quadberry lost his gamble at Emory Hospital in Atlanta. The brilliant surgeon his age lost him. Quadberry died. He died with his Arabian nose up in the air.

That is why I told this story and will never tell another.

ON THE ROAD

JOAN DIDION

Where are we heading, they asked in all the television and
radio studios. They asked it in New York and Los Angeles
and they asked it in Boston and Washington and they asked
it in Dallas and Houston and Chicago and San Francisco.
Sometimes they made eye contact as they asked it. Sometimes they closed their eyes as they asked it. Quite often
they wondered not just where we were heading but where
we were heading "as Americans," or "as concerned Americans," or "as American women," or, on one occasion, "as
the American guy and the American woman." I never
learned the answer, nor did the answer matter, for one of
the eerie and liberating aspects of broadcast discourse is
that nothing one says will alter in the slightest either the
form or the length of the conversation. Our voices in the
studios were those of manic actors assigned to do three-
minute, four-minute, seven-minute improvs. Our faces on
the monitors were those of concerned Americans. On my
way to one of those studios in Boston I had seen the mag-
nolias bursting white down Marlborough Street. On my
way to another in Dallas I had watched the highway lights
blazing and dimming pink against the big dawn sky. Outside

one studio in Houston the afternoon heat was sinking into the deep primeval green of the place and outside the next, that night in Chicago, snow fell and glittered in the lights along the lake. Outside all these studios America lay in all its exhilaratingly volatile weather and eccentricity and specificity, but inside the studios we shed the specific and rocketed on to the general, for they were The Interviewers and I was The Author and the single question we seemed able to address together was *where are we heading.*

> "8:30 A.M. to 9:30 A.M.: LIVE on WFSB TV/THIS
>   MORNING.
> "10 A.M. to 10:30 A.M.: LIVE on WINF AM/THE
>   WORLD TODAY.
> "10:45 A.M. to 11:45 A.M.: PRESS INTERVIEW with
>   HARTFORD COURANT.
> "12 noon to 1:30 P.M.: AUTOGRAPHING at BARNES
>   AND NOBLE.
> "2 P.M. to 2:30 P.M.: TAPE at WDRC AM/FM.
> "3 P.M. to 3:30 P.M.: PRESS INTERVIEW with THE
>   HILL INK.
> "7:30 P.M. to 9 P.M.: TAPE at WHNB TV/WHAT
>   ABOUT WOMEN."

From 12 noon to 1:30 p.m., that first day in Hartford, I talked to a man who had cut a picture of me from a magazine in 1970 and had come round to Barnes and Noble to see what I looked like in 1977. From 2 p.m. to 2:30 p.m., that first day in Hartford, I listened to the receptionists at WDRC AM/FM talk about the new records and I watched snow drop from the pine boughs in the cemetery across the street. The name of the cemetery was Mt. St. Benedict and my husband's father had been buried there. "Any Steely

Dan come in?" the receptionists kept asking. From 8:30 a.m. until 9 p.m., that first day in Hartford, I neglected to mention the name of the book I was supposed to be promoting. It was my fourth book but I had never before done what is called in the trade a book tour. I was not sure what I was doing or why I was doing it. I had left California equipped with two "good" suits, a box of unanswered mail, Elizabeth Hardwick's *Seduction and Betrayal*, Edmund Wilson's *To the Finland Station*, six Judy Blume books, and my eleven-year-old daughter. The Judy Blume books were along to divert my daughter. My daughter was along to divert me. Three days into the tour I sent home the box of unanswered mail to make room for a packet of Simon and Schuster press releases describing me in favorable terms. Four days into the tour I sent home *Seduction and Betrayal* and *To the Finland Station* to make room for a thousand-watt hair blower. By the time I reached Boston, ten days into the tour, I knew that I had never before heard and would possibly never again hear America singing at precisely this pitch: ethereal, speedy, an angel choir on Dexamyl.

Where were we heading. The set for this discussion was always the same: a cozy oasis of wicker and ferns in the wilderness of cables and cameras and Styrofoam coffee cups that was the actual studio. On wicker settees across the nation I expressed my conviction that we were heading "into an era" of whatever the clock seemed to demand. In green rooms across the nation I listened to other people talk about where we were heading, and also about their vocations, avocations, and secret interests. I discussed L-dopa and bio-rhythm with a woman whose father invented prayer breakfasts. I exchanged makeup tips with a former

Mouseketeer. I stopped reading newspapers and started re-
lying on bulletins from limo drivers, from Mouseketeers,
from the callers-in on call-in shows and from the closed-
circuit screens in airports that flashed random stories off
the wire ("CARTER URGES BARBITURATE BAN" is one
that got my attention at La Guardia) between advertise-
ments for *Shenandoah*. I gravitated to the random. I swung
with the nonsequential.

I began to see America as my own, a child's map over
which my child and I could skim and light at will. We spoke
not of cities but of airports. If rain fell at Logan we could
find sun at Dulles. Bags lost at O'Hare could be found at
Dallas/Fort Worth. In the first-class cabins of the planes on
which we traveled we were often, my child and I, the only
female passengers, and I apprehended for the first time
those particular illusions of mobility which power American business. Time was money. Motion was progress. Decisions were snap and the ministrations of other people
were constant. Room service, for example, assumed para-
mount importance. We needed, my eleven-year-old and I,
instant but erratically timed infusions of consommé, oatmeal, crab salad, and asparagus vinaigrette. We needed
Perrier water and tea to drink when we were working. We
needed bourbon on the rocks and Shirley Temples to drink
when we were not. A kind of irritable panic came over us
when room service went off, and also when no one answered in the housekeeping department. In short we had
fallen into the peculiar hormonal momentum of business
travel, and I had begun to understand the habituation many
men and a few women have to planes and telephones and
schedules. I had begun to regard my own schedule—a
sheaf of thick cream-colored pages printed with the words
"SIMON & SCHUSTER/A DIVISION OF GULF & WEST-

ERN CORPORATION"—with a reverence approaching the mystical. We wanted twenty-four-hour room service. We wanted direct-dial telephones. We wanted to stay on the road forever.

We saw air as our element. In Houston the air was warm and rich and suggestive of fossil fuel and we pretended we owned a house in River Oaks. In Chicago the air was brilliant and thin and we pretended we owned the twenty-seventh floor of the Ritz. In New York the air was charged and crackling and shorting out with opinions, and we pretended we had some. Everyone in New York had opinions. Opinions were demanded in return. The absence of opinion was construed as opinion. Even my daughter was developing opinions. "Had an interesting talk with Carl Bernstein," she noted in the log she had been assigned to keep for her fifth-grade teacher in Malibu, California. Many of these New York opinions seemed intended as tonic revisions, bold corrections to opinions in vogue during the previous week, but since I had just dropped from the sky it was difficult for me to distinguish those opinions which were "bold" and "revisionist" from those which were merely "weary" and "rote." At the time I left New York many people were expressing a bold belief in "joy"—joy in children, joy in wedlock, joy in the dailiness of life—but joy was trickling down fast to show-business personalities. Mike Nichols, for example, was expressing his joy in the pages of *Newsweek*, and also his weariness with "lapidary bleakness." Lapidary bleakness was definitely rote.

We were rethinking the sixties that week, or Morris Dickstein was.

We were taking another look at the fifties that week, or Hilton Kramer was.

I agreed passionately. I disagreed passionately. I called room service on one phone and listened attentively on the other to people who seemed convinced that the "texture" of their lives had been agreeably or adversely affected by conversion to the politics of joy, by regression to lapidary bleakness, by the sixties, by the fifties, by the recent change in administrations and by the sale of *The Thorn Birds* to paper for one-million-nine.

I lost track of information.

I was blitzed by opinion.

I began to see opinions arcing in the air, intersecting flight patterns. The Eastern shuttle was cleared for landing and so was lapidary bleakness. John Leonard and joy were on converging vectors. I began to see the country itself as a projection on air, a kind of hologram, an invisible grid of image and opinion and electronic impulse. There were opinions in the air and there were planes in the air and there were even people in the air: one afternoon in New York my husband saw a man jump from a window and fall to the sidewalk outside the Yale Club. I mentioned this to a *Daily News* photographer who was taking my picture. "You have to catch a jumper in the act to make the paper," he advised me. He had caught two in the act but only the first had made the paper. The second was a better picture but coincided with the crash of a DC-10 at Orly. "They're all over town," the photographer said. "Jumpers. A lot of them aren't even jumpers. They're window washers. Who fall."

What does that say about us as a nation, I was asked the next day when I mentioned the jumpers and window washers on the air. *Where are we headed.* On the twenty-seventh floor of the Ritz in Chicago my daughter and I sat frozen at the breakfast table until the window washers glided safely out of sight. At a call-in station in Los Angeles I was told by the guard that there would be a delay because they had a jumper on the line. "I say let him jump," the guard said to me. I imagined a sky dense with jumpers and fallers and DC-10s. I held my daughter's hand at takeoff and landing and watched for antennae on the drive into town. The big antennae with the pulsing red lights had been for a month our landmarks. The big antennae with the pulsing red lights had in fact been for a month our destinations. "Out I-10 to the antenna" was the kind of direction we had come to understand, for we were on the road, on the grid, on the air and also in it. *Where were we heading.* I don't know where you're heading, I said in the studio attached to the last of these antennae, my eyes fixed on still another of the neon FLEETWOOD MAC signs that flickered that spring in radio stations from coast to coast, but I'm heading home.

FALLING

JAMES DICKEY

A twenty-nine-year-old stewardess fell . . .
to her death tonight when she was swept
through an emergency door that suddenly
sprang open . . . The body . . . was found . . .
three hours after the accident.
   —*The New York Times*

The states when they black out and lie there rolling   when they turn
To something transcontinental   move by   drawing moonlight out of the great
One-sided stone hung off the starboard wingtip   some sleeper next to
An engine is groaning for coffee   and there is faintly coming in
Somewhere the vast beast-whistle of space. In the galley with its racks
Of trays   she rummages for a blanket   and moves in her slim tailored
Uniform to pin it over the cry at the top of the door. As though she blew

The door down with a silent blast from her lungs   frozen   she is black
Out finding herself   with the plane nowhere and her body taking by the throat
The undying cry of the void   falling   living   beginning to be something
That no one has ever been and lived through   screaming without enough air
Still neat   lipsticked   stockinged   girdled by regulation   her hat
Still on   her arms and legs in no world   and yet spaced also strangely
With utter placid rightness on thin air   taking her time   she holds it
In many places   and now, still thousands of feet from her death she seems

306

FALLING

To slow   she develops interest   she turns in her maneuverable body

To watch it. She is hung high up in the overwhelming middle of things in her
Self   in low body-whistling wrapped intensely   in all her dark dance-weight
Coming down from a marvellous leap   with the delaying, dumfounding ease
Of a dream of being drawn   like endless moonlight to the harvest soil
Of a central state of one's country   with a great gradual warmth coming
Over her   floating   finding more and more breath in what she has been using
For breath   as the levels become more human   seeing clouds placed honestly
Below her left and right   riding slowly toward them   she clasps it all
To her and can hang her hands and feet in it in peculiar ways   and
Her eyes opened wide by wind, can open her mouth as wide   wider and suck
All the heat from the cornfields   can go down on her back with a feeling
Of stupendous pillows stacked under her   and can turn   turn as to someone
In bed   smile, understood in darkness   can go away   slant   slide
Off tumbling   into the emblem of a bird with its wings half-spread
Or whirl madly on herself   in endless gymnastics in the growing warmth
Of wheatfields rising toward the harvest moon.   There is time to live
In superhuman health   seeing mortal unreachable lights far down seeing
An ultimate highway with one late priceless car probing it   arriving
In a square town   and off her starboard arm the glitter of water catches
The moon by its one shaken side   scaled, roaming silver   My God it is good
And evil   lying in one after another of all the positions for love
Making   dancing   sleeping   and now cloud wisps at her no
Raincoat   no matter   all small towns brokenly brighter from inside
Cloud   she walks over them like rain   bursts out to behold a Greyhound
Bus shooting light through its sides   it is the signal to go straight
Down like a glorious diver   then feet first   her skirt stripped beautifully
Up   her face in fear-scented cloths   her legs deliriously bare   then
Arms out   she slow-rolls over   steadies out   waits for something great
To take control of her   trembles near feathers   planes head-down
The quick movements of bird-necks turning her head   gold eyes the insight-
eyesight of owls blazing into the hencoops   a taste for chicken overwhelming
Her   the long-range vision of hawks enlarging all human lights of cars
Freight trains   looped bridges   enlarging the moon racing slowly
Through all the curves of a river   all the darks of the midwest blazing
From above. A rabbit in a bush turns white   the smothering chickens
Huddle   for over them there is still time for something to live
With the streaming half-idea of a long stoop   a hurtling   a fall

307

That is controlled   that plummets as it wills   turns gravity
Into a new condition, showing its other side like a moon   shining
New Powers   there is still time to live on a breath made of nothing
But the whole night   time for her to remember to arrange her skirt
Like a diagram of a bat   tightly it guides her   she has this flying-skin
Made of garments   and there are also those sky-divers on TV   sailing
In sunlight   smiling under their goggles   swapping batons back and forth
And He who jumped without a chute and was handed one by a diving
Buddy. She looks for her grinning companion   white teeth   nowhere
She is screaming   singing hymns   her thin human wings spread out
From her neat shoulders   the air beast-crooning to her   warbling
And she can no longer behold the huge partial form of the world   now
She is watching her country lose its evoked master shape   watching it lose
And gain   get back its houses and peoples   watching it bring up
Its local lights   single homes   lamps on barn roofs   if she fell
Into water she might live   like a diver   cleaving   perfect   plunge

Into another   heavy silver   unbreathable   slowing   saving
Element: there is water   there is time to perfect all the fine
Points of diving   feet together   toes pointed   hands shaped right
To insert her into water like a needle   to come out healthily dripping
And be handed a Coca-Cola   there they are   there are the waters
Of life   the moon packed and coiled in a reservoir   so let me begin
To plane across the night air of Kansas   opening my eyes superhumanly
Bright   to the damned moon   opening the natural wings of my jacket
By Don Loper   moving like a hunting owl toward the glitter of water
One cannot just fall   just tumble screaming all that time   one must use
It she is now through with all   through all   clouds   damp   hair
Straightened   the last wisp of fog pulled apart on her face like wool revealing
New darks   new progressions of headlights along dirt roads from chaos

And night   a gradual warming   a new-made, inevitable world of one's own
Country   a great stone of light in its waiting waters   hold   hold out
For water: who knows when what correct young woman must take up her body
And fly   and head for the moon-crazed inner eye of midwest imprisoned
Water   stored up for her for years   the arms of her jacket slipping
Air up her sleeves to go   all over her? What final things can be said
Of one who starts out sheerly in her body in the high middle of night
Air   to track down water like a rabbit where it lies like life itself

Off to the right in Kansas? She goes toward   the blazing-bare lake
Her skirts neat   her hands and face warmed more and more by the air
Rising from pastures of beans   and under her   under chenille bedspreads
The farm girls are feeling the goddess in them struggle and rise brooding
On the scratch-shining posts of the bed   dreaming of female signs
Of the moon   male blood like iron   of what is really said by the moan
Of airliners passing over them at dead of midwest midnight   passing
Over brush fires   burning out in silence on little hills   and will wake
To see the woman they should be   struggling on the rooftree to become
Stars: for her the ground is closer   water is nearer   she passes
It   then banks   turns   her sleeves fluttering differently as she rolls
Out to face the east, where the sun shall come up from wheatfields she must
Do something with water   fly to it   fall in it   drink it   rise
From it   but there is none left upon earth   the clouds have drunk it back
The plants have sucked it down   there are standing toward her only
The common fields of death   she comes back from flying to falling
Returns to a powerful cry   the silent scream with which she blew down
The coupled door of the airliner   nearly   nearly losing hold
Of what she has done   remembers   remembers the shape at the heart
Of cloud   fashionably swirling   remembers she still has time to die
Beyond explanation. Let her now take off her hat in summer air the contour
Of cornfields   and have enough time to kick off her one remaining
Shoe with the toes   of the other foot   to unhook her stockings
With calm fingers, noting how fatally easy it is to undress in midair
Near death   when the body will assume without effort any position
Except the one that will sustain it   enable it to rise   live
Not die   nine farms hover close   widen   eight of them separate, leaving
One in the middle   then the fields of that farm do the same   there is no
Way to back off   from her chosen ground   but she sheds the jacket
With its silver sad impotent wings   sheds the bat's guiding tailpiece
Of her skirt   the lightning-charged clinging of her blouse   the intimate
Inner flying-garment of her slip in which she rides like the holy ghost
Of a virgin   sheds the long windsocks of her stockings   absurd
Brassiere   then feels the girdle required by regulations squirming
Off her: no longer monobuttocked   she feels the girdle flutter   shake
In her hand   and float   upward   her clothes rising off her ascending
Into cloud   and fights away from her head the last sharp dangerous shoe
Like a dumb bird   and now will drop in   SOON   now will drop

In like this   the greatest thing that ever came to Kansas   down from all
Heights   all levels of American breath   layered in the lungs from the frail
Chill of space to the loam where extinction slumbers in corn tassels thickly
And breathes like rich farmers counting: will come along them after
Her last superhuman act   the last slow careful passing of her hands
All over her unharmed body   desired by every sleeper in his dream:
Boys finding for the first time their loins filled with heart's blood
Widowed farmers whose hands float under light covers to find themselves
Arisen at sunrise   the splendid position of blood unearthly drawn
Toward clouds   all feel something   pass over them as she passes
Her palms over *her* long legs   *her* small breasts   and deeply between
Her thighs   her hair shot loose from all pins   streaming in the wind
Of her body   let her come openly   trying at the last second to land
On her back   This is it   THIS

                                All those who find her impressed
In the soft loam   gone down   driven well into the image of her body
The furrows for miles flowing in upon her where she lies very deep
In her mortal outline   in the earth as it is in cloud   can tell nothing
But that she is there   inexplicable   unquestionable   and remember
That something broke in them as well   and began to live and die more
When they walked for no reason into their fields to where the whole earth
Caught her   interrupted her maiden flight   told her how to lie she cannot
Turn   go away   cannot move   cannot slide off it and assume another
Position   no sky-diver with any grin could save her   hold her in his arms
Plummet with her   unfold above her his wedding silks   she can no longer
Mark the rain with whirling women that take the place of a dead wife
Or the goddess in Norwegian farm girls   or all the back-breaking whores
Of Wichita. All the known air above her is not giving up quite one
Breath   it is all gone   and yet not dead   not anywhere else
Quite   lying still in the field on her back   sensing the smells
Of incessant growth try to lift her   a little sight left in the corner
Of one eye   fading   seeing something wave   lies believing
That she could have made it   at the best part of her brief goddess
State   to water   gone in headfirst   come out smiling   invulnerable
Girl in a bathing-suit ad   but she is lying like a sunbather at the last
Of moonlight   half-buried in her impact on the earth   not far
From a railroad trestle   a water tank   she could see if she could
Raise her head from her modest hole   with her clothes beginning
To come down all over Kansas   into bushes   on the dewy sixth green

Of a golf course   one shoe   her girdle coming down fantastically
On a clothesline, where it belongs   her blouse on a lightning rod:

Lies in the fields   in *this* field   on her broken back as though on
A cloud she cannot drop through   while farmers sleepwalk without
Their women from houses   a walk like falling toward the far waters
Of life   in moonlight   toward the dreamed eternal meaning of their farms
Toward the flowering of the harvest in their hands   that tragic cost
Feels herself go   go toward   go outward   breathes at last fully
Not   and tries   less   once   tries   tries   AH, GOD—

THE GOLDEN TRIANGLE

LINDA YABLONSKY

It's seventeen hours to Tokyo in a jumbo jet without a single
unoccupied seat. Everyone but us is Japanese. Before the
movie starts there's a newsreel. The big news is a midair
crash of a Japan Air Lines plane. There are a few survivors,
somehow—I don't get how, the broadcast's in Japanese.
Three of the survivors, a child and two young women, appear in interviews, heads bandaged, necks braced. Fire has
left one badly burned. Our cabin is quiet. This is Japan Air
Lines.

Seven hours into the first leg of the trip, I get dopesick
in my seat. I'm choking on my tongue, can't swallow. My
skin feels loose on my skeleton, my eyes are running. So's
my nose. The fellow in the seat next to me offers a pack of
Kleenex, asks if I want any help from the crew. No, no, I
say, and head for the John. I can see Mary Motion sitting a
few rows behind me, her eyes wide and wondering, and
Mario on the other side of the plane, pretending he doesn't
know me.

In my bag I've got a couple of methadone biscuits,
some Lomotil and codeine, but no dope. I've been too cautious. Didn't want to travel with powder. What a jerk. What

am I making this trip for, if not to carry? I stumble into the loo and bite off a piece of a meth biscuit, swallow a codeine. A minute later, it comes back up. My entire body retches, but nothing else is in it. I catch myself in the blue-green light of the tiny bathroom mirror. I have a sense there isn't a drop of fluid left inside me, no bile, no blood. I don't know how I can still be alive. If appearances mean anything, I'm not.

I swallow another piece of meth. Before I return to my seat, a stewardess brings me the sugar I ask for in little packets; down they go. I stare at her, eyes full of tears, I'm choking on my breath "More sugar, please," I gasp. She hesitates a moment, gets me another handful. Soon the hacking cough stops, but I'm far from feeling right. My arms seem a very long distance away, my hair feels false. Maybe this is normal, I think, as I notice the other passengers. They look green, too.

At the Tokyo airport, we change to a smaller jet for the trip to Bangkok, another five hours away. Everyone on this plane is Indian, they're going to Kashmir. Three men dressed in flimsy white leggings and long flowing blouses, their heads wrapped in white turbans, their faces hidden by full graying beards, are the only passengers in the first-class seats. I'm at a window in coach. I don't know why I feel resentful—this is their part of the world. White skin doesn't always bestow privileges. I stare out the window. The sky's black.

For dinner we get soba noodles, seaweed, and some kind of bean cake for the third time since the trip began. Breakfast, lunch, dinner, the menu's always the same. So is the entertainment: the plane-crash news. Over the summer of 1985, there have been more crashes than at any one time in the history of commercial aviation. I try to sleep. No use.

It's midnight when we arrive in Bangkok. Police are everywhere, soldiers too. There's been a coup, the borders are closed. Our cab driver says, "It's nothing."

Many more sleepless hours pass in the hotel room I share with Mary, who falls out the minute we get inside. The thin carpet is red, the bedspread is red, the curtains are red. The walls appear to be yellow, I'm not sure. We haven't bothered with the lights. The neon glow from the street outside provides all the illumination I can bear.

Mario spends the night in the hotel bar, chatting up a "sexteen"-year-old girl, one of many. I stay in my room, chipping at the codeine. I'm trying to save the meth. We don't know how long it'll be before we can score—maybe hours, maybe days. I find more packets of sugar from the plane, eat them. I pull the thin bedsheet over my head. First I'm freezing, then I'm sweating. All night long I'm turning the air conditioner off and on, on and off, opening and closing the window. The air outside is rank. I listen for gunfire, hear nothing.

In the morning I force myself into the shower. The water rails against my skin like pellets of thin steel. I order coffee from room service. It arrives in a steaming pot. I drink all of it.

At the hotel travel agency, I buy our plane tickets north. We're headed for Chiang Mai, a town in the hills near the Burmese border, popular with tourists. "It's cooler there," the ticket agent tells me. "May I arrange your hotel?" Angelo's already given me the name of the place he wants us to stay. The agent reserves three rooms.

My hands are shaking so badly I can't hold the tickets. I stuff them in my bag, approach the hotel dining room. A breakfast buffet is set up on the bar, staffed by men in olive-and-gold bus jackets, standing where the hookers had been the night before. The men are all short and all have the same haircut, styled, possibly, with an ax. They look pock-marked and sallow. I down another coffee, try to swallow a piece of fruit, settle for a few bites of sticky rice. Mario comes in, smiling, clean-shaven, wet from the shower. The girl was very nice, he says. It was fun in the bar last night. He had a nice massage. We should have come on down.

We still have a few hours to kill before plane time. In the narrow street outside the hotel, the air is so muggy and thick with smog I can hardly move my legs. Again I wish I'd brought something with me. Ridiculous, leaving all the dope at home. I'm much sicker than I ever expected, but I don't want to take a chance on buying something here from a total stranger.

We hail a cab, because it's air-conditioned. The driver wants to sell us a nickel bag of pot. I frown at this but Mario thinks it's great. I try to convince him otherwise. Everyone knows cabdrivers are cops, and besides, marijuana's not what we're here for. When I'm not looking, he buys it any-way. "Everyone does it," he whines.

"We're not everybody," I reply.

He looks dubious.

We drive along the Patpong Road, a main drag, strip joints mostly, a few jewelers. Bangkok's a stinking place. Where are the temples of gold? Families are living in the street, tending their woks over fires in the gutter, cooking breakfast. The sickening smell of frying palm oil wafts through the trees. With the auto exhaust fumes and heavy humidity, the air's nearly impossible to breathe. I bite off another piece of meth.

It's only eleven a.m., but we head for a bar and knock back a few beers. I don't taste them. My tongue feels bloody. I'm biting it. My eyes swim in my head. Mario wants a plate of French fries. They carry the stench of that sickening oil. I'll kill him, I think, before this is over.

We've all lost interest in a tour of the city's canals recommended in my guidebook. Klongs, they call them. "King Klongs," I say to Mary, who looks as glum as I feel. We walk back to the hotel.

It's almost noon and the equatorial heat has steeply escalated. All along the sidewalk, food vendors sitting under striped umbrellas display edibles we can't identify. Never have I seen food like this: strange shapes, unnatural colors, horrid odors. Shops advertise silk and linen suits made to order in a day. Men and women in thin polyester clothing rush to jobs. What about that coup? No sign of an army anywhere. I buy an English-language newspaper. The coup was a failure, but a couple of English journalists were killed and the borders are still closed. There's an article about the Thai Queen's visit to the Paris collections. A woman in low-heeled leather pumps passes by. Everyone else wears flip-flops.

The Bangkok airport looks different in daylight, clean and not too busy. The only activity on the tarmac surrounds a Vietnamese plane loading cargo. The terminal's metal detector buzzes as I pass. Two attendants approach, and a nearby guard. They want to search my bag. At the bottom of an inside pouch, I have a small plastic paper-cutter with a retractable blade. It doesn't look any more threatening than the prize in a Cracker Jack box. The blade is barely a half-inch long but it's sharp enough to cut a piece from a solid rock of dope—or a face. There's a small pocketknife in there, too, and a prescription bottle with my various pills. The guard seems more interested in my Polaroid. I waste a picture on him, and he lets me pass.

The trip north takes less than an hour. A man holding a sign with the name of our hotel takes us to a van, where a perky young woman is waiting, all smiles. I notice her skin—not a line, not a wrinkle—her cheeks are naturally rosy. She wears her hair short, cut in a subtle flip. Her dark eyes dance into mine. I haven't seen anyone like her since high school.

She says her name is Taffy. This makes me laugh and she takes me for a jolly person. I laugh again. She's a student at a nearby college and she's very congenial. How long will we be staying in Chiang Mai? she asks, very cheerful, never losing the smile. Where are we from? Would we like to take a tour of the temples?

Sure, I say. Temples? Sure. She hands me a four-color brochure. It describes several different excursions, some whole-day, some half-day, some two-day. I pick the first one scheduled for the morning, a half-day. Taffy seems happy at this. Her cheeriness is contagious. Could she be stoned? No, I don't think she's ever smelled dope in her life.

I thumb through the rest of the brochure. There are thirty-six temples within the walls of Chiang Mai, eighty more in the country around it. Taffy says if we stay another day, we can take in a few mountain villages, too. In one all they make is umbrellas. In another, silks. Which, I wonder to myself, is the one where they make the heroin?

At the hotel we drop our bags and go outside to get the lay. Mario says it's too early to check in with the connection. I didn't know we had an appointment. They have hours, he tells me. I give out an involuntary sigh. It's the same all over, isn't it?

The streets of Chiang Mai are deserted. Though it's late afternoon, there's hardly a shadow. The sky's blue-on-blue, not a cloud, the air so hot and pink and quiet it feels like a dream. 1 keep thinking the road's unpaved but it isn't— some kind of dusty illusion. The whole town seems built on straw. A high fence of loosely tied wooden poles runs down one side of the street, shielding the jumble of rickety houses behind it. On the other is a low line of stuccoed shops, most of them shuttered against the sun. A skinny Caucasian fellow lurches toward us with that telltale junkie buckle to his knees. His hair is long and stringy, his black jeans torn at the seat and dusty as the street. He hasn't had a bath or a meal in a while. His skin is just this side of human, his eyes have rolled back in his head. Mary makes a sound. "Well," she smirks. "We've come to the right place."

We're going to carry the dope in our intestines, packed tight in knotted condoms. We need to find a drugstore right away. The hotel concierge has told us there's one just down the road. There is. Poking through the crowded shelves, we look for laxatives and lubricants, condoms, and tuberculin spikes. Behind the counter, a middle-aged Thai man and woman, husband and wife, serve us without comment or question. No Taffy here. No "Where are you from? Do you like our town? Will you stay long?" None of that. They don't ask if we're related or what brought us. They know.

I stay many minutes at the shelves, as absorbed in the colorful boxes and shapely bottles as I was as a kid in the old courthouse that was my hometown library. George Washington had slept there; it had atmosphere. Intoxicated by the smell of polished wood and library paste, lulled by the metronomic ticks of a grandfather clock in the reading room, I lost myself then, as now, in a world of the senses, ruled by a habit of mind. But here products come from China, Egypt, Vietnam, and Germany—George Washington never saw anything like this.

My hand reaches for a small Chinese box with blue lettering. I feel a shallow breath behind my ear. "You don't want that," says a voice. The Thai man is standing at my shoulder, gesturing at the box. "That's not for you," he says. Really? I want to know what it is. The man is loath to say. I have to be careful. I don't want to make a scene. I replace the box and pick up a tube of toothpaste. The man smiles then, trades glances with his wife; we're all very friendly. Mary Motion and I buy a tube of K-Y jelly each, several boxes of condoms, some strong laxative tabs, a couple of clean gimmicks. I pretend this is business-as-usual. In Chiang Mai, maybe it is.

Back on the street it's like a sauna, hot but dry, better than the muggy air of Bangkok, anyway. In the heat even the distant hills look pooped. In the hotel parking lot, pedicab drivers in native costume nap in the passenger seats. We stop in the hotel bar, take a table. The tourists are all out with Taffy or one of the other guides; we're the only customers, one waiter, one barmaid. Mary wonders if they know why we're here. She's too paranoid. "We're tourists," I say. "We're seeing the world."

Mario checks his watch, downs his drink. "Time to go," he says in his thin, reedy voice, forever jovial. Everything to him is a yuk. I don't trust him but he's the one with the directions, which he doesn't share with us. Orders from Angelo, he smiles. I don't.

"Don't forget to bring back a sample," I growl. He gives me a high-sign and a gap-toothed grin. When he's gone I tell Mary we should follow him.

"Not me," she says, looking around uncomfortably. "I'll wait here." We're sitting near a large picture window, just out of the sun. I watch Mario climb into a pedicab and go off. We order another round.

I can't get drunk enough. I ate my last meth biscuit hours ago, it's wearing off. After the long journey, the stultifying heat and sleepless nights, after the vodka I've consumed, I'm in a state of semi-withdrawal. Forty hours ago I was buckling my seat belt at JFK. Now I'm staring into a glass, wishing it didn't have a bottom.

Mary and I wait for Mario and drink. We talk about New York, about the free time we'll have for shopping in Singapore, whether or not we should "lose" our passports there. Singapore is our vacation cover. The Thailand stamps dated only days apart might look funny at customs. Well, we can always get new ones. Mary says you just drop the passport in a mailbox somewhere and tell the consul it's been stolen. People steal American passports all the time.

"I wouldn't mind spending an extra day in Singapore," she giggles. "Maybe we could have some suits made." I wonder how she has the strength to laugh. I want to have cocktails on the veranda at Raffles, the hotel where Somerset Maugham used to stay. Nothing but tourists we are, after all. Taffy will never know the difference, anyway.

Other people are in the bar now, the sun's beginning to drop. We order another round. Suddenly Mario's standing by the table, again with the silly grin. Without a word we troop through the lobby to the elevators. I'm very drunk and a little stooped but at least I'm not noticeably sick. On the wall behind the check-in desk a line of clocks shows the time in every major city in the world. In New York it's about the same time as it is here, but not the same day. We've lost one or gained one, I can't remember.

In my room upstairs Mario explains that the deal is done but we've arrived too late to make the pickup. Tomorrow, he says. Two p.m.

Shit. I was hoping we'd be gone by then. Now we'll have to take Taffy's eight a.m. tour. She's going to call the room at seven.

I ask about the sample. Mario hands me a red condom balloon, its bottom heavy with perfect white powder. I dive into my bag for the pieces of aluminum foil I took from the hotel breakfast bar in Bangkok. I roll up a straw, untie the balloon, smooth out another piece of the foil. I lay down a clump of powder, light it easily. Smoke it. In a second it's gone. In a minute I can feel my eyes sparkle, my back straighten up. "I can walk!" I cry. "I can walk!" I'm suddenly in a party mood, but the other two are busy.

Mario's got a hit in his cooker, a bottlecap from a beer. He's tying off, looking anxious. Mary snorts a line off her compact mirror.

The Golden Triangle, I think, eyeing the mirror, the foil, the cooker. The Golden Triangle. We made it.

Mario boots. Couldn't I have guessed? He's down on the floor with the needle in his arm.

"Oh shit," says Mary.

Mario's going out.

"Let's get him on his feet," I say with a sigh, thinking, Here we go again. Damn.

She doesn't move. I give her a look. She's fucking stoned. Mary's no junkie, just a mule, and now she's stoned. Fucking A.

Finally she reaches over and we pull Mario to his feet. He's heavy. I curse him, take the needle from his arm. He wobbles, down he goes again, but the dope's made us powerful and we pull him up. Mario giggles. His face is scarlet. He's enjoying this! I'm yelling at Mary to wash out the spike, go down to the restaurant, steal some salt. I'm screaming at Mario, "You dumb asshole! Talk to me! Say something!" But all he can do is smile. That lazy, soporific honeymoon smile. I want to wring his neck.

Ten minutes later, Mary returns with the salt. "Forget that," I say. "Help me walk him."

It's another hour or so before we get him looking regular again. Those light eyes of his could give us away in a second. I'm so pissed I could spit. Hungry, too. I want to get some food, but while the others are taking showers I chase a little dragon instead. "I'm holding the sample from now on," I tell them. "We can't have anything like this happen again." They don't argue, I've put myself in charge. From now on, whatever I say goes.

The dead streets of daytime Chiang Mai have become a teeming river of human bodies drifting through the night. Bright paper lanterns float on the breeze, lighting the portals to windowless storefronts. Their doorways are crowded with carved wooden fetishes, some five or six feet tall. All manner of brass orientalia shines from within. Bamboo and straw mats hang everywhere. Flimsy card tables sit edge to edge on the sidewalk, laden with knockoffs of every sort of Western fashion, bending under the weight of Siamese collectibles, ivory and black lead elephants, tiny Buddhas and princesses, scores of beads and lacquerware, some pottery. Hawkers stand before every shop, their eyes shifting over the crowds thronging the street like a mall. Kung-fu music blares from loudspeakers wired to overhanging roofs. Even with all the noise and color, something's missing. It takes me a while to figure out what. It's light. There aren't any signs, no neon, no hanging shingles. None of the shops have names. Even movie houses are marked only by comic-book murals painted on the walls of corner buildings.

According to Taffy, the big draw in Chiang Mai after dark is the Night Market. It's set in a couple of large, two-story rough plank buildings, stall after stall of vegetables and dry goods of every description, fabrics, more elephants, T-shirts, shoes, statues. Each of us buys a few trinkets and a couple of cheap linen.

Someone's watching us now—a sun-browned skinny Thai, a guy about thirty, unusually tall. We can call him "Joe," he says. He speaks a slangy English I imagine he picked up from American soldiers during the Vietnam War, very Burger King with a hard-on. He must have done real well in the 1960s, a street-smart kid pandering to the GIs, showing them a good time in the brothels. We try several times to shake him, but every time we turn around, he's there.

He wants to sell us pot. "Thai stick," he says. "You know Thai stick?" He puffs out his bony chest, full of pride and confidence. His teeth are chipped, his eyes hop. I think he wants to fuck me. I look at Mary. It's obvious she thinks he does, too. Mario, his eyes still lit by the dope, seems to find this amusing. Joe lets a hand hover over his cock, which I can make out pretty well through his chinos. I'm feeling good now, but not that good. I don't want him in my hotel room. I decline the pot, but Joe doesn't let up. He looks me in the eye. "I know what *you* want," he says.

"What do I want?"

"Powder," he says, whispering. "You want white powder."

Mario slides an eyeball my way. "I don't know what you're talking about," I say, looking at Joe.

"No? Okay, I show you."

"Where?" Mario asks.

"Not far, just outside town," says Joe. "Ten miles. You married?" he asks, pointing at me and Mario, Mario and Mary.

"Yeah," we all say together. "No," we say then. Joe makes a face. He asks which hotel we're in, how long we're staying, where we're from. I can see his mind work; he's a hustler. If he gets his hooks into us, we'll be spending all our available cash paying for his silence.

A lot of Thais, Mario has told us, will get real friendly, take your money, even turn you on to a major source, then turn you in to the border guards just as you're leaving the country. We might have to bribe our way out. We've talked about what it takes to buy a general—anywhere from two to ten thousand dollars, maybe more, and then that might not be the end of it, not till we land in jail.

Joe's too cunning not to play every angle. He knows we're no kind of tourists. Mario, stoned as he is, knows this too, but Joe knows a place where the girls are the most beautiful girls in the land and the heroin's the best in the world. Cheap, too, he adds. "Very good price, okay?"

"See you around," I say.

"No, wait!" he calls out, alarmed. "I'm Joe! Joe is A-okay. Ask anybody." He gestures vaguely at the street. "Come on, we have a blast."

"What is this place, exactly?" I ask.

A massage parlor. I might have guessed. They're mentioned everywhere in the guidebook. Massage parlors seem to be this country's main source of income, not including you-know-what. Mario says he really needs a massage. He rubs his ass. He bruised himself falling down earlier.

"It's a trap," I tell him, out of Joe's hearing. "This Joe guy's full of it."

"I don't know ..."

"We can't do this," I say.

"Maybe we should check it out," Mario decides. "We don't have to buy anything. We can just get a massage."

Mary Motion shrugs. "Maybe he's harmless," she says.

"Aren't these places just for men?" I ask Joe. Now I'm certain he means to turn us in, that he has to be an informer.

"No, no," he says, his thin hands parting the air. "Massage for women, too. You like this massage," he insists. "You ever have Thai massage?" I shake my head slowly, no. "Ah! Thai massage very special, you like it. Make you feel *good*. Very *relax*. You have good time," he enthuses. "I show you. Okay?"

"Joe's gonna show us a good time," I say to Mary.

She laughs. "I'm done shopping," she tells me. "Might as well see a little of the country."

"Beautiful scenery," Joe agrees.

"What can we see at night?" I ask.

"Much more to see in the night than the day," he tells me. "I show you."

I don't want to go. I'm hungry again, and tired, edgy. Mary says she is, too, but now we're afraid to eat. Our stomachs have to be empty when we pick up the dope. When you're carrying fifty thousand dollars worth of heroin up your ass, you don't want to have to stop and take a shit.

Joe says we can eat at this place in the woods if we want to. It's a private club. Generals go there. Politicians.

325

"Food good, too," he says, rubbing his belly. "Everything good at this place. Everything A-okay."

"I don't like it," I say.

Joe looks at me in mock horror. "You still don't trust me? But I'm your friend, I am *Joe*. Practically *American*. Joe is A-okay! Ask anyone, they tell you. Everything good with me, everything *okay*.

"He's okay," says Mario. "This is Okay Joe." He gives the guy a brotherly pat on the back. Mario's truly an innocent, I think. He comes from a little town in northern Italy where all he knows is pasta and sunshine—all he ever needs to know. "How long will it take to get there?" he says.

I shake my head. It's Angelo I'm running this trip for and I can't let his only brother go off in the woods alone, not the way he is, stoned, a stupid child. Joe says again it's okay, everything we do with him is okay. "Okay, lady?" he asks. "This is a happy place—check it out."

I don't know what to say. All I can think is, Generals go there.

"What's your name?" Joe asks me.

"Evelyn," I tell him.

He can't pronounce it. "This is Judy," I say, pointing to Mary "She's Judy and I'm Evelyn and this is Joe."

Mario looks at me and laughs. Joe laughs, too. "Ho, Joe! Everything okay, now. Everything way okay." He says he'll get the car.

Okay Joe's "car" turns out to be whatever passing tuk-tuk will stop to take us on. The only one that will is a little three-HP truck, hardly more than a glorified scooter with a cab over the tiny front wheels. A roofed-in pickup affair is attached to the rear with two hard benches along its sides. A piece of thin pink fabric hangs where a window might be between the cab and the back. It's a Thai-sized version of the contraption Anthony Quinn and Giulietta Massina live in in *La Strada*.

"I love that movie," Mario tells me. He hops into the truck.

Our driver motions the rest of us inside. His wife and two small children cram into the front seat, three more remain in back with us. The rear end is open to the street. Vehicles similar to ours stretch beyond as far as I can see, their headlights inching along in the traffic with pedicabs, scooters, public shuttle buses, and bicycles. People on foot are everywhere. "It's the evacuation of Saigon," I say.

Joe looks at me quizzically. His hands are in his lap. "You can sit here," he offers. I'm happy where I am. Not really.

I'm sweating again. So is Mario, profusely. Mary can't get comfortable, either. She tries talking to the children, but they don't speak English. Joe talks to the driver, shouting over the noise of the traffic, the grinding of gears. In ten minutes, we move about a hundred yards.

Another ten minutes pass and we don't move at all. Horns are honking like crazy. Joe keeps up his rap—how great the Thai pot is, how fine the Thai massage, how private the club, how cool the woods, how expert the girls, how young and beautiful, how lucky we are to have met him. "I've gotta get some air," I say and climb out of the truck. Mario and Mary leave with me. We don't look back.

When we reach the Night Market, Joe's there waiting. "Hey, Ef-*leen*," he says. "Why'd you go?" He tugs at my elbow and pulls me toward an alley between the buildings. He has something to show me. Still holding my arm, he reaches in a trash can and removes a rolled-up newspaper. A spray of flowers shows at the top. "You like?" he asks. He tells me to look inside the paper. Under the flower stems I see the marijuana. "I don't think so," I tell him. He's exasperated. Mario gives a yawn.

The Night Market's closing now, it's ten p.m. We're starving. Like wolves we prowl the now-quiet streets, looking for a restaurant that will seat us. The best ones have already stopped serving. A man in the street tells us about an Italian place. We go there. I plead with the owner to stay open a few minutes more. I can't imagine eating Italian food in a place like Chiang Mai, but the thought of Thai food, everything fried, everything riced, disagrees with me more. No matter, the restaurant refuses to stay open.

"But we're from New York," I protest. It makes no impression; clearly, this isn't Italy. Calling the town as many names as we can think of, we walk back to the hotel, back to the bar, to the vodka. We buy a bottle and sit at the one empty table. The restaurant's full up now. There's a band playing, a lounge act with a girl singer doing American pop tunes in three languages. She sings a honking version of "Fever" in English, and "I Left My Heart in San Francisco" in Thai. I set aside my glass and drink from the bottle.

"I'll wake you at seven," I say to Mario when it's done.

"Don't bother," he tells me. "I like sleeping late."

Alone in my room I smoke another line from the sample. It's good stuff, all right. The best.

THE GIRL ON THE PLANE

MARY GAITSKILL

John Morton came down the aisle of the plane, banging his luggage into people's knees and sweating angrily under his suit. He had just run through the corridors of the airport, cursing and struggling with his luggage, slipping and flailing in front of the vapid brat at the seat assignment desk. Too winded to speak, he thrust his ticket at the boy and readjusted his luggage in his sticky hands. "You're a little late for a seat assignment," said the kid snottily. "I hope you can get on board before it pulls away."

He took his boarding pass and said, "Thanks, you little prick." The boy's discomfiture was made more obvious by his pretense of hauteur; it both soothed and fed John's anger.

At least he was able to stuff his bags into the compartment above the first seat he found. He sat down, grunting territorially, and his body slowly eased into a normal dull pulse and ebb. He looked at his watch; desk attendant to the contrary, the plane was sitting stupidly still, twenty minutes after takeoff time. He had the pleasing fantasy of punching the little bastard's face.

329

He was always just barely making his flight. His wife had read in one of her magazines that habitual lateness meant lack of interest in life or depression or something. Well, who could blame him for lack of interest in the crap he was dealing with?

He glanced at the guy a seat away from him on the left, an alcoholic-looking old shark in an expensive suit, who sat staring fixedly at a magazine photograph of a grinning blonde in a white jumpsuit. The plane continued to sit there, while stewardesses fiddled with compartments and women rolled up and down the aisles on trips to the bathroom. They were even boarding a passenger; a woman had just entered, flushed and vigorously banging along the aisle with her luggage. She was very pretty, and he watched her, his body still feebly sending off alarm signals in response to its forced run.

"Hi," she said. "I'm in the middle there."

"By all means." The force of his anger entered his magnanimity and swelled it hugely; he pinched his ankles together to let her by. She put her bag under the seat in front of her, sat down, and rested her booted feet on its pale leather. The old shark by the window glanced appraisingly at her breasts through her open coat. He looked up at her face and made smile movements. The stewardess did her parody of a suffocating person reaching for an air mask, the pilot mumbled, the plane prepared to assert its unnatural presence in nature.

"They said I'd missed my flight by fifteen minutes," she said. "But I knew I'd make it. They're never on time." Her voice was unexpectedly small, with a rough, gravelly undertone that was seedy and schoolgirlish at once.

"It's bullshit," he said. "Well, what can you do?" She had large hazel eyes.

She smiled a tight, rueful smile that he associated with women who'd been fucked too many times and which he found sexy. She cuddled more deeply into her seat, produced a *People* magazine, and intently read it. He liked her profile—which was an interesting combination of soft (forehead, chin) and sharp (nose, cheekbones)—her shoulder-length, pale-brown hair, and her soft Mediterranean skin. He liked the coarse quality in the subtle downturn of her lips, and the heavy way her lids sat on her eyes. She was older than he'd originally thought, probably in her early thirties.

Who did she remind him of? A girl from a long time ago, an older version of some date or crush or screw. Or love, he thought gamely.

The pilot said they would be leaving the ground shortly. She was now reading a feature that appeared to be about the wedding of two people who had AIDS. He thought of his wife, at home in Minneapolis, at the stove poking at something, in the living room reading, the fuzzy pink of her favorite sweater. The plane charged and tore a hole in the air.

He reviewed his mental file of girls he'd known before his wife and paused at the memory of Andrea, the girl who'd made an asshole of him. It had been twelve years, and only now could he say that phrase to himself, the only phrase that accurately described the situation. With stale resentment, he regarded her: a pale, long-legged thing with huge gray eyes, a small mouth, long red hair, and the helpless manner of a pampered pet let loose in the wilderness.

The woman next to him was hurriedly flipping the pages of *People*, presumably looking for something as engrossing as the AIDS wedding. When she didn't find it, she closed the magazine and turned to him in a way that invited conversation.

She said she'd lived in L.A. for eight years and that she liked it, even though it was "gross."

"I've never been to L.A.," he said. "I picture it being like *L.A. Law.* Is it like that?"

"I don't know. I've never seen *L.A. Law.* I don't watch TV. I don't own one."

He had never known a person who didn't own a TV, not even an old high school friend who lived in a slum and got food stamps. "You must read the newspapers a lot."

"No. I don't read them much at all."

He was incredulous. "How do you connect with the rest of the world? How do you know anything?"

"I'm part of the world. I know a lot of things."

He expelled a snort of laughter. "That's an awfully small perspective you've got there."

She shrugged and turned her head, and he was sorry he'd been rude. He glanced at her profile to read her expression and—of course; she reminded him of Patty LaForge, poor Patty.

He had met Patty at Meadow Community College in Coate, Minnesota. He was in his last semester; she had just entered. They worked in the student union cafeteria, preparing, serving, and snacking on denatured food. She was a slim, curvy person with dark-blonde hair, hazel eyes, and remarkable legs and hips. Her beauty was spoiled by the aggressive resignation that held her features in a fixed position and made all her expressions stiff. Her full mouth had a bitter downturn, and her voice was quick, low, self-deprecating, and sarcastic. She presented her beautiful body statically, as if it were a shield, and the effort of this presentation seemed to be the source of her animation.

Most of the people he knew at Meadow were kids he'd gone to high school and even junior high with. They still lived at home and still drove their cars around together at night, drank in the small bars of Coate, adventured in Minneapolis, and made love to each other. This late-adolescent camaraderie gave their time at Meadow a fraught emotional quality that was like the shimmering fullness of a bead of water before it falls. They were all about to scatter and become different from one another, and this made them exult in their closeness and alikeness.

The woman on the plane was flying to Kentucky to visit her parents and stopping over in Cincinnati.

"Did you grow up in Kentucky?" he asked. He imagined her as a big-eyed child in a cotton shift, playing in some dusty, sunny alley, some rural Kentucky-like place. Funny she had grown up to be this wan little bun with too much makeup in black creases under her eyes.

"No. I was born there, but I grew up mostly in Minnesota, near Minneapolis."

He turned away, registered the little shock of coincidence, and turned back. The situation compounded: she had gone to Redford Community College in Thorold, a suburb much like Coate. She had grown up in Thorold, like Patty. The only reason Patty had gone to Meadow was that Redford didn't exist yet.

He felt a surge of commonality. He imagined that she had experienced his adolescence, and this made him experience it for a moment. He had loved walking the small, neat walkways of the campus through the stiffly banked hedges of snow and harsh morning austerity, entering the close, food-smelling student union with the hard winter air popping off his skin. He would see his friends standing in a conspiratorial huddle, warming their hands on cheap cups of coffee; he always remembered the face of a particular girl, Layla, turning to greet him, looking over her frail sloped shoulder, her hair a bunched dark tangle, her round eyes ringed with green pencil, her perfectly ordinary face compelling in its configurations of girlish curiosity, maternal license, sexual knowledge, forgiveness, and femininity. A familiar mystery he had meant to explore sometime and never did, except when he grabbed her butt at a Halloween party and she smiled like a mother of four who worked as a porn model on the side. He loved driving with his friends to the Red Owl to buy alcohol and bagged salty snacks, which they consumed as they drove around Coate playing the tape deck and yelling at each other, the beautiful ordinary landscape unpeeling before them, revealing the essential strangeness of its shadows and night movements. He loved driving with girls to the deserted housing development they called "the Spot," loved the blurred memories of the girls in the back seat with their naked legs curled up to their chests, their shirts bunched about their necks, their eyes wide with ardor and alcohol, beer and potato chips spilled on the floor of the car, the tape deck singing of love and triumph. He getting out of the car for a triumphant piss, while the girl daintily replaced her pants. In the morning his mother would make him "cowboy eggs," eggs fried on top of bacon, and he would go through the cold to Meadow, to sit in a fluorescent classroom and dream.

"Did you like growing up in that area?" she asked.

"Like it? It was the greatest time of my life." Some extremity in his voice made her look away, and as she did, he looked more fully at her profile. She didn't look that much like Patty; she wasn't even blonde. But the small physical resemblance was augmented by a less tangible affinity, a telling similarity of speech and movement.

Patty belonged to a different crowd at Meadow. They were rougher than the Coate people, but the two groups were friendly. Patty was a strange, still presence within her group, with her hip thrust out and a cigarette always bleeding smoke from her hand. She was loose even by seventies standards; she had a dirty sense of humor, and she wore pants so tight you could see the swollen outline of her genitals. She was also shy. When she talked she pawed the ground with her foot and pulled her hair over her mouth; she looked away from you and then snuck a look back to see what you thought of her. She was accepted by the Thorold people the way you accept what you've always known. The stiffness of her face and body contradicting her loose reputation, her coarse language expressed in her timid voice and shy manners, her beauty and her ordinariness, all gave her a disconnected sexiness that was aggravating.

But he liked her. They were often a team at work, and he enjoyed having her next to him, her golden-haired arms plunged in greasy black dishwater or flecked with garbage as she plucked silverware from vile plates on their way to the dishwasher. She spooned out quivering red Jell-O or drew long bland snakes of soft ice cream from the stainless-steel machine, she smoked, wiped her nose, and muttered about a fight with her mother or a bad date. Her movements were resigned and bitter, yet her eyes and her nasty humor peeked impishly from under this weight. There was something pleasing in this combination, something congruent with her spoiled beauty.

It was a long time before he realized she had a crush on
him. All her conversation was braided together with a fly
strip of different boys she had been with or was involved
with, and she talked of all of them with the same tone of
fondness and resentment. He thought nothing of it when
she followed him outside to the field behind the union,
where they would walk along the narrow wet ditch, smoking pot and talking. It was early spring; dark, naked trees
pressed intensely against the horizon, wet weeds clung to
their jeans, and her small voice bobbed assertively on the
vibrant air. The cold wind gave her lips a swollen raw look
and made her young skin grainy and bleached. "So why do
you let him treat you like that?" "Ah, I get back at him. It's
not really him, you know, I'm just fixated on him. I'm working out something through him. Besides, he's a great lay."
He never noticed how often she came up behind him to
walk him to class or sat on the edge of his chair as he
lounged in the union. Then one day she missed work, and
a buddy of his said, "Hey, where's your little puppy dog
today?" and he knew.

"Did you like Thorold?" he asked the girl next to him.

"No, I didn't." She turned toward him, her face a stac-
cato burst of candor. "I didn't know what I was doing, and
I was a practicing alcoholic. I kept trying to fit in and I
couldn't."

"That doesn't sound good." He smiled. How like Patty
to answer a polite question from a stranger with this emotional nakedness, this urgent excess of information. She
was always doing that, especially after the job at the cafeteria ended. He'd see her in a hallway or the union lounge,
where normal life was happening all around them, and
she'd swoop into a compressed communication, intently

336

twining her hair around her finger as she quickly muttered that she'd had the strangest dream about this guy David, in which a nuclear war was going on, and he, John, was in it too, and—

"What did you do after Redford?" he asked the girl next to him.

"Screwed around, basically. I went to New York pretty soon after that and did the same things I was doing in Thorold. Except I was trying to be a singer."

"Yeah?" He felt buoyed by her ambition. He pictured her in a tight black dress, lips parted, eyes closed, bathed in cheap, sexy stage light. "Didja ever do anything with it?"

"Not much." She abruptly changed expression, as though she'd just remembered not to put herself down. "Well, some stuff. I had a good band once, we played the club circuit in L.A. for a while six years ago." She paused. "But I'm mostly a paralegal now."

"Well, that's not bad, either. Do you ever sing now?"

"I haven't for a long time. But I was thinking of trying again." Just like Patty, she looked away and quickly looked back as if to check his reaction. "I've been auditioning. Even though . . . I don't know."

"It sounds great to me," he said. "At least you're trying. It sounds better than what I do." His self-deprecation annoyed him, and he bulled his way through an explanation of what he did, making it sound more interesting than selling software.

A stewardess with a small pink face asked if they'd like anything to drink, and he ordered two little bottles of Jack Daniel's. Patty's shadow had a compressed can of orange juice and an unsavory packet of nuts; their silent companion by the window had vodka straight. He thought of asking her if she was married, but he bet the answer was no, and he didn't want to make her admit her loneliness. Of course, not every single person was lonely, but he guessed that she was. She seemed in need of comfort and care, like a stray animal that gets fed by various kindly people but never held.

"Will you get some mothering while you're at home?" he asked.

"Oh, yes. My mother will make things I like to eat and . . . stuff like that."

He thought of telling her that she reminded him of someone he'd known in Coate, but he didn't. He sat silently, knocking back his whiskey and watching her roll a greasy peanut between two fingers.

Out in the field, they were sitting on a fallen branch, sharing a wet stub of pot. "I don't usually say stuff like this," said Patty. "I know you think I do, because of the way I talk, but I don't. But I'm really attracted to you, John." The wind blew a piece of hair across her cheek, and its texture contrasted acutely with her cold-bleached skin.

"Yeah, I was beginning to notice."

"I guess it was kind of obvious, huh?" She looked down and drew her curtain of hair. "And I've been getting these mixed signals from you. I can't tell if you're attracted to me or not." She paused. "But I guess you're not, huh?"

Her humility embarrassed and touched him. "Well, I am attracted to you. Sort of. I mean, you're beautiful and everything. I'm just not attracted enough to do anything. Besides, there's Susan."

"Oh. I thought you didn't like her that much." She sniffed and dropped the roach on the raw grass; her lipstick had congealed into little chapped bumps on her lower lip. "Well, I'm really disappointed. I thought you liked me."

"I do like you, Patty."

"You know what I meant." Pause. "I'm more attracted to you than I've been to anybody for two years. Since Paul."

A flattered giggle escaped him.

"Well, I hope we can be friends," she said. "We can still talk and stuff, can't we?"

"Patty LaForge? I wouldn't touch her, man. The smell alone." He was driving around with a carload of drunk boys who were filled with a tangle of goodwill and aggression.

"Ah, LaForge is okay." He was indignant for Patty, but he laughed anyway.

"Were you really an alcoholic when you lived in Thorold?" he asked.

"I still am, I just don't drink now. But then I did. Yeah."

He had stepped into a conversation that had looked nice and solid, and his foot had gone through the floor and into the basement. But he couldn't stop. "I guess I drank too much then too. But it wasn't a problem. We just had a lot of fun."

She smiled with tight, terse mystery.

"How come you told me that about yourself? It seems kind of personal." He attached his gaze to hers as he said this; sometimes women said personal things to you as a way of coming on.

But instead of becoming soft and encouraging, her expression turned proper and institutional, like a kid about to recite. "If I'm going to admit it to other alcoholics in the program, I can admit it in regular life too. It humbles you, sort of."

What a bunch of shit, he thought.

He was drinking with some guys at the Winners Circle, a rough pickup bar, when suddenly Patty walked up to him, really drunk.

"John," she gasped. "John, John, John." She lurched at him and attached her nail-bitten little claws to his jacket. "John, this guy over there really wants to fuck me, and I was going to go with him, but I don't want him, I want you, I want you." Her voice wrinkled into a squeak, her face looked like you could smear it with your hand.

"Patty," he mumbled, "you're drunk."

"That's not why. I always feel like this." Her nose and eyelashes and lips touched his cheek in an alcoholic caress. "Just let me kiss you. Just hold me."

He put his hands on her shoulders. "C'mon, stop it."

"It doesn't have to mean anything. You don't have to love me. I love you enough for both of us."

He felt the presence of his smirking friends. "Patty, these guys are laughing at you. I'll see you later." He tried to push her away.

"I don't care. I love you, John. I mean it." She pressed her taut body against his, one sweaty hand under his shirt, and arched her neck until he could see the small veins and bones. "Please. Just be with me. Please." Her hand stroked him, groped between his legs. He took her shoulders and shoved her harder than he had meant to. She staggered back, fell against a table, knocked down a chair, and almost fell again. She straightened and looked at him as if she'd known him and hated him all her life.

****

He leaned back in his seat and closed his eyes, an over-weight, prematurely balding salesman getting drunk on an airplane.

"Look at the clouds," said the girl next to him. "Aren't they beautiful?"

He opened his eyes and silently looked.

Shrewdness glimmered under her gaze.

"What's your name?" he asked.

"Lorraine."

"I'm John." He extended his hand and she took it, her eyes unreadable, her hand exuding sweet feminine sweat.

"Why do you want to talk about your alcoholism publicly? I mean, if nobody asks or anything?"

Her eyes were steadfast, but her body was hesitant. "Well, I didn't have to just now. It's just the first thing I thought of when you asked me about Thorold. In general, it's to remind me. It's easy to bullshit yourself that you don't have a problem."

He thought of the rows and rows of people in swivel chairs on talk-show stages, admitting their problems. Wife beaters, child abusers, dominatrixes, porn stars. In the past it probably was a humbling experience to stand up and tell people you were an alcoholic. Now it was just something else to talk about. He remembered Patty tottering through a crowded party on smudged red high heels, bragging about what great blow jobs she gave. Some girl rolled her eyes and said, "Oh, no, not again." Patty disappeared into a bedroom with a bottle of vodka and Jack Spannos.

He remembered a conversation with his wife before he married her, a conversation about his bachelor party. "It was no women allowed," he'd told her. "Unless they wanted to give blow jobs."

"Couldn't they just jump naked out of a cake?" she asked.

"Nope. Blow jobs for everybody."

They were at a festive restaurant, drinking margaritas. Nervously, she touched her tiny straws. "Wouldn't that be embarrassing? In front of each other? I can't imagine Henry doing that in front of you all."

He smiled at the mention of his shy friend in this context. "Yeah," he said. "It probably would be embarrassing. Group sex is for teenagers."

Her face rose away from her glass in a kind of excited alarm, her lips parted. "You had group sex when you were a teenager?"

"Oh. Not really. Just a gang bang once."

She looked like an antelope testing the wind with its nose in the air, ready to fly. "It wasn't rape," she said.

"Oh, no, no." Her body relaxed and released a warm, sensual curiosity, like a cat against his leg. "The girl liked it."

"Are you sure?"

"Yeah. She liked having sex with a lot of guys. We all knew her, she knew us."

He felt her shiver inwardly, shocked and fascinated by this dangerous pack-animal aspect of his masculinity.

"What was it like?" she asked.

He shrugged. "It was a good time with the guys. It was a bunch of guys standing around in their socks and underwear."

Some kid he didn't know walked up and put his arm around him while he was talking to a girl named Chrissie. The kid's eyes were boyish and drunkenly enthusiastic, his face heavy and porous. He whispered something about Patty in John's ear and said, "C'mon."

The girl's expression subtly withdrew.

"What?" said John.

"Come on," said the kid.

"Bye-bye," said Chrissie, with a gingerly wag of her fingers.

He followed the guy through the room, seizing glimpses of hips and tits sheathed in bright, cheap cloth, girls doing wiggly dances with guys who jogged helplessly from foot to foot, holding their chests proudly aloof from their lower bodies. On the TV, a pretty girl gyrated in her black bra, sending a clean bolt of sex into the room. The music made his organs want to leap in and out of his body in time. His friends were all around him.

A door opened and closed behind him, muffling the music. The kid who'd brought him in sat in an armchair, smiling. Patty lay on a bed with her skirt pulled up to her waist and a guy with his pants down straddling her face. Without knowing why, he laughed. Patty twisted her legs about and bucked slightly. For a moment he felt frightened that this was against her will—but no, she would have screamed. He recognized the boy on her as Pete Kopiekin, who was thrusting his flat, hairy butt in the same dogged, earnest, woeful manner with which he played football. His heart was pounding.

Kopiekin got off her and the other guy got on; between them he saw her chin sticking up from her sprawled body, pivoting to and fro on her neck while she muttered and groped blindly up and down her body. Kopiekin opened the door to leave, and a fist of music punched the room. John's body jumped in shocked response, and the door shut. The guy on top of Patty was talking to her; to John's amazement, he seemed to be using love words. "You're so beautiful, baby." He saw Patty's hips moving. She wasn't being raped, he thought. When the guy finished, he stood and poured the rest of his beer in her face.

"Hey," said John lamely, "hey."

"Oh, man, don't tell me that. I've known her a long time."

When the guy left, he thought of wiping her face, but he didn't. She sighed fitfully and rolled on her side, as if there was something under the mattress, disturbing her sleep, but she was too tired to remove it. His thoughts spiraled inward, and he let them be chopped up by muffled guitar chords. He sat awhile, watching guys swarm over Patty and talking to the ones waiting. Music sliced in and out of the room. Then some guy wanted to pour maple syrup on her, and John said, "No, I didn't go yet." He sat on the bed and, for the first time, looked at her, expecting to see the sheepish bitter look he knew. He didn't recognize her. Her rigid face was weirdly slack; her eyes fluttered open, rolled, and closed; a mix of half-formed expressions flew across her face like swarming ghosts. "Patty," he said, "hey." He shook her shoulder. Her eyes opened, her gaze raked his face. He saw tenderness, he thought. He lay on her and tried to embrace her. Her body was leaden and floppy. She muttered and moved, but in ways he didn't understand. He massaged her breasts; they felt like they could come off and she wouldn't notice.

He lay there, supporting himself on his elbows, and felt the deep breath in her lower body meeting his own breath. Subtly, he felt her come to life. She lifted her head and said something; he heard his name. He kissed her on the lips. Her tongue touched his, gently, her sleeping hands woke. He held her and stroked her pale, beautiful face.

He got up in such a good mood that he slapped the guy coming in with the maple syrup a high five, something he thought was stupid and usually never did.

The next time he saw Patty was at a Foreigner concert in Minneapolis; he saw her holding hands with Pete Kopiekin.

Well, now she could probably be on a talk show about date rape. It was a confusing thing. She may have wanted to kiss him or to give Jack Spannos a blow job, but she probably didn't want maple syrup poured on her. Really, though, if you were going to get blind drunk and let everybody fuck you, you had to expect some nasty stuff. On the talk shows they always said it was low self-esteem that made them do it. If he had low self-esteem, he sure wouldn't try to cure it like that. His eyes rested on Lorraine's hands; she was wadding the empty nut package and stuffing it in her empty plastic cup.

"Hey," he said, "what did you mean when you said you kept trying to fit in and you couldn't? When you were in Thorold?"

"Oh, you know." She seemed impatient. "Acting the part of the pretty, sexy girl."

"When in fact you were not a pretty, sexy girl?"

She started to smile, then caught his expression and gestured dismissively. "It was complicated."

It was seductive, the way she drew him in and then shut him out. She picked up her magazine again. Her slight arm movement released a tiny cloud of sweat and deodorant, which evaporated as soon as he inhaled it. He breathed in deeply, hoping to smell her again. Sunlight pressed in with viral intensity and exaggerated the lovely contours of her face, the fine lines, the stray cosmetic flecks, the marvelous profusion of her pores. He thought of the stories he'd read in sex magazines about strangers on airplanes having sex in the bathroom or masturbating each other under blankets.

The stewardess made a sweep with a gaping white garbage bag and cleared their trays of bottles and cups.

She put down the magazine. "You've probably had the same experience yourself," she said. Her face was curiously determined, as if it were very important that she make herself understood. "I mean doing stuff for other people's expectations or just to feel you have a social identity because you're so convinced who you are isn't right."

"You mean low self-esteem?"

"Well, yeah, but more than that." He sensed her inner tension and felt an empathic twitch.

"It's just that you get so many projections onto yourself of who and what you're supposed to be that if you don't have a strong support system it's hard to process it."

"Yeah," he said. "I know what you mean. I've had that experience. I don't know how you can't have it when you're young. There's so much crap in the world." He felt embarrassed, but he kept talking, wanting to tell her something about himself, to return her candor. "I've done lots of things I wish I hadn't done, I've made mistakes. But you can't let it rule your life."

She smiled again, with her mouth only. "Once, a few years ago, my father asked me what I believed to be the worst mistakes in my life. This is how he thinks, this is his favorite kind of question. Anyway, it was really hard to say, because I don't know from this vantage point what would've happened if I'd done otherwise in most situations. Finally, I came up with two things: my relationship with this guy named Jerry and the time I turned down an offer to work with this really awful band that became famous.

He was totally bewildered. He was expecting me to say 'dropping out of college.'"

"You didn't make a mistake dropping out of college." The vehemence in his voice almost made him blush; then nameless urgency swelled forth and quelled embarrassment. "That wasn't a mistake," he repeated.

"Well, yeah, I know."

"Excuse me." The silent business shark to their left rose in majestic self-containment and moved awkwardly past their knees, looking at John with pointed irony as he did so. Fuck you, thought John.

"And about that relationship," he went on. "That wasn't your loss. It was his." He had meant these words to sound light and playfully gallant, but they had the awful intensity of a maudlin personal confession. He reached out to gently pat her hand, to reassure her that he wasn't a nut, but instead he grabbed it and held it. "If you want to talk about mistakes—shit, I raped somebody. Somebody I liked."

Their gaze met in a conflagration of reaction. She was so close he could smell her sweating, but at the speed of light she was falling away, deep into herself where he couldn't follow. She was struggling to free her hand.

"No," he said, "it wasn't a real rape. It was what you were talking about—it was complicated."

She wrenched her hand free and held it protectively close to her chest. "Don't touch me again." She turned tautly forward. He imagined her heart beating in alarm. His body felt so stiff he could barely feel his own heart. Furiously, he wondered if the people around them had heard any of this. Staring ahead of him, he hissed, "Do you think I was dying to hear about your alcoholism? You were the one who started this crazy conversation."

He felt her consider this. "It's not the same thing," she hissed back.

"But it wasn't really a rape." He struggled to say what it was. He recalled Patty that night at the Winners Circle, her neck arched and exposed, her feelings extended and flailing the air where she expected his feelings to be.

"You don't understand," he finished lamely.

She was silent. He thought he dimly felt her body relax, emitting some possibility of forgiveness. But he couldn't tell. He closed his eyes. He thought of Patty's splayed body, her half-conscious kiss. He thought of his wife, her compact scrappy body, her tough-looking flat nose and chipped nail polish, her smile, her smell, her embrace, which was both soft and fierce. He imagined the hotel room he would sleep in tonight, its stifling grid of rectangles, oblongs, and windows that wouldn't open. He leaned back and closed his eyes.

The pilot roused·him with a command to fasten his seat belt. He sat up and blinked. Nothing had changed. The woman at his side was sitting slightly hunched, with her hands resolutely clasped.

"God, I'll be glad when we're on the ground," he said.

She sniffed in reply.

They descended, ears popping. They landed with a flurry of baggage-grabbing. He stood, bumped his head, and tried to get into the aisle to escape, but it was too crowded. He sat back down. Not being able to leave made him feel that he had to say something else. "Look, don't be upset. What I said came out wrong."

"I don't want to talk."

Neither do I, he thought. But he felt disoriented and depressed amid these shifting, lunging, grabbing people from all over the country, who had been in his life for hours and were now about to disappear, taking their personal items and habits with them.

"Excuse me." She butted her way past him and into the aisle. He watched a round, vulnerable piece of her head move between the obstructions of shoulders and arms. She glanced backward, possibly to see if he was going to try to follow her. The sideways movement of her hazel iris prickled him. They burst from the plane and scattered, people picking up speed as they bore down on their destination. He caught up with her as they entered the terminal. "I'm sorry," he said to the back of her head. She moved farther away, into memory and beyond.

JACK, THE ROAD, AND ME

GARY HORN

As an undergraduate at Columbia University in the early 1980s, I became taken with the mythology surrounding Jack Kerouac and his picaresque adventures in *On the Road*. It made perfect sense to me, and my friends, holed up in our rat-infested dormitory on upper Broadway, that life's mysterious truths could only be discovered "out there" (wherever that was), and that the only logical path to take after graduation, student loan debt notwithstanding, was one of seeing as much of the world as possible. After all, Kerouac had dreamed the same dreams when he was a Columbia student in that very dorm.

And look what happened to him.

And then I sustained a spinal cord injury in a diving accident.

I was getting measured for my first wheelchair when I asked the occupational therapist, "Can I travel in this thing?"

"Yeah," she said. "No problem." But her eyes told me something different. Twenty-seven years later, my instincts have proven correct, exponentially so. I knew I wasn't going to let my chair keep me from seeing the world; but I was going to have to learn to be flexible—really flexible—

and to utilize the advice of another of my favorite authors from my college days, Hunter S. Thompson:

"When the going gets tough, the weird turn pro."

My first flight as a disabled person was on a People Express jaunt from Newark to Miami, en route to a physical therapy assessment. I must have called the airline a dozen times beforehand to make certain that everything would go smoothly. I rolled up to the gate (which looked more like a subway station than an airport, as People Express was the first wholesale airline) more than a little nervous, and checked in. I looked up to see a half-dozen huge men, familiar faces all, seated in the waiting area, passing a pair of lit joints between them. They belonged to a junket of WWF professional wrestlers, and although I now forget their names, I recall that, in heading down south for a little R & R, they were getting an early start on their partying.

The Haitian orderlies in the rehab hospital had turned me into a late-night wrestling devotee. And now a four-hundred pound, overalls-wearing behemoth with a chest-length beard named Hillbilly Jim waved me over to join them. Suddenly, my nervousness wafted away . . . People Express had no jetways, but Hillbilly Jim and his crew happily carried me, and my wheelchair, up the flight of stairs to the cabin. When we landed, they then carted my luggage around Miami International Airport.

This was going to be easy.

But, alas, in the hundreds of flights that have followed, I've never again encountered a group of professional wrestlers. The routine of arriving at the airport, checking myself and my chair onto the flight, transferring into an aisle seat, flagging down the appropriate personnel to get me on and off of the plane, ensuring that my chair arrives at our destination in one piece, and breaking down and assembling the chair, has largely been up to me (with acknowledgment to my wife, ex-wife, and two children, who have witnessed some of what follows).

Persistently, the most difficult part of the process is communicating with the harried airline personnel, who would rather be doing anything but helping someone with needs, special or otherwise. Ideally, I am pre-boarded, in their hopes of avoiding the rush of passengers along the jetway. However, this often turns out not to be the case.

One memorable time, while switching planes in Denver en route to Minneapolis, several of my fellow passengers, members of a women's hockey team, were in a hurry, apparently to get to their seats. Attempting to whisk past me, they knocked over the Asian security guard who was assisting me in my transfer.

The security guard, who stood no more than five feet tall, bounced off the floor, and drop-kicked the largest of the women (I'm assuming a defenseman), decking her, too. A full-scale brawl ensued, me in the middle, covering up like Sylvester Stallone in the final *Rocky* installment.

To his credit, the pint-sized security guard held his own quite nicely, as his cohort, radioing for help, yelled frantically:

"We need backup, immediately. Everybody is kung-fu fighting."

This jetway incident was surpassed in strangeness only one time, in my memory, at LAX, when I was being pre-boarded by a trio of American Airlines personnel who, after dropping me on the jetway floor, began screaming at one another in three different languages, prompting another traveler to step from his place in the pre-boarding queue and call out to me, with urgent concern, in a vaguely familiar voice.

"Would you like some help?"

I looked up. It was Stevie Wonder.

Once I have entered the plane, the transfer to the aisle seat is the next part of the process; the most physically demanding for those assisting me, and thus the one providing the most unique moments of hysteria and extreme behavior. As most wheelchairs are too wide to roll into a plane's cabin, the wheelchair user is lifted onto a ten-by-ten-inch stool on wheels, and rolled up the aisle to his or her assigned seat. In its design stages, this may have been a seamless process, but there were a number of small oversights:

1) No non-anorexic human being above the age of eleven possesses a ten-by-ten-inch ass, creating what the airline legal fine print has deemed "a rear-end overflow" situation.

2) Airplane aisles are not built according to a uniform width requirement, so many planes do not accommodate the aisle chair.

3) The core function of the FAA is to ensure that flights take off on time. Networks of airports, hundreds of thousands of travelers, the midair safety of hundreds of planes, etc., are affected if one flight should be delayed . . . You see what's coming . . .

4) Especially since the flight attendants' union forbids its membership from helping disabled passengers until they are deemed to be officially in their ticketed seats, leading to . . .

5) The inevitable conflagration, in which the overworked, understaffed airport personnel (always male) responsible for rolling the paraplegic passenger through the cabin on the aisle chair (from which the paraplegic passenger is sliding onto the floor) is urged, forcefully, by the nearby flight attendants (who are, again generally, either tastefully gay in the Neil Patrick Harris way or sporting pants suits and resembling Sarah Palin) to hurry up. And al-

ways with a smile that says: "Put him in his fucking seat, and do it now, or the flight will be late, and I will personally deport you. And do not dare ask me for help."

It is at this exact moment, while falling from the aisle stool, that I have witnessed some of the most entertaining racist, sexist, homophobic tirades imaginable.

At JFK once, I looked on as a heavily tattooed Puerto Rican man beckoned a nearby stewardess who, oblivious to his struggle at keeping me upright, refused to look up from her Starbucks and the male fashion spread she was reading in *Cosmo*.

"You *puta!* I wouldn't fuck you with his dick!" he said, gesturing at the photo of Antonio Banderas. Perplexed, she nodded and continued reading. In Boston, I watched as an aproned male flight attendant, sporting a perfect spray-on tan and enough cologne to fill several airplanes, responded to being called a "bumba clot faggot" by pouncing on the offending Jamaican airport worker and delivering an MMA-caliber headlock. Both of them tumbled into the galley amid a wild exchange of dreadlock-pulling and forcefully inflicted noogies.

And I was in Florida to witness what was, surely, one of the most memorable moments in twentieth-century travel, when a fellow wheelchair passenger, a three-hundred-pound Hasidic man, was lifted from the stool into his airplane seat, and then asked by the suddenly visibly uncomfortable airport worker who was assisting him, "What's that smell, mon?"

"I just had a bowel accident. A big one. I could use a little help . . ."

On airplanes I have witnessed trays of mimosas thrown in fury; lawsuits threatened; security and police summoned. But nothing to rival when that airport worker, without blinking, turned to the horrified flight attendant nearby (picture Marie Osmond dosed with a very powerful hit of LSD) and informed her, "That's your job, baby. The rabbi here is in his seat now . . . I think you need to get busy."

Why would I fly at all? I ask myself that question every time I click on Expedia to book my next trip.

The answer might be sex.

The Mile High Club is something to which many aspire, but very few have actually experienced. And, certainly, for the wheelchair-using passenger who is unable to leave his seat during flight, a virtual impossibility.

But isn't the pursuit of a dream more important than its realization? I have no idea. But I recommend it.

During my days as a single person, I most often flew on my own. And, as a sexually charged male, socially weaned in New York City in the late 1970s, I was hardwired to approach every situation in an enclosed area with two hundred or more people whom I have never met (half of them female) as if I were entering a disco.

So on those occasions when I have found myself seated beside an attractive woman with several hours to kill, I gleefully reverted to instinct. And the results combine to illustrate the following long-held theory: There are two types of women one meets when he spends his days in a wheelchair. Some will reject out of hand the notion of being with a disabled person. Others are not swayed one way or the other by the chair, or by preconceived prejudice. And there actually is a third, very small, supremely bizarre group of women who *prefer* being with someone in a chair—but that's a narrative for another book.

If you will, picture this scenario: I am seated on an airplane, my wheelchair is in a storage bin. I have been pre-

boarded so I've usually had limited contact with other passengers at the gate. To a stranger sitting down beside me for
the first time, I'm a six-foot-four, blue-eyed man, in pretty
good shape, with a pleasant-enough smile. Not Brad Pitt, but,
despite my receding hairline, I'm a good-looking guy.

And that is how I present myself. In my mind, I'm not
me, who is a disabled person. I am, simply, me. And so, on
a plane, when conversation leads, naturally, to drinking,
and then more conversation, and, depending on the length
of the flight, more drinking still, two people can affect a
faux . . . intimacy.

Yes. Intimacy.

And even wind up, when lights are turned off and
everyone else is asleep, in deep lip-lock, or thereabouts.

Now, imagine that you have been similarly intimate with
a woman for, say, the time it takes to get from Los Angeles
to, say, London. And you are paraplegic, and she has no
idea. And then, after ten or so hours of this, the lights are
turned on. She's eagerly suggested plans to see you that
night, at your hotel. And, yes, to repeat: she has no idea.

You are aware that some shit is gonna hit the fan at
baggage claim, when she sees you in your wheelchair, but
it's been really sweet, after all.

Have you ever seen a drunken thirty-year-old woman
(who has spent the last half a day hooking up on an airplane) freak out in the middle of Heathrow?

I have.

Thereafter, when finding myself approaching a similar
situation, I have always made sure to be forthcoming about
you-know-what. Months later, having been bumped to First
Class on a technicality, I found myself seated beside a female
rock star, whose name I shall not mention out of respect. Or
fear of legal reprisal. Suffice it to say that, from a fan's per-

spective, I had always ogled her; and, lo and behold, there she was, an armrest away, for six hours, coast to coast.

And she liked me. She was interested. To the point of putting down her book and asking me questions. At which point they brought out more champagne.

And then I told her.

Whereupon she looked deep into my eyes and uttered, "That's cool."

Maybe I secretly hoped that my being so forthcoming would unlock a door between us . . . that blurred boundary that separates friends from lovers. She was already evolved beyond the point where it would matter. She didn't care about spinal cords. She cared about me.

We continued discussing James Joyce, or James Brown, or William James, or whatever was floating by in our shared, spa cuisine–fueled stream of consciousness.

She was jumping around with the same enthusiasm she displayed on stage. I remember the excitement of her body language, and trying to steer the conversation back to "You want to get together later?"

She wasn't having it. The plane landed. Then, as everyone got up to leave, she gave me this great kiss—the kind that reverberates through your whole body.

It felt like it might still happen.

It didn't.

But I was left with a story.

And that, ultimately, is what traveling leaves us with, long after the curios are lost and the photos disappear. When we share them, our stories meld to create a mosaic that, hopefully, makes us all feel, for a moment or two, as if we never had to go anywhere in the first place. That everything's fine, right here. And then we go out and get more stories. The way Jack Kerouac did.

THE MYTH OF THE FREQUENT FLIER

JONATHAN TEL

I think you could fairly trace my obsession to a conversation
that took place some years ago on Aerolineas Argentinas
Flight AR185 from Buenos Aires to Auckland, the red-eye
that departed at 22:30, if my memory serves me right; reasonably commodious; I had been upgraded to first class; I accepted the champagne but waved away the food—and after
I had put in an hour or two at my laptop, and listened to a
snatch of Mozart through the headphones, it occurred to me
it might be for the best if I napped; however, (my internal
clock was not corresponding to that of the longitude) I felt
not in the least tired, and so, contrary to what had been my
self-imposed rule, listened gravely while a stewardess (in her
early forties, I should judge; some wrinkles around the eyes
[the flying does that to them: they try to counteract it with
moisturizer, but even so] and a pleasant smile, I thought, and
a poppy in her lapel though possibly it was a pin in the shape
of a heart this particular stewardess was wearing {the flower
having pertained to a stewardess six months or so earlier on
Alitalia 406 from Naples to Capri (among the most scenic
flights I have ever had the pleasure of)}]) told me a story.

She did not vouch for it personally. She said she had been told it by another stewardess, an employee of Cathay Pacific, in an airport washroom in Vientiane; the Cathay Pacific person herself had learned it from a Swissair purser. All the same, the Argentinean said, it could very well be true.

In brief, the story was about a man (she was fairly certain the person was male; the name she had forgotten, if she had ever been told it) who travels on scheduled airlines. As do we all: but the point is he never does anything but. (Not literally "never"—he has to transfer from flight to flight, of course, involving walking from gate to gate, and waiting patiently to board the next flight; and should the flight be international he would be required to go through Customs and Immigration—but as much as anyone ever could, he flies nonstop.) He sits in an airline seat; he eats airline food; he listens to airline music through airline headphones and watches airline films; he reads airline magazines; he makes the kind of conversation with the person or persons next to him that one does make on airlines; airline socks go on his airline feet, airline earplugs in his airline ears, an airline mask over his airline eyes, and he dreams airline dreams.

He has adopted this lifestyle by choice. He is presumed to be not unhappy.

As to how this had come about . . . She had been told he had won a competition of the I LOVE BRITISH AIRWAYS BECAUSE _____ (complete in not more than ten words) sort, for which the prize had been a pass entitling the bearer to travel as much as desired, for life. Naturally the airline had supposed the winner would use the pass a few times a year; little had they suspected he would choose to stay aloft whenever possible. They had offered him a lump sum in lieu; he had refused to accept it.

And was the airline he flew on in fact British Airways? I sought to make the story more specific, and so more verifiable.

She wasn't certain, but she thought that was what the woman in the Vientiane washroom had told her she'd been told. But possibly she (the woman from Aerolineas Argentinas, that is) was misremembering the detail, she conceded; or then again Cathay Pacific might not have got it quite right; or the fault might lie in Swissair, or somewhere further back.

I did not think much of the story; I filed it to the back of my mind. And then, about two and a half months later, in a seafood bar in the new Denver airport (notorious for its automated baggage transfer system that kept breaking down) from the man serving the lobster salad, I heard another version. In this retelling, the traveler was from North America, and his name (the lobster salad thought) began with a J, or at least had a J in it—John, Jack, Jean-Jacques, Roger—something like that . . . I had a 727 to catch to Mexico City, and heard no further details.

But by then I was alerted and listened out for further installments. Over the years since, whenever I have had need to travel, I have made a point of chatting with the aircrew and the ground crew, and airport employees, and I'm no longer surprised by how often variations on this story come up. An urban myth, you could call it; but not exactly urban, since it is told (to the best of my knowledge) only in the air world. Call it an airborne myth, then. An updated version of an ancient legend.

Who is he? Where is he from? What impels him to keep doing it? Will he ever stop?

In all the variora I have come across, the frequent flier is described as male (though it is conceivable a female avatar may exist somewhere). He is middle-aged to elderly, never young. His country of citizenship, though, is open to question. The one constant is that he is always a foreigner, never the same nationality as the informant. In the curious airport in Jakarta, modeled on a traditional Javanese longhouse yet constructed in concrete and glass, a security guard told me the eternal traveler is Malay. In the Albuquerque airport a vendor of Native American turquoise trinkets assured me he is Salvadorian. The fellow employed to chivvy goats off the Axum airstrip swore he is Somali. During the short hop from Sikkim to Katmandu, he is Chinese. In Heathrow he is Irish. In O'Hare he is Canadian. On the polar route from Osaka to Copenhagen, he is Australian.

I was not too surprised to come across (indeed, with the wisdom of hindsight one might characterize it as inevitable) a version of the tale in which he finds a mate. It was a Filipina, employed as a toilet cleaner in the Dubai airport, who first revealed this aspect of his character. The cleaner herself had a Harlequin romance in Tagalog translation stuffed in the pocket of her apron, yet the story she told me was not one of love.

You see, she explained, there was a clause in his prize to the effect that he could take a spouse with him on his travels. And somewhere on his journeys, at some random terminal, he had found a woman who had agreed to marry him—a woman much like herself, in fact, in her mid-thirties, originally from Zamboanga, who might well have dreamed of an aristocrat with flashing green eyes but who had known that a hunched, rumpled middle-aged frequent flier was the best she could hope for. The nuptials had been celebrated in an airport chapel. Thereafter the two of them were flying the world together.

Mrs. Frequent Flier never complains. She sits beside her husband, whether in economy, business, or first class. She massages his swollen feet. She serves him his dinner, selecting choice morsels from the reheated airline tray. She talks when he wants to hear her voice, and listens when he wants to speak, and when he needs silence she sits beside him, awake, gazing beyond him at the ailerons shifting on the wing.

One cannot help wondering what else the two of them get up to. It is late at night, on a red-eye, and I am unable to sleep. Are they, at that very moment, side by side on some other jet, slumped and snoring in economy? Or are they crammed conjointly in the washroom? Or—give them the benefit of the doubt—they are in first, a blanket is draped over them, sweet romantic music is wafting from the headsets . . . their coupling might be lovelier than we'll ever know. Or, of course, in their time zone it might be midday. Wide awake, he pages through the *Financial Times*. Her knitting needles click.

And it should be stressed that the wife is evanescent. In the majority of versions she does not exist, or is unmentioned at least. She is non-canonical as Mrs. Noah. And when she does manifest herself, her ethnicity and appearance vary as much as his. In Abu Dhabi she is from Ghana. During the Kunming–Chiang Mai shuttle she is Hmong. In Stockholm he has a gay partner (though given the appearance and mannerisms of the flight attendant who told me, I wouldn't put too much credence in that).

Just a few months ago, on Ryanair from Liverpool to Dublin (in retrospect, amazing this version had not turned up sooner), a sauntering copilot advised me the frequent flier, a Frenchman, is a proud father. His German wife gave birth in the first-class washroom during the Rome–Tripoli run. The child, a healthy three-kilogram boy, was named Alitalia by the proud parents.

A legend is not a fixed thing. It evolves; it grows. Since then, I have heard several times that he and his wife have twins, a boy and a girl. (Always the child or children are described as babies, mind you. Impossible to imagine their adolescence; the myth would shatter.) Personally, I can swallow the wife but not the children; let's face it, a jetliner is no place to bring up a family; and if one uses proper precautions, it need never happen. And even the wife, she too may yet prove to be apocryphal, and fade out of the tale.

But here we come to the crux. Is this legend based on a true story? Several times I have questioned British Airways flight attendants during Heathrow–JFK—they declared no such traveler existed on their airline, indeed the prize of a lifetime pass had never been offered. Of course this does not preclude the possibility they were mistaken, or lying, or that the frequent flier was in fact on a different airline. And the whole prize shenanigans might be a red herring anyway. There are versions with much circumstantial detail asserting the frequent flier is a millionaire eccentric, a retiree with an American Express platinum card and time on his hands. There are related versions in which he is doing it for a bet, or he has a moneyed backer, or he is obsessive-compulsively researching an article for a travel magazine, or he is an independently wealthy performance artist or freak or monk. Indeed, he would not need to be particularly well-funded. I performed a rough calculation on the back of my Emirates Airlines in-flight magazine. Assume he restricts himself to the cheapest long-distance runs (London–New York, Hong Kong–Kuwait, and so forth). Assume he travels by night, and spends daytimes in transit lounges. Assume he buys his tickets through consolidators and "bucket shops" and quasilegal resellers of bump-tickets and unneeded mileage, via the Internet or in those markets where the vagaries of currency and airline pricing policies result in the cheapest possible rates (I could recommend Penang). If so, I guesstimate he could travel for as little as $170 per day, 365 days per year (366 in a leap year): call it $60,000 per annum. Granted, he would need to cover out-of-pocket expenses, and of course the total would be greater if he chose to fly by way of more exotic airports, say Ouagadougou or Aspen . . . but still, his outgoings would be no greater than those of a settled man with a house and a mortgage in any city in the developed world.

And what is his motive? Is he running away from something, or is he in search of it? Is he cursed or is he blessed? Will he ever find peace? There are those who say they have met him personally, though none has absolute proof. Once or a few times I think I might have glimpsed him myself—being turned away from the Royal Orchid lounge at Bangkok airport; asking the way to the Kansas City Terminal 2 Burger King in impeccable Spanish; running to make the connection at Keflavik . . . but I could tell you nothing that would convince a skeptic.

Yet I am sure he exists. I keep traveling from airplane to airplane, from airport to airport, from departures to arrivals to departures again . . . One day I shall find him.

BIRDS IN FALL

BRAD KESSLER

It's true: a few of us slept through the entire ordeal, but others sensed something wrong right away. We grew restless in our seats and felt what exactly? An uneasiness, a movement in the air, a certain quiet that hadn't been there before? Several men craned their necks about the cabin. We caught each other's eyes, exchanged searching looks, and just as quickly—embarrassed—glanced away. We were eighty minutes into the flight. Orion on our left, the bear to the right. The motors droned. The cabin lights dimmed. The whoosh of the engines was the sound of erasure: *Shhhhh*, they whispered, and we obeyed.

The woman beside me clicked on her overhead light and adjusted a pair of reading glasses. She laid a folder of sheet music on her tray. Thin, black-haired, she smelled vaguely of breath mints. Her blue cello case lay strapped to the seat between us. She was giving a concert in Amsterdam and had booked an extra ticket for her instrument. I'd joked about her cello on the tarmac: Did she order special meals for it on flights? Did it need a headset, a pillow? She was retying hair behind her head and cast me a barely tolerant smile.

365

When the drink cart passed, she ordered a Bloody Mary—
I, a scotch. Our pygmy bottles arrived with roasted nuts. I
reached across the cello case and touched her plastic cup.

To your cello, I tried again. Does it have a name?

She nodded tepidly over the rims of her glasses.

Actually, she said, it does.

I couldn't place her accent. Something Slavic. Roman-
ian perhaps. She wore a lot of eye shadow. She returned to
her music. I could just make out the title of the piece:
Richard Strauss's *Metamorphoses: A Study for Twenty-
three Solo Strings*.

Over the Gulf of Maine, the moon glittered below us. I
wanted to point out to the cellist as I would to my wife,
Ana, that the moon hung actually *beneath* us. I wanted to
tell her we were near the tropopause, the turning point between the stratosphere and the troposphere, where the air
is calm and good for flying; *tropo* from "turning," *pauso*
from "stop" (I prided myself on my college Latin). And surely
she'd know these musical terms. But the woman was counting bars now. Across the aisle, a man in a wine-colored
sweater lay snoring, his mouth opened wide.

Somewhere over the Bay of Fundy the cabin lights
began to flicker. The video monitors went dead (they'd
been showing a map of the Atlantic, with our speed, altitude, and outside temperature). The cellist looked up for a
moment, her lips still moving with the sheet music. Then
the cabin fell entirely dark, and a strange silvery light
poured into the plane through each oval portal and bathed
the aisles in a luminous, oddly peaceful glow. One by one,
people tried to press their dome lights on, not yet in alarm
but bewildered, to be up so far in the atmosphere, bathed
in that frozen blue moonlight. A flight attendant marched
up the aisle and told us to keep our seat belts on. The

clouds lay effulgent below, edged in gold; another attendant shouted that there was nothing to be alarmed by. The
lights blinked, faltered, turned on again. A sigh rose from
the seats, and the cellist glanced at me with nervous relief.

The captain came over the intercom then. He apolo-
gized and mentioned we were going to make a "short stop"
in Halifax "before we get on our way." He was trying to
sound unfazed, but in his Dutch accent—we were flying
Netherland Air—his comments sounded clipped and startling. He got back on the intercom and added that we might
want to buckle our belts for the rest of the ride and—inci-
dentally—not to get out of our seats.

The cellist turned to me.

What do you think it is? she asked.

I don't know, I shrugged.

Her glasses had slid halfway down the bridge of her
nose. She squared her sheet music on the tray table. The
man in the wine sweater had awakened and was demanding answers. People flipped open their cell phones—to no
avail. Outside, the tip of the wing looked laminated in moonlight, the Milky Way a skein above. We had started sinking
fast, that much was clear, the nose of the plane dipping downward; and there was a curious chemical smell, not exactly
burning, more like a dashboard left to bake in the sun.

The man in the wine sweater bolted from his seat and
ran toward the bathrooms at the rear galley of the plane. Beside his empty seat a young Chinese woman in leather pants
lay sleeping, earphones on her head, seat belt cinched across
her hips. She wore an eyemask across her face.

Someone ought to wake her, the cellist said.

She's better off sleeping, I replied. Besides, it's probably nothing.

Probably, she whispered.

Tell me, I asked, about your instrument.

She looked at me with disbelief.

My cello?

Yes, I urged. I wanted to distract her; I wanted to distract myself. Then, as if she understood the reason for the query, she swallowed and began talking about her cello, how it was built by one of the great Italian cello makers, a man named Guadagnini, and how he traveled between Cremona and Turin, and how his varnishes were famous, though they varied with each place he worked. She talked of the thinness of the plates, the purfling, the ivory pegs, the amber finish he was known for. I could barely hear her voice; she kept toying with one of her earrings. I asked if it was old and she said, yes, it was built a few years before the execution of Marie Antoinette.

She snapped off her glasses and drained the meltings of her Bloody Mary and placed the cup back in its bezel. Her hands were trembling slightly. The Chinese girl hadn't moved; we could hear the tinny sound of hip-hop through her earphones.

For several minutes neither of us said a word. Clouds shredded past the windows. The cabin rattled unnervingly. The entire plane was silent now, save the shaking and the whisper of air in the vents. The name Moncton appeared on the video map. We were being passed from one beacon to the next, a package exchanged between partners, Boston Control to Moncton Control. The cabin grew noticeably hot. The moon was now the color of tea.

I told the cellist I had a particular interest in orientation and flight. In birds, actually. That I was an ornithologist, my wife too; I told her about the study skins and museum collections. She nodded, clenching and unclenching a cocktail napkin in her fist. I rabbited on to fill the empty space, so my voice might be a rope that both of us could cling to; and I told her about polarization filters and magnetic fields, the tiny pebbles, no larger than poppy seeds, found between the skull bones of migratory birds. Magnetite, I said. Black ore, which helps them home, to the same nest or tree across an entire hemisphere. I kept the patter going, reeling and threading out more rope, whatever came to mind, cladistics, the systematics laboratory, how we needed new bird specimens for their DNA (which you couldn't obtain from the old study skins), and how I collected birds (killed them actually), and that I was going to Amsterdam to deliver a lecture and then visit the Leiden Museum to inspect their collection of Asian Kingfishers. I told her about Ana as well, her work with Savannah Sparrows and migration—but the cabin was growing hotter by the minute, my collar sponged now in sweat, the little hairs on my arms damp. The plane shuddered and pitched and my heart leapt and I could hear the cellist's breath catch beside me. "Gravity" comes from the Latin *gravitas*, I explained. Heavy, grave, a lowness of pitch. The impulse of everything toward the earth. Newton's universal law, Kepler's "virtue." Someone vomited in their seat; we heard the vile gurgle, then smelled the sickening odor. The cellist yanked the paper bag from her seat pocket.

Shut up! she hissed.

Was I still talking? I hardly knew. She fished inside her pocketbook and fumbled a tube of lipstick and a hand mirror, and held the trembling glass in front of her face. Her forehead gleamed. She skull-tightened her lips but kept missing, dabbing dots of pigment on her cheeks.

Fuck! she screamed and clicked the compact and tossed it in her purse.

Then she pushed up the cotton sleeve of her black blouse. Her arm was slender and pale. With the lipstick, she composed an *E* just below her elbow. I watched as she wrote each letter on the inside white of her arm: *E*, then *V*, then *D*, then *O*.

When she finished it spelled "Evdokiya."

She handed the opened tube across the cello.

What do I do with this? I asked.

You write your name.

You're being dramatic.

Am I? she asked.

The name of the lipstick was Japanese Maple. Against her pale skin, the letters looked lurid and blotchy.

The Japanese maple on our roof was slightly more purple than the lipstick. Its leaves in fall the color "of bruises," Ana once said. She would have looked good wearing that pigment. I held the glistening tube in my hand, not knowing what to write or where. I wanted to write Ana's name, or both our names, as though we were a piece of luggage that, lost, would find its way back to our loft. So I put our address down, taking care with each number, each letter: 150 First Avenue; and then I showed my arm to the cellist, and she said: Your *name*. Yet I couldn't bring myself to write it down.

The smoke seeped in slowly and curled to the ceiling. The smell of burning plastic was distinct now. The video monitors were still working and showed we were twenty miles from Halifax. A man in a silk prayer shawl stood bobbing up and down in the aisle, the white cloth a cowl over his head. The girl with the earphones still lay fast asleep; no one apparently had woken her. Now and again a pilot or a flight attendant raced up the aisle, urging us to keep calm. We all had our life vests on by then—some inflated theirs against instructions, and you could hear the alarming *pffffff* of them filling with air. The cellist found my hand across the cello case and burrowed her fingers into mine, as if to hide them there. Others were grabbing hands across the aisles. I kept jerking open my jaw to pop the unbearable pressure in my ears; the cellist was doing the same. I imagine, in the end, we all looked like fish.

An eerie whistling filled the fuselage like someone blowing into a soda bottle. The cellist named the notes as we were going down. The pilot was uttering the word "pan, pan, pan." We could hear it over the intercom. It sounded as if he were shouting for bread.

We dropped between layers of atmosphere. Clouds tore past the wing. The whistling lowered to a gentle warble, the fuselage a flute with one hole left open, an odd arpeggio in the rear of the plane. Someone shouted *land!* and I pressed my forehead to Plexiglas and saw, between scraps of cloud, lights below, pink clusters like brush fire, four or five of them, the brief flames of villages and towns checkerboarded, scalloped along the coast, yet distant; and some began to cheer, thinking, We will make it; we are so close to land, Halifax couldn't be far. We were coming over the spine of the world, out of the night, into the welcoming sodium lights of Canada. We hit clouds again and the plane shuddered; the ocean hurled to the left, and the plane rammed hard to the right.

Oxygen masks sprang from the ceiling panel and swung in front of our faces. I caught mine and helped the cellist with hers. The plastic was the color of buttercups.

She took the belt off her cello and unfastened the buckles.

Help me! she screamed through her mask. She was in a sudden rush, fumbling, standing, a flight attendant shouting for her to sit. I helped her prop open the shiny plastic case and saw inside the instrument—amber-toned, varnish gleaming, the grain a fine and lustrous brown. In its capsule of red velvet it looked like a nesting doll. She slipped a finger in through the F-hole and touched the sound post and closed her eyes. The instrument was humming a sympathetic vibration.

It's the D, she whispered.

It'll be safer with the case closed, I said.

She leaned over and kissed the cello's neck and let the cover drop.

The cabin rattled. The bulkheads shook. The overhead bins popped open. Bags, briefcases, satchels rained down. The cellist clenched her eyes. I felt her fingers tightened on mine—but it was Ana I felt beside me.

We broke cloud cover and dropped into a pool of dark. The bones around my cheeks pressed into my skull. I saw the sheet music flattened like a stamp on the ceiling. The metamorphoses. I couldn't tell which way was up and which was down and out the window a green light stood on the top of the world, a lighthouse spun above us, a brief flame somewhere in the night.

Did I feel it then, the beginning of this pilgrimage, from air to thinner air, from body to body, before the impact? Was it then or after or in between, before the seat belts locked our pelvises in place and unleashed the rest of us. The ilium. Why is it the same name for Troy? Ana once asked, tracing the upper bone of my hip with her finger. Because it's a basin, I said, and told her the Latin word *ilia*. More like wings, she said and climbed above me and laid the two points of her hips on top of mine. Our bones tapped together, like spoons.

The cabin burst into light, sunbright, dazzling, an orange edging around it. I could see the bones beneath my flesh like pieces of pottery. And then we were entering the sea.

INSIDE THE TUBE

MEGHAN DAUM

They gather in small, blonde clusters at the gate, sipping coffee from the Terminal C Nathan's Famous, their clean hair swept carefully out of their clean faces. They cannot possibly be real, these uniformed creatures, these girls with matching luggage and matching shoes, these warm-blooded extensions of that hulking, spotless aircraft.

Neither passenger nor pilot, the flight attendant is the liaison between the customer and the machine. She is somehow blonde even when she's not blonde, a girl even when she's a guy. Part bimbo and part Red Cross, she is charged with the nearly impossible task of calming the passenger down while evoking enough titillation to suggest that there remains, even in the twenty-first century, something special about air travel.

Flight attendants are fetishized and mocked in equal measure. They are both fantasy and punch line, the players in hackneyed sex jokes and the guides through smoke and fire to the emergency exit. Since the beginning of commercial flying, back in the 1930s when flight attendants were required to be registered nurses, the profession has symbolized an unearthly female glamour. Until the 1960s, flight attendants were not allowed to be married. On many airlines they were required to have a college degree and speak a foreign language. Their skin was periodically checked for blemishes, their hair was not allowed to touch their collars, and if they were, say, five-foot-four, they could not weigh more than 115 pounds. Until the 1970s they were called "stewardesses," real girls who were treated like ladies.

There is no small amount of perverted nostalgia in all of this. When people today talk about what's happened to flying, about why any given transcontinental flight bears a heavy resemblance to a Greyhound bus ride from Memphis to Louisville, they often claim to be talking largely about the absence of ethereal waitresses serving seven-course meals in first class. No longer does the starchy hiss of the uniform sound a note of almost military kinkiness. Back in the old days, flight attendants were as sleek and identical as F-16s flying in formation. Back in the old days, they may as well have all been twin sisters. There was a time when you could pinch their asses and they'd buy you a martini. These days they will stop serving you drinks when you've had enough. If you do anything that they feel interferes with their duties, you could be charged with a felony. There are restraints in the cockpit should such an occasion arise. These days you have your fat ones, your ugly ones, and worst of all, your old ones. It used to be they had to quit when they turned thirty. Today, with no retirement age, there are a few as old as seventy-seven.

But even now, perhaps even this morning when you boarded some generic flight to some generic airport, you looked at them in search of some whiff of the past—you looked for a cute one, someone who might like you more than the others, someone to whom you pretended you might give your phone number. You wanted to consider

these possibilities but chances are those possibilities simply weren't there. She's not in your league. Her sole education requirement is a GED. She's some bizarre relic. And,
like the fact that your flight was oversold and delayed and
some used-car salesman in a Wal-Mart suit inexplicably
ended up seated next to you in business class, you are
more than a little heartbroken about the whole thing. This
is because the sex appeal of the flight attendant, like the
sex appeal of flying, is gone forever. As much as you act
like you have it over her, you somehow still long for an earlier era, back when there was no question that she had it
over you.

The sky is a strange place to be. Eustachian tubes are
tested up here. The human lung is not designed for the air
outside. The food is nuked, the forks are plastic, the dirty
words have been edited out of the movie. There's a good
chance that the flight attendants, who may be hamming it
up during the oxygen mask announcement and giggling in
the rear galley like sauced-up Tri Delts, had not met each
other until they boarded the plane.

When I board an evening flight on US Airways from
Philadelphia to San Francisco, accompanied by a flight attendant who agreed to participate in a magazine article, no
one else on the crew has met me or had any warning that
I'd be coming along. I tell them that I am writing a story
about flight attendants for a glossy men's magazine (the
story, in the end, was killed by the editor because it lacked
the prurient details he'd hoped for). After a few requests
that I change their names—"I want to be called Lola!"—we
are getting along like old high school pals. They're connois-
seurs of bonding, high skilled socializers. If a reporter
showed up to my workplace and announced that she'd be

there for the next thirty-six hours I'd duck out for coffee and never come back. But there's plenty of coffee here already. They can't leave and their ability to deal with this fact is pretty much Job One.

This is called a turnaround, a day-and-a-half stint during which this crew will fly from their base in Philadelphia to San Francisco and then to Charlotte before returning to Philadelphia. We are on a Boeing 757—a "seven-five," in airline speak. All of the flight attendants are in their thirties or forties, four are women, three of whom are married, and two are men. All have been flying for at least ten years.

To contemplate what it means to be a flight attendant for ten or more years is to consider, after getting past the initially ludicrous notion of serving drinks at 37,000 feet, the effects of the relatively recent, popular tendency to put flying in a category that also includes walking and driving. To say that flight has become pedestrian is something of a Yogi Berra-ism. But to say that air travel has infused itself into the human experience without leaving marks or building up potentially problematic immunities is to view technology in a Pollyanna-like manner that may have gone out of fashion when applied to phenomena like the Internet and surveillance cameras but continues to thrive in the realm of travel. When it comes to technology's hold on our quality of life, cyber porn may be insidious, but jetliners are by now almost quaint, older than Peter, Paul, and Mary, as common as the telephone.

This is true and not true, a dilemma that often emerges when, as is the case in air travel, the glorious evolves into the stultifying and we are forced to come up with ways to re-experience, if not the original novelty, some form of entertainment. This is where the flight attendant appears onstage. When flying began, she was part of the show, as slick as the aircraft itself. Even through the 1970s, passengers were moneyed and expensively outfitted; ladies wore gloves on DC-4s. To deplane using a movable staircase was, for a moment, to do as rock stars and presidents did, and respect was paid accordingly. The idea has always been that the persona of the flight attendants should reflect that of the flying public. In that respect, little has changed. The only difference is that today the flying classes seem a little more public than in the past. The flight attendant, too, is given to the bad manicures and bad perms of any girl next door. She's still part of the entertainment, it's just that this is a lower-budget production. This may gnaw at passengers, but those holding $99 tickets to Miami may do well to look at the larger picture. Perhaps the flight attendant wouldn't remind us so glumly of the girl next door if so many of us didn't live close to the airport.

Still, passengers pay attention to flight attendants, not during the safety announcements, when they're supposed to, but later, while flight attendants are eating dinner or reading *Cosmo* or doing normal things that are somehow rendered out of sync because of the uniform. During our five hours and twenty-six minutes to San Francisco, we hit some "light chop" twice—airlines discourage pilots from using the word "turbulence," which frightens passengers— and the seat belt sign goes on. Passengers get up anyway. They visit the flight attendants in the galleys. They ask for playing cards and more drinks and hand over their garbage to be thrown out. Wayward business travelers amble around the first-class galley and take stabs at the same kinds of conversations they impose on people sitting next to them. "Where do you live? Do you like it there?" and then "Could you get me another drink?"

Even as he accepts an empty pretzel bag from an unshaven, Reebok-wearing passenger, Carl, who is working in the main cabin tonight, manages to put a spin on his role as service provider. "We're a few notches below celebrity status," he says. "The moment people see a crew member, their eyes are on you constantly. People will come into the galley and just stare while you eat dinner. You have to watch everything you do and say."

Carl is thirty-six and has been a flight attendant with US Airways for twelve years. I am asking him questions in the aft galley ("aft" is used to describe anything located behind the wings) where he and Jim, his friend and colleague, have fashioned a seat for me out of a stack of plastic crates because I'm not allowed to sit in the flight attendant–reserved jump seat. They have poured salad dressing left over from first class into a plastic cup and are eating it off of their fingers. "We have a needy bunch tonight," Carl says. "But not as bad as if we were going to L.A. Certainly nothing like Florida."

A lot of call buttons have been ringing tonight. A lot of people cannot seem to figure out how to use their headsets to watch the in-flight screening of *Tomorrow Never Dies*. A fleshy, spacy eleven-year-old boy repeatedly visits the aft galley asking for more soda, more peanuts, some ice cream. "You're a pretty demanding kid," Carl says with just enough smirk so that I notice but the kid does not. Carl and Jim disagree as to whether the boy qualifies for the unofficial passenger shit list that is compiled on every flight.

"He's a pain in the ass," says Carl.

"No, he's obviously slow," says Jim. "I feel sorry for him."

Still, no one is punching anyone in the nose tonight. No one has threatened a flight attendant with bodily harm or become obstreperously drunk or engaged in the sort of activity that would merit a presentation of those restraints stored in the cockpit. The fact that these sorts of incidents are ascending at an alarmingly steep angle, mostly for those pesky reasons having to do with the invasion of a public mentality into what was once perceived as a private space, dominates much of what is written and discussed about flight attendants these days. It is part of the reason that I am here in the aft galley dipping my finger in salad dressing tonight, the other part having to do with discerning whether the deglamorization of the job is the cause or the symptom of all that aggression.

What is at first most noticeable about flight attendants is the chronic disorientation that follows them both on and off the job. With work space measured by aisle widths and hours either stolen or protracted by virtue of time changes and date lines, flight attendants occupy a personal space that must prove stronger than the artificial and ever-changing scope of "real" time and geography. Flight attendants are always tired and usually bored and, though they are required to wear a working watch at all times, understand distinctly the difference between knowing what time it is and feeling what time it is. A forty-five minute break on a transatlantic flight demands the ability to fall asleep instantly on the jump seat. They must learn to literally sleep on cue.

But there is another layer in the psyche of flying that transcends the burdensome working conditions of flight attendants. It's a set of notions that has a lot to do with life on the ground and yet can best be unpacked by examining the ebb and flow of life on an airplane. Just as air pressure will make one martini in the air equal two on the ground, the malaise of modern life extends its claws in cartoon-like proportions on an airplane. It's a sickness aggravated by tiny bathrooms and recirculating air and laptop computers that allow no excuse to take a break from work. "What I hate is when passengers won't put the computer away when I try to bring them dinner," Theresa, a sinewy Mexican-American flight attendant for US Airways, tells me. She is in the first-class galley eating chocolate syrup out of a plastic cup. "They never look up, never take a break to enjoy the flight. They never just look out the window and see how beautiful it is."

This is a disease of plastic and its discontents. It is what happens when sleep becomes a greater novelty than gravity defiance. It is what happens when the concept of New York to London seems more like changes in a movie set than a journey involving thousands of miles of empty sky, five degrees of longitude, an ocean. It is what happens when the miraculous becomes the mundane, when we are no longer amazed by flying but bored by it at best and infuriated by it more often than not. And it is this hybrid of nonchalance and aggression that has largely come to define the modern air traveler. It's what causes passengers to punch, slap, spit, swear, make obscene gestures, grope, and fling food at flight attendants and each other. It's what makes people dismantle smoke detectors, throw tantrums when they don't get a meal choice, and threaten to get a crew member fired over such infractions as not having cranberry juice. That the flight attendant must act as an agent for the big, impenetrable aircraft as well as for the small, vulnerable passenger is both a corporate conflict and a metaphysical conundrum. As boring as the airplane may be at this point, its technology remains distancing and unnerving, sometimes even terrifying. And whether the flight attendant is aware of it or not, her duty is to bridge the gap between the artificiality of the cabin and the authentic human impulses that play themselves out in that cabin. She has to shake her ass yet still know how to open the exit door.

The more tangible reasons for her condition have to do with numbers. Every year more seats are squeezed on to planes, seat width has become narrower, flights are over-sold, and cheap tickets attract passengers that would otherwise be taking the bus. Flight attendants blame the overcrowding on federal deregulation, which occurred in 1978 and essentially legislated that airlines were allowed to spend as little money as possible per flight as long as they did not violate federal safety standards. This introduced significantly lower ticket prices; it costs an average of twenty-four percent less to fly today than before deregulation.

Out of this was born the era of the $99 ticket. It also meant an abrupt end to luxury air travel; the pillbox hats were traded in for unwashed hair. "We're taught in training that people can't get on board if they have curlers in their hair or no shoes on," said Tracy, another US Airways flight attendant. "And if they have to publish that [in training manuals], that's frightening."

"They show up wearing jogging suits," Carl says. "And I doubt that they're wearing any underwear under those things."

"I hate it when people in the exit row put their feet up on the bulkhead," a Delta flight attendant told me a few weeks later. "If you were a guest in someone's house, would you put your feet on the wall?"

It seems like such a small complaint, but then again this is the sort of gesture that shapes the psyches of those who work in the air. This is *not* her house. And yet it is.

This is not a house at all, and yet it's the place where a huge number of people spend a huge amount of time. As more and more Americans carry the detritus of earthbound life to this tube in the air, measures must be taken to make them feel at home without allowing the frontier to become lawless. "When the door closes, we must play every role," said Britt Marie Swartz, a Delta flight attendant who began her career at Pan Am in the late 1970s and actually cooked eggs to order in 747 galleys. "We're doctors, lawyers, travel agents, therapists, waitresses, and cops. No one would demand all of that from a normal person."

The first thing aspiring flight attendants learn when they attend a recruitment meeting at the American Airlines training school near the Dallas/Fort Worth airport is that, if hired, they will make a base starting salary of around $14,000 a year. The second thing they must do is fill out a lengthy questionnaire designed to give recruiters an idea of their basic character makeup. When I visit the training facility, I am not allowed to see this questionnaire, although I am told that the nature of their answers will lead to what interviewers call "probing points," wherein candidates are asked to talk about themselves in ways that may or may not indicate personality traits incompatible with airplane social dynamics. "There was one grammar outburst," a recruiter says as he emerges from an interview. "I think I detected a double negative." Although I must sign a release saying that I will not print or repeat any of the questions asked of candidates, I am allowed to print the answers they give. And as I spend an hour watching a sweet and painfully sincere twenty-four-year-old from Arkansas hang herself on the basis of about two answers, I am amazed at what an art the recruiters (all of whom are former or working flight attendants) have made out of selecting their co-workers. The candidate, carefully outfitted in an Arkansas version of a power suit, complete with Fayva-type pumps and a neckerchief, seals her fate based on the following responses:

"I would say 'I don't find that type of humor funny' and walk out of the galley," and, "If nothing else worked, I wouldn't lie. I guess I would say, 'Your feet seem to be causing an odor. Can you please put your shoes back on?'"

The woman is sent back to Arkansas with the promise that she will be notified by letter within six weeks, which means that she most certainly will never be hired. Though the recruiter, who looks and speaks almost exactly like the weatherman on my local ABC television affiliate, cannot put his finger directly on what turned him off to her, he tells me it has something to do with apparent inflexibility.

During the week that I observe training, I spend most of my time with a class of sixty students. They have been selected from an original pool of 112,000 applicants, all but 4,000 of whom were eliminated via an automated telephone screening system. American has one of the most rigorous training programs in the industry—flight attendants from other carriers frequently refer to them as the "Sky Nazis"—but it is also among the most sought-after employers, both for its reputation and its pay scale, which is high by industry standards.

The training facility is an awe-inspiring complex. Occupying a large building next door to the flight academy, it contains a hotel, conference center, and salon, as well as a multitude of offices, lecture halls, and several life-size cabin simulators. The simulators, which fill up large rooms, look like movie sets of airplanes. They hold real seats, real galleys, and real doors. The windows are filled in with

painted renderings of fluffy white clouds. The flight attendants practice serving real food to their classmates and are
observed closely by their instructors. Part of their training
involves getting accustomed to erratic hours and last-
minute schedule changes; their day can begin as early as 3
a.m., and individual students often receive telephone calls
in the classroom from a mock scheduling unit, which in-
forms them that drills or simulated flight times have been
reassigned. Business attire must be worn at all times. This
means jackets and ties for the men and no skirts above the
knee for the women. Flight attendants both in and outside
of American have referred to this training program as Bar-
bie Boot Camp. New hires consult at least once with the
American Airlines salon manager, who suggests suitable
hairstyles—the French twist is especially popular—and
teaches the women how to apply makeup, which is to be
worn at all times during training. Several of the students
privately refer to the image consultant as Sergeant Lipstick,
who is known to keep tabs on the freshness of application.

Throughout the week I am escorted at all times by a
representative from the corporate communications office,
an impeccably groomed and perfectly nice woman who
leads me through an itinerary that has been set up specifically for me. Almost all of the classes I observe have to do
with aircraft evacuation. One class involves food service,
another is centered almost entirely around a device called
the Automated External Defibrillator, which American recently acquired for most of their overseas jets and which,
I am told several times, many other airlines do not have. To
my disappointment, I have apparently missed the phase of
training that involves personal appearance standards.
When I ask twice if I can relocate to the hotel at the training
center in order to interview the experienced flight atten-

dants who are housed here for their annual recurrent training, I am subtly put off both times; like a demanding passenger, I am denied my request without ever hearing the word "no."

It seems to me that flight attendant training has relatively little to do with the actual job of flight attendant. Although the trainees have ostensibly been hired based on a vibrancy of personality and the good sense not to say "I don't find that type of humor funny," there is something so sterile about the vibe of this education that it's hard to imagine how their lessons will ever mesh with the reality of dealing with actual people in the actual sky. In an entire week of observing classes, I never once hear the word "crash." Instead, a strange semantic code seems to be in place. Several times I hear the term "crispy critter," which, apparently, is what the flight attendants will be if they can't maneuver a clear path through fire. "If you do not go through the protected area and there's a fire," chirps an instructor at 7:15 one morning, "who's the crispy critter? You!"

Though American may have earned its "Sky Nazi" wings by maintaining a somewhat overzealous tone when it comes to corporate culture, their personnel bear little resemblance to the "coffee, tea, or me" drones of the past. Recruiters say that they work hard to hire crews that will reflect the demographic makeup of the passengers and from the looks of things, they're succeeding. The class I observed had several men and women over forty and a number of people of color, including a thirty-six-year-old former North Carolina highway patrolman with two children who said he just always wanted to fly. "The times that I've felt down about being here, I just go to the airport and watch the planes take off and land," he says in a group interview that's been set up for me by company supervisors.

That's a poetic sentiment, and American Airlines doesn't mind that kind of sound bite. But the theme music they really want played is all about "customer service," a term that the company repeats like a mantra, much like the Boy Scouts' "Be Prepared." Things get tricky, however, when it becomes clear just how difficult it is to uphold Ritz-Carlton–like service philosophies in an arena that is accessible to almost all walks of life. Customer service may be the gospel here, but it isn't necessarily the law. "Our company no longer holds fast to the policy that the customer is always right," says Sara Ponte, a flight attendant recruiting supervisor. "If a passenger consistently causes a disturbance, then that's not a passenger we want on our airline." Although no one at American will confirm or deny any rumors, company myths have it that a few celebrities, including Kim Basinger and Charlie Sheen, have been banned from the airline because of in-flight misconduct. Basinger's tantrum was allegedly sparked after she was refused ice cubes made from Evian water.

Herein lies the central conflict of flight attendant training, and it is the conflict that factors most heavily into the larger identity crisis of airborne life. Cabin crews are supposed to maintain an aura of exclusivity by making passengers feel special. But how can this be done when the very customers they're trying to please are anything but exclusive? By definition, the public is not private, nor are flight attendants high-priced personal assistants who consider the maintenance of freshly starched shirts a higher priority than feeding 173 people in under one hour or, for that matter, being able to evacuate 173 people in less than ninety seconds. That airlines continue to advertise themselves as luxury watering holes that, it so happens, will get you across the country in five hours is both a disservice to the flight attendant and one more way that the passenger is distanced from the actual concept of flying. Singapore Airlines, which is considered to have the highest level of customer service of any carrier in the world, has long touted their flight attendants as their major selling point. In the 1980s, the airline's slogan was "Singapore Girl, You're A Great Way to Fly." While it's doubtful that any United States carrier could get away with this kind of ad copy, all flight attendants carry the burden of this kind of public image. They are expected to represent the sex in their airline while remaining utterly nonthreatening. They are symbols of technology and symbols of flesh, and this is where their religion and their rules begin to come unglued.

When new hires are asked to leave American Airlines's training program, they always disappear instantly. Students can be eating lunch together only to find a classmate gone permanently an hour later. In this class of sixty, seven left early, some for reasons no one quite understands. When I try to talk to the students, they happily accommodate my questions until they realize that everything they say will be within earshot of my escort from corporate communications. A woman waiting to practice a drill tells me that she was forced by the company salon to cut her hair and now feels bad about it. Back in the classroom, half an hour later, she clams up on me. When I press her, she finally slips me a note that reads, "I can't really talk now."

Though I cannot be sure, I have inklings that my escort from corporate communications is keeping an eye on me when I visit the ladies' room. We eat lunch together every day. We walk down every corridor together. As I throw questions at anyone I can find she lingers next to me, reducing every flight attendant to the bland politeness of the first-class cabin. Though my escort has offered to pick me up at my hotel and drive me to the training center every morning, I have a rental car and assure her that I can find my way on my own. One afternoon, after parting ways in the parking lot, we get separated by a few cars as we pull onto the road that leads to the freeway. As I drive along I notice that she's pulled over to the shoulder so I can catch up. "How nice," I think to myself. "She's making sure I don't get lost." Hours later it occurs to me that she might have been making sure I didn't sneak back to the training center to interview people without her. I had indeed considered staying behind by myself, only to discard the idea for fear I'd be sent home.

Back on our US Airways flight to San Francisco, I learn that Carl and Jim have a penchant, during mid-flight seat belt checks, for taking note of male passengers who have fallen asleep and developed erections. They then go into the galley and whisper something in the neighborhood of "Check out 26C" and send other flight attendants, one by one, to do the old corner-of-the-eye glance while moseying on by. This is considered a necessary distraction and an entirely acceptable way to while away the hours. They also play a game called "Thirty-Second Review," wherein they have thirty seconds to walk through the cabin and make a note of the seat number of the passenger they would most like to have sex with.

As I research this story, I am told about flight attendants who work as prostitutes on the side, flight attendants who give mid-flight blow jobs to pilots, flight attendants who are transsexuals, and flight attendants who carry separate business cards for their drag queen personae. A friend of mine can tell a story about a flight attendant who gave him a hand job in the business-class section of a 747 during her half-hour break on a flight from New York to São Paulo. A cab driver who took me home from the airport a few months ago described meeting a flight attendant on the way to Orlando and shacking up with her for a week at a hotel near Disney World. "Of course, I had to pay for everything," he said to me as we careened over the Triborough Bridge. "She had it all figured out."

None of these actions or examples, weighed on their own, register enough scandal to send the airlines into collapse. As sensational as some of them are, these are the exceptions that prove the rule that most flight attendants are regular people with regular aspirations, many of which do not require business cards at all. But the fact that such tales are recounted so readily, both by people outside of the job and by flight attendants themselves, reveals a trait that is shared by just about everyone who works in the air. As the remoteness of the sky threatens to render them something less than human, they have no choice but to make themselves almost exaggeratedly human, hyperreal characters who rely on wild behavior and raunchy mythologies in order to outsmart the numbing effects of the airplane.

These stories, apocryphal or not, serve to sustain humanity inside the artificiality of the tube. A particularly dark plotline involves the widely held belief that the so-called Patient Zero, to whom over forty of the first AIDS cases were traced back, was an Air Canada flight attendant named Gaeten Dugas. More common are ambitious passengers seeking membership into the Mile High Club. Carl recalls a couple from Dayton who sheepishly offered him twenty dollars to allow them to enter the lavatory together (he waived the fee). An American Airlines flight attendant recounts what he swears is a "true rumor" about identical twins who worked as flight attendants for Eastern Airlines in the 1980s. The sisters worked together on wide-body aircrafts like the DC-10 and L10-11 that had lower-level galleys accessible from small elevators, which could, in effect, be locked by keeping the door open downstairs. Together they would solicit a male passenger and take him down into the galley for clandestine three-way sex. Afterward, they would serve him champagne.

Such rituals have been in place since the inception of commercial air travel. Pan Am stewardesses regularly taped centerfolds to the backs of safety cards when flying United States troops on military-contracted flights to Vietnam. Even into the late 1970s, flight attendants on Pacific South Airlines wore uniforms that featured miniskirts and go-go boots. The difference today is that these rituals are played out on the sly. As airlines fight harassment and discrimination lawsuits, keeping strict watch over potentially solicitous pilots or questionable behavior on layovers, these antics are mind games more than parlor games. There is considerably more talk than action going on. The influence of gay male culture cannot be ignored either. It is perhaps no accident that stereotypically gay male styles of social behavior seem custom-made for the flight attendant lifestyle. "For a lot of the gay guys it's been a wonderful ride," says Carl, who came out the same year he began flying. "The airlines have been a friendly atmosphere for being ourselves. But it's more social than sexual."

Jim, who is also gay, is quick to jokingly add that there is no better job for him *because* he is gay. This is a valid point, but not in the way that probably first comes to mind. While there are plenty of male flight attendants who are not gay, the cabin is dominated by an unquestionably campy sensibility; the boys help the girls with new hair styles, the girls loudly evaluate the boys' asses. It's a vibe that points toward the tolerance on which flight attendants pride themselves. But it also scratches the itch of their central contradiction. They are at once erotic figures and cartoon characters, raunchy talkers who wouldn't be out of place in the cast of Up With People. Their penis jokes have the ring of a junior high school cafeteria; words like "meat" or "fruit" cannot be spoken without some degree of sophomoric innuendo. Flight attendants live in a state of permanent chaos, and thrive on it. Unlike their passengers, whose systems are still adjusting to the transient new world, the flight attendant has successfully adapted to surroundings that are neither here nor there. For better or worse, she represents the nervous system of the future.

Kew Gardens, Queens, near JFK and LaGuardia airports in New York City, is the sometime-home to approximately two thousand flight attendants and pilots. I visit an apartment complex that houses two hundred of them in dorm-like apartments that are cleanly furnished with drab sofas, Formica dinette sets, and the perfunctory $24 halogen torch lamp. The building's landlord actively seeks out airline personnel, who each pay a monthly rent of $150 for their maximum stays of seven days. Each unit has two or three bedrooms that hold two sets of bunk beds with the exception of the errant single-occupancy pilot's room, one of which is elaborately outfitted with stereo equipment, a computer, and a wall-mounted, large-screen television affixed with a Post-it that reads "Seinfeld 11:00." A lot of pilots, however, drift in and out of a nearby place nicknamed

Animal House, which is considered a prime spot for crew parties and fraternity-style debauchery.

But things are pretty calm tonight in unit C-2, where several flight attendants, many of whom have just returned from places where today is still yesterday, are gathered in the common room watching the Weather Channel. Janet is thirty-eight, divorced, and worked on the ground for Delta until she got a company transfer and began flying in 1993. She commutes to this crash pad from her home in Atlanta, and, like many of her colleagues, admits that her transient lifestyle can get in the way of her personal life. A typically prepubescent maxim in aviation goes like this: "What does AIDS stand for? Airline Induced Divorce Syndrome." For every crew member who relishes the personal space inherent in her job, there is another who feels her relationships have been sabotaged by it.

"A lot of the girls from my class are divorced now," she says, finding herself unable to keep from getting up to refill my drink before I even finish it. "Guys you meet think it's kind of fascinating, the whole mystique of being a flight attendant. I dated a guy who I swear wanted me to wear my uniform when we went out. But they don't really want to have a relationship with someone who is gone so much. They'll come home at five o'clock and you're not there."

Later we go across the street to Airline Night at the local dive bar. There are hundreds of flight attendants and a few scattered pilots ordering two-for-one drinks and rubbing each other's shoulders. Even out of uniform, there is something about the crowd that is unmistakably airliney. With their clean fingernails and neat hair, they seem like they come from nowhere, as if they're extras in a made-for-TV movie. Like people in an airport, they are a smorgasbord of regional accents and styles. Though most will fly together only rarely, they tend to touch each other a lot, giving bear hugs and wet kisses and pulling familiar figures aside saying, "I remember you from the seven-two, a couple years ago."

Not unlike the main cabin of an airplane, this bar is jammed with representatives from every town in every state. Hired to assist and identify with the country's disenfranchised, disoriented air travelers, the primary job requirement seems less about handling an emergency than diffusing the side effects of hours spent in the hothouse that is the plane. Very few say they fear an accident, and most maintain a Zen-like philosophy about the possibility of crashing. "I figure when it's my time to go, it's my time to go," a thirty-two-year-old flight attendant named Len says. Of all the flight attendants I spoke with, about half had experienced incidents like engine explosions or faulty indicator lights that required returning to the airport. Within that group, only a tiny fraction had ever evacuated their plane. Britt Marie Swartz says that early in her Pan Am career she was scheduled for a trip that she had to cancel at the last minute. "The plane crashed. After that I was never afraid. I figure my time will come when it comes."

No one is allowed to die on an airplane. The worst thing you can do to a flight attendant is try to die on her. It won't work. She'll have to give you CPR no matter how evident your passing may be. Upon making an emergency landing, after they cart you away, the plane will be impounded. There will be the inevitable lawsuits.

"We are told unofficially that no one is allowed to die on the airplane," a Delta flight attendant in Kew Gardens told me. "Maybe they died on the jetway, but not on the airplane." Flight attendants are not allowed to declare death, and doctors, if there are any on board, are often reluctant to speak up when called for because of liability issues. In 1997, Lufthansa lost a million-dollar lawsuit against the family of a man who had died of a heart attack on the plane.

There is an unparalleled creepiness about airplane deaths, perhaps because we most often associate them with the gothic horror of news footage when there is a crash. But while air crashes occupy a far larger place in the popular imagination than they do in realistic odds, medical emergencies are relatively common. Every flight attendant in this story described situations which were sometimes harrowing enough to rival an episode of *ER*—strokes, seizures, childbirth, psychotic reactions to drugs, broken bones, a catheter that needed to be changed in heavy turbulence.

In the sky, denial is not just human instinct, it's a job requirement. A flight attendant for Canadian Airlines remembers an elderly man who, unbeknownst to his wife, died in his sleep. "I put a blanket on him," she says. "His wife was right beside him and I let her believe he was asleep until we landed. It was the best thing to do given the situation."

"A colleague of mine said that last week a woman traveling with her husband knew he had died twenty minutes into the flight," says Shannon Veedock, a Chicago-based American Airlines flight attendant. "They had made a stop in Dallas, stayed on the plane, and continued on to New York. She kept telling the crew he was asleep. She'd even called her son from the plane and told him what was going on. She was determined to get him home."

Here again lies the contradiction of flying, smatterings of the grotesque on a sublime canvas, heroism one minute and *Beavis and Butt-Head* behavior the next. A flight attendant with a major airline explains to me how she and her co-workers spent two hours and forty-five minutes giving CPR to a passenger who was vomiting on them and saved his life. Five minutes later in our conversation she recalls a particularly nasty passenger who demanded an extra lime for her gin and tonic. "She'd been snapping her fingers at other crew members, snapping her fingers at me, and so I took her glass into the galley, got two pieces of lime and shoved them up my nostrils and wiggled them around. Then I plopped them back in the glass and cheerfully brought it back to her."

The night I am flying home from my turnaround with the US Airways crew, I find myself overtaken with an uncontrollable urge to become a flight attendant, to join the living up here among the sleeping, to wear the uniform. It's the uniform that gets me where I live, that hideous, dazzling, itchy ensemble of unnatural fibers, that homage to country and corporation. It embodies all the contradictions of airplane life, contradictions which, in the end, make more evident the crisis of national identity: the need to be free versus the need to be sewn inside an organized structure. With their insignia and their rebellion, I can't help but think that flight attendants are, in a sense, quintessential Americans. They are at once rootless souls and permanent fixtures, vagabonds who can't stay anywhere too long and plain folks trying to restore equilibrium to a crowded, light-headed world.

This 757 is a tube of intersecting lives, a pressurized cross section of the entire population, a flying nation. In a few hours we will land at an airport that looks like a shopping mall. We will stay in a hotel that gives no clue as to what city we're in. In a world whose pace and legroom is controlled by the speed of technology, a glance down this length of darkened cabin gives a pretty fair indication of the shape we're in. One hundred ninety-four passengers are curled up asleep in what little space they have, their coats tucked under their heads, their knees tucked under their chins. Laptop computer screens are glowing. The air smells of coffee and peanuts and bodies. It's such a specific aroma, bottled in its giant container, sponged off the skins of 194 people who think it must be coming from the person sitting next to them. But this is what an airplane always smells like. It is the scent of the house where the entire world lives.

THE BAGGAGE CAROUSEL

THOMAS BELLER

Later in life it came back to him at odd moments. As a rule he avoided talking about it but then it arrived in the foreground of his thoughts, unannounced, and he had to stare at it, the memory. Girlfriends were curious, of course. This was due, in part, to his curiosity about how it happened for them. With whom. If they wanted to. If they liked it. When they asked him the same question he would roll out the story grandly, getting up on an elbow in the dark, the sheets all curled around them; it was a moment of solidarity and confession. But he came to realize that he never made it to the end of the story, in part because whomever was listening seemed so *amused*.

Then, at a friend's wedding, he found himself telling the story to a group of people, all of them giddy as he unfurled the narrative. He did the whole thing, the bathroom, everything, omitting only the end. The crowd of people, which included several good friends, but also this couple from Philadelphia whom he hardly knew, laughed and slapped their thighs and said, "Really? You're kidding. Really?"

****

The flight was from Washington, D.C. to Houston. Sam was
going to spend a weekend with his cousin, Jason, who was
ten years older and known in the family as a bit of a degen-
erate. His mother had wrung her hands when Sam first announced that Jason had invited him and that he would like
to go, venting out loud about the pros and cons. The main
pro was that it might be good for Sam to spend some time
in the company of an older man. The main con was that
Jason was a musician and someone who gave every impression of having bad habits of the sort that are highly
transferable to an impressionable fourteen-year-old.

Sam kept his mouth shut about it and let his mom work
out the issues with her sister, Jason's mom. Sam had never
told his mother that over the years Jason had taken every
opportunity to extol the virtues of sex, group sex when possible, drugs, alcohol, the Allman Brothers, and various jazz
fusion artists. Jason had once advised Sam to spit as often
as possible when walking with a girl, because although
they would complain and find it gross, girls ultimately were
more likely to have sex with you if at some strategic moment you grossed them out.

In the end his mother let him go. The ticket was bought
and for a brief moment it seemed like his mother would
want him to wear one of those plastic pouches around his
neck containing his identification, like he was a pet, or a
minor, which she pointed out he still was, technically.

After the plane had been aloft for twenty minutes the re-
freshments cart rattled down the aisle and the chirpy sing-
song voice of the stewardess drifted over the ambient hum.
The phrase "Juice-or-coffee?" was inter-cut with the sound
of ice being poured into plastic cups. Sam deferred to the

woman sitting next to him when the cart arrived at their
row. Mid-twenties, a lot of tousled brown hair, wedding
ring. Sam was a precocious noticer of wedding rings, having observed at an early age that his mother did not wear
one. When he asked her why she said, "Because, sweetie,
I'm not married."

"Bloody Mary, please," said the woman sitting next to
him.

The stewardess was pulling together the Bloody Mary.
He glanced sideways at the woman who had ordered it. She
was attractive but kind of overweight—the sort of girl, he
thought, that you look at and think "God, it would be fun to
pork her," and then, "But it would suck if anyone saw me
with her!" Then, with a shudder, Sam thought, "Please tell
me that sentiment is universal and I'm not going to hell."

He did not believe in heaven, hell, or God. But every
now and then he felt something, or someone, looking over
his shoulder, wanting to give advice. He had once shared
this thought with his shrink and, in the silence that followed, added, "Do you think it's my father?" But the shrink
hadn't answered.

The stewardess was doing a semi-limbo—shoulders
back, bending at the knees, rummaging through the shelf of
cans. She could have bent forward, but instead she did this
awkward limbo-like gesture and Sam wondered if maybe it
was because if she bent forward it meant her ass would
stick out and she didn't want her ass sticking out right into
someone's face.

"No Bloody Mary mix. Would tomato juice be OK?" she
said. "Or I could check in the back when I finish."

Tomato juice was fine for the woman sitting beside
him. Sam took the can, the cup of ice, and finally the little
vodka bottle and handed them across to his neighbor.

"Thank you," she said. She was wearing jeans and a heavy knit sweater within which lurked an intriguing fullness and heaviness whose contours he couldn't quite make out. As he handed her each item, he noticed her hands. The nails were manicured and a deep red. The hands themselves were a bit strangled-looking and tired.

"And you, sir?" said the stewardess.

"Same for me."

"I'm going to need to see some ID," said the stewardess.

"I don't have it on me, ma'am," he said.

"Then I'm afraid I can't serve you, sir," she said, totally perky. "Is there anything else I can get you?"

"I can't believe I'm being carded on an airplane," he said.

"We have laws up here the same as on the ground," she said. "Actually a lot more of them."

"I just don't think it's reasonable . . . it's not like the captain is going to come out and . . ." He dropped off into the silence of defeat. Then he said, "You're a stewardess, not a bartender." He was just lashing out, he knew. He felt bad about it.

"Actually we like to be called flight attendants. Can I offer you soda or juice?"

He recovered his composure and said, "I'll have the tomato juice, ma'm, and a lemon."

"Sure thing!"

"I'll have a second bottle of vodka," said the woman sitting next to him.

"Okie doke, that will be four dollars for the second bottle," said the flight attendant, her smile tight. She handed the beverage to him and then the bottle of vodka and stood there to make sure he passed it over. He held onto it while

THOMAS BELLER

the woman beside him attacked the interior of her purse. At last she produced a twisted, strangled-looking clump of bills, which he passed along. The flight attendant and her cart moved on to the next aisle. "Juice-or-coffee?" chirped out again and Sam sat there contemplating the red viscous liquid in the cup on his tray.

The woman mixed her drink. The second bottle sat there, unopened. The initial thrill of her request, which Sam was sure meant that she would give it to him, was starting to turn into a kind of mortification. Would she make him ask for it? He peered at her hand. The diamond ring pivoted like a top as she stirred in circles, round and round.

When his mother made her remark about not being married there was a brief short circuit in his mind—the synapses fired one after the other like the blue lights lighting up one after another to illuminate a runway that lead to his dead father lying beneath a collapsed roof. In this picture his father's hands and feet were sticking out of the rubble, like in a cartoon.

There was no actual photograph of this image. It was a figment of his imagination. But it was real, too, since this is apparently what had happened to his father when Sam was two years old. The image was a sad photographic heirloom which he kept buried in the backyard of his mind. But his mother's remark led his gaze to this buried treasure and exhumed it. Confronted with the image of his father under rubble his circuits shorted, sparks flew, and then it all vanished, except for an awareness, hovering like smoke that lingers after the bullet is long gone, of her absent wedding ring, and all wedding rings.

****

When the woman next to him finally said, in a small, conspiring voice, "Would you like this?" there was so much tension between them it was as though a whole conversation had transpired already.

He poured the vodka and they toasted.

"Cheers," she said, smiling, her eyes squinting in a way that struck him as familiar.

She asked him questions about himself. "What grade are you in?" she said. "Who do you hang out with?" "I bet you have a lot of girlfriends." He went back and forth between answering her honestly and trying to calibrate what would give him the biggest advantage. He wasn't sure to what end he wanted an advantage. She was an adult, and he reflexively spoke to adults with an eye toward some hidden agenda, that was the game, except she was an unusual kind of adult. She conspired with him on another bottle of vodka. He felt pleasantly light. She was animated. She seemed to want something from him, some acceptance into a club, his club. He couldn't imagine what his club had to offer, other than that he was in it. Perhaps it offered her a chance to be a teenager. She acted like nothing would make her happier than to be able to be in the lunchroom when he walked in so they could sit together.

She sipped the plastic cup with her pinky in the air. Dainty little slurps with her eyebrows raised. Her mascara was caked on her lashes. A wave of lust and antipathy passed though him like a tremor. It gripped him in a manner similar to the reverie he'd had repeatedly about Ms. Deluca, the biology teacher with enormous breasts and a kind of fullness and sadness to her mouth about whom he fantasized while she lectured on vertebrates. Finally there was that one class where genus and species and so forth was discussed, at the end of which he'd raced out as soon as the bell sounded and sequestered himself in the restroom stall to madly relieve himself of his need.

When he opened his clenched eyes he was a little stunned, and couldn't quite orient himself until he looked down and saw what he had released in the clear water of the toilet bowl. It drifted down like a frozen sculpture, or someone falling through the air in the slow motion.

When he told the story at the wedding he ended with a line of hers, "Oh you dear boy, I hope I haven't corrupted you," and everyone laughed and laughed.

He was in the midst of explaining the logic he used by which he could claim success in school.

"It's like a contest," said Sam.

"What does that mean?" she said.

"It's like, who can do worse? If you do worse, you win. You know? And I am very competitive."

"The winner is the big loser?"

"That's not how I would phrase it. I mean, loser is, you know."

"Yeah, it's not good."

"Well the point is whoever fucked up the most was winning. So you weren't a loser. You were a winner. And needless to say I am often winning."

"If you say so."

"That's what I'm telling you. That's what we called it. Winning. Which I suppose is fucked up."

"You curse a lot."

"It's because I'm jaded and have seen too much of the world."

"Whether or not you have seen too much of the world, I will not venture to say. But jaded you are not."

"I'm not?"

"No."

"Why do you say that?"

"I don't know. You're not jaded. You're sweet."

"Thank you. I know you're much older than me but . . . "

"You make me feel like an old lady."

"I just mean, you know, older."

"OK, I am definitely older than you, yes. You were going to say something."

"I forgot."

"Rats. It sounded like it was going to be a compliment."

"Well I was going to say that you seem really sweet, too."

"You were?"

"No, actually. Not really. I mean you are sweet but sweet is not a word I usually use unless it's like, you know, that song is sweet, or whatever. It's like a girly word. But since you said it . . . OK you know what I am thinking?"

"No. What are you thinking?"

"I'm thinking that you remind me of this girl I go to school with."

"Oh yeah? What's her name."

"Vickie."

"You're kidding! That's my name, too!"

"Your name is Vickie?"

"Yes!"

"That is a shocker. That's really, really weird. I may need another drink to settle my nerves."

"And what's the deal with the other Vickie?"

"Vickie is, I don't know, I kind of like her and hate her."

"Wow. I remind you of someone you hate?"

"No, no, I don't hate Vickie it's just that she pisses me off but I also like her."

"And what pisses you off about her?"

"You sound like my shrink."

"You see a shrink?"

"A bunch of people in my grade have shrinks. I've been seeing mine for a year."

"Is there something . . . wrong with you?"

"I don't know. Maybe. I mean, what does wrong mean?"

"You're a very interesting kid."

"It was my idea," he said. "I told my mother I was underachieving and I thought I should see a therapist."

"That's very proactive of you," she said. "I'm impressed. You were telling me about Vickie. I was reminding you of her. What do we have in common?"

"I don't know, you look alike a little bit I guess."

"And are you into her? You like her? Does she know that? And you said you hated her, too? What's the deal with that?"

"She takes a lot of shit. I wish she wouldn't take so much shit."

"What does that mean?"

"Well, they call her Vickie the Quickie."

"Who is they?"

"Everyone. My friends. People. She tends to smile and giggle like an idiot and not say anything. And it's not true."

"She's not a quickie?"

"You use that word very easily."

"Oh I didn't mean it like that, to pile on. Oh . . . you like this girl, don't you."

"Of course, that's why I'm pissed at her for being such a doormat."

"Do you ever stand up for her?"

"Stand up for her? What do you mean?"

"Defend her against the people who call her Vickie the Quickie."

"What's to defend? She sits there smiling like an idiot."

"And this is the person I remind you of!"

"In a good way."

"Oh, dear boy," she said, and she reached out and petted his hair.

Then out of the blue she said "I'm going to the bathroom . . . want to come?"

Without thinking, he said "Yeah," and he slid into the aisle behind her and walked staring at his shoes, which he followed into the bathroom. In the cramped space she whispered, "Sit down," and he did, and looked up at her with fear. She sat down on his lap. Her weight crushed him. She started kissing him. Her tongue in his mouth in small lizard licks. The fluorescent lights and the smell made him feel as though some medical procedure was taking place. To say his dick was not growing was an understatement. It was trying to crawl into itself and vanish. She stopped kissing him. For a moment he sat there with his mouth ajar and his eyes closed. He shut his mouth but took another moment before he opened his eyes. He was afraid of what he would see. He wanted to leave.

She stroked his hair, stroked his face, purred into his ear, "You are such a beautiful boy. This is going to be so special."

When he opened his eyes he saw that she was looking at him with this matter of fact expression while unbuttoning her blouse. There had been a fullness to her breasts that he had keyed into right away, but it didn't prepare him for the sight of her pale flesh pressing against her bra, and then their forward thrust when she unhooked it. She pushed her breasts into his face. He was suffocating, drinking of them, he was the thirstiest man in the world now swimming in a pool of clear water, drowning and drinking, and very hard. She pulled down his jeans and then hers, and straddled him on the nasty little toilet.

"Maybe we should use a condom," he mumbled, and decided that the effort counted, and it would protect him against AIDS, everything. She put her hand down there, squatted. He was inside her. He thought for a moment it would snap off inside her. It felt huge and something separate from him. He gasped a fearful sound, a sound he might make if he heard the engine of the plane sputter. It was a gross animal sound. She replied with a whimper, tender, a little predatory, his mind raced contemplating if she would now change dramatically, if this was a trick, some nasty version of candid camera.

"Baby, baby, baby," she said. She bounced on him, lightly at first, but she quickly became more forceful. The whole experience began to feel like a water rocket that you pumped pumped pumped and then pressed the button and it exploded. She crashed down on his lap, he was aware of the smell, the awful bathroom smell, and along with it the lemony and slightly acrid smell of her body, her breasts, one of which she was guiding into his mouth. He thought fleetingly of Vickie, not her face or anything she said, but of the exasperation he felt, and a curious kind of feeling welled up within to accompany the animal rutting that now consumed him, something along the lines of vengeance. He tried to get a nipple in his mouth but it was too hectic there wasn't time he was being molested he thought he might sustain an injury something enormous was rushing out of him . . . "Oh God," she said as he exploded. She banged up and down extra hard.

He made a grunt and a whimper, a bit like a sound his old dog Charlie once made when its paw got run over. And suddenly a home movie began playing against the dark screen of his tightly shut eyes, the golden lab whimpering loudly as the car eased out of the garage and then quickly limping away, trotting, walking it off, walking it off in circles while his mother threw open the door and exclaimed, "Oh, Charlie!" almost irritated, like it was the dog's fault. After a few minutes Charlie stopped whimpering. But he never really stopped limping.

He opened his eyes, more for the purpose of interrupting this movie than to see where he was.

Vickie was tearful again, gazing at him, her tits there between them.

"Oh baby you are such a beautiful boy," she was saying.

"You are, too," he said. He didn't know if he meant it. He was elated. His thighs hurt.

"Oh God, oh my beautiful boy. Oh dear, oh boy. Oh boy! Oh boy oh boy oh boy!" She laughed. She sniffled. "I hope I haven't corrupted you, my dear beautiful boy," she said, and she smiled at him apologetically. With that she stood, grabbed a tissue, and shoved it between her legs. He was afraid he would not be able to stand. His legs seemed useless, damaged. He hoisted himself onto his feet with his arms. His legs were fine. A few moments later they pushed out of the tiny space. The male flight attendant was standing there fiddling with a coffee pot. He looked over at them, beaming. "You guys are in big trouble!" he whispered. His hair was heavily moussed and had blond streaks. It occurred to Sam that he was gay. This seemed appropriate. Gays thought a lot about sex, this was necessary because they had to decide that they were gay. It was like he had now joined the Sex Club, where people did more than talk or think about it, they had it, did it, rolled around in it, ground against one another in airplane bathrooms and got winked at when they emerged.

"I have a weird favor to ask you," he said when they were again seated.

"Anything you want," she said.

"It's just so I can remember this experience," he said, which he thought was as delicate a way of putting it that was both true and that would also satisfy this sudden primal need, which was proof.

She listened to his request and tilted her head, as though to look at him from a new angle. What did she see? He held a frozen grin. The grin of a shoplifter at the moment a security guard asks, "Excuse me, can you show me what is in your bag?"

"Of course, honey," she said after a moment.

She took his journal, and wrote feverishly, with her own pen, while the plane descended. Her hair blocked his view of the page.

"Don't read it till we split ways," she said, handing it back. "Promise?"

He promised. The plane was landing. The static hum of noise that had created a soft muffling between them, a kind of privacy, became louder, his ears were blocked, and they sat beside each other gathering themselves up to say goodbye.

He was going to be met by Jason, and was already giddy at the thought of sharing this recent development.

The first thing he did was go to the bathroom, pee, and stare briefly at his dick to make sure it didn't look diseased. It looked like it always did, but different. Alone, disease-free, and no longer a virgin, he stared at himself in the mirror for a few moments and then threw his arms up like a boxer who has just knocked out his opponent. He didn't make a sound. It was a pantomime of joy.

He wanted to read his journal right there but he didn't want to sit on a toilet like a fugitive. So he went out and found a bench near baggage claim to read what she had written before he got in the car. Just as he reached into his bag, he saw her, waiting there with everyone for the baggage carousel to start moving, looking dumpy and unremarkable and, he now thought, though he hadn't before, a bit used. He had been awakened to the potential for sex in any situation. He studied her for clues as to how he might discern those underlying tendencies in other women. But this errand, which he processed while he stared, was interrupted and overruled by another feeling, a really sad kind of feeling that came with seeing her standing there alone waiting for the baggage carousel to start, with no one there to pick her bag up. He imagined that the bag would be a little too heavy for her, and she would drag it off the carousel and then stand there for a minute recuperating.

Just then her head swiveled casually and her eyes locked on him looking at her. A smile appeared on her face. It was knowing and confident somehow and he felt stupid for all the pity he had just been feeling and a little embarrassed to have been caught staring.

He stood up and waved. He was sure, for some reason, that she had written her number down in his journal. He had no intention of ever calling it. But he liked that he had it. It made turning from her with a wave and walking away much easier.

****

Years later, when he told this story to girlfriends, or at the wedding, and everyone got so amused, it insulted his memory of the whole thing, which is why he could never get to the end of the story. Everything got so abstract as soon as they parted. The excitement of their connection didn't translate into real life, and it didn't translate at all into his grown up life, and yet he felt it still. Or maybe it had to do with the feeling of being conned somehow, that there was something off about it all in a way he couldn't quite see at the time, that fleeting feeling he had in the bathroom, of this being a con, the worry that the con and real life were intermingled, a feeling that was always provoked by that amusement that greeted his attempts at telling the story, and kept him from getting to the end.

Jason was there at the airport with a huge grin, arms outstretched, wild blond hair tamed a bit, but still brittle like a Brillo pad. Sam always marveled that he was related to this Brillo pad hair. They clapped backs and rushed to the car—an El Camino, a car of pure criminality, Sam thought with admiration—and on the way Sam kept saying he had the most amazing news.

"No fucking way dude," said Jason when Sam spat it out at last. "In the friggin bathroom? That is so awesome. You're kidding me, right?"

"I'm not kidding! I knew you would say that. I have proof!"

"I believe you, kid. Crazy shit happens with babes all the time. They're just dying for it. That's what most people don't understand. There was this one time . . ."

"I want to show you the proof," said Sam. He wasn't ready to yield the floor just yet.

"Dude don't show me no disgusting tissue or something."

"She wrote in my journal! I made her write it down in my journal! Right here!"

"You keep a journal? You gotta be careful about that."

"I haven't even read it yet. Let me read out loud. 'Beautiful boy, you have been a delicious dream,'" he began.

"Get the fuck out of here," said Jason. "You wrote that yourself."

"Dude, is this my handwriting?"

"I'm driving kid, I can't be reading your journal."

Sam looked back to the page.

There, right below his most recent entry ("I'm on a ski lift. It's fucking cold. Snow last night, fucking powder, I'm going to kill. The Stockwells and the whole chalet scene is getting me down, but two blonde girls and their mom checked in last night with about a thousand suitcases and a deviant . . ." after which he had dropped the pen) was her handwriting. It had round letters which in their roundness suggested that, with only a little effort, they could have been turned into an illustration of a bunny, or something else cuddly and nice. There was something about it that reminded him of the other Vickie. It also had a hopefulness to it that made him uncomfortable. He drowned these feeling with the sound of his own voice.

"Beautiful boy," he began again, reading loudly. "You have been a delicious dream, as though you were an angel sent to enter my thoughts and draw them out for me to see in the plain light of day—or this airplane—what a shambles my life has become and how much richer and more fun it could be. My dad used to beat me and my husband kicked the shit out of me just before I left D.C. I was in such a low place when I got on this plane. But it was a gift to talk to you and it was a gift what we had together in that little bathroom—the Mile High Club! I hope I didn't corrupt you, you innocent beautiful boy! That was really and truly the most beautiful and tender and deep sexual experience I ever had. Thank you."

Sam closed his journal. He stared out the window, and a creeping exhaustion began to overtake him. It wasn't until later that he realized that she didn't leave her number. And so the remaining lingering image, like when you look at a bright light and then close your eyes, was not the wild bouncing in the skanky bathroom and the big tits in his face and his huge explosion. It wasn't the image of her leaning towards him after getting that second Bloody Mary and starting to look at him as though every word that popped out of his mouth was the perfect word and it was guiding them down the path of an unseen maze towards a prize. What stayed with him was the image of her at the baggage carousel waiting for it to start, and then it lurching into motion and starting to snake around and around without anything yet on it, which was weird, because that was an event he hadn't even been there to see.

I MET A WOMAN ON THE PLANE

GRACE PALEY

she came from somewhere around Tampa
she was going to Chicago
I liked her a lot
she'd had five children
no she'd had six   one died
at twenty-three days

people said   at least you didn't
get too attached

she had married at sixteen   she
married again twenty years later
she said she loved her first husband
just couldn't manage a life

five small children? I said
no not that
    what?   him?
no   me she said
I couldn't get over that baby girl
everyone else did   the big
kids   you'll drive us all crazy
they said   but that baby   you can't

GRACE PALEY

believe her beautifulness
when I came into the kids' room

in her little crib   not a month old
not breathing   they say get over it
it's more than ten years   go away   leave
us for a while   so I did that   here I am she said
where are you going

UP IN THE AIR

WALTER KIRN

To know me you have to fly with me. Sit down. I'm the aisle, you're the window—trapped. You crack your paperback, last spring's big legal thriller, convinced that what you want is solitude, though I know otherwise: you need to talk. The jaunty male flight attendant brings our drinks: a two percent milk with one ice cube for me, a Wild Turkey for you. It's wet outside, the runways streaked and dark. Late afternoon. The first-class cabin fills with other businessmen who switch on their laptops and call up lengthy spreadsheets or use the last few moments before takeoff to punch in cellphone calls to wives and clients. Their voices are bright but shallow, no diaphragms, their sentences kept short to save on tolls, and when they hang up they face the windows, sigh, and reset their watches from Central time to Mountain. For some of them this means a longer day, for others it means eating supper before they're hungry. One fellow lowers his plastic window shade and wedges his head between two skimpy pillows, while another unlatches his briefcase, looks inside, then shuts his eyes and rubs his jaw, exhausted.

Your own work is done, though, temporarily. All week
you've been out hustling, courting hot prospects in fran-
chised seafood bars and steering a rented Intrepid along
strange streets that didn't match the markings in your atlas.
You gave it your all, and for once your all was good enough
to placate a boss who fears for his own job. You've stashed
your tie in your briefcase, freed your collar, and slackened
your belt a notch or two. To breathe. Just breathing can be
such a luxury sometimes.

"Is that the one about the tax-fraud murders? I'm hearing his plots aren't what they used to be."

You stall before answering, trying to discourage me. To
you, I'm a type. A motormouth. A pest. You're still getting
over that last guy, L.A. to Portland, whose grandson was
just admitted to Stanford Law. A brilliant kid, and a fine
young athlete, too, he started his own business as a teen
computerizing local diaper services—though what probably clinched his acceptance was his charity work; the kid
has a soft spot for homeless immigrants, which pretty
much describes all of us out west, though some are worse
off than others. We're the lucky ones.

"I'm on page eleven," you say. "The plot's still forming."

"It hit number four on the *Times* list."

"Don't read that paper."

"You live in Denver? Going home?"

"I'm trying."

"Tell me about it. Nothing but delays."

"Foul weather at one of the hubs."

"Their classic line."

"I guess they don't take us for much these days."

"Won't touch that. Interesting news about the Broncos
yesterday."

"Pro football's a farce."

"I can't say I disagree."

"Millionaires and felons—these athletes sicken me. I do enjoy hockey, though. Hockey I don't hate."

"That's the Canadian influence," I say. "It ameliorates the materialism."

"In English?"

"I talk big when I'm tired. Professor gasbag. Sorry. I like hockey, too."

The atom was split by persistence; you relax. We go on chatting, impersonally at first, but then, once we've realized all we have in common—our moderate politics, our taste in rental cars, our feeling that the American service industry had better shape up soon or face a crisis—a warmth wells up, a cozy solidarity. You recommend a hotel in Tulsa; I tip you off to a rib joint in Fort Worth. The plane heads into a cloud, it bucks and shudders. Nothing like turbulence to cement a bond. Soon, you're telling me about your family. Your daughter, the high school gymnast. Your lovely wife. She's gone back to work and you're not so sure you like this, though her job is only part time and may not last. Another thing you dislike is traveling. The pissy ticket agents. The luggage mix-ups. The soft hotel mattresses that twist your spine. You long for a windfall that will let you quit and pursue your great hobby: restoring vintage speedboats. The water—that's where you're happiest. The lake.

Now it's my turn. I make a full report. Single, but on the lookout—you never know, the woman in 3B might be my soul mate. Had a wife once, the prospect of a family, but I knew her mostly through phone calls across time zones. Grew up in Minnesota, in the country; father owned a fleet of propane trucks and served as a Democrat in two state legislatures, pressing a doomed agricultural agenda while letting his business slip. Parents split while I was in college, an eastern hippie school—picture a day care run by PhDs—and when I got home there was nothing to come back to, just lawyers and auctioneers and accusations, some of them true but few of them important. My first job was in computers. I sold memory, the perfect product, since no one has enough of it and everyone fears some competitor has more. Now I work as a management consultant, minoring in EET (Executive Effectiveness Training) and majoring—overwhelmingly, unfortunately—in CTC (Career Transition Counseling), which is a fancy term for coaching people to understand job loss as an opportunity for personal and spiritual growth. It's a job I fell into because I wasn't strong, and grew to tolerate because I had to, then suddenly couldn't stand another hour of. My letter of resignation is on the desk of a man who will soon return from a long fishing trip. What I'll do after he reads it, I don't know. I'm intrigued by a firm called MythTech; they've put out feelers. I have other logs in the fire, but no flames yet. Until my superior flies back from Belize, I work out of Denver for ISM, Integrated Strategic Management. You've heard of Andersen? Deloitte & Touche? We're something like them, though more diversified. "The Business of Business," we say. Impressed me too, once.

As the hour passes and the meal comes (you try the Florentine chicken, I take the steak, and neither of us goes near the whipped dessert), the intimacy we develop is almost frightening. I'd like to feel it came naturally, mutually, and not because I pushed. I push sometimes. We exchange cards and slot them in our wallets, then order another round and go on talking, arriving at last at the topic I know best, the subject I could go on about all night.

You want to know who you're sitting with? I'll tell you.

****

Planes and airports are where I feel at home. Everything fellows like you dislike about them—the dry, recycled air alive with viruses; the salty food that seems drizzled with warm mineral oil; the aura-sapping artificial lighting—has grown dear to me over the years, familiar, sweet. I love the Compass Club lounges in the terminals, especially the flagship Denver club, with its digital juice dispenser and deep suede sofas and floor-to-ceiling views of taxiing aircraft. I love the restaurants and snack nooks near the gates, stacked to their heat lamps with whole wheat mini-pizzas and gourmet caramel rolls. I even enjoy the suite hotels built within sight of the runways on the ring roads, which are sometimes as close as I get to the cities that my job requires me to visit. I favor rooms with kitchenettes and conference tables, and once I cooked a Christmas feast in one, serving glazed ham and sweet potato pie to a dozen janitors and maids. They ate with me in rotation, on their breaks, one or two at a time, so I really got to know them, even though most spoke no English. I have a gift that way. If you and I hadn't hit it off like this, if the only words we'd passed were "That's my seat" or "Done with that *Business Week*?" or just "Excuse me," I'd still regard us as close acquaintances and hope that if we met again up here we wouldn't be starting from zero, as just two suits. Twice last October I sat in the same row, on different routes, as 1989's Miss USA, the one who remade herself as a Washington hostess and supposedly works nonstop for voting rights. In person she's tiny, barely over five feet. I put her carry-on in the overhead.

But you know some of this already. You fly, too. It just hasn't hooked you; you just don't study it.

Hey, you're probably the normal one.

Fast friends aren't my only friends, but they're my best friends. Because they know the life—so much better than my own family does. We're a telephone family, strung out along the wires, sharing our news in loops and daisy chains. We don't meet face-to-face much, and when we do there's a dematerialized feeling, as though only half of our molecules are present. Sad? Not really. We're a busy bunch. And I'm not lonely. If I had to pick between knowing just a little about a lot of folks and knowing everything about a few, I'd opt for the long, wide-angle shot, I think.

I'm peaceful. I'm in my element up here. Flying isn't an inconvenience for me, as it is for my colleagues at ISM, who hit the road to prove their loyalty to a company that's hungry for such proof and, I'm told, rewards it now and then. But I've never aspired to an office at world headquarters, close to hearth and home and skybox, with a desk overlooking the Front Range of the Rockies and access to the ninth-floor fitness center. I suppose I'm a sort of mutation, a new species, and though I keep an apartment for storage purposes—actually, I left the place two weeks ago and transferred the few things I own into a locker I've yet to pay the rent on, and may not—I live somewhere else, in the margins of my itineraries.

I call it Airworld; the scene, the place, the style. My hometown papers are *USA Today* and the *Wall Street Journal.* The big-screen Panasonics in the club rooms broadcast all the news I need, with an emphasis on the markets and the weather. My literature—yours, too, I see—is the bestseller or the near-bestseller, heavy on themes of espionage, high finance, and the goodness of common people in small towns. In Airworld, I've found, the passions and enthusiasms of the outlying society are concentrated and whisked to a stiff froth. When a new celebrity is minted in the movie theaters or ballparks, this is where the story breaks—on the vast magazine racks that form a sort of trading floor for public reputations and pretty faces. I find it possible here, as nowhere else, to think of myself as part of the collective that prices the long bond and governs necktie widths. Airworld is a nation within a nation, with its own language, architecture, mood, and even its own currency—the token economy of airline bonus miles that I've come to value more than dollars. Inflation doesn't degrade them. They're not taxed. They're private property in its purest form.

It was during a layover in the Dallas Compass Club, my back sinking into a downy sofa cushion and coarse margarita salt drying on my lips, that I first told a friend about TMS, my Total Mileage System.

"It's simple," I said, as my hand crept up her leg (the woman was older than me and newly single; an L.A. ad exec who claimed her team had hatched the concept behind affinity credit cards). "I don't spend a nickel, if I can help it, unless it somehow profits my account. I'm not just talking hotels and cars and long-distance carriers and Internet services, but mail-order steak firms and record clubs and teleflorists. I shop them according to the miles they pay, and I pit them against each other for the best deal. Even my broker gives miles as dividends."

"So what's your total?"

I smiled, but didn't speak. I'm an open book in most ways, and I feel I deserve a few small secrets.

"What are you saving up for? Big vacation?"

"I'm not a vacation person. I'm just saving. I'd like to give a chunk to charity—to one of those groups that flies sick kids to hospitals."

"I didn't know you could do that. Sweet," she said. She kissed me, lightly, quickly, but with feeling—a flick of her tongue tip that promised more to come should we meet again, which hasn't happened yet. If it does, I may have to duck her, I'm afraid. She was too old for me even then, three years ago, and ad execs tend to age faster than the rest of us, once they're on their way.

I don't recall why I told that story. Not flattering. But I wasn't in great shape back then. I'd just come off a seven-week vacation that ISM insisted I take for health reasons. I spent the time off taking classes at the U, hoping to enrich an inner life stretched thin by years of pep-talking the jobless. My bosses matched my tuition for the courses: a creative writing seminar that clawed apart a short nostalgic sketch about delivering propane with my father in a sixty-mile-per-hour blizzard, and a class called "Country-Western Music as Literature." The music professor, a transplanted New Yorker in a black Stetson with a snakeskin band and a bolo tie clipped with a scorpion in amber, believed that great country lyrics share a theme: the migration from the village to the city, the disillusionment with urban wickedness, and the mournful desire to go home. The idea held up through dozens of examples and stayed with me when I returned to work, worsening the low mood and mental fuzziness that ISM had ordered me to correct. I saw my travels as a twangy ballad full of rhyming place names and neon streetscapes and vanishing taillights and hazy women's faces. All those corny old verses, but new ones, too. The DIA control tower in fog. The drone of vacuum cleaners in a hallway, telling guests that they've slept past checkout time. The goose-pimply arms of a female senior manager hugging a stuffed bear I've handed her as we wait together for two security guards—it's overkill; the one watches the other—to finish loading file cubes and desk drawers and the CPU from her computer onto a flat gray cart whose squeaky casters scream all the way to an elevator bank where a third guard holds down the "open" button.

I pulled out of it—barely. I cut that song off cold. It took a toll, though. Because I seldom see doctors in their offices, but only in transit, accidentally, my sense of my afflictions is vague, haphazard. High blood pressure? No doubt. Cholesterol? I'm sure it's in the pink zone, if not the red. Once, between Denver and Oklahoma City, I nodded off next to a pulmonary specialist who told me when I woke that I had apnea—a tendency to stop breathing while unconscious. The doctor recommended a machine that pushes air through the nostrils while one sleeps to raise the oxygen level in one's blood. I didn't follow up. My circulation is ebbing flight by flight—I can't feel my toes if I don't keep wiggling them, and that only works for my first hour on board—so I'd better make some changes. Soon.

I'm talking too much. I'm dominating this. Are you interested, or just being polite? Another bourbon? I'll have another milk. I know it's been discredited as an ulcer aid, but I come from dairy country. I like the taste.

Anyway, I should wrap this up—we'll land soon. You're meeting me in the middle of my farewell tour, with only six days and eight more cities to go. It's a challenging but routine itinerary, mixing business and pleasure and family obligations. There are people I need to see, some I want to see, and a few I don't know yet but may want to meet. I'll need to stay flexible, disciplined, and alert, and while it won't be easy, there's a payoff. Every year I've flown further than the year before, and by the end of this week, conditions willing, I'll cross a crucial horizon past which, I swear, I'll stop, sit back, and reconsider everything.

A million frequent flyer miles. One million.

"That's obsessive," you say. Because you care for me, not because I'm annoying you, I hope. "It's just a number. It doesn't mean a thing."

"Pi's just a number," I say.

"It's still obsessive."

The engines reverse thrust and here comes Denver.

"It's a boundary," I say. "I need boundaries in my life."

They open the doors and seat belts start unsnapping. Maybe I'll see you again, though it's unlikely. Next Monday the boss gets back from chasing marlin and the first thing he'll do after sifting through his in-box will be to cancel my corporate travel account, which he's often accused me of abusing, anyway. I need my million before then, and on his dime.

Deplaning now. As we stride down the jetway toward whatever's next for us, two lottery balls tossed back into the barrel, a mini cassette tape falls out of my coat and you see it before I do, and bend down. It's the last favor you'll ever do for me and it occurs in slow motion, a tiny sacrament.

"Thanks," I say.

"Have a good one."

"You too."

"I'll try."

You're gone, a fast walker, off to see the family. I hope you're not mad that I kept you from your book. I didn't want to spoil things by telling you, but I read it when it was in hardback. There's no plot.

AFTERBIRTH

SHEILA M. SCHWARTZ

At first when the captain's voice came on over the intercom and made the announcement, she felt almost glad. Not gleeful exactly, but a sudden ching! of recognition coursed through her; events fell into place. She was glad she'd had her weekend at the hotel, glad for her swim in the hotel pool, for sleeping late, for the free hot coffee available in all the lobbies, tables laid out formally with linen napkins and china trimmed with gold leaf. She was glad, most of all, that she was flying alone; her husband and children hadn't come with her as they'd threatened to at the last minute. She was glad to be so selfless knowing that they were safe on the ground.

The captain's voice echoed her mood. It had a cheery lilt to it, like someone in a cartoon with a bubble over his head. It was his sightseeing voice he used as they passed over the runway then abruptly surged upward again into the clouds above the lake. His tone seemed to imply that this just might be a Christmas miracle, the kind in a made-for-TV movie about the yin and yang of self-sacrifice, as the engines churned forward, then picked up speed, the wings hovering and dipping like an uncertain insect. "Ah, well,

427

folks," the captain said, "it looks like we've got a little problem here. Our landing gear light is shining red, and we don't know what it means. That's why we did that little dress rehearsal back there." He paused to chuckle at his own wit for a minute, dryly, then turned sober and reassuring. He banked the plane again for emphasis. "Now don't worry yet—it may not mean a thing. We'll just fly around for a little bit and check out some systems. Try to be patient with us, if you please."

Donna looked around to see what her reaction should be. No one else seemed to be panicked yet. An elderly couple across the aisle exchanged a look with her, a grim little smile that said, "We go through this every day." Other passengers, seasoned business travelers, were pretending to read their newspapers, thumbs paging casually, tenderly, through the *Wall Street Journal*. They were pretending to read computer printouts, legal briefs. Two seats up was a teenager who hadn't even heard the announcement. He had his Walkman on, turned up high enough for Donna to hear the bristle of drums, the angry thud of voices protesting some teenage issue—bad drugs, bad sex at the multiplex, exams without curves. She wondered if she ought to tell him, tap him on the shoulder gently and mouth it, "Honey— could you turn that down a bit? We're going to crash." (Donna had called everyone under thirty "honey" since her children were born, as if she'd suddenly and irrevocably catapulted into maturity, responsible for the frail moods of all souls. She practiced smiling when people were rude and ill-tempered, understanding for the first time how these were linked to a yearning for innocence, for the brick wall of mother love that would accept them.)

The boy swung his head back and forth, "No . . . no no no . . ." His smile was squeezed tight in a sullen orgasm of rebellion. "No . . . no no no . . ."

No no no no . . . , Donna mouthed to herself, but the captain interrupted, this time twinkling. "Yep! Still here, folks. Now just sit tight. We haven't found anything specific yet, and things are stacked up over the airport, anyway, as per usual. So we'll keep cruising. If you'd like another beverage, our personnel will be coming through the cabin to serve you."

At this cue the flight attendants broke their huddle at the cockpit. They clattered trays and carts, hoisted coffeepots, sprang soda tabs with a merry "Pffft!," jingled change for beer and whiskey, all the while smiling as if they were just here to perk up a weary office party. They moved quickly to fend off questions. They handed out extra bags of peanuts, as if this were one of the perks of crash landings. Their eyes were a geometry of evasion.

"And what would *you* like?" The flight attendant smiled, acting her part flawlessly—grace under pressure. "Coffee or tea? A beer, maybe? We're not charging for alcoholic beverages." And though Donna wanted to ask her, What do you *really* know? What did the captain tell you up there?, she did not want to be the one to ask nor to undo the carefully composed mood of the cabin. "Diet Pepsi," Donna said, "if you don't mind."

"No bother." The flight attendant nodded gravely as if it were not only appropriate but wise to choose, as one's last beverage on earth, something low-cal. Her gestures were a ballet of calm. "We're here to make you as comfortable as possible."

****

Donna had heard of masquerades like this one before. She'd heard of captains like this. Their bravery put ordinary humans to shame. In times of catastrophe, they could sound like a training manual. They could go through all the niceties of protocol as if death didn't mean a thing. They followed their procedures. They enunciated their last words clearly into the black box. There was a captain like that a couple of years ago she'd read about—somewhere over Iowa—who saved the lives of more than half the people on his plane by his expertise, his presence of mind. He was able to speak about the crash moments after the plane landed in a cornfield, able to explain how he'd decided on that particular site based on wind velocity, angle of engine failure, forward thrust and momentum, air to ground time. The empty field was a miracle, though, the God-given aspect of the situation. It opened up like a mirage just in the nick of time.

Of course, Donna thought, everyone knew there was nothing *but* cornfields in Iowa—what else would open up there? What interested Donna was how quickly the captain refocused the disaster into something positive. He didn't exactly gloss over the ninety-seven people who'd been killed, but he made it seem as if they'd beaten the odds, anyway. Two hundred and twelve people had been saved in a crash that might have killed everyone. He didn't bother to describe the burning bodies, entire families wiped out in one fell swoop. He didn't describe the particular horrors she'd read about later, the passenger accounts. One woman in particular had written an article for a parents' magazine, pleading with readers to pay for an extra seat on a plane trip to transport an infant in a carrier that could be secured with a seat belt. Donna wondered if Captain Marvel had read *that* article, if he'd read the mother's description of her child's trusting look as she tried to soothe him before they crashed. "I love you," she murmured to him, her hand poised across his brow, as if to check for one last fever. "I love you, little Bobby, little dear one. You've had a beautiful life." Then she kissed him over and over until the end. She wasn't able to hold on to him when they struck the ground. He'd hurtled forward through time and space, a frail illustration of the laws of physics, the rest of his life condensed to a few brief seconds of fear. Donna wondered how a mother could survive such a thing.

She was glad that she might not have to. That was one of her greatest fears, the possibility of outliving her children, imagining the hundred different ways she could lose them: fire, car crash, inhaled balloons, the impervious marble of bathtubs, the magnetism of empty electrical sockets. The thought of a knife too close to the edge of the kitchen counter sometimes made her gasp right out loud.

Now she might be spared all these—though there still weren't any clear signs of doom from the flight attendants. They were hurrying through the aisles like precursors of the Christmas rush, balancing cups and trays, swinging sprays of tiny liquor bottles that chimed succinctly into the trash.

The plane itself seemed quiet as it plowed through the muffled darkness of clouds. The engines had smoothed to a hum, not loud and grinding like the plane she'd taken on the trip out to St. Louis. That one had needed a tune-up, she'd joked with a fellow passenger after landing, a man about ten years older than she. He had a tiny crease in his ear from a long-gone rhinestone, like a fossil imprint of his wild youth. She watched the discreet cascade of emotions that rippled across his face before he answered her: surprise, boredom, curiosity, lust, and, finally, lethargy. "Yeah. Well, that's what you get for flying a bankrupt airline," he said. He faced forward into the crowd of departing passengers and made his eyes glaze over.

She hadn't meant to pick him up or anything. It was just a remark to make while deplaning, her face pressed into the wool of someone's back as everyone crowded to get off. A thought like that hadn't occurred to her in years—she was a woman so thoroughly married, she'd lost all gender. Though she didn't mean that with any special bitterness. It was just the inescapable result of being married, of being a mother, of parading nakedly through the streets with a double-stroller.

And since she thought of herself that way, as a bad mystery ("The Case of the Revolting Mother"), it seemed ironic how this trip itself had come up. An old college friend had offered her a chance to be on a panel: "How Images of Women in the Helping Professions Have Changed Since the Feminist Movement of the Seventies." She didn't really qualify for the panel—she had no image. She'd been a literacy volunteer before the children, had quit five years ago when Jackie was born, but she hadn't ever been a professional anything, had never done anything with vehemence or discipline except maybe waiting. She'd made a profession of that—waiting to grow up, waiting to leave home, waiting for her first love affair, her first husband, house, child. Her own mother had taught her to do this, had made her understand that happiness always seemed like a distant hill, just far enough away to look pleasant at twilight.

Like this trip. Something she'd anticipated for months, since her third child, Michael, had been born. It was an anniversary present from Tom, but she'd waited almost a whole year to do it, to be sure that as she walked out the door to the taxi, Michael's cries wouldn't draw her back. They circled her, but she shrugged them off, shrugged off the rationale behind Tom's gift—time to "rediscover" herself. *His* words. What could she find in a weekend? What could possibly be left?

She shivered now to think how eager she'd been to leave home, how it all might turn out to be a bad omen in a few short minutes—Tom's offer, the conference, her reunion with her friend, the man on the plane who'd snubbed her, the man at the conference who didn't. It had seemed like an opportunity at the time. Now it seemed like a mirage, a trap; it was her fault because she'd been so happy to leave her family. The plane was going to crash because of her, because she couldn't stand how much her children needed her, how they screamed every time she left the room, even if it was just to get their pajamas from the linen closet.

When she'd slammed the front door, departure day, it made an airtight seal. On her side, there was cool, clean air, trees as light-hearted as ghosts. On their side, sealed in amber, three despairing faces. Abandoned forever? Time was like that for children. A few minutes seemed like a lifetime.

She wondered if they'd gotten to the airport yet, Tom and the children, whether they were already waiting, her babies with their noses pressed to the glass, caroling: Mommy! Mommy! Mommy! They'd be wearing their new snowsuits, their tender faces haloed in bunny fur. She wondered how long they'd stand there watching for her plane before Tom dragged them away to check the board, what the word DELAYED would signify to them except that

Mommy hadn't kept her promise; she was supposed to burst through the door right away like an angel and save them. Life for them was one rescue after another—from boredom, broken toys, premature bedtimes.

Someday they'd be too old to want her, and that would be worse. They'd be like that boy in the next row, oblivious, uncaring. His headphones were still on, and he was sound asleep, the static at the end of the tape whirred on and on, the mantra of all electrical equipment. Why didn't anyone wake him? Even the flight attendant speeding by, the jolt of her hip, an inadvertent nudge to his lolling head, didn't rouse him.

The flight attendants were gathered again at the door to the cockpit, waiting for further instructions, whispering the way nurses do outside the door of a terminal patient. Predictably the captain's voice reappeared again, not quite so cheery this time. It sounded strained, muffled, as if he'd placed a handkerchief over his mouth to hide his true identity.

"Sorry to keep you waiting," he sighed. "We're still checking our systems and coming up blank here, so we're going to try something a bit different. We're going to come around again over the airport and buzz the tower. They'll check us through their binoculars to see if our landing gear is intact. If it looks okay, we'll make one more pass again then proceed with our landing." The captain's voice dwindled. Even now he was unwilling to say what they'd do if their landing gear wasn't intact. "Sorry to keep you," he added.

Of course that was what the red light meant—no landing gear. Donna felt a chill yawn open inside her, a mouth to a secret cave. She tried to remember any similar cases she'd read of—a plane landing in that condition, what were their chances of surviving?— but all she could picture was an explosion, their plane, pregnant with passengers, bursting open, trailing fire as they skidded down the runway, plowing red searing scars into the tarmac.

Now everyone else seemed nervous, too. They tucked their heads down and checked their seat belts. They stared out the darkening windows to grapple with fate, with clouds shifting form, disappearing into the night. Donna heard a rush of air that might have been the engines accelerating or the sudden whispering of everyone around her, lips forming wishful prayers. "I've been in worse situations," she heard someone say, but who? Not the teenager. He was as still as the moon. Not the old couple across the aisle. They were holding hands, peering at one of their tickets, maybe rereading the provisions for sudden death. What sorts of allowances would be made in such a case? Who would benefit?

Only the businessmen three rows back seemed to still be taking this in stride, though at a slightly higher pitch. They shook their heads as if this were just another part of their job description. They were swigging beers, rattling bags of potato chips, their faces flushed with scorn for the other passengers. It was as if this were an office party they didn't want to break up, a Xerox of other near-tragedies that could be averted by a loud voice, a jovial attitude. They were laughing to keep the mood from changing, telling stories of near-misses they'd had, crashes they'd avoided by accidental rebookings, malfunctions that didn't pan out, emergency landings.

"I've been on a lot of dud runs," one of them said.

"And I've been drilled in shit," said another, "and lived to do the deed!"

"What deed?" his friend across the aisle asked. "What the hell does that mean?"

Who knew? What did it matter?

They rambled on rapturously as if these were war stories or tales of sexual conquest. There were mountainous fogs they'd braved, shorn engines, battered wings, smokers in lavatories who set off alarms, were caught shamefaced with their pants down around their ankles stubbing out the evidence of their pleasure into their palms. There were baggage holds that split apart and cabins that lost pressure. There were drunken captains, incompetent ground crews who de-iced windows instead of wings. There was wind shear in their voices, tailspin in their eyes.

Of course all three of them had ordered several rounds of whiskey from the flight attendant on her last trip through. And then chasers. A few more chasers. All three wore London Fog raincoats buttoned and belted, ready to bolt when the plane came down. Their briefcases were poised across their laps, though the flight attendant chided them now to stow these safely in the overhead until they landed. (*When* they landed. *If* they landed.)

"Let's not get too grammatical," one of them said.

Which reminded his friend of another story which he told as soon as the flight attendant flickered back up the aisle. "I knew this guy once who boarded his live snake in the compartment in a lunchbox of all things. What an incredible jerk! I told him not to do it, but he claimed he didn't want to freeze it in baggage—it was a tropical snake! When we hit some turbulence, the compartment sprang open and out fell the snake—it had been crawling around in there loose the whole flight. A constrictor or something—long as my ass, long as a witch's tit." (*What* is that expression?) "At any rate, all hell broke loose. Somebody yelled, 'Help! Snakes! Terrorists!' One lady peed her pants—I swear! She wet the seat. You could see this big dark stain. That was one landing we made over water!"

The other two laughed uproariously, but Donna suddenly wanted to cry. What if they were really going to be killed? What if the last thing she heard was some horrible stupid story? What if she never saw her children again? Or Tom? She should concentrate on remembering them, press her feelings and memories into thumbprints, leaf stains. They probably had at least a half an hour left. Fifteen minutes, anyway, before they circled all the way over the airport and found their landing gear definitely gone.

Donna tried to picture them—Tom, with his arms around the children like a family portrait, grinning his gigantic smile, so sure that life was just right, that things would work out eventually if she wouldn't worry so much. Then she tried to review each of her children separately, their perfect limbs, their subterranean smiles, but they seemed to streak right past her without stopping, too small to be held. All she could clearly remember was the moment of their births, feeling them gush from her legs in a waterfall of pain, their tiny heads pushing, pushing, pushing her aside. Those were the only real moments of her life, it seemed, for the last five years. If not forever. The three births. Jackie. Allen. Michael. One right after another. Her life with Tom was over as soon as her life with them began. It was horrible but true—why bother to disguise it now? They both knew it, though they were too polite to say so. She would never think of Tom first ever again, would always feel that the best nights of her life were those first nights spent with each child, alone in the hospital room, their tiny lips pressed to her skin, soft as flowers; all night their infant moans of pleasure as she nursed them. They were perfect children untouched by memory. Perfectly safe. Perfectly hers.

Donna wondered if the other passengers were having thoughts like this. Weird thoughts. Desperate thoughts. What exactly were you supposed to be thinking at a time like this? Something profound, no doubt. Something that would change the course of your life forever, brief as that course might be. Dwelling on old sins, maybe. Or new ones. Maybe that's why they were so quiet.

She certainly had enough to keep *her* busy for the rest of the trip. That man at the conference, for instance. As different from Tom as she could make him. A lot like the businessmen behind her. A complete stranger. Horrible to her in most ways, frightening, even, with his briefcase filled with monetary funds and annuities, his eyes set thirty years ahead on retirement, as if what happened in between was neither principle nor interest.

They'd met at the pool, where she could see his skin stippled with scars, pockmarks, maybe. His white legs underwater thrashed as if there were a strong current. They grappled desperately with unseen forces. Donna had been a swimmer all her life and scorned people like this—hellbent on the rituals of exercise. They bought expensive swimsuits, put plugs in their ears, showered with gusto, strode to the edge of the pool, and peered down as if it were Niagara Falls. Then—plunge!—dove in with such a splash, the waves knocked everyone else out of the water. It was people like this who broke their necks diving into the wrong end. That was their idea of real get up and go.

Predictably he surfaced heartily, thrusting up an array of water, gulping air. His backwash dislodged her goggles. "Nice dive," she told him, and he was pleased.

438

"Thanks much," he said. His great round head nodded with slippery satisfaction. He was the least desirable man at the pool, so she chose him, to punish herself for what she was about to do.

"How about a drink?" he asked her, waiting around and waiting around until she'd showered and dried her hair. She didn't believe in saunas but lingered to try out the free soaps and lotions in their tiny bottles, neat as family heirlooms. It fascinated her, a bathroom like that, with carpeting and silvery wallpaper, silk flowers nodding in crystal vases—a locker room decorated for an assignation.

Like the restaurant where they went to grab a bite beforehand. No time to waste. Part of the hotel's package deal. Though it was only nine-thirty in the morning, the bar was already open and fluid with customers leaning over candles in red glass jars flickering knowledgeably, without warmth. Maybe it was the management's idea of romantic, implying checkered Parisian tablecloths and tree-lined boulevards from some bygone era. That was the meaning of the red carpet, the crystal chandeliers and brass sconces, a timeless bar for timelessly tacky love.

She didn't mind that they went there. She wanted it to be tacky. And fruitless. She planned in advance that he'd disgust her, to prove to herself, maybe, that touching someone other than Tom would make her sick. It was good that his arms were too thin, his chest was too hairy. She hoped that when it happened, after these last hollowed-out years of her marriage, his lips would feel sticky, like pieces of a burst balloon. He would kiss her too long here. Not long enough there. He'd hold her afterward in a noncommittal way as if this were a demographic—the average length of post-coital grip. Wow! Wow!

That's what he said at the end but in a voice that rang of sex manuals. Do this. Do that. Express urgency.

There was no real way to explain what she'd done (what excuse could she possibly give? "At least I didn't have to pay for a babysitter"?), and now, maybe no need. When she looked out the window again, they were lowering through the clouds, coming closer to the airport once more, waiting for their moment of truth. Donna recognized features of the landscape they'd just passed a while ago, an hour ago maybe? Who knew how long it was when your mind was wandering free of responsibility, of logic. They passed over the usual grids of suburban neighborhoods just like hers: tree, lawn, house, tree lawn house, treelawnhouse—a series of what must be golf courses with tiny perfect ponds, miniscule flags waving, roads that looped around like elegant, handwritten O's. They crossed the marshy discarded fields that surrounded the airport, the glowering highway filled with rush-hour cars staring up as the plane roared over with the unreal magnitude of a blimp. So close. Donna could feel the magnetic pull of the landing strip (a battery of twirling lights from fire trucks already waiting for the crash) as they approached, the desire to kiss earth drew the plane downward, but they resisted; the plane rumbled over the tower slower than gravity, then shot upward again, expelling a loud groan.

The engines demurred, showed fear for the first time. "Goddammit," the captain muttered, "goddammit to hell," then realized the intercom was on and revised himself, "Oops!" as if this were a program for children and he might have to be recast. His voice wavered up and down a notch, searching for the right key. He cleared his throat. "Well, folks. Ahem," he said. (A-hem. Two syllables.) "I have some good news and some bad news. The bad news is we're missing something. Part of our landing gear must have fallen off somewhere along the way. Folks over Des Moines probably thought they saw Kahoutec." He paused as if to let his audience recollect this forgotten comet of the seventies. A murmuring filled the plane, but not of recognition. "Also, the tower has figured out the runway here is too short for a gear-up landing, and we've now burned up too much fuel to go to another airport. The good news is— there have been many successful landings over water."

Water? A water landing? A shiver ran through them, a collective ripple of terror and reluctance.

The teenager two rows up screamed finally, but in his sleep, of all things, as if their bad karma had jumped ship and ignited him, made him dream his tapes were all snarled, unwinding for no reason into thin shining slivers that rustled onto the floor. Words tumbled from his mouth: *Help! Help! I hate you!* like an echo to all their thoughts.

Even the businessmen seemed unnerved for the first time. Puzzled. Their deadlines were tangled. Their calendars were really boxed up. A checklist of disappointment welled up on their faces: Death. Water. Death. Water. Death. Jesus Christ—not Death!

Death.

Clearly they weren't made for crash landings, though the flight attendant seemed to think so. She slid up the aisle smooth as glass to tap two of them on the shoulder, the two in the aisle seats, as soft and lightly as an angel, and pointed to the third in the window seat, her finger outstretched, serene, granting them pardon, or grace.

These men, her gesture seemed to say, were in the exit row—that was a privilege and an honor. These men were potential heroes—from where she stood, they were still neatly ironed. They could be guardians of the water slide, masters of the emergency chute *and* life rafts. The flight attendant warned them she'd be back in just a minute to give them further instructions, but they could reread their passenger safety cards in the meantime. They could hold themselves steady. Keep their heads up and look chipper. Smile those brushed white smiles.

Her words were light and frothy, much lighter than the air holding the plane up, still heavy enough to lift all three of them partway out of their seats. They leaned forward in unified protest, their smiles frozen in overdrive. "God Almighty," one of them muttered—the snake charmer. He screwed up his lips as if to spit, but nothing came out, just words made plain and grammatical by fear, "God Almighty—did she really mean that?"

"We're going to be pretty busy up here for a while," the captain announced, jumping in to divert their panic into smaller, more manageable streams. "It's going to take us some time to position ourselves, and the emergency ground crews are consulting with the Coast Guard about the best possible landing sites." He made it sound so simple, like a car pool, but he wasn't really fooling anyone.

All up and down the aisles there was motion, an animated universe of gestures like branches suddenly tossed by a hurricane, thrashing to get away, though the flight attendants warned them to stay in their seats with their belts fastened. The captain signed off again and left them alone without giving them any specific notion of time. Would he be back again? Did "some time" mean five minutes or two hours?

How much fuel did they have left? Maybe they would just cruise around until everyone had made his separate peace with God. Well—why not? She'd once been in a plane with engine trouble over Peru. That was long before she'd met Tom. She'd been a different person then, high above the clouds, someone with a sense of mystery, who believed in magic beads and the advice of tea leaves. She'd gone to Peru on a whim to learn to "see," a phrase she'd borrowed from a popular mystic she barely understood. She'd had a couple of ambiguous moments (maybe spiritual, maybe not)—chewing coca leaves with an Indian on the train to Machu Picchu, again at the peak of a volcanic mountain she'd assumed was extinct until it rumbled. (She hadn't bothered to read her guidebook.)

Then there was that *real* moment, the one she'd thought was real, flying over the Andes, above a lake of clouds, when she was sure it was all over, felt the shining pinnacle of her body dissolving into the sun, had thought how light and casual it felt, like snow melting on a bright winter's day, pleasant almost—the way she'd repeated her own name out loud, several times, as if it might survive her. It had thrilled her then that no one knew she was on that plane, no one at all had the slightest idea where she was. Her entire history could be erased in a single minute, and there'd be nothing left to remember her. She was twenty-five years old and hadn't accomplished a single thing.

This time it was a completely different story. What *wouldn't* she leave behind? Everything she'd ever touched would become an artifact. Every word she'd ever said to her children would be a mystery.

If they could even remember what she'd said—words beyond "No, no, naughty!," words beyond "Don't touch!" Had she ever said anything meaningful, something they might remember as the years went by that would still glow for them like the birthday ring Tom had given her, a sapphire with rays of shifting light?

She tried to think, but space seemed to be roaring around her, as if it weren't infinite and desperately wide but small and crushing, shutting her in. She could only think of one conversation she'd had verbatim, with Jackie, her oldest boy—at Christmas, a year ago. They'd been walking around the neighborhood together looking at displays of lights when suddenly a meteor had fallen, had moved across the sky slowly and deliberately as if pushed by an unseen hand. Donna had gasped and exclaimed, "I can't believe it! I can't believe it! We saw the Christmas star!" Though Jackie had no idea what that was, he smiled for her, then exclaimed back, "That's nice, Mommy!" He still was young enough he'd say anything to please her. She tried hard to explain to him the star meant they were lucky; they were special. Maybe it meant they were blessed.

Now she saw it was just another crazy moment in a long line of them. It lifted her out of her skin for just a glimmer, and that was it.

All up and down the plane, they were remembering their own crazy moments as they stowed away their last belongings—books, magazines, extra jackets, needle-pointed pillows that whiled away the time. They wouldn't while away the time now. Barely time to remember who they were, where they'd been for the last twenty, thirty, sixty years. No way to define it except in glimmers, as she had done.

What were they thinking? What last memories? The old couple—were they remembering their grandchildren? What medications they'd forgotten to take that morning? Were the businessmen thinking about statistics? Or that special lunch at the Four Seasons, how lucky some of their clients were to eat caviar as casually as Spam?

It was bad to be bitter in one's last moments—that's what Tom would say. But how would he ever know? Nothing in the clouds to tell her what her attitude should be. They were a gray shroud, a thick, indecipherable tissue. They were still as an x-ray, silent as ice. As were her fellow passengers, riveted in their seats by expectation, facing straight forward, not speaking, not even swallowing. No one looked to see if there were life jackets underneath their seats; no one felt to see if their seat belts were properly fastened. No one looked to find the nearest emergency exit, as if, even at this late hour, that would be the grossest possible lapse in taste, to seem as if you were wondering how you could be the first person to leave the plane.

Not that Donna had ever been much for good taste. She didn't care much if her children were muddy, if they used their forks and spoons to eat. Tom blamed her for things like that, for socks that never matched, for the tone of voice she sometimes used to yell at the children, and him ("I feel like a dog that just peed on the carpet—"); sometimes she thought he blamed her for everything, right from the moment they met, years before, at a barbecue to celebrate the summer solstice. It was two months late because the hosts had been too stoned to organize on time. As if that were *her* fault. The party was held at their farm, a never-say-die commune that had long since collapsed into private ownership. The members believed in total honesty, and that was how her friend had introduced her to Tom. "Now *this* is a woman worth sleeping with." That was marriage brokering in those days. It didn't seem to deter him. They went off to pick buckets of blueberries that stained their hands and lips dark as ink, a tribal rite—"We're marked for life," Tom had said.

This was clearly romantic, but later there was a pig roast, despite some vegetarians who objected, who took their tofu burgers and set up camp in another part of the field far away from where the pig smouldered in a deep pit plowed over with leaves and mud. Like a murder victim unearthed by accident. They dug the body up to eat it, subdivided the parts with a huge carving knife, waved forelegs, hindquarters. Donna and Tom sat next to each other and giggled at how weird it all was.

Though not as weird as the little 8 mm film of a home birth brought along by a newlywed couple to celebrate the first harvest and offered proudly as a follow-up to the dessert of blueberry pie and ice cream. What was it supposed to be? Entertainment? Erotica?

That's how Tom had labeled it afterwards—"porno lite," though this really missed the essence. But so did the barbecue crowd, chanting: "New life! New life! Go! Go! Go!" as the screening progressed.

Still, the couple was proud. Their timing couldn't have been better. As luck would have it, the birth coincided with their wedding day—the film was still rolling from the ceremony when the bride felt the first contraction. She took off her wedding gown to labor right there in the field, got down on all fours to push the baby out into the billowing mess of her veil. Donna couldn't believe how the woman's haunches had clenched, unclenched, clenched, unclenched, in a demonstration of sheer animal fury. There was no sound, thank God, to explain her wide open mouth, but Donna could feel the screams as if they were her own as the woman swayed from side to side, grinding her belly into the earth.

Donna and Tom left before the placenta came out, after the top of the baby's head had popped in and out several times like a shy woodchuck peeping from its hole. That was one of the few times Tom was ever at a loss for words. Even at the birth of their own first child, he'd been composed, had whispered something into her ear about launching a new ship. Back then, though, he'd said, "Is it *me*, or is this the most disgusting thing you've ever seen?"

Back then Donna had agreed, but she didn't think so now. What could be more disgusting than dying before you were ready to?

That's what everyone else was thinking, she was certain, except for that crazy, comatose teenager still sleeping up there. Donna leaned forward in her seat, ready to wake him, just as the night attendant passed by, already, in the act. She ran one bright red fingernail across his forehead, then shook him by the shoulder for good measure. "Wake up, sir," she said firmly. "You can't sleep now. We need your attention."

The boy opened his eyes and cursed. "What the hell?" but she was already gliding away to another destination, another crisply performed task. "Damn," the boy muttered again, as if she'd interrupted something truly special—a memory of rollerblades or a bright green Mohawk, maybe the first time he told his parents to go screw themselves.

Nothing sentimental in *his* face. It was a map of pain and boredom—bored to be alive, bored in the U.S. of A., bored by the sound of rain pattering along the drainage ditch in his suburban cul-de-sac. A boy with just one parent. Or maybe four, six, eight. The wrong number, at any rate—all his exponents were mixed up. He was the kind of boy she was afraid her sons might grow up to be, the kind she always saw at shopping malls, too tall and skinny to be handsome, bent like a praying mantis over the record rack, worshipping the latest dance mixes, the type of boy who'd sit on the floor of a coffeehouse in the dirt and cigarette butts, enthralled by the sound of the espresso machine (hissing, hissing . . .); he probably liked to have his tongue vacuumed at the dentist, any sensation as long as it was unpleasant. A plane crash wouldn't bother him at all. He shrugged when the flight attendant warned him of what was to come. "Who cares?" he asked with such bitterness it was almost touching, "We're all gonna crash sooner or later." Then, bolstered by his own wit, he readjusted his headset, tucked the spongy earpieces tenderly back into the hollows of his ears, and closed his eyes, breathing deeply, face tilted to his airjet as if it were glue.

They were handing out final instructions, holding up the laminated cards that looked so simple. There was the plane cruising midair. There was the plane nestled in the ocean, waves lapping gently. There were the merry passengers taking their turns obediently, zipping down the chute like a great water slide adventure.

"This is your flotation device," the flight attendant said. She held up a seat cushion and waved it. "You'll want to take this with you on your way out. After we're safely in the water, you'll need to dislodge it and take it with you down the emergency slide. Don't take any belongings. You'll want to get out as quickly as possible. This is the only thing you'll need—it will help you to remain on the surface of the water while we wait for rescue."

The flight attendant moved backwards several rows to give her spiel again. As she passed by, heat rose from her uniform like steam. (She was really nervous after all, despite the look on her face of frozen glee.) Her body trailed perfume—rose or lilac? She moved forward in a cloud of goodwill and determination. "Now *these* gentlemen," she said heartily when she reached the businessmen, "these fine gentlemen—" She waved her hand across them like a magic wand. "They're going to help you," she explained as she rotated a half-circle to face them. Her voice had a bright glare to it as she said, "You. You. *You.*"

She pointed to the one in the window seat. "You will open the emergency door when we land. And you," she tapped the middle one with her long fingernail, "will help him place the door in the row behind you. Don't throw it outside, or you might puncture the evacuation slide, which will deploy automatically." She nodded to the snake charmer across the aisle, *"You* will move to the window seat, and you will remove the door yourself and deposit it in the next row. After you do that, jump down the slide. The three of you, don't stay and try to assist people. You'll only block the passage for the other passengers."

She paused there, as if this were a moment in her script that deserved some thought. Donna marveled at her composure, the way her voice balanced on the ledge of a tall building. Her lipstick still gleamed thick as a layer of frosting. She could be dropped underwater, and she'd keep right on ticking. Though none of *them* could. They'd be at the bottom of the lake in just a few minutes, enshrined beneath the fierce upswellings of cold, of industrial waste, an occasional algal bloom. Their mouths would be clogged with ice, or fish, or stones. In summer the beer cans would rain down on their skulls, boats would roar across them, suntan lotion would seep towards them through the water slow as tears.

There was silence in the plane now, as if they'd all just shared the same bizarre fantasy, but the flight attendant didn't miss a beat. She treated this silence as if it were a loud and drunken outburst, as if she were waiting for the man to say, "Hell, no, lady—I won't do that. You're some crazy bitch if you think I'll do that—crazier than a witch's tit!" but he just shook his head—once, twice. His mouth was screwed up as if to spit, but nothing came out.

Donna felt sorry for the man. She nodded in sympathy like everyone else on the plane. Who was the flight attendant kidding? Even assuming that a safe water landing was possible, gentle as Icarus tumbling into the sea. She thought of a father watching from shore, his son burning up like a meteor, then of Tom shielding the children's eyes as the plane exploded. Luckily they'd be too far away to see her. If they saw anything, it would be like fireworks, like a far-off sparkler.

"This is a very important job," the flight attendant tried again, as devoted to her job as a mother. "It entails a great deal of responsibility," she added, as if this were something to add to a résumé later: 1) Dispatched rescue equipment. 2) Saved face in plane crash. She bent towards the man to pat his shoulder, but he turned away and pressed his face to the window. This made the flight attendant nod once more, agreeably. "Okay," she said. "That is perfectly all right. If you feel you are unable to perform your duties properly, then will you please change seats with someone who feels more confident? Can I have a volunteer?" She peered down the aisle expectantly, a glimmer of a smile on her face. Be brave, the smile said, be noble, be the kind of person you've always wanted to be! "We haven't much time," she chided.

As if to reaffirm this, Donna saw the lake appear below them, waves as sharp as fingerprints, the tiny festive dots of boats crawling over the hard surface of the water. She knew just how hard it would be when they hit, like iron, like Tom's face if she lived to tell him what she'd done that weekend, how she'd betrayed him as an experiment to see what it would feel like to do something absolutely wrong, to take on the shape of another life, a shadow that would glide between them, silent and dark, filling in the space her children had made that couldn't be explained, not the moments of crisis, not the moments of ecstasy, but those absolutely plain moments that were sheer as ice—tucking them in at night, washing their hair, pulling up their pants, their little socks that fell around their tiny ankles, pouring corn flakes into their bowls each morning, tenderly, measuring their sleep in hours, weeks, sometimes in seconds, reading them the same books over and over again ("Spot likes to chase his bouncy red ball . . ."), careful to vary the rhythms of her sentences, the pitch of her voice, patting a piece of bread with a smidgen of butter, a smidgen of jelly, smoothing her palm across each forehead as if she could instill something divine in them, make them healthy, better than she and Tom had ever been, better than they ever would be. "My children!" she thought. "My little babies." As if this were the most complete idea she'd ever had, the most enlightened.

"Okay," Donna said. "I'll do it. *I'll* do it, I'm willing," though the flight attendant didn't hear her. Everything was suddenly out of order, shaking to pieces as they went down, tipping over towards one wing, and then the other, unsure of gravity, where it might take them, the captain calling one last time over the intercom, "Hold on now, folks—this is a little sooner than we expected!" the teenager in front wagging his head back and forth as if this were some far-out beautiful rhythm, plane crash as performance art. He was

SHEILA M. SCHWARTZ

shaking his shoulders. He was beating the armrests with both hands. He was yelling, "Yes! Yes! Do it, Mama! Do it to me, do it to me *now!*"

"You be quiet," the old lady across the aisle leaned over to glare at him. "Have some respect, young man," as if they were in a church, a reverent movie theater, and suddenly Donna knew it was okay. His craziness would save them. This was *his* crash, not theirs; he was the only one who believed in it. Everyone else still believed it couldn't happen to them, not today, not with so much unfinished business, so much misunderstood, not with a husband and three babies waiting down below, their lives not yet unfolded, crushed up in cocoons of adoration, still wet with joy and love.

CRYBABY

DAVID SEDARIS

The night flight to Paris leaves JFK at 7.00 p.m. and arrives at de Gaulle the next day at about 8:45 a.m. French time. Between takeoff and landing, there's a brief parody of an evening: dinner is served, the trays are cleared, and four hours later it's time for breakfast. The idea is to trick the body into believing it has passed a night like any other— that your unsatisfying little nap was actually sleep and now you are rested and deserving of an omelet.

Hoping to make the lie more convincing, many passengers prepare for bed. I'll watch them line up outside the bathroom, some holding toothbrushes, some dressed in slippers or loose-fitting pajama-type outfits. Their slow-footed padding gives the cabin the feel of a hospital ward: the dark aisles are corridors; the flight attendants are nurses. The hospital feeling grows even stronger once you leave coach. Up front, where the seats recline almost flat, like beds, the doted-on passengers lie under their blankets and moan. I've heard, in fact, that the airline staff often refers to the business-class section as "the ICU," because the people there demand such constant attention. They want what their superiors are getting in first class, so they complain incessantly, hoping to get bumped up.

There are only two classes on the airline I normally take between France and the United States—coach and something called Business Elite. The first time I sat there, I was flown to America and back for a book tour. "Really," I kept insisting, "there's no need." The whole "first-to-board" business, I found a little embarrassing, but then they brought me a bowl of warm nuts and I began to soften. The pampering takes some getting used to. A flight attendant addresses me as "Mr. Sedaris," and I feel sorry that she's forced to memorize my name rather than, say, her granddaughter's cell phone number. On this particular airline, though, they do it in such a way that it seems perfectly natural, or at least it does after a time.

"May I bring you a drink to go with those warm nuts, Mr. Sedaris?" the woman looking after me asked—this as the people in coach were still boarding. The looks they gave me as they passed were the looks I give when the door of a limousine opens. You always expect to see a movie star, or, at the very least, someone better dressed than you, but time and time again it's just a sloppy nobody. Thus the look, which translates to, Fuck you, Sloppy Nobody, for making me turn my head.

On all my subsequent flights, the Business Elite section was a solid unit, but on this particular plane it was divided in two: four rows up front and two in the back. The flight attendant assured everyone in my section that although we were technically in the back, we shouldn't *think* of it as the back. We had the same rights and privileges as those passengers ahead of us. Yet still they were *ahead* of us, and I couldn't shake the feeling that they'd been somehow favored.

On the way to New York, I sat beside a bearded Frenchman, who popped a pill shortly after takeoff and was out until we landed. On the leg back there was no one beside me, at least not for the first half hour. Then a flight attendant knelt in the aisle beside my seat and asked if I might do her a favor. That's how they talk in Business Elite. "I'm wondering, Mr. Sedaris, if you might do me a favor?"

Chipmunk-like, my cheeks packed with warm nuts, I cocked my head.

"I've got a passenger a few rows up, and his crying is disturbing the people around him. Do you think it would be OK if he sat here?"

The woman was blonde and heavily made-up. Glasses hung from a chain around her neck, and as she gestured to the empty window seat beside me, I got a pleasant whiff of what smelled like oatmeal cookies. "I believe he's Polish," she whispered. "That is to say, I think he's from Poland. The country."

"Is he a child?" I asked, and the flight attendant told me no.

"Is he drunk?"

Again she said no. "His mother just died, and he's on his way to her funeral."

"So people are upset because he's *crying over his dead mother?*"

"That's the situation," she told me.

I'd once read that a first-class passenger complained—threatened to sue, if I remember correctly—because the blind person next to him was traveling with a Seeing Eye dog. He wasn't allergic, this guy. Labrador retrievers on the street didn't bother him, but he hadn't paid thousands of dollars to sit next to one, or at least that was his argument.

If that had seemed the last word in assholiness, this was a close second.

I said of course the man could sit beside me, and the flight attendant disappeared into the darkness, returning a few minutes later with the grieving passenger.

"Thank you," she mouthed.

And I said, "No problem."

The Polish man might have been in his mid-forties but seemed older, just as people in my parents' generation had. Foreign blood, or an abundance of responsibility, had robbed him of the prolonged adolescence currently enjoyed by Americans of the same age, so his face, though unlined, seemed older than mine, more used. His eyes were red and swollen from crying, and his nose, which was large and many-faceted, looked as if it had been roughly carved from wood and not yet sanded smooth. In the dim light, he resembled one of those elaborate, handcrafted bottle stoppers—the kindly peasant or good-natured drunk who tips his hat when you pull the string. After settling in, the man looked out the darkened window. Then he bit his lower lip, covered his face with his remarkably large hands, and proceeded to sob, deeply. I felt that I should say something, but what? And how? Perhaps it would be better, less embarrassing for him, if I were to pretend that he wasn't crying—to ignore him, basically. And so I did.

The Polish man didn't want dinner, just waved it away with those king-sized mitts of his, but I could feel him watching as I cut into my herb-encrusted chicken, most likely wondering how anyone could carry on at a time like this. That's how I felt when my mother died. The funeral took place on a Saturday afternoon in November. It was unseasonably warm that day, even for Raleigh, and returning from the church we passed people working on their lawns as if nothing had happened. One guy even had his shirt off. "Can you beat that?" I said to my sister Lisa, not thinking of all the funeral processions that had passed me over the years—me laughing, me throwing stones at signs, me trying to stand on my bicycle seat. Now here I was eating, and it wasn't bad, either. The best thing about this particular airline is the after-dinner sundae. The vanilla ice cream is in the bowl already, but you can choose from any number of toppings. I order the caramel and chopped nuts, and the flight attendant spoons them on before my eyes. "Is that enough sauce, Mr. Sedaris?" she'll ask, and, "Are you sure you don't want whipped cream?" It would be years before I worked up the courage to ask for seconds, and when I finally did I felt like such a dope. "Do you think, um . . . I mean, is it possible to have another one of those?"

"Well, of course it is, Mr. Sedaris! Have a third if you like!"

That's Business Elite for you. Spend eight thousand dollars on a ticket, and if you want an extra thirteen cents' worth of ice cream, all you have to do is ask. It's like buying a golf cart and having a few tees thrown in, but still it works. "Golly," I say. "Thanks!"

In the years before I asked for seconds, my sundae would be savored—each crumb of cashew or walnut eaten separately, the way a bird might. After those were gone, I would recline a bit and start in on the caramel. By the time the ice cream itself was finished, I'd be stretched out flat, watching a movie on my private screen. The control panels for the seats are located on a shared armrest, and it would take me a good three or four flights before I got the hang of them. On this trip, for instance, I kept mashing the buttons, wondering why they failed to work: feet up, feet down, head back, head forward. I was two seconds from calling the flight attendant when I looked to my right and saw the Polish man keening and bucking against his will. It was then that I realized I had the wrong control panel. "Sorry about that," I said. And he held up his pan-sized hand, the way you do when you mean "No hard feelings."

When my empty bowl was taken away, I leafed through the in-flight magazine, biding my time until my neighbor's dizziness wore off and he could fall asleep. In an effort to appear respectful, I'd already missed the first movie cycle, but I didn't know how much longer I could hold out. Up ahead, in the cheerful part of Business Elite, someone laughed. It wasn't the practiced chuckle you offer in response to a joke, but something more genuine, a bark almost. It's the noise one makes when watching stupid movies on a plane, movies you'd probably never laugh at in the theater. I think it's the thinness of the air that weakens your resistance. A pilot will offer some shopworn joke, and even the seasoned fliers will bust a gut. The only funny announcement I've ever heard was made by a male flight attendant, a queen, who grabbed the microphone as we were taxiing down the runway in San Francisco. "Those of you standing in the aisles should have an excellent view of the Fasten Seat Belt sign," he said.

My memory of him and his stern, matronly voice was interrupted by my seatmate, who seemed to have suffered a setback. The man was crying again, not loudly but steadily, and I wondered, perhaps unfairly, if he wasn't overdoing it a bit. Stealing a glance at his blocky, tearstained profile, I thought back to when I was fifteen and a girl in my junior high died of leukemia, or "*Love Story* disease," as it was often referred to then. The principal made the announcement, and I, along with the rest of my friends, fell into a great show of mourning. Group hugs, bouquets laid near the flagpole. I can't imagine what it would have been like had we actually known her. Not to brag, but I think I took it hardest of all. "Why her and not me?" I wailed.

"Funny," my mother would say, "but I don't remember you ever mentioning anyone named Monica."

My friends were a lot more understanding, especially Barbara, who, a week after the funeral, announced that maybe she would kill herself as well.

None of us reminded her that Monica had died of a terminal illness, as, in a way, that didn't matter anymore. The point was that she was gone, and our lives would never be the same: we were people who knew people who died. This is to say that we had been touched by tragedy, and had been made special by it. By all appearances, I was devastated, but in fact I had never felt so purposeful and fulfilled.

The next time someone died, it was a true friend, a young woman named Dana who was hit by a car during our first year of college. My grief was genuine, yet still, no matter how hard I fought, there was an element of showmanship to it, the hope that someone might say, "You look like you just lost your best friend."

Then I could say, "As a matter of fact, I did," my voice cracked and anguished.

It was as if I'd learned to grieve by watching television: here you cry, here you throw yourself upon the bed, here you stare into the mirror and notice how good you look with a tear-drenched face.

Like most seasoned phonies, I roundly suspect that everyone is as disingenuous as I am. This Polish man for instance. Given the time it would take him to buy a ticket and get to JFK, his mother would have been dead for at least six hours, maybe longer. Wasn't he over it yet? I mean, really, who were these tears *for?* It was as if he were saying, "I loved my mother a lot more than you loved yours." No wonder his former seatmate had complained. The guy was so competitive, so self-righteous, so, well, over the top.

Another bark of laughter from a few rows up, and it occurred to me that perhaps my sympathy was misplaced. Perhaps these tears of his were the by-product of guilt rather than sorrow. I envisioned a pale, potato-nosed woman, a tube leaking fluids into her arm. Calls were placed, expensive ones, to her only son in the United States. "Come quick," she said, but he was too caught up in his own life. Such a hectic time. So many things to do. His wife was getting her stripper's license. He'd been asked to speak at his son's parole board hearing. "Tell you what," he said. "I'll come at the end of dog racing season." And then . . . this. She rides to her death on a lumpy gurney, and he flies to her funeral in Business Elite. The man killed his mother with neglect, and because of that I can't watch a movie on a plane?

I pulled my private screen from its hiding place in my armrest and had just slipped on my headphones when the flight attendant came by. "Are you sure I can't get you something to eat, Mr.. . . ?" She looked down at her clipboard and made a sound like she was gargling with stones.

The Polish man shook his head no, and she regarded me with disappointment, as if it had been my job to stoke his appetite. *I thought you were different,* her eyes seemed to say.

I wanted to point out that at least I hadn't complained. I hadn't disrespected his grief by activating my screen, either, but I did once she'd retreated back into the darkness. Of the four movies playing, I had already seen three. The other was called *Down to Earth* and starred Chris Rock as an aspiring stand-up comic. One day he gets hit and killed by a truck and, after a short spell in Heaven, he's sent back among the living in the body of an elderly white man. The reviews had been tepid at best, but I swear I've never seen anything funnier. I tried not to laugh, I really did, but that's a losing game if ever there was one. This I learned when I was growing up. I don't know why it was, exactly, but nothing irritated my father quite like the sound of his children's happiness. Group crying he could stand, but group laughter was asking for it, especially at the dinner table.

The problem was that there was so much to laugh at, particularly during the years that our Greek grandmother lived with us. Had we been older, it might have been different. "The poor thing has gas," we might have said. For children, though, nothing beats a flatulent old lady. What made it all the crazier was that she wasn't embarrassed by it— no more than our collie, Duchess, was. It sounded as if she were testing out a chain saw, yet her face remained inexpressive and unchanging.

"Something funny?" our father would ask us, this as if he hadn't heard, as if his chair, too, had not vibrated in the aftershock. "You think something's funny, do you?"

If keeping a straight face was difficult, saying no was so exacting that it caused pain.

"So you were laughing at nothing?"

"Yes," we would say. "At nothing."

Then would come another mighty rip, and what was once difficult would now be impossible. My father kept a heavy serving spoon next to his plate, and I can't remember how many times he brought it down on my head.

"You still think there's something to laugh about?"

Strange that being walloped with a heavy spoon made everything seem funnier, but there you have it. My sisters and I would be helpless, doubled over, milk spraying out

461

of our mouths and noses, the force all the stronger for having been bottled up. There were nights when the spoon got blood on it, nights when hairs would stick to the blood, but still our grandmother farted, and still we laughed until the walls shook.

Could that really have been forty years ago? The thought of my sisters and me, so young then, and so untroubled, was sobering, and within a minute, Chris Rock or no Chris Rock, I was the one crying on the night flight to Paris. It wasn't my intention to steal anyone's thunder. A minute or two was all I needed. But in the meantime here we were: two grown men in roomy seats, each blubbering in his own elite puddle of light.

DARK MAN AT THE AIRPORT

SAÏD SAYRAFIEZADEH

It was my great misfortune to be traveling from New York City to Paris just two months after 9/11.

For while my passport is American and clearly states that I was born in New York, there is no getting around the fact that the name printed beside the photo of a dark-haired, dark-eyed, and slightly unshaven young man, is "Sayrafiezadeh, Saeed." *Saeed* being the variant spelling that my Iranian father and American mother chose for my birth certificate, and which subsequently became the spelling on every one of my legal documents. It was also, regrettably, the same spelling as Saeed al-Ghamdi, the twenty-one-year-old from Bahah Province, Saudi Arabia, who helped hijack United Airlines Flight 93 before it crashed into the field in southwest Pennsylvania, killing all forty-four people on board.

"You're going to have problems at the airport," a friend cautioned.

"I know," I said.

It made no difference, of course, that I didn't speak one word of Persian, or that I'd never been anywhere in the Middle East, or that I was generally presumed to be Italian,

463

or that my mother was an American Jew from Westchester. My name doomed me to a life of being Middle Eastern. It was a name that, in the end, did not matter if it was spelled Saïd or Saeed or Syeed.

And another friend, hoping to bring some levity to my impending day of departure, suggested that after I collect my belongings at the x-ray machine I yell out, "My god is greatest god!" We laughed at this.

But it reminded me of a story I once heard about two Brazilian men who had been detained at the airport under suspicion of drug smuggling. The men were completely innocent and had come to the United States for a week's vacation. Nevertheless, the authorities kept them handcuffed in an airport room, interrogating them on and off for six hours, before eventually strip-searching them. Discovering nothing, they were freed. The damage had been done, though, and the men returned to Brazil the very next day. The message, according to them, had been heard loud and clear: *we don't want you in our country.*

As for myself, I had been fully expecting to experience some form of xenophobia ever since that Tuesday morning I stood on the West Side Highway and watched the second airplane crash into the World Trade Center, hoping that it might be due to some sort of mechanical failure. Later that same day, bleary and dazed, I sat across from my girlfriend Karen at the only restaurant we could find open, and declared that being Middle Eastern in America in 2001 would soon be tantamount to being Jewish in Germany in 1939.

"You heard it from me first," I said.

My prediction didn't turn out to be true. At least not by the time Karen and I were to leave for our Thanksgiving in Paris. We had booked the vacation nearly six months in advance, and then proceeded to count the days with delicious anticipation. Now the concept of traveling was fraught. I had briefly argued for canceling our trip, but less than a week after 9/11 a friend of ours had flown to Toledo on business without incident, and then someone flew to the Bahamas, and it was quickly apparent that air travel had resumed to normal. Not to go to Paris would be an act of cowardice. Moreover, I was convinced that it would only contribute to a general sense of hysteria that was slowly enveloping the country, a hysteria that would soon target every Middle Eastern person regardless of their actual nationality, parentage, or place of birth. My predicament, thus, was twofold: I was afraid of the airplane nearly as much as I was afraid of the airport.

And then, four days before we were to leave for Paris, American Airlines Flight 587 lost a rudder right after take-off and crashed into Queens, killing all two hundred and sixty people on board and five on the ground.

Karen and I arrived at JFK on Friday evening, November 16, three hours before our 10:55 p.m. departure, since three hours had replaced the customary two hours for international flights in order to accommodate increased security delays.

The airport was as crowded as ever. But a soldier dressed in camouflage and holding a submachine gun ambled through the concourse. I could detect an edginess at check-in, as if people expected at any moment something was about to happen. Karen and I stood together in the long line, slowly inching our suitcases closer to the counter. I had the sensation that I was being observed by someone, somewhere. A dark man and dark woman, possibly Middle Eastern, stood in a line adjacent to ours, and as we neared them I tried to make eye contact, wishing to convey a feeling of fraternity. In the foreground, I could see the soldier passing back and forth. His presence unnerved me. It also irritated me.

"Who do you think he's looking for?" I asked Karen. "Blond guys with blue eyes?" And for a moment I worried I might have said it loud enough for him to hear me.

Karen looked at the soldier and shrugged. "He's just here to make people feel safe."

I stewed silently. Then finally I said, "He's adding to the hysteria."

When it was our turn at the Air France counter, I did my best to put on a happy, confident, untroubled face that would assure the female attendant that all was well with *Sayrafiezadeh, Saeed* and that he had no concern whatsoever with presenting his passport.

But I could tell right away this was not going to be easy. The attendant looked at me curiously and then at my photo. She typed something into the computer and then hit the return button hard. I followed her eyes following the screen. What was she reading? I could feel the back of my neck grow warm.

"Traveling to Paris?" she asked. It sounded like an accusation.

"Yes," I said. A tight, crisp *yes*. A *yes* without an accent. She typed, she waited. Her gaze was alert and mistrustful.

"Are you checking any luggage?"

"No." A causal *no*. A *no* that accentuated the *yes*. See, I'm a casual American guy.

Meanwhile, a steady stream of suitcases moved along the conveyer belt behind her. Endless and without interruption. A thousand black suitcases of varying sizes. A million. Differentiated only by an occasional colorful tag or ribbon. For so long we had all lived under the assumption that we would be safe as long as our suitcases were safe.

And then the attendant printed something out, tore it sharply along its perforation, folded it in thirds, placed it an envelope, and said, "Enjoy your trip."

I walked briskly through the concourse, passing the soldier with his submachine gun who struck me now as a harmless, comical figure. "Doesn't he kind of look like Mick Jagger?" I snickered. My passport was in my back pocket and I touched it to make sure it was still there, and then I touched it again—happy that it was an American passport. And then ashamed that I was happy. I thought of my Iranian father having to live his life beneath the heavy yoke of an Iranian passport. After that I thought of my Jewish mother and 1939.

At security we were greeted by an overweight black man who looked exhausted. I smiled at him but he didn't seem to care about smiles. I knew from recent articles in the *New York Times* that he earned somewhere between six and seven dollars an hour and most likely had a second job, which all worked in my favor because he appeared to have no investment in any of the documents I presented to him. He opened my passport with a slow hand and made a show of studying the picture, but just as quickly closed it, handed it back, and waved us through to the line that wound toward the metal detectors. The machines beeped and beeped. Here I could feel the edginess again, the expectation. The line surged forward then stopped. Then crawled. The beeping grew more frequent. How was it humanly possible, I wondered, to catch everything? White men in white uniforms stood along a wall watching the column of people filing through. These men were not the same as the underpaid security screeners. They were professionals and they meant business. Years ago the metal detector had gone off on me and as a joke I had said, "Don't worry, that's just my bomb."

"I can arrest you right now," the guard had told me. I was eighteen and had wanted to display my wit. Instead, I had been frightened and humiliated. The guard had let me go but the lesson was learned.

My god is greatest god popped into my head. The sad humor of how easily I could jeopardize myself. I looked at Karen, who was beginning to empty her pockets into the plastic bins. I looked at the white men in their white uniforms. I looked at the belt that I had just taken off, making my pants sag, leaving me feeling helpless and exposed like a little boy in a schoolyard. People had mocked the government's new prohibitions on things like tweezers and straight-edged razors and cutlery as bumbling attempts by an incompetent government, but they had all missed the point : what was really being x-rayed in the end were *people*.

And I suddenly knew, without the slightest doubt, that I was heading for trouble.

Into the plastic bin went my belt, my jacket, my wallet, my *passport*, disappearing into the dark tunnel of the x-ray machine. I watched it all float away. Karen walked through the metal detector with no sound, crossing one step closer to Paris. And then I lifted our two suitcases onto the conveyer belt and crossed through myself. There was no beep. But I knew there would be no beep. I knew that my peril was in the guards in white, who now surrounded me, three of them, asking, "Sir, is this your luggage?" "Sir, can we see your boarding pass?" "Are you traveling with anyone, sir?" "Yes," I said. I tried for a crisp *yes*, but there was no longer any crispness.

"This way, sir." And I followed dutifully to a metal table where the men unzipped my suitcase, because they could unzip my suitcase if they wanted, they could search me if they wanted, they could detain me if they wanted, for years if they wanted. Because this is the reality of America post-9/11.

"Oh, that's mine," Karen said, referring to the object in question that one of the guards held in his hand. A long, brown cylinder that indeed looked like a weapon, but in actuality was an EpiPen Auto-Injector that Karen carried everywhere because she was allergic to peaches and plums and eggplant and if she were ever to eat any by accident she would need to quickly give herself a shot of adrenalin in her thigh. She explained this to the guards and showed them the prescription from her doctor.

"Enjoy your trip," they said.

At the gate Karen and I found two seats against the wall and talked excitedly about everything we were going to do in Paris, and all the museums we were going to visit, and all the things we were going to eat. Croissants, crepes, croque-monsieurs.

"What about frogs' legs?"

We both laughed. No way! Ha ha ha. Maybe snails, though.

There were still thirty minutes before it was time to board and so we started a game of Scrabble on the little travel set that I had bought Karen for her birthday. The game was soothing and I spelled the simplest of words. I realized there had been a pounding in my head since I first arrived at the airport and I could feel it begin to recede. An older couple sat down next to us speaking French, and Karen looked at me romantically.

Midway through the game I asked Karen if she was nervous about flying.

"No," she said. "Well, maybe a little." And after a pause she asked, "What about you?"

"Not anymore," I said.

We played on and then Karen took a pee break. I sat there thinking about nothing, and then I thought about boarding the airplane, and putting my luggage away, and whether my seat would be any good . . . And suddenly, no longer having anything to worry about concerning my ethnicity or my nationality or *Sayrafiezadeh, Saeed*, I was gripped by the thought of that plane that had lost a rudder and crashed in Queens just four days earlier. And I thought also of standing on the West Side Highway on that Tuesday morning and watching United Airlines Flight 175 come over from New Jersey, growing closer and closer, wondering if that was the airplane that was coming to put out the fire. I thought of bin Laden's declaration that Americans will never be safe until Palestinians have a homeland. And I remembered those hallucinations in the days immediately after 9/11 where I was so sure I saw planes flying too low over the city. Once I had panicked at the sight of a Goodyear Blimp heading directly toward the Empire State Building, heading, heading, heading, until I realized that my depth perception was distorted and the blimp was actually miles away. And I thought of TWA Flight 800 that had plunged into the Atlantic Ocean in 1996, just twelve minutes after it had taken off from JFK. It had also been flying to Paris. I had known a woman on that plane. A friend of a friend. We had had dinner together once, just the two of us on the Upper East Side. She was rich and I was broke and I had spent the entire meal hoping she would pick up the tab, which she had. The next I heard, she had died on that plane. Everyone had suspected terrorism right away. But it had never been proven. I had thought of her often after that, how her body was lying somewhere on the ocean floor. How horrible it was to picture that. And how horrible it was to picture Karen and me now flying over that same ocean, at night, heading in that very same direction.

And it was then that I saw him: a young man about my age, but whose skin was a shade darker than mine. He was standing. Why was he standing, I wondered, when there were plenty of seats available. And he seemed anxious. Anxious, why? He had no luggage with him. No bag. No briefcase. No book. Who boards an eight-hour flight with nothing? He was wearing a white shirt that flowed loosely past his waist, and which, to my untutored eye, had a vague Arab influence. A shirt that, under any other circumstance I would have seen as stylish but that now seemed like a subtle warning of sorts. No, there was nothing overtly Middle Eastern about this young man, but hadn't that been the great misconception about the hijackers? That they had stood out conspicuously at the airport in their robes and turbans. In truth they had looked just like *regular* people. Regular people who happened to have dark skin and dark features and box-cutters.

For a moment I was seized by the idea that maybe this man was the twentieth hijacker I had heard spoken of. Then I pushed that idea out of my head. Or maybe he was the twenty-first hijacker. Was there a twenty-first? And I recalled the chilling story that the actor James Woods had told about how, one month before 9/11, he had flown first class with four men who looked like they could have been Middle Eastern. They had had no luggage either, no carry-on, no newspaper. They did not speak or eat or drink the entire flight. Instead, they sat and observed everything. Woods had told the flight attendant about his concern, and she, along with the pilot, had filed a report with the FAA, but the report had been lost beneath a mountain of reports and nothing ever came of it. And yes, Woods had later confirmed that at least two of the men on that flight in August were the ones who hijacked the planes on 9/11.

I had disbelieved that story when I had first heard it. To me it had smacked of xenophobia, told by a blatantly xenophobic man who had once referred to Arabs as "towel heads." But now I saw myself as James Woods. If only he could have done something more when he had seen those men. If only he could have made people listen to him. Perhaps things would have turned out differently for all of us.

I must say something, I thought. I must say something *right now*. I will go to the attendant at the counter and tell her. That is what I will do. And if she does not believe me, I will stand on a chair and I will shout at the top of my lungs: *Attention everyone! There is someone among us . . .*

But what if I was wrong and falsely accused this man? I imagined the endless shame and embarrassment. Would he forgive me? Of course he would. He would have to. We would have a good laugh about it afterward. I would put my arm around his shoulder and say, "These are strange times we're living in, brother."

But what if he did not forgive me? *Could* not forgive me? Would I have inflicted irreparable harm on him, on his soul? I thought again of the story of those unfortunate Brazilian men and their vacation of trauma.

No, I decided, I must not say anything.

But what if I was *not* wrong? What then?

My quandary was suddenly inflamed by the image of a thousand suitcases passing by on the conveyer belt, of a thousand people walking through the metal detectors, of a weapon that was really an EpiPen, of the Atlantic Ocean waiting in the darkness. *It is not humanly possible to catch everything.*

And then, from out of the low rumble of the airport, I heard the most frightening thing of all: "Air France Flight 9 is now ready for boarding."

THE ADVENTURES OF *HAZY LILY*

BERNARD CHABBERT

The sun was just rising over the central Pacific Ocean in the early hours of July 2, 1937, when a fuel-starved, twin-engine monoplane crashed into the water, a few miles from its destination. A spit of sand one mile long and half a mile in width, Howland Island had no trees, nor even a hill. It remained undisturbed. The aircraft, a silver and orange Lockheed Electra named after a star in the constellation of Taurus, was never recovered. Its pilot, Amelia Earhart, and her highly respected navigator, Fred Noonan, were never seen again.

Seventy-one years later and several thousand miles away, an American film production company needed an Electra for its upcoming motion picture feature, *Amelia*.

This is where I come in: I happen to own one.

Now, if you are insane enough to possess one of the dozen or so Electras still in circulation, you have probably fantasized about such a scenario. You have probably also developed a tendency to consider your Electra a masterpiece of 1930s Art Deco sophistication. Her wings alone embody an endless potential for adventure.

The film company's request arrived to me via e-mail, while I was skiing in the Alps. *Amelia*'s star was to be Hilary Swank. Earhart's husband, George Putnam, would be played by Richard Gere. The richly talented Mira Nair would direct. The cinematographer was Stuart Dryburgh of *The Piano*. It sounded like a dream.

There was a catch, however.

In order for the dream to materialize, my Electra had to travel from France to South Africa, where it would then be used to shoot aerial scenes along seven different locations. To put this in context, following its departure from California in 1937, the real Amelia's Electra flew a total of seventeen thousand nautical miles before disappearing forever. Including the filming flights, my Electra would have to cover nineteen thousand nautical miles.

Hazy Lily, as my Electra was nicknamed, was sixty-seven years old. Men now dead had long since filled *Lily*'s logbook with details of her service with the U.S. naval attaché in London, where she flew as a liaison aircraft during World War II. From 1946 to 1952, she fell into the hands of Sydney Cotton, a businessman and renowned spy for Her Majesty's Intelligence Service who had been the model for James Bond. So, by extension, *Lily* is James Bond's aircraft! And although there's no formal proof, rumor has it that Michael Curtiz even used *Hazy Lily* for the filming of *Casablanca*.

But all these years later, *Lily*'s age was taking a toll. In fact, at the time of the film company's request, she was stranded inside a hangar without engines or propellers. Some air scoops had been badly bent the autumn before during an electrical glitch, while she was taxiing. Her landing gear retracted on its own; she had ended up on her belly.

The film company needed *Lily* in South Africa by the third Sunday in July, giving us only four months to find two new engines and build from scratch two new propellers. Organizing this eccentric trip around Africa presented an array of obstacles. Crawling across the whole length of the African continent aboard our slow and low-flying machine, for example, we would be burning aviation gasoline in a world now using kerosene for its fast jets. We would have to negotiate with African bureaucracies for a small piece of sky amid continent-leaping liners.

In 1937, such a voyage would have appeared on the front pages of all of the world's newspapers. Now we would be nothing but an aeronautical nuisance. And although *Lily* would clock roughly the same number of nautical miles as Amelia's plane had during her failed world tour, we were going to all of this trouble just to perform some flying shots in a movie. Our motivation, in the end, came from a world star and a dreamer: Amelia herself. We decided to do our best to commemorate her legacy, hopefully realizing our own dreams in the process.

Our team consisted of friends and family—mostly pilots—addicted to flying this very old, eccentric machine. Most of us, starting with my son, Antoine, were professionals, and worked for airlines. Some had experience flying in Africa. Eve, my wife, spent twenty-five years working as a flight attendant (half of them on the Concorde). In fact, the idea of buying the nearly wrecked Electra in 2000, and restoring it to impeccable flight status, had originally been Eve's. So *Hazy Lily* had a connection with women. And women bring magic.

We organized the trip in three parts: first came the flight down along the west coast of Africa. Second were the filming flights across South Africa. Third was the return flight along the continent's eastern coast. Each part would require its own crew.

Still, in spite of our meticulous planning, our preparations were plagued with setbacks. *Lily*'s new engines, fresh from the workshop in Oklahoma, got stuck in a customs warehouse for ten days, waiting for some stamp. Just before the planned departure date for Africa, the propellers suffered a similar fate.

With only two and a half weeks before the first planned day of shooting, the *Hazy Lily*, fresh from the French civil aviation inspection, lifted off from Annemasse airfield, near Geneva, towards the east coast of Spain. Given our limited time for advance test-flying, the old girl behaved like a real adventurer, and flew without a hiccup.

Two days later, *Lily* crossed the Straits of Gibraltar and landed in Tangiers. From there, the crew notified us that credit cards were not readily accepted for landing fees, gasoline, and hotels across Africa.

Eve rushed to the local bank where she created a commotion asking for a big envelope filled with banknotes of all currencies. Then she continued to the nearest airport, and found an afternoon flight to Casablanca, arriving just in time to deliver the cash to the crew.

White skies saturated by blinding sun and bad visibility were expected for most of the trip down the African coast. We anticipated the usual rows of thunderstorms found this time of the year between the tropics. And, sure enough, heavy warm rains did converge, with low drifting dark gray atomic cells skimming along the ground. Still things continued to go relatively smoothly. We were keeping to our very tight schedule.

Then in Bamako, on Sahara's southern border, the weather became less cooperative. The crew had to scratch one full day of flight because of torrential rains. Then they headed to Lomé, on the Gulf of Guinea shore, only to discover that, despite e-mail and fax confirmations to the contrary, there was no aviation gasoline anywhere available.

With only two hours of fuel left in *Lily*'s tanks, we faced two options: we could either fly east into Nigeria (our insurance company said this was too dangerous and vetoed the idea), or we could fly west—backward—to Accra. There, according to airfield rumors, we might find some leftover avgas . . .

The crew landed in Accra with fifty minutes of flight left in the tanks. After some searching, they found gas of questionable quality and paid a small fortune for it. The morning after, they took off for a flight across the shark-infested Gulf of Guinea, towards Libreville.

Lily bumped into huge clouds, and zigzagged for hours around heavy rainfalls. Still, flying low and slow, almost skimming the waves, she steered a more or less steady course. Then she crossed an island named Malabo. The crew radioed the local airport to ask if, by chance, they had any avgas. The answer from the tower was "No, sir, we don't, and as you did not request landing clearance, you are not authorized to land."

Lily flew on, once again over the ocean. A short while later Malabo called back, announcing that, after closer inspection, they had discovered some avgas. Landing clearance was granted. *Lily* turned back.

No sooner had she landed than the crew was surrounded by a dozen uniformed men holding Kalashnikov AK-47 assault rifles. Charged with violating Equatorial Guinea's airspace, the crew was detained for three days in Malabo's only hotel. With the help of some French diplomats, an agreement was reached the following Monday morning, with a cash payment of 7,500 euros required to cover the violation.

The crew paid the fine, then returned to the Electra, only to discover that the onboard cash box, containing 3,500 euros, had disappeared while the airplane was under watch by the local police. It had proven to be an expensive stop.

As a member of the second flying crew, I was already in Capetown, where I had to explain to the 175-person film crew that *Lily*'s timely arrival at the Cape was not at all assured. My stress level—as well as that of my team—was off the charts.

After Douala and Libreville, *Lily* still had to cross Angola, Africa's largest oil producer. When, again, no avgas was available in Luanda, we chartered a small twin-engine cargo aircraft in northern Namibia. Loaded with five drums of gas, it flew to Luanda. It took five hours to carry the fuel north, five more to bring the cargo back south. The total cost set what must be a record for the world's most expensive refill: forty-two dollars per gallon.

Late Friday afternoon, the exhausted and elated crew landed in Capetown. But we barely had time for a beer and congratulations, since *Lily*'s original surface still needed to be stripped and repainted in Amelia's signature silver and orange. We managed to complete this procedure within the allotted twenty-four hours only because of a miraculous rally on the part of the film props specialists. On Sunday, as planned, the aircraft was ready.

Naturally, we were zonked. But now came the very purpose of our trip: filming.

After *Lily*'s long flight down, we needed to make sure she would perform. This required many hours of tender, loving, care and oily, dirty work. *Lily*, our graceful, old lady of the skies, instantly became a part of the cast. Everybody called her "the Electra." Hilary Swank, for one, immediately acted as if she really were Amelia and *Lily* her beloved aircraft.

There were precious, rare moments, such as Hilary's birthday, when we were filming at Rand Airport, Johannesburg. During a lunch break inside a hangar, cakes were set on the tables while we all sang "happy birthday, Hilary." Richard Gere went on to serve cake to each of the more than seventy women, all of whom waited, smiling and courteous.

Later that afternoon, Hilary got locked in the cockpit for several takes. With the sun beating the aluminum fuselage, it gets hot in there. That day it also smelled of gasoline and oil. Hilary, sitting on the pilot's seat, began to feel unwell. Antoine was with her, crumpled on the cockpit floor, invisible to the camera, to help her if necessary.

After the umpteenth take from outside the cockpit windshield, Hilary suddenly became quiet. Then, in a low voice, she said, "When I was a little girl, I wanted to be a film actress. I really wanted that. And now it's my birthday, and here I am, a film actress . . ."

Chased by the film crew's camera-equipped helicopter, we crisscrossed South Africa from one location to the next.

Old *Hazy Lily* never coughed, even during difficult scenes, like Amelia's last take-off from Lae, in New Guinea. Decades ago, the real-life Electra had been so overloaded with fuel that, after barely lifting off from the airstrip above the beach, she needed to dive toward the sea to pick up some desperately needed airspeed. Now, reenacting that scene took twenty-two hair-raising attempts.

Another scene of Amelia's takeoff from Calcutta under monsoon rains at night required four takes in a row. *Lily* was no longer just a prop when she rallied in almost total darkness, with the unlit dust strip lost under the stars in the high bush north of Capetown.

The pilots worked with the film crew, offering ideas they thought would add drama. In all of our minds were the aviation scenes from the film *Out of Africa*, which we all loved, but were determined to improve upon them.

Filming became our life. And after flying the old machine low above Victoria Falls, skimming the Okavango Delta desert, slipping between vertical mountain slopes, and caressing endless soft beige sand dunes near Port Elizabeth, we felt supremely grateful to have been involved with something so extraordinary and unique.

Then, brutally, it was over. *Lily* and her crew were left alone in Johannesburg, with only the return flight to look forward to.

It was a slow voyage back. The crossing of Lake Victoria, which usually lasts an hour and a half, took three days because of certain stamps not arriving on certain strategic papers. We crossed all of Sudan using car gasoline of dubious quality, because there was no avgas at all. Nor was there any way around unsafe places like Juba, where we heard gunshots not far from the airstrip during a night stop.

In Cairo, we were charged thirty dollars a gallon for gasoline, and thousand dollars to park the Electra for one night under the stars in the corner of a deserted tarmac. After a magical flight over Entebbe, and flying along the Nile up to Luxor, low and slow above history and so many stories, *Lily* finally landed at her home base near Geneva.

She had clocked a total of 170 hours in eight weeks in the hands of seven aviators, who shared with her the adventure of their lives. And she hadn't missed a beat. Not only that: she had brought all of us on a tour of history and taught us about Amelia Earhart.

My only regret is that Hilary never flew the Electra. Her inner Amelia would have loved it.

A few days after *Lily* was returned to her hangar, I went through Purdue University, in effect to cure my post-filming blues. I'd decided to poke through Amelia Earhart's archives. My father had been an aviator with Aeropostale and Air France. For years, beginning in 1929, he had flown the mail between France and South America. He was posted in Dakar, Senegal, when Amelia landed there a few weeks before she disappeared near Howland Island. He used to tell me how he'd met her then. He'd gotten some technicians from Air France to help her with some mechanical problems.

I'd examined rows and rows of photographs when, suddenly, I spotted four that were labeled "Amelia at the Aero Club dinner, Dakar." And there they were: Amelia, Fred, and my father, standing by a table ready for a colonial banquet.

It was an apt end to a dream come true. And I couldn't help but wonder if fate wasn't up in the sky somewhere, directing it all, to her great amusement.

MY FRIENDS: THERE IS NO ORCHESTRA SO OLD IT CANNOT BE ENLIVENED BY THE ADDITION OF A NEW AND HEARTFELT PLAYER

JOHN BOWE

I used to travel as often as I could, everywhere I could, from Little Rock to Luang Prabang, Ouagadougou to Porto Velho. The point wasn't to see the world so much as to listen to its jokes, its complaints, the music of its voice. For years, collecting conversation was my favorite thing. Monk, trucker, soccer mom, prostitute; everyone I met pollinated my curiosity. Until the day I met motherfucking Chippy.

LAX to LaGuardia. I had a window seat near the toilet, and Chippy sat next to me in the aisle. His name wasn't really Chippy. That's just the name I came up with for internal reference. He was sort of pixie-ish, about twenty-three, twenty-four years old, with blond hair that looked streaked. "Sun-kissed," I've heard it called. I asked him where he was from: San Diego. At the time, I didn't really know anything about San Diego. It was like a dead spot in a cellular network. I should have had San Diego covered, but I didn't.

"What do you do in San Diego?" I asked.

"I install satellite dishes."

Now, normally everyone I met became an instant member of the orchestra of my worldview, the John Bowe Philharmonic, in which we all play a tune, we're all beautiful, we're all one, etcetera, etcetera. And "satellite dishes" should have been yet another novel opening note from the symphony that never ends. It should have stimulated the filigree tendrils of my curiosity, and I should have welcomed Chippy as a new member of the band: Welcome, San Diego! But something about Chippy's mien—or lack therof—I just wasn't getting much by way of a vibe beyond the sun-kisses. He was there. He was not-there. He was pleasant. But undifferentiated. I'm making this too complicated.

In the year or two before the expedition, I'd taken acid about a hundred and fifty times (like I said, I was into curiosity pollination). This trip had been my first exploration of southern California, and had been loosely themed around the idea of my somewhat unhappy family visiting some old friends of my mother's, a proportionately unhappy family. But I think what had affected me most was honest grief at seeing for the first time the fabled banality of southern California.

Neither consciously nor un-consciously, I allowed myself to associate the grief with Chippy, to assign him the role of mascot for or emblem of both banality and environmental degradation. Or something. I found provocative the idea of himself driving around, parking his sun kisses in a white van in a series of southern California cul-de-sacs, in front of a series of houses, each one virtually alike, one after one after one, installing with his sun kisses enormous radar dishes made out of toxic compounds as the planet spun around, slowly gassed by the particular lifestyle choices unfolding by the millions around him. ("Hey, how

483

are you doing today, Marybeth?" "I'm driving a lot, Jim!
How are you doing?" "Great!")

During my years of travel, through high worlds and low,
I'd met any number of crude, dirty, self-interested, and even
repugnant characters, but Chippy alone provoked in me
this specific spiritual revulsion derived from no other cause
than a signal association between ecological disaster and
some sort of moral nonfeasance. What about Buddhism's
Eight-fold Path? Right speech, right action, right livelihood,
and so on? Nowhere did I recall anything about radar dish
installation. To some extent I'm ranting for fun, but I'm also
not.

Revulsion is very nearly the opposite of curiosity, and
the less curious I became about Chippy, the more he
wanted to talk. I'd reflexively turned him on. But at that
point of my life, the John Bowe Philharmonic Orchestra
had no off switch. Chippy certainly didn't. He'd by now
gamboled into a series of tales about his life as a satellite
dish installer, doling out with loving detail and embellish-
ment every aspect of the profession: the pay, the boss, the
co-workers, the promotional opportunities, the house-
wives—ooh-la-la! And just to be very clear, if he had been
talking about any other profession, it would have been fine.
In fact, the year before, I'd met a German refrigeration specialist in Cuba who held me spellbound with vocational an-
nals. But TV, specifically satellite TV, southern California,
sun kisses, the color of the sand that passes for soil and the
shrubbery that passes for vegetation surrounding the
houses Chippy mounted with his sun kisses, the way the
houses he mounted looked against the sky, blue and vigorous and smoggy with contrail zests—it did me in. And as
my senses, brain, and spirit numbed into a sort of shit taffy,
it became absolutely clear that all this was only a prelude.

Because the installation of radar dishes was not the be-all end-all of Chippy's existence. The considerable time we'd lavished upon the one subject thus far was merely a prelude to a much more vigorous, in-depth discussion of Chippy's activities.

Chippy's principal leisure activity, it would soon emerge, was installing stereo speakers in his car. Vast numbers of them. In fact, Chippy was only one of a thriving tribe of southern Californians for whom car stereo speaker installation was the acme of existence. Glowingly, he told me about this friend's car and that friend's truck, and how they'd managed to get seventeen speakers in this car, and twenty-two speakers into that truck. One of Chippy's friends' fathers owned a car stereo shop, he said, and because of this, the kid, Chippy's friend, could get awesomely cheap speakers. This friend had installed thirty-four speakers inside his rebuilt Volkswagen Beetle. It was rad. It was gnarly. So much so that the subject apparently bore repetition ad nauseam, and in this vein Chippy went on for perhaps thirty more minutes. So I'm estimating, but if this had all started more or less above San Bernadino, and we were by now flying somewhere over Kansas, I'd been hearing about radar dishes and stereo speakers for over a thousand miles, a third of a great nation, a desert, and a mountain range traversed to the tune of mindless and in fact apocalyptic prattle.

When I write "apocalyptic," it might seem like I'm joking, ranting again for fun's sake. But I'm not, really. Chippy's was prattle of a peculiarly unhinging sort. When most people blather on (as we all do), even if they're going on about something that doesn't interest me, I'm able to ingest, meditate, penetrate: what is this person really after? Are they lonely? Do they need affirmation? How can I relate? But

my moral imagination simply wasn't prepared to ingest
such a radically cultureless person as Chippy, who seemed
to live so unquestioningly in a fundamentally material
world, demarcated only by varying degrees of sensation
and stimulation. It wasn't that Chippy was bad. It was that
he was the first person I'd ever met who really wasn't interesting. Because he wasn't there. He'd been absorbed by the
speakers and radar dishes. He didn't care if I thought he
was cool or liked him or any such thing—*because there
was no more him*. There was no us. There was only the
fact of speakers. Or rather, the fact that speakers are cool.
This, apparently, was the sum total of existence.

Pre-Chippy, I'd always been extremely open to different people's views. Good people, bad people—agreeing
with them or liking them had never been the point.

On a flight from Denver to Seattle, I met Jeff W., a roly-
poly, late-thirty-something dude-type American. Jeff had
worked as an electrician in rural Washington state. One day
he met a woman, who, it turned out, didn't mind snorting a
little crystal methamphetamine now and then. The first
night they did it together, they stayed up all night long having sex. Shwing!

In short order, Jeff W. became an addict, a car thief, and
a minor drug lord. His life took on the proportions of a low-
grade thriller, replete with rip-offs, overdoses, good deals gone
bad, visits from armed friends at 5 a.m., ratting girlfriends,
cops knowing his first name, a three-month stretch in jail and
a roller-coaster weight loss from 255 pounds to 200 pounds.

His very first car chase began with him circling his
home town at 110 miles per hour. Act two commenced with
him breaking through a police roadblock. A mile down the
road with four cruisers in pursuit, he told me—and I believed him—he hit a ramp on a curve and "caught air." And

then he said, matter-of-factly, "You know when you're on a curve, and you catch air, you're going to come down hard. Cuz the steering wheel is going to want to jerk straight. If you keep your hands on the wheel, it's gonna yank your wrists hard enough to break them. So you have to know to take your hands off the wheel." I asked him where he got the expertise for this kind of thing, and he shrugged. Movies? He had no idea. He just didn't want to get caught. I stayed in touch with Jeff for years, trying to publish his story. I loved it because it had no moral. Jeff did wrong, he paid no price. The cops had him on a variety of charges, but let him go if he promised to quit "the lifestyle." He quit. Now he sold jewelry cleaning paste now, shlepping from one jewelry show to the next, savoring his memories of the days he lived large. No regrets. Thanks for coming to the show.

On a flight from Minneapolis, I met a stewardess. Her name, let's say, was Lori, and she was built like a porn star: fake boobs, jet-black hair and dramatic, flashing, Spanish eyes. "Are you a writer?" she asked, seeing my laptop and some notes. "So am I," she continued. "I write poetry. It's deep." She bucked her head like a show horse, gave me a free wine, and later, two more. I think it would be fair to say that Lori—and her attentions to me—would hit the bullseye of most male fantasy scenarios. Except for one problem: I was returning home from my father's deathbed. My sexual appetite was lamentably far, far away. I got her email address, but my heart wasn't in it.

She later sent me some of her poetry. I remember one, riven with torment, about how men see "the outer Lori" and thought of her as a sex toy, an object. They saw her fake boobs and didn't take her seriously. But the "inner Lori" knew better. The "inner Lori" experienced life as pure, unremitting pain, as broken glass raking across her face and her insides for eternity, a constantly breaking tidal wave of loneliness, anger, misunderstanding.

Lori!

And now, here was Chippy, bumming me out. It wasn't that Chippy's monologue was boring, per se. The fact was that I'd truly never met anyone like him. But the thought of he and his friends, centering their lives around car stereo speakers—I don't know—what about sex? God? Art? Killing people. Something! This kind of small, pointless focus was truly the end of times, the end of days. Wouldn't it be more fun or at least stimulating to be a flagellant, marching through the medieval streets, flogging oneself and one's pals into a frenzy? At least that would have been environmentally sustainable.

At the time, I was still too midwestern to know how to politely beg off from unwanted conversations by claiming fatigue or pretending to work, so after about forty-five minutes, I embarked upon a magnificently passive-aggressive and weird stratagem I'd played with. I decided to be as bland, meaningless, and dumb as it took to get Chippy to disengage. I decided to respond with sentences or phrases that contained some form of the word "freak" in them—until it became too weird to continue.

So after Chippy's next bit about economy pickup trucks or speaker wattage, I answered "Whoa. Freaky."

Another bit, and I rejoined, "Freakin' out!"

Two or three nonsense-gambits later, I upped the ante, held my folded *New York Times* inches from my eyeballs, and continued. "Aow! Get me a freakagectomy!"

"Freakalicious!"

And so on.

I deployed thirteen phrases in a row with the word "freak" in them, and to my enraged surprise, I got absolutely nowhere. Not only did I not find Chippy interesting, but I found myself confronting the heretofore impossible. I didn't *like* Chippy. Very simple. I didn't like him, I didn't like what he was all about, and I didn't want him talking to me anymore, filling my head with his nonsense. I finally sputtered and told Chippy, "Listen, do me a favor. Tell your friend with the thirty-four speakers that you met a complete stranger on a plane who told you that he *hates* him!"

I'd never said anything so curmudgeonly in my life. Ever. I was sort of surprised at myself. And so was Chippy, it seemed. He balked for maybe a second, as if recognizing that what I'd said had been somewhat intense. And then, without another nanosecond's thought, he barreled forward again, back to the buddy with the thirty-four car stereo speakers in his pickup truck.

I don't remember the end of the story. But I had never said anything deliberately mean before like that. It was, in its own very small way, a total breakdown. A part of me had died, or at least, become transformatively vigilant, and it was the part that had been interested in hearing any and all stories from strangers, especially on airplanes.

I became more circumspect. I learned how to dampen and modulate my friendliness. Nowadays, I sit down in my seat, and deliberately do not engage beyond say, Engagement Level Three. Out of ten. I smile. I'm pleasant. I express sympathy, as with the Filipino who was visibly terrified when turbulence hit us during mealtime (back when there was such a thing) and our trays were literally flopping up into the air. Or with the mother of seventeen, juggling her sobbing children. And if a flight attendant needs to complain in the middle of the night on a fifteen-hour flight to Hong Kong, I'm there. Because she's earned it. But while

I'm interested in *good* stories, no longer am I interested in *all* stories. And that's the way it's been for years.

Recently, I flew from Salt Lake City to L.A. I'd been reporting a very depressing story about labor exploitation, which *The New Yorker* later killed, for which I was therefore paid one third of the originally agreed-upon sum. I had flown from an island in the Pacific, where I was then living, to Thailand, Maui, L.A., Salt Lake City, and finally, back to my Pacific island. Exhausted. I took my seat in a full-ish plane, and was elated to find an empty seat by my side. Passengers streamed past me, boarding, boarding, boarding, but no one took the seat. It was my personal little friend, karma, giving me a little break—because I'm the kind of guy who writes depressing stories about labor exploitation and then has them killed and gets paid one third of the original agreed sum! Yes! I was inwardly rubbing my hands with glee. And then, the second before the doors closed, here he came: a gimpy African guy with a weird walk. He was very small, almost midget-sized, and as he weeblo-wabbled down the aisle, I just knew it: he's gonna sit next to me. And of course, he did.

Now, it might sound mean to talk negatively or uncarefully about an African, a person of color, a person with obvious body defects. But my travels have been such that I have become a man of the Earth and all its people, which is to say, I have spent time with virtually every kind of person on the planet, and am comfortable with both them and my level of open-heartedness. If I don't want someone sitting next to me, it makes no difference whatsoever whether it's a German supermodel or a weeble-wabbling, semi-midgetous African with an unevenly football-sized hump protruding from his chest.

I ignored him. He took the window seat next to me. His sunglasses stayed on, an affect I've always found somewhat vulgar. He wore a suit, and took advantage of his diminutive size by scrunching his legs up in front of him and falling asleep for the majority of the flight.

As I flipped pages of whatever book I was reading, I checked him out. Hair: clean. Suit: very neat. Hump: weird. How did a person get a hump like that? Ah——ah—I could hear my old curiosity welling, and I willed it to back off. But then a funny thing happened.

During the descent into L.A., he woke up, and somehow, through no flexing of my sinister talents for conversation-making, we began to talk. It just happened. It turned out he was going to Sudan. From Salt Lake City to L.A. to London to Khartoum. When I remarked that there weren't a whole lot of people these days going *to* Sudan, he told me he was going back home.

And then he told me that he was one of the Lost Boys of Sudan.

And this was very funny, because I, who obviously knew everything, and had been everywhere, had never heard of them, even though, apparently, everyone else in the universe, including, probably, Chippy, knew all about the Lost Boys of Sudan. The guy didn't lay it on thick at all, but explained to me, very matter-of-factly, that the Lost Boys are a group of children from southern Sudan whose parents were killed by soldiers from the north during Sudan's civil war, and that they'd marched by the thousands for many long miles in a ragtag group to the border of Kenya, where many had lived ever since in a refugee camp. In 2001, four thousand of them were admitted to the U.S., he among them.

I asked him if he was with a missionary group, and he shook his head. He'd become an analyst in a bank, and he just wanted to see his homeland. Now he was on his way, thirty hours each way. In coach. I was suddenly honored to meet him. We shook hands and said goodbye, and I felt a little bit of the dewy sensation I used to feel whenever the John Bowe Philharmonic would tune its instruments. On the way to the baggage claim, I remembered an intense daydream that hits me sometimes when I see a plane whizzing overhead. I imagine the outer shell of the plane removed and three or four hundred people sitting in rows, six miles above the ground, jetting through the heavens. There's no point to the dream. I just like to think of them all, making friends, making judgments, getting annoyed, waiting for the bathroom.

WHITE SKY

RACHEL CANTOR

James has already walked down the aisle once to look at me. He tipped to the left as the plane tipped to the right, tipped right as the plane tipped left. And smiled, slightly. I looked up from my in-flight magazine, ran my tongue over my lips. I couldn't help myself, though we have an understanding about the need for discretion.

I walked past him, too. I pretended to be looking for the ladies' room, though I knew I wasn't allowed in first class. I stepped on his toes. He was sleeping, though, and didn't wake up.

But he's awake now. Maybe he's getting nervous about Paris: I just heard him order a whiskey. No mistaking that voice: the baritone that's thrilled millions. Yes, millions have thrilled to that voice—no less than to his marriage to that singer, the one he discovered in Budapest, the one he made famous in America long before he discovered me singing on a street corner with my guitar. Me he didn't make famous; me he kept for himself.

I've never seen James drink whiskey—I've never seen him drink anything, maybe out of consideration for my *condition*. I want to see if he looks like he drinks whiskey

493

often when I'm not around. I walk again down the aisle, one row to the red curtain, two rows beyond that, clinging to chair backs. I stop in front of him, apparently in full shock.

"Hang on there!" I say in a loud voice. "Hang on there! I know you! Don't tell me, *I know who you are!*" I point my finger at him, smile widely, look around for witnesses.

James doesn't know whether he should be amused. He rubs his eyes, looks around to see who might be watching.

"You're James McManus, the world-famous opera singer, right? You've thrilled millions with your Grammy Award–winning song stylings. *The Best of Disney*, right?"

James doesn't think I'm funny. He looks confused, he searches my face. He probably thinks I've fallen off the wagon.

"You sang the National Anthem at last year's World Series, didn't you? You're *famous!* You've sung with the Muppets!"

All of first class watches us now. Passengers look at me, they look at him, then back at me. James is helpless. Usually his fans amuse him: he enjoys their attention, he likes to be *genial.* Now he runs his hands through his black hair, he doesn't know what to do.

I sit down on the armrest across the aisle.

"You're married to Magda, that sexy rock-and-roll star from Hungary, aren't you? You know, people think I look like her. What do you think? I'm younger, of course. And I don't have a problem with *barbituates.*" I turn to the man sitting in front of him: "I read about Magda's *barbituate* problem in the *National Enquirer.*"

I don't know why I'm doing this. I seem to be pushing him to make some sort of declaration, to admit he has an empty seat beside him, which he bought so he wouldn't

494

have to share. I want him to admit that I'm a better singer than Magda will ever be, only I came too late to be discovered. To admit that he's afraid of losing his voice, and dreams that he's falling into the pit at the Met, falling and falling—and when he screams he screams with the voice of a boy, a thin, high voice that attracts no attention. I want him to admit that he can't sit in a window seat, because of all that space below, the space between him and solid ground.

A flight attendant with a navy skirt, a well-etched mouth, eyes ringed too tight with violet moves between us as I'm about to ask about this dream, to ask if it's true he can no longer reach that high A, if he's anxious about his consultation with the Parisian throat specialist, if they're true, the rumors he's seeing an ex-alcoholic ex–coffee-house singer on the sly.

"I'm afraid you have to return to your seat," the attendant says.

"Has Maestro McManus complained that I'm disturbing him? Maestro, am I disturbing you?" I ask, craning my neck around the flight attendant.

James shrugs at the attendant, as if to say, things like this happen to me all the time.

"Please, miss," the flight attendant says, putting her red-laquered fingertips on my shirt sleeve. "It's time you left Mr. McManus alone."

I stand up and look at James.

"Is it time?" I ask. "Is it time I left you alone?" And I'm afraid now, because James won't look at me. He smiles, apologetically, he shrugs his shoulders—this time at the woman who sits diagonally across. I'm afraid because the flight attendant is pushing me back to my seat, I can feel her fingernails against my back, afraid because I'm returning to my seat, which doesn't go back because it's broken, and because I'm sitting between a five-year-old with a runny nose and six coloring books, and a fat man who snores and whose thigh pushes against mine, and because I'm nothing more than a coffee-house singer with stringy hair who sings on street corners to pay the rent, and loving James won't change that, and because from the corner of my eye I catch a glimpse of white sky, white sky and nothing else.

HEART MACHINE TIME

BILL BROUN

"Alcohol gave me wings to fly,
Then it took away the sky."
—from Alcoholics Anonymous

Martin, a man I sponsor in AA, calls my cellular phone to
say he is cleaning his underwear in his kitchen sink. He acts
like I'm to blame for this situation.

"You don't understand how bad off I am," he says. "You
don't know."

"I think you sound pretty bad, Martin." I have to shout.
I'm on an airport tarmac, close to the International Terminal. Heat ruffles up from the ground, making the brownish
pink clouds near the horizon quiver and glisten. Jet engines
scream around me. "Hold on," I say. I put the phone on the
pavement. The jets sound like circular saw blades shot at
me from all directions. I yank a bag stitched with swirled
flowers from a moving belt—the end of a load from Paris.
I chuck it into the last cart on the cart train, and pick up
the phone again. I get on the belt motor—a sort of drivable
ramp, like a giant cardiac exerciser on wheels—and pull
out.

497

I say, more humanly, "Stay with me just a minute more, Martin."

"This isn't that important," he says. "I'm being a baby."

"Just wait!"

I head back, trying to cradle the phone on my lap. I swerve under a wing, ducking, then coast into the enormous Quonset hut called the baggage bank. I drive toward the square opening in the cargo floor, "Hades," where we shove the suitcases and hat boxes, the ski poles and sticky baby chairs. The bags all ride the underground conveyor until they pop onto the chrome merry-go-rounds where passengers grapple.

This morning we moved three hundred frozen cobras for a veterinary college. Each snake costs a fortune. They'd come from a laboratory in India, via Charles de Gaulle. Another ramp rat, Jimmy K., broke open one of the flight cartons for us. "Oops!" he mocked, ripping off the first of the tape. Then he went wild. "Oops, oops, oops!" No one laughed though. One by one, we all took our look. The snake came in clear bag of blue jelly, like a spiral in a marble. It was small and pale, almost a worm. It gave us all this bad feeling. Personally, I didn't think the prank was too funny; in sobriety, in AA, we're supposed to play by society's rules. But I didn't want to nark on Jimmy; plus, he'd start one of his rants—about our low pay, how they deserved it. I quietly went back to work. I felt all confused and guilty, slamming suitcases around like bricks in Hell, and finally I had to call my own AA sponsor, Buzz. Buzz said, "One snake? Let it go."

"But won't I be some kind of accomplice?"

"If this Jim character had taken five or six snakes," said Buzz, "I'd say report him. One cobra? Just forget this. It's a matter of proportion. And remember: You're mainly responsible for yourself. You can't fix the world."

I told Buzz, "Thanks, Buzz. Thanks for being Buzz." And I was grateful for my sponsor.

After break, Jimmy, looking worried, carefully bundled the rubbery snake and the membranous mess into Taco Bell food wrappers. He thrust it all deep into a white plastic F.O.D. bucket, which is, weirdly enough, for "foreign object debris." I still felt distracted—"too into myself," as Buzz would say. So I was actually glad when, during our next plane, Martin called.

"I think my intestines are sort of rotting or something," he says now.

I say, "I believe you, Martin."

He has been defecating all over his apartment this morning. He's spilling a lot of blood, too, yet he refuses to go to the hospital. What can you say? This is what happens to Martin after just two days of drinking nowadays. But I'm only making an educated guess when I say, "Martin, I think if you don't stop drinking you're going to die."

You should see Martin. He's handsome, with icy blue eyes and the boxy chin of a fairy-tale prince. He has three interesting nervous "habits," besides alcoholism. One is that he blinks frequently. The second is puckering his forehead and parting his lips slightly before he speaks. Together, they give him the appearance of someone trying to drink from a fire hydrant. The third habit—I'll get to that.

At age thirty-nine, Martin is a failed actor. He's also one of these people who seems to both punish and pathetically elevate himself by reminding you of his failures, the more agonizing the better. He lives off his parents, who send money from Massachusetts. His claim to fame at our AA meetings is he doesn't believe in God.

We once told him: "No one's asking you to worship any god." We told him—we were kind of holier-than-thou, I recall—all about the New York City atheists who helped start AA. In London, we said, there were still meetings where they'd bawl you out if you dared mention God. "See, you can be an atheist and it's OK."

He shook his head and started blinking. He has this way of making our platitudes seem like spiteful ploys. He said, "Now you guys are getting creepy. And that's all I'm saying." Yet Martin kept coming around to Commonwealth House, sitting on the back couches. He wanted to be left alone, he made clear. But he "kept coming back," as we AAs say. Once, after the third or fourth time he relapsed, I saw him berate himself for letting down his family. "Don't get your hopes up for me," he said. "I think I'm doomed. I'm a piece-of-crap son and I don't deserve help." Of course, in AA, these sorts of words are supposed to grab your conscience. So I made it my mission to be Martin's friend.

Now he's saying, "I've got it coming out both ends." I hear him pause, taking a deep breath. "First I noticed blood in my vomit, just some red bits. Then it started coming up like motor oil." He makes a sarcastic *phuuu* noise through his teeth, like static on Radio Nowhere. "It was fucking horrible."

I can't think of what to say. Martin never accepts my sympathy. What he wants are eyewitnesses. So I say, "Wow."

"I'll be OK," he says. "Don't get upset. I'm going to stay put."

I say, "Why can't you just let a doctor check you out?"

"No doctors," he says. "I know what they'll do. They'll shove me through all their neato machines!" He says it like that, like a punch line. "Ha! No. No way. Ha!" I've imagined the dark mental screening room in Martin's head, with its wry, blinking audience of other Martins in seat rows, each with their auburn hair parted perfectly on the side. There's a grim nervousness in there, too. You hear it throughout Martin, seismic tremors far beneath Movie Land, making all the sulky Martins restless in their seats.

"How do you feel right now?" I say. Through a wall, I hear the intercom in the terminal, an echoey monotone, like a snail's song. "I mean, right this second?"

"I don't know how I feel—trapped. I've got the shakes," he says. "I know the shakes. I'll be all right. I'm just not having loads of fun."

Last year, for a little while, Martin and I seemed to have a nice time together. He was terribly lonely, and, really, I was too. We'd sit at his computer, firing violet-red rays into space aliens shaped like ripply tusks. We knew it was stupid, but we couldn't stop. I'd hit the key marked "CTRL" and he'd commandeer the ship with his joystick, offering pessimistic commentary. "This is a Cyberian ambassador ship. It's not supposed to attack us, but . . ." Or, "This pulsar will drag our engines down. Just watch." Then, one night, we got tired of the game. He went to the kitchen to make us coffee. I heard him talking on the phone. He was checking on Sabro, another AA who couldn't often stay sober very long. Poor Sabro has no hands, but flippers. When we say the Lord's Prayer at the end of our meetings, I sometimes get to hold Sabro's flipper. It is a beautiful thing to grasp, like a limb too perfect for earth. You can almost feel the ghost hand in it, swimming nimbly in its flawless world.

Martin came back holding his heavy chin high, out like an elbow. It was as if he was finally in charge of something.

"Sabro's OK," Martin said curtly. "He just needs someone to talk to."

I could tell Martin really loved Sabro, and after talking

about Sabro, we got on the subject of how it was, if anything else, good to have friends.

"And you're good, too," I told him. "I think you're a really good person trying to break out."

Martin's face got red. "Don't hand me too much of this formalized intimacy stuff, OK?"

"I'm sorry," I said. "What I'm trying to say is, I like you."

"Well, you don't have to force it."

That night, amazingly, I almost convinced him to go with me to this chapel I know about, a place for people like him and me. It's a giant cube painted maroon inside.

"We won't pray," I promised. "We'll just sit and soak up whatever's there."

Martin had said, "Hmm." He'd made with his blue lips the softest smile.

But instead of going, Martin brought out a messy stack of photographs of himself in films I'd never heard of. Some of them fell on the carpet and he left them there. He handed them over and sat on his couch. "Get ready. You're in for a laugh," he said. I took a slow look. There was a flash of a thinner, younger version of Martin in loose swim trunks, feeding a dark fish to a happy dolphin in a pool. There was Martin as a dismal chauffeur, opening a limo door for a tall women in foxes. The one I remember most was Martin as a medieval monk, he and his jug of holy water getting whacked aside by two bearded men who battled with broadswords. The water flew into the air like a visible shriek. There was something that went beyond the cliché of that image, Martin's princely face and long, gentle mouth, its surprise and weariness and insult. In all of them, Martin was decidedly placed at the edge of each frame. I laughed alright, but they were sharp, hard little laughs.

Now he says, bitterly, "At this point, if this binge kills me, that's fine. That's perfectly fine." Then he adds, "You won't have to worry about old Martin anymore. That ought to make your life a lot easier, huh?"

I say, "Don't."

And that's it. He hangs up forever, for Martin's third habit is trying and not trying to stage suicide attempts. What I heard later was that Martin drunkenly swallowed a bottle of aspirin. He was already hemorrhaging, and the aspirin did him in. He'd tried to walk out into the street and stop a car. They found him beside the building, in a parking lot of asphalt cracked to pieces.

That day—it wasn't so long ago—turned out to be a very hard one. It was more than Martin.

A fairly young DC-10, one I'd helped cargo, was taking off for Mexico City International on Runway Eighteen. We were on break in the baggage bank, eating our lunches, playing dominoes. Because we'd removed our headphones, we heard the bang. We'd have heard it anyway. It sounded like a car backfiring, only ten times louder. We jumped. Everybody jumped. Jimmy K. dropped a box of dominoes. The black rectangles bounced off the shiny floor. By the time we sprinted out of the hut, the fire engines were screaming bloody murder and racing toward the end of Eighteen.

I hopped on my motor and speeded toward the plane. This wasn't exactly authorized, but something took over in me. Already, the bright yellow inflatable chutes were dangled out the sides of the DC-10, their segments trembling in the wind. Men and women in silver suits unraveled long white hoses from the fire trucks. Passengers burst down the slides. Nothing was calm or orderly about it. You can imagine. I could see the plane was OK. No smoke, no fires. Perhaps a gull had flown into an engine. Just a scare. But the passengers, mostly men in dark suits, they didn't care. They were way beyond any suggestions. They hit the ground, then scrambled from the plane.

I got to about two hundred yards from the plane and stopped. I stayed on the grass median, a bumpy area riddled with rabbit holes. There are regulations for cargo personnel. For some reason, one desperate woman spotted my belt motor and its tilting ramp and, of all the vehicles shooting toward the plane, thought I was the kind of help she needed. She looked about forty. She wore a light green dress, but was barefoot. Her dark hair was still styled into neat, lustrous waves. She ran toward me and my ramp, waving her arms. Her face was twisted horribly. She screamed, "Please, O God!" She fixed her huge eyes on my face.

I suddenly got this mental picture of Martin, lying on his shit-covered couch beside a carton of elderberry wine. Of course, I didn't know Martin was really going to die at this point. I don't know. I wanted to pull the ramp back, away from the woman, to step on the accelerator and get out of there and not look back.

But the woman clambered onto the seat and clutched the safety bar. It was as if she'd just caught the last subway from the edge of the earth. She turned one of her brown forearms over and over, flexed her fingers in and out. She bent down and checked her feet. She looked at all the body she could see, panting. She kept fidgeting. But she never took both hands off the chrome bar at the same time.

I didn't know what to say. So I said, "I just unload the bags." She didn't say anything to that. She looked at me like I was nuts. Then, somehow, she bumped the lever with the green ball on its end and the belt on the ramp started trundling upwards.

We rode toward the terminal, not talking, the belt rolling, and you know—I wondered about her bags. This is what I remember. I knew we wouldn't get to touch the DC-10 for hours. It was silent and breezy. I felt very lucky to be alive and yet sad about Martin hanging up on me. There was going to be a long break this afternoon. All the other planes had stopped flying.

When I parked the ramp, the woman just sat there, staring around the baggage bank. "How can I help you?" I asked. She said nothing. She shook her head no. She glanced up, into the cave-like ceiling with its shadowy green trusses showing like faint ribs. When a jumbo takes off, the roof screeches a bit and shudders, and it feels like being inside Godzilla. But all you could hear now was the squeaking sound of the rollers on my belt motor. The woman had both hands on the safety bar. It became clear she wasn't going anywhere. And then I had a funny impulse. I climbed up onto the rumbling belt, stood up and started walking down it—walking in place. It's a regular joke with the ramp rats. It's our secret. We call it Heart Machine Time. It's only six feet high, so no one gets hurt. But I'd never tried it before. Of course, Heart Machine Time was one of Jimmy K.'s specialties; and now here I was, Mr. Law and Order, making long uncertain strides. "Hey, look at this," I told the woman. "It's heart machine time." I tried to make a sweet face. I tried to walk the weirdness out of the situation. "You walk and you get better." I said something Jimmy K. always says: "The doc says my heart is breaking. So it's heart machine time." She took one unsure hand off the bar and wiped her nose. A glistening streak ran along her cheek. The other rats stood around, watching, pulling on their green reflector vests. Some of them smiled and some didn't. There'd almost been a major airline disaster, after all. Yet Jimmy croaked, "You got it!" He turned a lever, and the belt really started hustling. "Is this boy going to live?" he said. The woman glanced quickly at everybody's faces, and then she cracked a tiny, shocked smile. "You muthafuckers is crazy," she said. I began to trot down the moving belt, faster and faster. I could barely breathe. I imagined Martin blinking at all this, scrunching his forehead, opening his mouth to condemn the God none of us understood. Maybe I felt I'd never been enough for my poor friend, and somehow I knew he was going away from us that day. But I wanted to get distance from him. I wanted to be happy. That's what I remember most. I couldn't bring myself to jump off because I felt like something was almost chasing me toward joy. I wanted to run, down and down the ramp. Then, stop, and ride the belt back up toward the edge.

PILOT, CO-PILOT, WRITER

MANUEL GONZALES

I.

We have been circling the city now at an altitude of between seven thousand and ten thousand feet for, according to our best estimates, around twenty years.

I once asked the Pilot—this was early into the hijacking, maybe a week—how we were in terms of gasoline and how he planned to refuel, but he did not tell me. He laughed and patted me on the shoulder as if we were good friends together on a road trip, and I had just asked him how we were going to get there without a map. Back in the cabin I asked a man who was an engineer if he knew how we had managed to stay aloft for so long, and he gave me a complex explanation, most of which I did not understand, centered around a rumored "perpetual oil."

"Is there such a thing?" I asked him. "Perpetual oil?"

"Well," he said. "I'm not sure that there isn't."

The Pilot called my name over the intercom a number of times before I realized it was me he was calling for. By the time I figured it out, the other passengers were leaning into the aisle and stretching over their seats to see who it was being summoned. I stood up and a low murmuring passed through the cabin. I suppose everyone assumed I was being called to be executed, since the hijacking had just happened a day or two before and we had been kept in the dark about it ever since. There had been speculation about demands, about actions, about executions, but nobody knew, really, what was going on or going to happen. I didn't blame the others for thinking that I had been called in to be the first casualty as I had assumed the same, though I wasn't sure why me instead of the man in front of me or the woman across the aisle or anyone else on board, one of the flight attendants, maybe. A woman grabbed my arm as I walked toward the front of the plane and shook her head, entreating me with her eyes not to go, to sit back down, but I didn't want to make the Pilot mad, so I pulled myself free and made my way.

When I knocked on the Pilot's door, I heard his voice say in a sing-song way, "Come in." He turned to look at me as I entered his cabin. "Sit, sit," he said, gesturing to the seat next to him, the co-pilot's seat.

I sat and he smiled and, without looking at me, said, "So you are the writer."

Unsure of what else to say, I said, "Yes. That's me."

"My name is Josiah," he said. "Josiah Jackson." He handed me a pad of paper and a pen. "Write that down," he said.

I wrote on the top of the sheet of paper, *Josiah*. And then, for good measure, underneath that, I wrote, *Josiah*

Jackson. I tore the sheet off the pad and gave it to him for his inspection.

He laughed as if I had made a very good joke, and then he said, "You are no less than what I had expected you to be."

We sat next to each other in silence for a moment, then two moments, until finally he said, "Okay. You can go now."

Feeling a certain amount of relief knowing that I wasn't to be executed and feeling confident in having made him, for whatever reason, laugh, I asked him why he had hijacked the plane and why we were still circling Dallas. At this he gave me a stern and serious look. "I do not usually answer questions, but since it is you: we are circling because I only know how to fly to the left." He looked at me and then laughed again, and said, "No, no. I'm only kidding." Then he turned back to look at the sky, which was now growing dark, and said no more.

The plane was full. The overhead compartments were full, too. The woman next to me had somehow managed to board the plane with more carry-on items than is normally allowed, but as she and I had been the last passengers to board, she was forced to cram as much as possible under the seat and then, noticing that I had not carried much with me onto the plane, she asked if she could place just one or two items under the seat in front of me.

"Just this small bag and this other small bag," she said. "You can just kick them out of the way, if you want. They're nothing but dirty clothes."

I told her I didn't mind, but in fact I minded a little, and after we had taken off and the seat belt light was turned off and she left for the restroom, I did kick one of the bags, but it wasn't filled with clothes and I heard, or felt, something break. I was waiting, after she came back to her seat, for a

good time to tell her that I had accidentally broken whatever it was that had been in her bag, but then the hijacking
happened and nobody thought about anything like their
bags or their connecting flights for a long time, and then, as
she was an older woman and as the years passed by, she
eventually forgot about almost everything else and passed
away in her sleep before I was ever able to apologize.

For a while, we all fought over the window seats because
no one believed me when I said that we weren't going anywhere, that we were merely circling and circling over the
same city. I was pulled out of my seat and pushed aside,
and even though I didn't care to look out the window anymore, knowing that it would be the same view again and
again, I didn't like being jerked away like that, and I
grabbed the guy who had pushed me by the back of his
jacket and pulled him roughly back, but he was lighter than
I expected him to be and the both of us fell into a pregnant
woman, who pushed into another passenger, and then we
all started fighting. After a while, we were pulled apart by
the Pilot, who said, "I have to fly the plane, and I can't keep
coming out here like this to babysit you. So sit down and
shut up."

Afterward, no one cared to look out of the windows
but me and a few others, and as the days and weeks and
months passed, these people, too, stopped looking, pulled
down their window shades, turned their heads to look anywhere else but outside at the Dallas skyline, because, they
said, their necks hurt and the sight of Reunion Tower only
made them depressed.

"Nobody move," is what he yelled. "This is a hold-up!" Then
he began to laugh at what he thought was a clever and ten-

510

sion-breaking joke. Since he was dressed as a pilot and had a softly southern accent, we laughed, too. But then, it turned out to be a hold-up, of sorts.

We weren't sure for a long time what had happened to the other pilots, the real pilots. Had they been abducted on their way through the airport? Were they now tied and gagged and locked in a broom closet, or possibly murdered? It wasn't difficult, despite his laughter and his slight paunch, to picture our Pilot engaging in such activities. But how had our Pilot managed to maneuver through security? How did he fool the flight attendants, who surely should have known he wasn't a real pilot?

Only later did we find out, from one of the flight attendants, that he was the real pilot. That he had been flying for ten years. That she had flown with him a number of times. But that no one knew what had happened to the co-pilot.

At one point, looking out the window at the city below and the streets and the highways and the trees and buildings, I saw a long freight train moving slowly along the tracks that run parallel to highway 635, and I was reminded of a story I had written in which a man had tried to build a scale model of nineteenth-century America and the trains that crossed it. He lived underground, as did a number of other people in this story, and so had no concept of how large exactly the continent was. Looking out the window at this height made me realize that such a model was now laid out before me, and I understood that I too had no concept of how large exactly the continent was. That the scope of my imagination was shown to be so much smaller in scale and weight than the continent that I had been trying to imagine through the eyes of a man who had never seen it before, depressed me, and so I closed my window-shade for the first time and leaned my head back against the seat and tried to sleep.

Sometimes I will go for weeks, months even, without looking at myself in the bathroom mirror. I know the bathroom well enough to be able to perform whatever human functions I need to perform with my eyes closed. Then, after a long enough time has passed, I will suddenly open my eyes and stare directly into my own face in the mirror, hoping the sight of age will shock me into feeling some kind of emotion, sadness or anger or humility, but I have decided that anything besides boredom and thirst and a dull, physical ache are beyond the reach of airplane passengers.

I have tried to write other things besides this since the plane was hijacked. The Pilot gave me pen and paper, and I at first expected that he expected it of me to chronicle the hijacking. I wrote a few pages—descriptions, mainly: the color of the woman's hair next to me; the stale, cold air of the cabin; etc., etc.—and showed them to him, but then he didn't want them, said he didn't have time to read them. "Don't you know I'm busy?" he said, laughing, but also, or so it seemed, peeved that I had bothered him. I've never been comfortable with rejection of this sort, and, for the first year or so, his words kept me from writing anything down at all. Then, slowly, I began to take notes for a story and then notes for a novel and then notes for another novel and another story, but all they have been are notes.

We were given permission to use our cell phones. The Pilot said he didn't care about signals or about whom we called.

Everything he said, he said with a laugh, though none of us could ever tell what he thought was so funny. We called our loved ones. I called my wife. I told her we had been hijacked. She knew, she said, because it was all over the evening news. We said those things we were supposed to say, but I felt that her heart wasn't in it; that maybe she was distracted by the news story on the television. Maybe my heart wasn't in it either. A baby had been crying for some time in the row or two rows behind me. We, my wife and I, didn't have kids yet and she wasn't pregnant and we had only been married for a short while, so I had a hard time feeling as bad for myself as for the old man who was missing his wife's birthday, who then missed—as time went on—their fortieth anniversary, and then her funeral; or the man whose pregnant wife was on board with us (the one I pushed down by accident), whose unborn child he might never see again. But then, they (the old man, the pregnant wife) never appeared to feel too sad about it all, either. Mostly, once I hung up with my wife, I felt worn out by the need to shout so much over the poor reception, and twice our phones hung up by mistake—lost signal, etc.—and each time involved a series of callbacks and messages until we were finally able to reconnect. Looking around the cabin at the other passengers as they also hung up with their loved ones, I had the feeling that they had been worn out, too. No one much used their cell phones after that first time and eventually all of the batteries died out, anyway.

My eyes adjusted so completely to looking at the city from high up that when I imagined myself on the ground, walking through the downtown area, or driving from north Dallas to Plano or Grapevine, I could not figure out how I would navigate from such a narrow perspective. How would I know my way around? How would I avoid being run over by a car or hit by a trailer truck?

As the years passed, I learned to pick out details, as if I were a hawk or an owl. I got to where I could see my parents' house, my wife's mother's house, the church where my wife remarried; not just see the general area where they should have been, but see them, in detail. Sometimes I will see a little boy or girl whose ball has bounced into the street run out after it unaware of the teenager speeding around the corner, or some situation like this, and the first couple of times I saw this, I yelled at the child (or dog or blind old man) to watch out, but I soon realized how foolish I sounded, how I startled the other passengers with my yelling, and so I stopped.

A young man in first class—a business executive or some such, I suppose—began a regimen of walking and stretching and worked very hard to convince everyone else on the plane to follow suit.

"This poor excuse for food," he complained, "will only make us sick and flabby."

He said, about our muscles, "Use them or lose them, people."

He would walk down the aisle and pat random bellies or he would jog down the aisle, bouncing on his toes, his arms up around his face as if he were preparing for a boxing match. A few of the passengers joined him. Calisthenics, jumping jacks, yoga stretches. Most of us, though, sat in our seats and watched him bounce up and down, his face sickly and pale and sweaty. It turned out that he wasn't eating the food at all, and it was really no surprise, in hindsight, that he was the first to go. After that, the exercise regimens came to a quick and quiet stop.

****

The phone in front of my seat rang once. It was my mother. I do not know how she knew how to contact me on the plane. Other phones rang at other seats, too, and I suppose it is possible that the airline gave these callers our numbers. She sounded the same on the phone as she had when I had last spoken with her, some seven or eight years before, but I knew that she must have looked much older than I remembered, and as we spoke, I closed my eyes and tried to add wrinkles and creases to her face, gray hairs to her scalp, liver spots to the back of the hand that held the phone.

She told me about my father. She told me that she had gone to my wife's second wedding, and that it was a nice, small affair. She asked me about what we had been eating, and, so she wouldn't worry, I did not mention the weight I had lost, or the flavorless liquid the Pilot had us drink. She asked if I had met anyone on the plane, a nice woman, perhaps, someone, anyone to keep me from feeling lonely. So she wouldn't worry, I told her about the pregnant woman, who had not been pregnant now for quite some time, but I was embarrassed talking about it on the phone since I knew that she could hear me saying these things to my mother even though both of us knew nothing had ever happened between the two of us except for one night, during a heavy storm, when the cabin lights blew out and she grabbed my hand out of fright. I tried talking to her once or twice after that night, but her son, who had grown into a rather big boy at seven years old, locked me in the bathroom when his mother wasn't looking and threatened to keep me locked in there unless I promised to leave his mother alone.

After a while, a second woman's voice came on the line and informed my mother and me that the call would end soon and that the phones would be disconnected and shut-off once we hung up. We said our good-byes. I told her to tell my wife hello. Then we hung up.

Early on, I figured that what I would miss most from my former life, assuming that we would not make it through the tragedy alive, would be my wife: the presence of her, the sound of her voice, the feel of her pressed next to me at night in our bed, her small soft hand enveloped by my own. But I have found, over these past relentless years, that, not being dead, not even being seriously injured, not being lost or, technically, alone, but instead finding myself in this plane, what I miss most are those basic qualities of life—standing up, walking around, sleeping lying flat, sex—and what I miss above all is food.

We ran out of the ham and cheese sandwiches within six weeks, despite the rationing, and the pretzels were eaten within the next month after that. At first, we were disappointed that we had no more food, until it dawned on us that, unless the Pilot wanted to starve himself, or, even if he had been hoarding his own supplies in the cockpit, unless he wanted to circle Dallas with a plane full of the starved and emaciated and, eventually, dead, he would have to finally land.

A full two days passed after the last bag of pretzels had been emptied before the Pilot finally came out of his cockpit. Expecting him to admit defeat, or to inform us of his plans to land in some remote island in the Pacific or simply to crash us into the earth (by then, anything would have been preferable to the constant sight of the city below us), we waited patiently for him to speak. He frowned and looked down at his feet. "As you are probably all now aware, we have run out of food, which means we must now draw straws to see who of us will be the first to be eaten." He paused as we each looked at our neighbor, and perhaps if he had actually made us try to eat one another, we would have then risen up, wrested control of the plane from him, found a way to land, ended the ordeal, but before we could do or say anything, he smiled broadly at us and laughed, saying, "No, no, no. I'm just joking." He then proceeded to walk down the aisle, pulling out a bag he'd hidden behind his back, and began to hand out small vials of a clear liquid to each passenger as he passed. With each vial handed out, he would repeat, "Two drops should do. No more than two drops. Don't want to over-do it. Two drops should do just fine." Once he was finished, he walked to the front of the plane again, turned to us and said, *"Bon appétit,"* and then stepped back into his cockpit, the door closing solidly behind him.

As we ran low on drops, the Pilot would bring us new vials.

I'm not sure how they work or what sustenance they provide. While I am still hungry after my two drops, while I still have an unnamable appetite (the drops at first had a mild grassy taste to them, but are now as good as flavorless, as I can't taste anything at all, or else I seem to have forgotten almost entirely what anything might taste like) and I have lost weight and will probably continue to lose weight, I have not starved. As far as I know, no one who has taken his drops has.

The Pilot would come out of his cabin twice or three times a day. As the years passed, as he grew older and became thicker around the middle and as his blond hair turned, in

517

places, white, I began to wonder how he felt in the mornings when he woke up, if he felt as old and tired as I sometimes felt.

I assumed he slept. He locked the cabin door at night, so none of us knew for sure. I asked him once if he slept and he didn't answer me and then I asked him, if he did sleep, who flew the plane. He laughed and patted his belly and said, "My co-pilot." When I asked him, recently, if his co-pilot would also be the one to fly the plane once he has died, he did not respond, pretending not to have heard my question.

It is surprising to me how quickly news of the hijacking spread. I called my wife within the hour of being told we had been hijacked, and she already knew. The people of Dallas organized a vigil that very night. We could see the huddled bunch of them with their candles standing on the tarmac of the Dallas/Fort Worth Airport. Someone—a gentleman from the rear of the plane—said, "Them standing there, we couldn't land even if we wanted to." In the morning, the same group of people (or perhaps a new group) stood in approximately the same formation, this time holding white posters with black letters on them that spelled out something too small for us to read.

For a while, I liked to think of my wife there among them, holding a candle or a piece of the message, but, in truth, my wife does not like crowds, and it's more likely that she was not.

Within a week, regardless of my wife's involvement or lack thereof, the vigils had stopped, the news reports, I'm almost certain, had stopped as well, and we had become a fixture of the Dallas skyline no different or more exciting than the neon Mobile Pegasus.

II.

I often find myself considering the man my wife married, by which I usually mean myself, a thought that then returns to me the fact that she has since remarried, and so I am forced to think of the two of us, her husband and I, side by side. This despite the fact that I have never seen him, which leads me, more often than not, to picture myself side by side my other self so that I might consider how the two of us have failed and how we continue to fail as husbands. I have a catalogued list in my head; it grows by the day, and it changes nearly constantly as faults are moved around, given more or less priority, my dirty underwear left on the bathroom floor moved down a rung by the peanut-butter crusted knife left for a week in the backseat of my car. When I get into this mood of rearranging faults—real and imagined—I begin to wonder, too, what the other passengers, those who are left, are thinking. We are not friends, any of us. Of course, we were all friends at first, or, at the very least, friendly with those people to our left or our right or across the aisle, as people on a plane tend to be, in that manner of searching for common ground in a book being read, a destination being reached, a vacation being taken. With the underlying sense that these friendships would last no longer than the few hours between Dallas and Chicago, we opened ourselves up to our neighbors. These relationships were made stronger once the plane was hijacked, as we felt bonded to each other by a shared sense of tragedy and uncertainty. Then, as time passed, as we continued to circle, as we realized just how long we might have to share the same space with each other, we—I am projecting, now—began to feel crowded, as if there wasn't enough room, and slowly we gathered ourselves inward, pulling knees into our chests, feet onto the seats, curling our arms around our shins, and placing our heads down or, if we could stomach the sight, pressing our faces away from our neighbors and against the windows. Now the plane is still and quiet and we have been moving with such regularity for so long that I have this sense of perfect unmovement, which creeps into the pit of my stomach and produces there a soft fluttering of wings and a welling anxiety, as if I had forgotten to do some minor but personal thing, or as if I am riding a child's ride at a fair, the dips not enough to be truly belly-rising, but raising, instead, a tingling awareness of gravity, or gravitas, in my arms and shoulders and legs: a feeling that is at once pleasant and upsetting.

When we were still talking—the other passengers and I—the woman who sat next to me and who had once asked that I store some of her bags beneath my seat told me, breathlessly and as she sat down, officially the last person to board the plane and take her seat, how she had nearly missed the flight and how she had had to beg and argue and plead with the gate attendants to let her on board. "I explained to them," she told me, "how the shuttle had had a flat and how someone was supposed to have called ahead to tell someone about the situation and that we had some- how convinced the first tow-truck driver to squeeze us into his cab and drive us to the airport so that we could all make our flights on time, but by then, with rush hour traffic, and even with the tow-truck flashing its yellow lights, it took us over an hour to move through the accidents and the stalled cars and by the time we arrived at the entrance to the airport, I only had fifteen minutes to get my baggage checked and run to my gate, and after all of that, do you believe that they almost didn't let me on the plane?" How did you convince them, I invariably asked, to which she replied, "Why, honey, with my feminine charm." It was an

amazing story the way she told it, embellished and repeated often to the others around her as we taxied down
the runway and in those first few minutes in the air before
the Pilot came out of the cockpit and hijacked us all, and
then, much later, she began repeating the story again,
though lamentably and with less energy, as if she were
reciting the Act of Contrition; and with each successive
dirge, more and more details of the story were removed
until finally, late one night a month or so into our circling,
she turned her head to me and confessed that in fact there
was no flat tire, no tow-truck driver, no real traffic even,
but that she had overslept, and that's why she had almost
missed her flight. "If only I had slept ten minutes longer,"
she said, and then she turned her head to face straight
again, and, while I'm sure she must have said something
else between then and the time she passed away, I cannot
remember what else that might have been. Now, however,
I repeat her story to myself, having adopted it as my own,
except that sometimes the tow-truck driver refuses to carry
us in his cab and we are forced to hail down a woman driving with her baby in a station-wagon, and she's the one who
brings us to the airport on time, and sometimes I will catch
myself thinking, If only she hadn't picked us up, and despite
the fact that the story, which is not even mine, has never
been true, I cannot help but feel a keen disappointment in
the fact that such an insignificant event has led me to this
end.

III.

When the Pilot died, it came to light that he in fact did have
a co-pilot. The pregnant woman's son, it·turned out, had
been spending more and more time in the Pilot's cabin,
learning the technique of flying, learning the secrets of our

perpetual oil. At first, we were relieved. The Pilot was gone, we could finally land, and the boy, now a young man, would certainly land the plane, just as his mother had asked him to. But, of course, why should he? In a way, it made more sense to us—perhaps not to the boy's mother—that we continued to circle Dallas even after the Pilot's death. In all of our time circling with the Pilot, we never learned, were never told why we could not land, why we had been hijacked. Now that the boy was in charge, though, what else should he have done? What other world did he know but this one inside the plane? Would he so easily give up its comforts, its familiarity?

Most of us had some memory of what it was like to stand straight, to walk on an object that does not so noticeably move, to breathe an air that has not been cycled and recycled a hundred thousand times, and even we were a little afraid of what our lives would become if we were to finally land on solid ground. The prospect of seeing a building up close and from below must have been a devastating and frightening one for the boy. Despite his mother's weeping and crumpled body outside the Pilot's door, he did not alter the Pilot's original course, not even to change the direction of our circle.

Shortly after the Pilot hijacked the plane, he had us pose for pictures taken with a Polaroid camera. As with everything else, he did not explain why he wanted these pictures. The flight attendants had us stand in front of the lavatory between first class and coach, and after the picture was taken and had developed, they let each of us look at our photograph before placing it in a box with the rest of them that was eventually handed over to the Pilot.

The Co-Pilot—he had a name, but since the Pilot's death, he refused to answer to anything but Co-Pilot— found these photographs and decided to take another series of them, and we lined up again and posed. Once these had developed, the Co-Pilot had his mother give everyone the original photograph and the new photograph. A sizeable pile of old pictures with no matching new ones remained in the box, and these, we decided, should be placed in the now empty seats, but once this had been done, we changed our minds and took them all back up and placed them back in the box and returned the box to the cockpit.

I had begun to put on some weight before my trip, and I remember feeling self-conscious about the way my pants had begun to fit. There is a difference of maybe thirty pounds between the first man pictured and the second man pictured. Still, the thinness looks no better on me than the extra weight did. Whereas my clothes once seemed uncomfortably small, they look, in the more recent photograph, ridiculously large. Furthermore, along with the weight, my face has lost whatever charm it once had. Oddly, and this seems to be the case with nearly everyone else's picture too, I am smiling in both.

IV.

I often find myself lost in thought trying to imagine the paths of our lives after we have landed. In this I am, I believe, alone.

Suppose the Co-Pilot falls ill and we are forced into an emergency landing, or simply, as he matures, he experiences an epiphany, a change of heart, a desire to do something more with his life. Whatever the reason, some small part of me would not be terribly surprised if one day the Co-Pilot were to step out of his cabin and ask, nonchalantly, "Does anyone know how to put us down?" I wonder, then, which we will choose: to rebuild our former lives or begin them anew. Is twenty years long enough to wipe away bad marriages, poor career choices, too many long hours spent following someone else's dreams? How many of us will return to our old homes, rented out to new tenants or boarded up or sold, settle ourselves back into old routines now occupied by new people?

Some of us have already made our choice. The former accountant practices sleight-of-hand tricks for hours on end. He has told me, while pulling quarters out of my ear, while filling and emptying the overhead bins with the wave of a blanket, that he plans to change his name, buy a few costumes, and take up the birthday party racket, or aim for the big time, the comedy club circuit. "Carpe Diem," he told me. For others, the choice seems to have been made for us. My wife, for instance, has remarried. It is likely that by now my parents have both died. The friendships I enjoyed have surely unkindled themselves after twenty years. I will step out of this plane and onto the tarmac with no human connection but to the people on board with me, most of whom I have not spoken to in months. I am afraid that I will, if I'm not careful, seek out a life that most closely resembles the one I have for twenty years been living. Perhaps, when we land, I will buy a bus ticket and ride the cross-town 404 as it loops through its never-ending circuit. Or I might rent or buy a car and drive to Belt Line Road and continue to circle the city in that way. It would be good to devise a plan to prevent this sort of life taking hold, but no such plan comes readily to mind. In my imagination, then, I often wind up on the side of the road, kicked off the bus by the driver or having run out of gasoline, forced then to continue my course on foot. These thoughts bring me little comfort, which explains, perhaps, why the others have given up such fruitless speculation and why all plans of overpowering our hijacker and taking control of the situation were long ago abandoned.

I will not be here for the more realistic ending, of course. How could I be? Though not yet the oldest person on the plane, I am not far from it, either, and it's not likely that I'll conspire to live as long as the Co-Pilot, who seems to be in excellent health. We can hear him perform his calisthenics every morning after he wakes and every night before he goes to sleep, a regimen he must have learned from the Pilot. When we glimpse it, his face has a ruddy glow.

As I imagine it, everyone else will have gone by then, too. Even now there is only the one flight attendant left and though younger than many of us, she has long since stopped taking her drops and her once pretty face is gaunt and withered. Soon, then, no members of the original crew will be left, and there will be only the seven other passengers who remain. And once we have all died and there is only the Co-Pilot, what then? It's unlikely that he will land—I doubt he even knows how. But he might become lonely. He might tire of the Dallas skyline, which has changed not at all since we first took off, and seek some new skyscape. Flying straight ahead for some time, east or west, toward sunrise or sunset, perhaps finding himself soon over the Pacific Ocean, wondering what this world is, blue above and blue below, that he's flown himself to, until, following the sunset each day, he eventually finds the Asian continent, or perhaps Africa, and then Europe, and then the Atlantic, and the Eastern Seaboard, until he reaches Dallas again, at which time perhaps he will turn left, or right, or continue on straight again, circling the world the way he has for so long circled Dallas. I can't see how it will or should matter to me, since I will have long since died by then, but at times I feel sorry for the boy, sorrier for him than for us. He will fly and fly and fly, until he one day slumps over in his Captain's chair, the dead weight of his body pushing the controls forward. I can feel my stomach lurch even as I imagine the nose dipping, the wings turning downward. The plane will break through the clouds, condensation beading up along the windows like rain. The world will rush past below, cars and buildings and trees and people becoming larger by the moment, as if they are rising to meet us, until at last, with great and terrible speed, the Co-Pilot finally lands.

AFTERWORD

DOROTHY SPEARS

The idea for this anthology arose in the summer of 2006, when I was writing a story for the *New York Times* about artists and writers who had pioneered Long Island's East End in the mid-twentieth century. As part of my research I read James Salter's memoir, *Burning the Days*. A fascinating piece of writing, it recounts, in Salter's spare, elegiac prose, the ambitions and humiliations he endured during his training at West Point, his service in the U.S. Air Force at the end of World War II, and then his experiences in Korea as a combat pilot.

Drawn to flying both as a subject for stories and an apt metaphor for navigating life, I decided to ask Jim Salter during one of our interviews if there were any other pilot-writers whose work he found interesting. He was quick to respond with a list of his favorites, among them Beryl Markham, Roald Dahl, and Antoine de Saint-Exupéry. "*Night Flight* is probably his best," he cautioned, referring to Saint-Exupéry.

I read Roald Dahl's fabulous memoir *Going Solo*, and his collection of short stories about flight, *Over to You*, as well as Beryl Markham's classic *West with the Night*, in quick succession.

In the process, my interest in flying literature blossomed into obsession.

Apart from the challenges pilots faced in finding their way through an infinite array of life-and-death circumstances, what repeatedly struck me during these readings was how flight presented a relatively new frontier for writing. I began to envision these flight stories, so riveting in their telling and so distinctive of voice, side by side in a book. Bringing these stories together, I suspected, would even deepen their individual impact.

In the basement of Manhattan's Strand bookstore were several shelves cluttered with books on aviation. Among them were *Miracle at Kitty Hawk: The Letters of Wilbur and Orville Wright*, *The Published Writings of Wilbur and Orville Wright*, Charles A. Lindbergh's *Spirit of Saint Louis*, Amelia Earhart's *Last Flight*, and Mary Lee Settle's *All the Brave Promises*. Fearing these historically significant texts would vanish out of print before I would ever have a chance to read them, I piled them in my arms, and bought them all.

A few weeks later, I approached Thomas Beller at Open City about publishing an anthology of stories about flying. He immediately said, "I want to do this book," and put me in touch with his co-editor, Joanna Yas. She expressed her excitement about the idea, and mentioned several stories previously published by Open City in which flying played a part.

In February 2008, I circled back to Jim Salter, and presented him with my idea for an anthology entitled *Flight Patterns*. His response was immediate. "Well, Dorothy," he said, "this is an interesting topic for you, because as far as I know your father was never a pilot."

Jim didn't know, because it hadn't even yet occurred to me: In 1968, shortly after our family moved to Connecticut, my father had gotten his pilot's license. I was in kindergarten at the time, which meant I was in school only for a half-day. During the other half of the day, my father would rent a Sessna at nearby Westchester Airport and take me up for rides.

I remember the thrill of watching the houses recede until the patchwork of buildings and streets looked like a real-life enactment of the miniature town in the title sequence of *Mr. Rogers' Neighborhood*. The cars resembled sparkling, scurrying beetles. Once when the plane dropped abruptly, I spontaneously vomited. My father, annoyed, asked me why I didn't grab an air bag, but now it was obviously too late. Staring glumly at the front of my coat and its slimy wooden buttons, I could hardly wait for the precarious bouncing wheels of our agile plane on the runway so I could clean myself off.

Around that time, the dreams began: I was running down the grassy hill in front of our house, my arms outstretched. Finally, my speed was adequate to lift me off the ground. I'd be flying. In one dream, a frightening giant caught hold of my foot, pulling me screaming down to the earth, and the danger of his snarling clutches. In another, I was flying alongside my father's Sessna. A bandana was wrapped around my mouth so I could breath. My mother, who sat beside my father in the cockpit, watched me impassively, as the bandana came looser and ever looser and I began to suffocate. My favorite dream by far featured me soaring over our house, above a beloved pair of fir trees, which were old and very tall and looked as if they were hugging.

My father told me recently that in learning to fly, he "had this naïve thought that we could go to Hyannis or East Hampton, then park the plane for a weekend and fly back."

The idea of flying to Lake Placid, climbing a mountain or two, then flying home, he said, particularly appealed to him. In this spirit, in November 1968 he took my mother, my two brothers, and me on a day trip to Martha's Vineyard. After landing at the tiny airport, we stopped for a quick meal in the cafeteria. "We were sitting there eating," recalled my father, "when I saw snowflakes coming down on the runway."

I remembered the snow, and how distraught my father had been at the sight of it. "There could be six inches of snow on the ground before this is over," he'd fretted. My father didn't have an instrument rating, he explained recently, so he was not permitted to fly into a cloudbank. "The clouds always had to be above you," he said.

I remember my parents urgently discussing the cost of keeping our rental plane overnight—we had to pay by the hour—and putting our family up in a hotel.

With no time to file a flight plan, my father decided to turn around and fly home.

We were lucky. Seven months later, my father was considering the joint purchase of a single-engine canvas-topped plane with a friend and business colleague. Around this time, a dear friend of his, Jim Ritchey was planning to fly to Rhode Island to visit his parents with his wife and three children.

A more experienced pilot than my father, Ritchey had taken off in haste, in order to beat some inclement weather. He had not registered his flight plan. Outside of Trumbull, Connecticut, when the clouds started closing in, my father recalled, "Jim came down to a lower altitude than he should have." Another pilot, having just taken off from Trumbull, decided he didn't like the weather, and "elected to do the safe thing, and come back," according to my father. The second pilot asked for permission to land and was given clearance.

His plane collided with the Ritchey plane outside of Trumbull. There were no survivors.

I remember when I first spotted my father from the stairs that morning. He was sitting on the TV room couch in his bathrobe, staring straight ahead. "The Ritcheys are gone," he said. We were friends with the Ritchey children, who were born at roughly the same intervals as my brothers and me. That our friends—an entire family—could simply vanish like that forever sounded impossible, but it was my father's despair that truly frightened me.

At the time that was my main worry about death, was being alone forever. "At least they were all together," I told him. "That way they can keep each other company." When my father didn't answer, I began to wonder—if they died in the air, then what happened to their bodies.

If they died in the air, I suggested, maybe they never came down, but just went straight up to heaven. After all, I reminded him, they were already practically there.

Nothing I said could make even a dent in my father's profound sadness.

My father said he flew at most twice, maybe only once after the Ritchey tragedy.

"I was just learning to fly and land a plane at night," he told me the other day, explaining that one had to accumulate a certain number of prescribed hours before earning instrument accreditation. At his next lesson after the crash, he said he realized his heart was no longer in it. The plane purchase "didn't pan out," he explained. "Flying was more time-consuming than I thought it would be. Then Mom and I decided this was much more dangerous than I'd like to admit."

"Jim was the inspiration for my flying," he added, after a pause. And that appeared to be his final word on the subject.

Since Jim Salter had brought my father up, I decided to tell him this story. After a long pause, Jim asked what sort of flying stories interested me most. I recalled his inscription of my copy of his novel, *Light Years*: "Life is weather, etc." It occurred to me that weather had figured prominently in *Burning the Days*, as well as in the writings of the Wright Brothers, Amelia Earhart, Antoine de Saint-Exupéry, and Beryl Markham. In fact, it didn't matter how far we'd come in terms of technological advancements. Weather remained flying's great neutralizer.

"I guess weather," I said.

Jim considered this. "Given your experience in Martha's Vineyard," he said, "that would make sense. And what authors speak most to you?"

In *Over to You*, I told him, there was this fascinating story called "They Shall Not Grow Old."

"I'm sure I've probably read it," Jim said, "I don't remember."

I told him how magical it was, how Dahl had this way of recounting the most terrifying things with a sense of humor.

"Tell me the story, Dorothy," said Jim.

I'd never done this before, told anyone the story of a story I'd read. But there was a quiet insistence in his voice, and I didn't dare say no.

"There were two pilots sitting on a runway," I began. "It was very hot. They were in Greece. They were on—" I couldn't remember the term.

"Alert," Jim said. "Go on."

"There was a third pilot who'd already been called up."

AFTERWORD

I continued. About two-thirds into the story, I told him, you find out that the pilot who had been called up was missing. You are seeing things from his perspective now and you are realizing that he has hit a cloud. He has been lost in the cloud for a day and a half. He sees a line of planes coming toward him. It's all the soldiers who have died during the war. As a reader you're not sure suddenly if his experience in the cloud is merely a wish on the part of the narrator that his friend was still alive. The friend could be dead. This could be the waiting pilots' way of dealing with the loss, imagining their friend lost in a cloud.

Jim has been silent for a long time. "Am I losing you?" I asked him.

"Dorothy," he said, his tone serious. "I've heard every word. Keep going."

I told him the pilot must have lived because they continue flying afterward. "Eventually the lost pilot gets shot down, but because of his experience in the cloud, he's not afraid."

The book is sitting on a cabinet in my office. I pick it up and read Jim the last few paragraphs, so he can hear for himself how it ends.

"Well, Dorothy, that's a charming story," he said. "And one only Roald Dahl could tell."

"So you see about the magic," I said.

"This is a serious collection," Jim said, finally, in that same sober tone.

As inclusive as I've attempted to be, this book could have expanded even further. For as I write this I'm reading *First Light: The True Story of the Boy Who Became a Man in the War Torn Skies above Britain*, by Geoffrey Wellum. Wellum's book and *Falling through Space* by Richard

533

Hillary, a favorite of Jim Salter's, could have fit in the middle part of this book. In their absence here, I highly recommend them. A story by one of the surviving World War II Kamikaze pilots featured in the 2007 documentary *Wings of Defeat* would also, undoubtedly, have proven interesting.

In an ideal world *Flight Patterns* would include a firsthand account by one of the Lost Boys of Sudan of a scene in the documentary film of the same name, when the boys are leaving Sudan and marvel over the various novelties of the aircraft and air travel. A story by one of the young Egyptian flight attendants from Etihad Training Academy in the United Arab Emirates describing how flight attendant jobs in the oil-rich Persian Gulf present a new form of social mobility for Arab women would have offered a poignant twist on tired flight attendant clichés. And the heroic testament of Chesley Sullenberger, the pilot who landed an Airbus A320 in the Hudson River, bringing all 155 passengers on board to safety, in a maneuver dubbed "the miracle on the Hudson," would surely be a crowd pleaser.

These possibilities—not to mention those that would inevitably follow since, for as long as humans inhabit the skies, stories about flight will continue to be written—would keep an editor busy for years. So for now, I am putting endpapers on the material I've assembled to date. The sooner to hand this book, in the words of Roald Dahl, *over to you.*

ACKNOWLEDGMENTS

This book wouldn't exist without the support of Open City co-editors Thomas Beller and Joanna Yas. Apart from their initial excitement about the book, their specific story suggestions, editing advice, and practical assistance kept *Flight Patterns* safely on course from start to finish. To them I'd like to extend my deep gratitude.

I'd also like to thank James Salter, Lee K. Abbott, Lorrie Moore, Julie Lasky, Pamela Reis, Kevin Hyman, and Nicholas Callaway for their generous suggestions. Many thanks also to Open City intern Emily Hunt, who helped with the tedious task of securing permissions for previously published stories.

Last but not least, I'd like to give special thanks to my partner, Alexis Rockman, and my two sons, Alex and Ferran Brown, for their consistent encouragement and love, and to my father for imparting in me the wonder of flying.

CONTRIBUTORS' NOTES

THOMAS BELLER is the author of two works of fiction, *Seduction Theory* and *The Sleep-Over Artist*, and *How to Be a Man*, a collection of essays. He has edited numerous anthologies, including the forthcoming *Lost and Found: Stories from New York*. A founder and co-editor of *Open City* and creator of the Web site *Mr. Beller's Neighborhood*, he teaches creative writing at Tulane University.

JOHN BOWE is co-writer of the film *Basquiat*, co-editor of *Gig: Americans Talk About Their Jobs*, and author of *Nobodies: Modern American Slave Labor and the Dark Side of the New Global Economy*. He has written for *The New Yorker*, *The New York Times Magazine*, *GQ*, and others.

BILL BROUN is an assistant professor of English at East Stroudsburg University. He is seeking a publisher for his recently completed novel manuscript, *A Night of the Animals*, the story of a semi-homeless man who releases dozens of animals from the London Zoo.

RACHEL CANTOR's stories have appeared in *The Paris Review*, *One Story*, *Ninth Letter*, *New England Review*, *DoubleTake*, and elsewhere. They have twice been nominated for a Pushcart Prize and have been shortlisted for *Best American Short Stories* and *The O. Henry Prize Stories*. She lives in Philadelphia, where she has just completed a collection and her first novel.

BERNARD CHABBERT, a senior editor at Europe 1, a French radio broadcasting network, has written extensively about aviation. He has flown over two hundred aircraft types, from antiques, such as his privately owned Electra, to the Concorde. Among his many documentaries is an eighty-minute portrait of Alberto Santos-Dumont, a Brazilian-born aviator who made his first flight while in Europe in 1906. Chabbert's father, a close friend of Antoine de Saint-Exupéry, was also a pilot for Aeropostale.

ROALD DAHL (1916–1990) was a salesman for Shell Oil in Tanzania during the outbreak of World War II. In spite of his towering height, six-foot-six, he was accepted into the Royal Air Force and learned to fly. *Over to You*, his collection of fiction based on flying, was published in 1946. His other books include *James and the Giant Peach*, *Charlie and the Chocolate Factory*, *Boy: Tales of Childhood*, and *Going Solo*.

MEGHAN DAUM is the author of the novel *The Quality of Life Report* and *My Misspent Youth*, a collection of essays. She writes a weekly column for the *Los Angeles Times*, which appears in the Op-Ed page every Saturday. Her essays and articles have appeared in *The New Yorker*, *Harper's*, and *The New York Times Book Review*, among other publications. She has contributed to NPR's *This American Life* and *The Morning Edition*. She lives in Los Angeles.

JAMES DICKEY (1923–1997), author of the best-selling novel *Deliverance*, enlisted in the U.S. Air Force in 1942. Between combat missions in the Pacific, he read poetry, and later pursued graduate work and devoted himself to writing. His collection, *Buckdancer's Choice*, won the National Book Award for poetry. Dickey served as Poetry Consultant to the Library of Congress, a position now known as Poet Laureate. He continued to write and publish poetry until his death in South Carolina after a long illness.

JOAN DIDION was born in California and lives in New York City. She is the author of five novels and eight books of nonfiction, including *Play It As It Lays*, *A Book of Common Prayer*, *The White Album*, and *Slouching Towards Bethlehem*. *The Year of Magical Thinking* won the National Book Award for nonfiction.

AMELIA EARHART (1897–1937), a staunch advocate of equal opportunities for women, took her first flying lesson in 1921. On June 17, 1928 she joined two other pilots on a Fokker F-7, and twenty-one hours later became the first woman to fly across the Atlantic Ocean. In 1937, after numerous record-breaking flights, and approaching her fortieth birthday, she set her sights on becoming the first woman to fly around the world. She departed on June 1 and was last heard from a month later, one hundred miles from a tiny Pacific atoll. President Roosevelt authorized a search, but after covering 250,000 square miles of ocean, the search was called off. No trace of the accident was ever found.

MARY GAITSKILL is the author of two novels and three collections of stories, most recently a collection titled *Don't Cry*. She lives in upstate New York.

MANUEL GONZALES lives and writes in Houston. He holds an MFA from Columbia University and has recently been published in *The Believer*, *Open City*, *Fence*, and *One Story*.

BARRY HANNAH's first novel, *Geronimo Rex*, won the William Faulkner Prize and was nominated for the National Book Award. He is the author of a dozen other books, including *Airships*, which won the Arnold Gingrich Short Fiction Award. His latest collection of stories, *High Lonesome*, was nominated for a Pulitzer Prize. He lives in Oxford, Mississippi.

JOSEPH HELLER (1923–1999) is widely regarded as one of the most influential post–World War II satirists. After joining the U.S. Army Air Corps in 1942, he was sent to Italy, where he flew sixty combat missions as a B-25 bombardier. He studied English on the G.I. Bill, earning his M.A. from Columbia University. His first novel, *Catch-22*, became a bestseller and was adapted for the screen. He went on to write such novels as *Something Happened* and *Picture This*. He died of a heart attack shortly after the completion of his final novel, *Portrait of an Artist, as an Old Man*.

GARY HORN's writing life began with the publication of *Swim in the Void*, a collection of his poetry, in collaboration with artist Alexis Rockman. He has gone on to write numerous screenplays, editorials for the *Los Angeles Times*, and an original television series for CBS and Wolfgang Petersen. Currently, he lives in Malibu, California, with his wife and young son (his greatest creative endeavor).

ERICA JONG graduated from Barnard College and earned her M.A. in eighteenth-century English literature from Columbia University. Although she began her literary career as a poet, her first novel, *Fear of Flying*, established her as leading voice of the 1970s women's movement. She has published many books of poetry, fiction, and nonfiction since, and was awarded the United Nations Award for Excellence in Literature. Her most recent collection of poems, *Love Comes First*, was published earlier this year.

BRAD KESSLER's novel *Birds in Fall* won the 2006 Dayton Literary Peace Prize and was named by the *Los Angeles Times* one of the top ten books of the year. He is the author of another novel, *Lick Creek*, and his nonfiction has appeared in numerous publications including *The New Yorker*, *The Nation*, *Kenyon Review*, and *Bomb*. Kessler is the recipient of the Rome Prize from the American Academy of Arts and Letters, and a Whiting Writer's Award.

WALTER KIRN has published a collection of stories, *My Hard Bargain*; a number of novels, including *Up in the Air* and *Mission to America*; and, most recently, a memoir entitled *Lost in the Meritocracy:The Undereducation of an Overachiever*. He lives in Montana.

CHARLES A. LINDBERGH (1902–1974) made the first solo nonstop flight across the Atlantic Ocean in 1927. Initially against U.S. intervention in World War II, Lindbergh eventually advised the United States Army and Navy in the Pacific theater. While flying approximately fifty combat missions, he developed cruise-control techniques for American fighter planes. Pan American World Airways later hired Lindbergh, who helped design the Boeing 747 jet. In 1953 his book about his transatlantic flight, *The Spirit of Saint Louis*, won a Pulitzer Prize.

BERYL MARKHAM (1902–1986) was born in England and grew up in East Africa, where her father trained and bred racehorses. In 1931 she began flying mail, passengers, and supplies to remote points in the continent, and in 1936 she became the first aviator to fly solo east to west across the Atlantic. *West with the Night*, published in 1942, is her most widely read book. She was living in poverty near the racetrack in Nairobi when *West with the Night* was released in 1983. The book provided her enough income to live in comfort until her death.

ALICE MUNRO is a Canadian short-story writer. Her first collection, *Dance of the Happy Shades*, won the Governor General's Award, Canada's highest literary honor. The many collections she has written since include *Something I've Been Meaning to Tell You*. Her stories appear frequently in *The New Yorker* and *The Atlantic Monthly*. In 2005 she won the Medal of Honor for Literature from the U.S. National Arts Club.

GRACE PALEY (1922–2007) was a widely praised poet, short-story writer, and social activist. Her *Collected Stories* (1994) was a finalist for both the Pulitzer Prize and the National Book Award. From 1986 to 1988, she was New York's first official state author. She was also Poet Laureate of Vermont. Her final book of poems, *Fidelity*, was completed just before her death.

ANTOINE DE SAINT-EXUPÉRY (1900–1944) began training as a military pilot when he was twenty-one. One of the pioneers of postal flight, he was assigned by Aeropostale to establish a route in South America. A pilot in the Spanish Civil War, he also served as a reconnaissance officer in the French Army during World War II. His novel *Night Flight* won the Prix Femina in 1931, and *Wind, Sand and Stars* received the Grand Prix of the French Academy in 1939. He is the author of the children's book *The Little*

Prince. He disappeared during a reconnaissance flight over the Mediterranean.

JAMES SALTER, a former combat pilot for the U.S. Air Force, has been called one of the most gifted writers of modern American fiction. *A Sport and a Pastime* and *Light Years* are among his best-known novels. His collection *Dusk and Other Stories* won the 1989 PEN/Faulkner Award. *Burning the Days: Recollection* is among his numerous books of nonfiction. A lifelong skier, Salter wrote the screenplay for the 1969 film *Downhill Racer*. He lives in Colorado and on Long Island.

SAÏD SAYRAFIEZADEH's is the author of *When Skateboards Will Be Free: A Memoir of a Political Childhood*, about his experiences growing up communist in the United States. His stories and essays have appeared in *Granta*, *The Paris Review*, *Open City*, and other publications.

SHEILA M. SCHWARTZ (1952–2008) is the author of *Imagine a Great White Light*, a short-story collection, and the novel *Lies Will Take You Somewhere*. Her work has appeared in *The Atlantic Monthly*, *Ploughshares*, and *Triquarterly*, as well as in the anthologies *The O. Henry Prize Stories* and *The Pushcart Prize*.

DAVID SEDARIS is a Grammy-nominated humorist and the best-selling author of *Naked* and *Me Talk Pretty One Day*. His essays frequently appear in *The New Yorker* and on NPR's *This American Life*.

MARY LEE SETTLE (1918–2005) was a novelist who also wrote several books of nonfiction. *All the Brave Promises* is a memoir of her experiences in England as a recruit in the Women's Auxiliary Air Force during World War II. After the war, she worked in magazines, and eventually moved to London where she wrote fiction, plays, and an etiquette column published under a pseudonym. Her novel *Blood Tie* won the National Book Award. In the fall of 1980, she launched the PEN/Faulkner Award, an annual prize for fiction.

JERRY STAHL is a screenwriter and author of the best-selling memoir *Permanent Midnight*. He has also published a story collection, *Love Without*, and the novels *I, Fatty, Perv—A Love Story, Plainclothes Naked*, and *Painkillers*. He lives in Los Angeles.

JAMES TATE's first collection of poems, *The Lost Pilot*, was published in 1967 when he was still a student at the University of Iowa Writers' Workshop. He has since published several books, including *Selected Poems*, which won a Pulitzer Prize, and *Worshipful Company of Fletchers*, which won a National Book Award. His father, an American pilot, was killed in World War II when Tate was five months old.

JONATHAN TEL is the author of the story collection *Arafat's Elephant* and the novel *Freud's Alphabet*. His stories have appeared in *The New Yorker, Open City, Granta*, and *Zoetrope*. He has worked as a quantum physicist and an opera librettist. His most recent book is, *The Beijing of Possibilities*, a collection of stories.

FLIGHT PATTERNS

TOM WOLFE is the author of a dozen books, among them *The Electric Kool-Aid Acid Test*, *The Right Stuff*, and *The Bonfire of the Vanities*. After receiving his BA from Washington and Lee University, he earned a PhD in American Studies from Yale University. While a daily reporter for the *New York Herald-Tribune*, he completed his first book, *The Kandy-Colored Tangerine-Flake Streamline Baby*, establishing himself as a pioneer of experiments in nonfiction now known as New Journalism. He lives in New York City.

TOBIAS WOLFF is the author of numerous books, including the memoir *This Boy's Life* and the recent story collection, *Our Story Begins*. He is also the editor of *The Vintage Book of American Short Stories*. Among his honors are the PEN/Malamud Award and the Rea Award, both for excellence in the short story; the *Los Angeles Times* Book Prize; and the PEN/Faulkner Award. He lives in northern California and teaches at Stanford University.

ORVILLE WRIGHT (1871–1948) and his brother Wilbur Wright (1867–1912) transformed modern life by building and flying the first airplane.

LINDA YABLONSKY is a novelist and art journalist who travels widely, in and out of New York, where she lives.

COPYRIGHT INFORMATION